Thomas Carlyle
Sartor Resartus
&
Selected Prose

Thomas Carlyle
Sartor Resartus
&
Selected Prose

Introduction by
Herbert Sussman

HOLT, RINEHART AND WINSTON
New York   Chicago   San Francisco
Atlanta   Dallas   Montreal   Toronto   London   Sydney

Contents

Contents

Past and Present 271

Introduction

To the Victorians, Thomas Carlyle was a prophet who, like the Biblical prophets, had come out of the wilderness, in this case rural Scotland, to preach to the sinful inhabitants of the city. He had been raised in a small Scottish village under a rigid Calvinist faith that taught a fundamentalist belief in the Bible, a distrust of pleasure as a snare of the Devil, and a conviction that work is a religious obligation, a form of duty by which men fulfill God's hidden purposes. When Carlyle left this severe rural world for Edinburgh University in 1809 he, like many poor but intelligent young Scots, planned to become a minister of this faith. But, like his autobiographical creation Diogenes Teufelsdröckh, his faith was shaken by the skeptical, scientific learning at the university. Rejecting plans for the ministry, unable to find a new profession, barely able to earn enough money for food, Carlyle fell into the despair and thoughts of suicide recorded in the "Everlasting No" chapter of *Sartor Resartus* (Book Second, Chapter VII). Faith returned, not through traditional religion, but through his reading of German transcendentalist philosophy, particularly that of Johann Fichte and Immanuel Kant, from whose chief work, *A Critique of Pure Reason*, Carlyle takes the title for Book Third, Chapter III of *Sartor*. By joining the metaphysics of transcendentalism with his fundamental Calvinist morality, Carlyle created for himself a viable faith.

Carlyle's transcendentalism, which shapes not only the content of his writing, but its very form, can best be seen as a refutation of the mechanistic assumptions that lay beneath the teaching at Edinburgh University and the increasingly scientific thought of the age. Philosophical mechanism follows from the assumption of Newtonian science that all material events have a physical cause. The implication of this seemingly simple belief is that since events must reach back to causes in an unbroken chain, all phenomena, even human actions, are determined by prior events. And thus the universe can best be understood using the analogy of a machine, for it is wholly material, its actions are predetermined and, without an Immanent God, it runs to no moral purpose. At the nadir of despair, Teufelsdröckh describes this mechanistic world in terms taken from contemporary technology, "To me the Universe was all void of Life, of Purpose, of Volition, even of Hostility: it was one huge, dead, immeasurable Steam-engine, rolling on, in its dead indifference, to grind me limb from limb" (Book Second, Chapter VII). It is this amoral, deterministic vision that Carlyle calls "The Everlasting No," for it denies the instinctive knowledge that we have a moral sense and that our will is free.

To preserve moral value and volitional freedom, Carlyle's transcendentalism posits the existence of two worlds—the phenomenal world, the area of ordinary sense experience which is accurately described by the causal relationships of Newtonian science, and the transcendental world, which lies beyond material appearances and the experience of our senses. This view calls for two different mental faculties: the practical reason, or what Carlyle calls "vulgar Logic" (*Sartor*, Book First, Chapter X), that can perceive the deterministic chain of causal connection, and the higher or "Pure Reason" (*Sartor*, Book First, Chapter X), an intuitive power that can go beyond ordinary sense experience to perceive the transcendental world revealing itself in the phenomenal. For Carlyle, space and time, the necessary categories of mechanistic philosophy, are created by the mind itself; they govern the phenomenal world, but do not apply to the transcendental. As Teufelsdröckh says in "Natural Supernaturalism" (Book Third, Chapter VIII), "Admit Space and Time to their due rank as Forms of Thought; nay even, if thou wilt, to their quite undue rank of Realities: and consider, then, with thyself how their thin disguises hide from us the brightest God-effulgences!" With the categories of space, time, and causality seen as applying only to the phenomenal world the application of determinism is limited, for the higher faculty of mind, the pure reason, can transcend these categories by perceiving moral purpose in the transcendental realm and by acting with freedom of will. At the crucial moment in *Sartor Resartus* when Teufelsdröckh defies the "Everlasting No," the mechanistic world view, with the words, "*I* am not thine, but Free, and forever hate thee!" (Book Second, Chapter VII), the very act refutes philosophic mechanism by showing a soul breaking out of the chain of cause and effect to make a free moral choice.

Carlyle's particular version of transcendentalism should not, however, be identified with the Platonic view that the material world is but a poor copy of a higher reality. The particular quality of Carlyle's philosophy is that while it provides a basis for his need to believe in moral purpose and volitional freedom, it also maintains the importance of the material world, the hard, palpable realm of everyday activity in which men can perform the moral obligations of work and duty demanded by his Calvinism. For Carlyle, the phenomenal and the transcendental are not only of equal value, but are interpenetrating. In Carlyle's terms, all phenomena are symbols and in the influential chapter of *Sartor* entitled "Symbols," he defines the term: "In the Symbol proper . . . there is ever, more or less distinctly and directly, some embodiment and revelation of the Infinite; the Infinite is made to blend itself with the Finite, to stand visible, and as it were attainable there. . . . The Universe is but one vast Symbol of God; nay, if thou wilt have it, what is man himself but a Symbol of God" (Book Third, Chapter III). For Carlyle, then, all phenomena, including human personality and historical events, show transcendental forces manifesting themselves through the material world. In the words of the Earth-Spirit in Goethe's *Faust*, the entire earth is the "*living visible Garment* of God" (*Sartor*, Book First, Chapter VIII); in the words of Diogenes Teufelsdröckh, all phenomena are clothing.

The extravagant clothes philosophy which Carlyle assigns to the German philosopher Teufelsdröckh is, then, a rich metaphor by which Carlyle can present his complex and often paradoxical world view. The material world considered as symbol is both a veil over the Divine Presence and the means by which the Divine manifests itself, just as clothing both hides the essential nature of man and, as Carlyle suggests in a multitude of ways throughout *Sartor*, symbolically reveals the true spiritual nature of the wearer. With only a slight shift of metaphor, clothing becomes the covering of the body politic, those traditional social institutions that, like outgrown clothing, bind the historical forces creating the industrial state and must be exchanged for new. But for all Carlyle's sense of the need to establish new institutions to fit the demands of industrialism, he is no believer in "Adamitism" (*Sartor*, Book First, Chapter IX); he is not one who wishes to discard entirely the necessary protective clothing of social institutions. The brilliant Swiftian vision in the chapter on "Adamitism" of the House of Lords stripped naked suggests not only the anachronistic quality of feudal institutions, but the ludicrous horror of men in a natural state, freed from the emblematic clothing society provides. The political implication of Carlyle's clothing metaphor is not primitivism, the belief that social institutions destroy the innocence of man, but a melioristic belief that, since social institutions are necessary, they must be reshaped, or "retailored" (a literal meaning of "Resartus") to fit the historical forces shaping the age. The creaking armor of the Champion of England (Book Third, Chapter III) must be exchanged for the simple black coat of the new hero whom Carlyle calls the Captain of Industry (See *Past and Present*, Book Fourth, Chapter IV).

Although these philosophical and social ideas form the basis of Carlyle's writing, the ideas should not be equated with or substituted for the literary work itself. Carlyle is above all an artist, who, like a poet or a novelist, creates a literary structure in order to make the reader feel upon his pulses the truth of the writer's particular vision. And for a literary masterpiece like

Sartor Resartus, the purpose of reading must not be to extract a schematic statement of Carlyle's "thought," but to understand how his vision is inseparable from the very form of his work.

Consider one of the most pervasive features of *Sartor,* the metaphorical style. We have already seen how the central metaphysical and social ideas are presented through an extended metaphor, that of clothing. The very texture of the prose, too, is metaphorical. Speaking of language, Teufelsdröckh says in "Prospective" (Book First, Chapter XI), "Language is called the Garment of Thought: however, it should rather be, Language is the Flesh-Garment, the Body, of Thought. I said that imagination wove this Flesh-Garment; and does not she? Metaphors are her stuff." Of this passage, the editor comments quite accurately, "Than which paragraph on Metaphors did the reader ever chance to see a more surprisingly metaphorical?" Certainly the passage is typical of Carlyle's style in not describing the subject by a logical structure but by an accumulation of metaphors. But for all its seeming lack of order, this "surprisingly metaphorical" style is quite appropriate for describing the symbolic universe. For the denotative and logical language of science can only describe the phenomenal world; metaphor, the structure of comparison, is the linguistic analogue of the symbolic world which is itself a sign of inexpressible spiritual meaning. Furthermore, the very obscurity of the style in its lack of concrete definition suggests the more general principle that in the symbolic world truth in all its fullness is ultimately unknowable.

Or consider another stylistic feature of *Sartor,* the extensive elaboration of seemingly trivial subjects. This movement from the low and particular to the general and often transcendent appears in the structure of such chapters as "Aprons," "Tailors," and in the elaborate developments of the meaning of George Fox's suit of leather in "Incident in Modern History" (Book Third, Chapter I). Carlyle even seems to relish the recondite, as seen in the extensive allusions in his prose, and the trivial, as in his use of Bulwer-Lytton's descriptions of high society (Book Third, Chapter X). In part, this attention to the obscure in the present and in the past is in keeping with the mind of the book's persona, a pedantic German professor. But more important, the very movement of the prose in developing the significance of modern trivia or in searching through history to draw meaning from obscure events of the past is in itself an exemplification of Carlyle's central principle—that in this symbolic universe even the most trivial object or seemingly unimportant event is a revelation, if we read it correctly, of the spiritual world. And to enter the imaginative world created by *Sartor Resartus* is to be absorbed into a new mode of seeing, which is sacramental, not scientific, and in which events are not mere links in the causal chain but revelations of an unseen power.

A similar literary complexity appears in the very early essay "Signs of the Times" (1829). Here Carlyle introduces the idea developed throughout his writing, that the nineteenth century is the "Age of Machinery, in every outward and inward sense of that word." As in *Sartor*, Carlyle's symbolic style creates both a metaphor adequate to the complexity of his thought and a form exemplifying his vision. The machine, in "Signs of the Times," is a particularly Carlylean symbol. By "Machinery" he means, of course, the new technology of industrialism; this is machinery in the "outward" sense of the term. And by "Machinery" he means, too, the "inward sense," both in the mechanistic science that created the machines and the rationalized social organization that technology demands. But in the Carlylean symbol the "inward" and "outward" senses interpenetrate; the material phenomenon and the spiritual principle cannot be separated. And the fusion of historical fact and philosophical doctrine into the single term "Machinery" illustrates in its very form the central idea that as much as mechanistic thought has created the machine, the success of the machine has contributed to an increasingly mechanistic cast of thought.

In *Sartor*, this same symbolic style is used to describe the protagonist, Diogenes Teufelsdröckh. For all the parallels between Teufelsdröckh's life and Carlyle's—a rural childhood, Calvinist upbringing, attendance at a university steeped in mechanistic science, an unhappy love affair, despair and conversion—the author cannot be wholly identified with his fictional creation. Carlyle, after all, never stood at the North Cape and frightened off a Russian smuggler. Nor is Carlyle's marriage included in the autobiographical sections. The point is that Teufelsdröckh is a fictional character created by Carlyle for particular literary purposes out of his own experience. Primarily, Carlyle has ordered the autobiographical material so that the life of Teufelsdröckh exhibits a clear moral progress. In the first stage of his conversion, Teufelsdröckh moves from a despairing belief in an indifferent universe to an affirmation of his own freedom of will in his almost existential denial of the absurd world he calls the "Everlasting No." In the final stage, which Carlyle calls the "Everlasting Yea" (Book Second, Chapter IX), the protagonist renounces the stirrings of self which were the very proof of his freedom for self-sacrificing submission to the imperatives of duty and work. "Love not Pleasure; love God."

Furthermore, for all the autobiographical element in this moral progress, the biographical sections do not have the naturalistic and psychological concerns of a novel. Teufelsdröckh is a larger-than-life character dimly perceived, almost as if in lightning flashes, by the editor. He is a symbol and, like all Carlylean symbols, ultimately mysterious; like all phenomena in the Carlylean vision he can never be fully comprehended, for his spiritual meaning is infinite. Paradoxically, like all phenomena, his life, while ultimately unfathomable, is also a revelation of transcendental forces working in the material world. The exaggerated qualities given to Teufelsdröckh transform him into a Carlylean hero, a figure who embodies the historical forces shaping a particular era. And the central imperative of the "Everlasting Yea," "Close thy *Byron*; Open thy *Goethe*," points to the necessity of finding a new hero for the age. For Carlyle, Byron is the quintessential romantic, and the figure of Teufelsdröckh is often almost a parody of the Byronic hero such as Manfred, who, like Teufelsdröckh in the "Everlasting No," defiantly sets his will against a hostile universe. Goethe, however, represents for Carlyle a new kind of hero, who rejects the egocentric posturings of a Byron in order to perform constructive work in this world. And in the renunciation of the infinite longings of the self for a life of self-submission in dutiful work, the conversion of Teufelsdröckh can be said to symbolize the change from the romantic to the Victorian era.

But what of Carlyle himself? Does Teufelsdröckh speak for him? Can Carlyle's voice be identified with that of his fictional creation? These questions must be asked because of the particular structure of the book. The clothes philosophy and the biographical account are gathered from fragmentary sources and presented to the reader by another fictional character, the editor. The editor, whose comments make up a good part of the book, is perplexed, hostile, and sympathetic by turns; he is the rationalistic, empirical Englishman to whom the transcendental message of the book is directed. But why should this often hostile voice be included? In part, the function of the editor is to anticipate the comments of the average English reader and thus allay his hostility to this strange Germanic message. But the comments of the editor often point shrewdly to the extravagance of Teufelsdröckh's transcendentalism. And this common-sense criticism is reinforced by a stylistic extravagance in the treatment of Teufelsdröckh. Perhaps the most difficult thing for a modern reader to feel about *Sartor Resartus* is that it is a humorous work, written in a mock-heroic style which satirizes not only Byronism, but the transcendental philosophy itself. There are, then, two voices, that of the rationalistic editor unable to comprehend the transcendental vision, and that of an often profound, often ludicrous, German sage. Neither is Carlyle's and both are Carlyle's. Each of the fictional characters, editor and professor, speak for Carlyle who, at this early stage in his career, was attracted by the doctrines of transcendentalism and duty, and yet could still perceive their limitations.[1] Furthermore, a literary form in which the full meaning of the work is created by an interaction between the empiricism of the editor and the transcendentalism of the philosopher is a fitting expression of Carlyle's belief that, in the symbolic universe, truth in all its fullness cannot be stated directly within the confines of language.

After *Sartor*, however, the voice of Teufelsdröckh became the voice of Carlyle. In *Past and Present* (1843), the extravagant style of Teufelsdröckh is no longer assigned to a fictional character, but is the voice in which Carlyle directly addresses the

[1] George Levine, " 'Sartor Resartus' and the Balance of Fiction," *Victorian Studies*, 8(1964), 131–160.

reader. In this work, Carlyle puts into practice the principle reached by Teufelsdröckh at the end of his spiritual progress; he has closed his Byron and opened his Goethe. If *Sartor* is still essentially a romantic, even a Byronic work, in its concentration on the inward struggles of a single soul, *Past and Present* is particularly Victorian in its renouncing thoughts of self in order to turn to the work at hand—improving the condition of England.

Following the enormous popular success of *The French Revolution* (1837), Carlyle began another historical work, on Oliver Cromwell. In carrying out his investigations in Cromwell's home country of eastern England, Carlyle was deeply moved by the sight of a poorhouse where able-bodied men sat in the sun, unable to find work. To a man who held the fundamental Calvinist belief in the religious obligation of labor, depriving men of the opportunity to work seemed the ultimate social sin. And the poorhouse seemed to Carlyle a sign of the social ills of the times. Simply, it symbolized the economic distress of the 1840s created by an industrial slump after a period of rapid expansion. More important, the poorhouse seemed to Carlyle a symbol of utilitarian thought, for the poor law required that the unemployed reside in the poorhouse in order to receive relief and that conditions within the poorhouse be set so little above the subsistence level that the poor would have no desire to avoid work. The assumptions behind this scheme, the idea that through a careful balancing of pains and pleasures the government could manipulate human actions, and the deeper belief that men are motivated solely by the hope of material well-being, are the main objects of Carlyle's criticism in *Past and Present.*

In this work Carlyle comments on the industrial present by contrasting it to a mythic past. Carlyle based the second section of the book, "The Ancient Monk," on a recently published twelfth-century manuscript, *The Chronica Jocelini de Brakelonda* in which a monk, Jocelin, tells of the life of Samson, first as a monk, then as Abbot of the monastery and, in effect, ruler of the surrounding lands. Working from this actual historical document, Carlyle fashioned his description of life in a medieval monastery into a utopian vision. Samson becomes a Carlylean hero; the chapter "Government" shows the newly-appointed Abbot bringing to the microcosm of his realm order and purpose where before there had been only indolence and confusion. Under Abbot Samson's firm control, the monastery exemplifies what Carlyle saw as the needs of the early industrial age: leadership by heroes, unself-conscious religious faith, the responsibility of leaders reciprocated by loyalty among the led, and a spiritually satisfying purpose restored to daily work.

For Carlyle, the symbol of the historical process that would bring these qualities to the industrial world was the Phoenix (*Sartor*, Book Third, Chapter V), the legendary bird that every five hundred years dies in flames, only to arise newly-born from the ashes. It was Carlyle's faith that from the flames of industrial unrest that he saw in Chartism would emerge a new kind of hero, the Captain of Industry, who would be as much the agent of the historical forces shaping the mechanized present, as Abbot Samson was an agent of the forces shaping the feudal past. Like Abbot Samson, the Captain of Industry would create the organic filaments (*Sartor*, Book Third, Chapter VII) of responsibility and loyalty so that even through mechanized labor, the worker could perform the sacramental duty of work. But as Carlyle grew older, he saw the reality of industrialism draw further and further from his vision of the technological hero. And his own writing grew more severe, his distrust of democracy more fierce. When the Reform Bill of 1867 extended the franchise, Carlyle responded with an essay entitled "Shooting Niagara: and After?" whose message was that in advancing toward democracy, society had gone over the brink to destruction. His idea of the hero grew more authoritarian; ties of loyalty became the discipline of an authoritarian state. And the industrial utopia he had envisioned for the present appeared to him as it appears to us, as remote as the feudal utopia he had imagined in the past.

Berkeley, California   Herbert Sussman
January 1970

Chronology

1795   Born in small village of Ecclefechan, Scotland.

1809–1814   Attends Edinburgh University.

1814–1818   Works as tutor, gives up plans for becoming a minister.

1818–1824   Period of great personal unhappiness. Supports himself by doing articles and translations. Undergoes the religious experience described in "Everlasting No."

1824   Translation of Goethe's *Wilhelm Meister's Apprenticeship*.

1826   Marries Jane Welsh.

1828–1834   Lives at Craigenputtock, an isolated farmhouse, where he writes "Signs of the Times" and *Sartor Resartus*.

1833–1834   Serial publication of *Sartor Resartus* in *Fraser's Magazine*.

1834   Moves to London.

1836   American edition of *Sartor Resartus*, prepared by Ralph Waldo Emerson.

1837   *The French Revolution* published and becomes great popular success.

1838   First English edition of *Sartor Resartus*.

1841   *On Heroes and Hero-Worship* published.

1843   *Past and Present* published.
1845   *Oliver Cromwell's Letters and Speeches* published.
1850   *Latter-Day Pamphlets*, a collection of social criticism, published.
1852–1865   Six volumes of *Frederick the Great* published.
1867   *Shooting Niagara: and After?* published, a work protesting the extension of the franchise by the Reform Bill of 1867.
1881   Dies and is buried in Ecclefechan.

Selected Bibliography

Text:

Works, Centenary Edition, ed. H. D. Traill. 30 vols. London, 1896–1901. [All texts in this Rinehart Edition are based upon the text of the Centenary Edition.]

Sartor Resartus, ed. Charles F. Harrold. New York, 1937. [A fully annotated edition.]

Biography:

Froude, James Anthony. *Thomas Carlyle: A History of the First Forty Years of His Life, 1795–1835.* 2 vols. London, 1882.

————. *Thomas Carlyle: A History of His Life in London, 1834–1881.* 2 vols. London, 1884.

Criticism:

Calder, Grace. *The Writing of Past and Present.* New Haven, 1949.

Cazamian, Louis. *Carlyle.* New York, 1932.

Deen, Leonard W. "Irrational Form in *Sartor Resartus,*" *Texas Studies in Literature and Language,* V (1963), 438–451.

Selected Bibliography

Holloway, John. *The Victorian Sage: Studies in Argument.* London, 1953. [Contains an excellent analysis of Carlyle's rhetoric.]

LaValley, Albert J. *Carlyle and the Idea of the Modern,* New Haven, 1968.

Levine, George, " 'Sartor Resartus' and the Balance of Fiction," *Victorian Studies,* VIII (December 1964), 131–160.

Neff, Emery. *Carlyle.* New York, 1932.

Sussman, Herbert L. *Victorians and the Machine: The Literary Response to Technology.* Cambridge, Mass., 1968. [Contains an analysis of Carlyle's reaction to industrialism.]

Tennyson, G. B. *Sartor Called Resartus: The Genesis, Structure and Style of Thomas Carlyle's First Major Work.* Princeton, 1965. [Excellent full-length study of *Sartor Resartus.*]

Signs Of The Times

"Signs of the Times"
was first published in the
Edinburgh Review,
Number 98 (June 1829).

Signs Of The Times

It is no very good symptom either of nations or individuals, that they deal much in vaticination. Happy men are full of the present, for its bounty suffices them; and wise men also, for its duties engage them. Our grand business undoubtedly is, not to *see* what lies dimly at a distance, but to *do* what lies clearly at hand.

> Know'st thou *Yesterday*, its aim and reason;
> Work'st thou well *Today*, for worthy things?
> Calmly wait the *Morrow's* hidden season,
> Need'st not fear what hap soe'er it brings.

But man's 'large discourse of reason' *will* look 'before and after'; and, impatient of the 'ignorant present time,' will indulge in anticipation far more than profits him. Seldom can the unhappy be persuaded that the evil of the day is sufficient for it; and the ambitious will not be content with present splendour, but paints yet more glorious triumphs, on the cloud-curtain of the future.

The case, however, is still worse with nations. For here the prophets are not one, but many; and each incites and confirms the other; so that the fatidical fury spreads wider and wider, till at last even Saul must join in it. For there is still a real magic in the action and reaction of minds on one another. The casual

3

deliration of a few becomes, by this mysterious reverberation, the frenzy of many; men lose the use, not only of their understandings, but of their bodily senses; while the most obdurate unbelieving hearts melt, like the rest, in the furnace where all are cast as victims and as fuel. It is grievous to think, that this noble omnipotence of Sympathy has been so rarely the Aaron's-rod[1] of Truth and Virtue, and so often the Enchanter's-rod of Wickedness and Folly! No solitary miscreant, scarcely any solitary maniac, would venture on such actions and imaginations, as large communities of sane men have, in such circumstances, entertained as sound wisdom. Witness long scenes of the French Revolution, in these late times! Levity is no protection against such visitations, nor the utmost earnestness of character. The New-England Puritan burns witches, wrestles for months with the horrors of Satan's invisible world, and all ghastly phantasms, the daily and hourly precursors of the Last Day; then suddenly bethinks him that he is frantic, weeps bitterly, prays contritely, and the history of that gloomy season lies behind him like a frightful dream.

Old England too has had her share of such frenzies and panics; though happily, like other old maladies, they have grown milder of late: and since the days of Titus Oates[2] have mostly passed without loss of men's lives; or indeed without much other loss than that of reason, for the time, in the sufferers. In this mitigated form, however, the distemper is of pretty regular recurrence; and may be reckoned on at intervals, like other natural visitations; so that reasonable men deal with it, as the Londoners do with their fogs,—go cautiously out into the groping crowd, and patiently carry lanterns at noon; knowing, by a well-grounded faith, that the sun is still in existence, and will one day reappear. How often have we heard, for the last fifty years, that the country was wrecked, and fast sinking;

---

[1] Aaron, brother of Moses, threw down before Pharaoh a rod which miraculously blossomed and bore fruit (Num. xvii.8).
[2] An Englishman who, in 1678, fabricated a tale of a Popish Plot in which Roman Catholics were to massacre Protestants. In the resulting agitation, many Catholics were killed.

whereas, up to this date, the country is entire and afloat! The 'State in Danger' is a condition of things, which we have witnessed a hundred times; and as for the Church, it has seldom been out of 'danger' since we can remember it.

All men are aware that the present is a crisis of this sort; and why it has become so. The repeal of the Test Acts, and then of the Catholic disabilities,[3] has struck many of their admirers with an indescribable astonishment. Those things seemed fixed and immovable; deep as the foundations of the world; and lo, in a moment they have vanished, and their place knows them no more! Our worthy friends mistook the slumbering Leviathan for an island; often as they had been assured, that Intolerance was, and could be nothing but a Monster; and so, mooring under the lee, they had anchored comfortably in his scaly rind, thinking to take good cheer; as for some space they did. But now their Leviathan has suddenly dived under; and they can no longer be fastened in the stream of time; but must drift forward on it, even like the rest of the world: no very appalling fate, we think, could they but understand it; which, however, they will not yet, for a season. Their little island is gone; sunk deep amid confused eddies; and what is left worth caring for in the universe? What is it to them that the great continents of the earth are still standing; and the polestar and all our loadstars, in the heavens, still shining and eternal? Their cherished little haven is gone, and they will not be comforted! And therefore, day after day, in all manner of periodical or perennial publications, the most lugubrious predictions are sent forth. The King has virtually abdicated; the Church is a widow, without jointure; public principle is gone; private honesty is going; society, in short, is fast falling in pieces; and a time of unmixed evil is come on us.

At such a period, it was to be expected that the rage of prophecy should be more than usually excited. Accordingly, the Millennarians have come forth on the right hand, and the Mil-

---

[3] The Test Act, requiring that all holders of public office take the sacrament of the Church of England, was repealed in 1828. Catholic Emancipation, passed in 1829, freed Roman Catholics from certain civil disabilities.

lites on the left. The Fifth-monarchy men prophesy from the Bible, and the Utilitarians from Bentham.[4] The one announces that the last of the seals is to be opened, positively, in the year 1860; and the other assures us that 'the greatest-happiness principle' is to make a heaven of earth, in a still shorter time. We know these symptoms too well, to think it necessary or safe to interfere with them. Time and the hours will bring relief to all parties. The grand encourager of Delphic or other noises is— the Echo. Left to themselves, they will the sooner dissipate, and die away in space.

Meanwhile, we too admit that the present is an important time; as all present time necessarily is. The poorest Day that passes over us is the conflux of two Eternities; it is made up of currents that issue from the remotest Past, and flow onwards into the remotest Future. We were wise indeed, could we discern truly the signs of our own time; and by knowledge of its wants and advantages, wisely adjust our own position in it. Let us, instead of gazing idly into the obscure distance, look calmly around us, for a little, on the perplexed scene where we stand. Perhaps, on a more serious inspection, something of its perplexity will disappear, some of its distinctive characters and deeper tendencies more clearly reveal themselves; whereby our own relations to it, our own true aims and endeavours in it, may also become clearer.

Were we required to characterise this age of ours by any single epithet, we should be tempted to call it, not an Heroical, Devotional, Philosophical, or Moral Age, but, above all others, the Mechanical Age. It is the Age of Machinery, in every outward and inward sense of that word; the age which, with its whole undivided might, forwards, teaches and practises the great art of adapting means to ends. Nothing is now done directly, or by hand; all is by rule and calculated contrivance. For

[4] The Millennarians and Fifth-monarchy men prophesy the imminent coming of the Kingdom of God. Millites is Carlyle's term for Utilitarians, followers of James Mill and Jeremy Bentham. The Utilitarians believed that all laws should be judged as to whether they would bring about the greatest happiness for the greatest number.

the simplest operation, some helps and accompaniments, some cunning abbreviating process is in readiness. Our old modes of exertion are all discredited, and thrown aside. On every hand, the living artisan is driven from his workshop, to make room for a speedier, inanimate one. The shuttle drops from the fingers of the weaver, and falls into iron fingers that ply it faster. The sailor furls his sail, and lays down his oar; and bids a strong, unwearied servant, on vaporous wings, bear him through the waters. Men have crossed oceans by steam; the Birmingham Fire-king[5] has visited the fabulous East; and the genius of the Cape, were there any Camoens now to sing it, has again been alarmed, and with far stranger thunders than Gamas.[6] There is no end to machinery. Even the horse is stripped of his harness, and finds a fleet fire-horse yoked in his stead. Nay, we have an artist that hatches chickens by steam; the very brood-hen is to be superseded! For all earthly, and for some unearthly purposes, we have machines and mechanic furtherances; for mincing our cabbages; for casting us into magnetic sleep. We remove mountains, and make seas our smooth highway; nothing can resist us. We war with rude Nature; and, by our resistless engines, come off always victorious, and loaded with spoils.

What wonderful accessions have thus been made, and are still making, to the physical power of mankind; how much better fed, clothed, lodged and, in all outward respects, accommodated men now are, or might be, by a given quantity of labour, is a grateful reflection which forces itself on every one. What changes, too, this addition of power is introducing into the Social System; how wealth has more and more increased, and at the same time gathered itself more and more into masses, strangely altering the old relations, and increasing the distance between the rich and the poor, will be a question for Political Economists, and a much more complex and important one than any they have yet engaged with.

[5] James Watt (1736–1819), developer of the modern steam engine, had his factory in Birmingham.
[6] Luis de Camoëns, in his epic poem the *Lusiad* (1572), celebrates the voyage of Vasco da Gama around the Cape of Good Hope in 1497.

But leaving these matters for the present, let us observe how the mechanical genius of our time has diffused itself into quite other provinces. Not the external and physical alone is now managed by machinery, but the internal and spiritual also. Here too nothing follows its spontaneous course, nothing is left to be accomplished by old natural methods. Everything has its cunningly devised implements, its prëestablished apparatus; it is not done by hand, but by machinery. Thus we have machines for Education: Lancastrian machines; Hamiltonian machines;[7] monitors, maps and emblems. Instruction, that mysterious communing of Wisdom with Ignorance, is no longer an indefinable tentative process, requiring a study of individual aptitudes, and a perpetual variation of means and methods, to attain the same end; but a secure, universal, straightforward business, to be conducted in the gross, by proper mechanism, with such intellect as comes to hand. Then, we have Religious machines, of all imaginable varieties; the Bible-Society,[8] professing a far higher and heavenly structure, is found, on inquiry, to be altogether an earthly contrivance: supported by collection of moneys, by fomenting of vanities, by puffing, intrigue and chicane; a machine for converting the Heathen. It is the same in all other departments. Has any man, or any society of men, a truth to speak, a piece of spiritual work to do; they can nowise proceed at once and with the mere natural organs, but must first call a public meeting, appoint committees, issue prospectuses, eat a public dinner; in a word, construct or borrow machinery, wherewith to speak it and do it. Without machinery they were hopeless, helpless; a colony of Hindoo weavers squatting in the heart of Lancashire.[9] Mark, too, how every machine must have its moving power, in some of the great currents of society; every little sect among us, Unitarians, Utilitarians, Anabaptists,

---

[7] Joseph Lancaster (1778–1838) popularized an educational method in which the older pupils in a school taught the younger. James Hamilton (1769–1831) developed a method of teaching languages by practice rather than from rules.

[8] The Bible Society, a popular nineteenth-century charity, distributed Bibles for use in missionary work.

[9] Lancashire was the center of the newly mechanized textile industry, which depended heavily on the export of cotton goods to India.

Phrenologists, must have its Periodical, its monthly or quarterly Magazine;—hanging out, like its windmill, into the *popularis aura*,[10] to grind meal for the society.

With individuals, in like manner, natural strength avails little. No individual now hopes to accomplish the poorest enterprise single-handed and without mechanical aids; he must make interest with some existing corporation, and till his field with their oxen. In these days, more emphatically than ever, 'to live, signifies to unite with a party, or to make one.' Philosophy, Science, Art, Literature, all depend on machinery. No Newton, by silent meditation, now discovers the system of the world from the falling of an apple; but some quite other than Newton stands in his Museum, his Scientific Institution, and behind whole batteries of retorts, digesters, and galvanic piles imperatively 'interrogates Nature,'—who, however, shows no haste to answer. In defect of Raphaels, and Angelos, and Mozarts, we have Royal Academies of Painting, Sculpture, Music; whereby the languishing spirit of Art may be strengthened, as by the more generous diet of a Public Kitchen. Literature, too, has its Paternoster-row[11] mechanism, its Trade-dinners, its Editorial conclaves, and huge subterranean, puffing bellows; so that books are not only printed, but, in a great measure, written and sold, by machinery.

National culture, spiritual benefit of all sorts, is under the same management. No Queen Christina, in these times, needs to send for her Descartes; no King Frederick for his Voltaire, and painfully nourish him with pensions and flattery: any sovereign of taste, who wishes to enlighten his people, has only to impose a new tax, and with the proceeds establish Philosophic Institutes. Hence the Royal and Imperial Societies, the Bibliothèques, Glyptothèques, Technothèques,[12] which front us in all capital cities; like so many well-finished hives, to which it is expected the stray agencies of Wisdom will swarm of their own accord, and hive and make honey. In like manner, among ourselves, when it is thought that religion is declining, we have

---

[10] "Breath of the populace."
[11] Street in London which was the center of the bookselling trade.
[12] Libraries, museums of sculpture and technology.

only to vote half-a-million's worth of bricks and mortar, and build new churches. In Ireland it seems they have gone still farther, having actually established a 'Penny-a-week Purgatory-Society'! Thus does the Genius of Mechanism stand by to help us in all difficulties and emergencies, and with his iron back bears all our burdens.

These things, which we state lightly enough here, are yet of deep import, and indicate a mighty change in our whole manner of existence. For the same habit regulates not our modes of action alone, but our modes of thought and feeling. Men are grown mechanical in head and in heart, as well as in hand. They have lost faith in individual endeavour, and in natural force, of any kind. Not for internal perfection, but for external combinations and arrangements, for institutions, constitutions,—for Mechanism of one sort or other, do they hope and struggle. Their whole efforts, attachments, opinions, turn on mechanism, and are of a mechanical character.

We may trace this tendency in all the great manifestations of our time; in its intellectual aspect, the studies it most favours and its manner of conducting them; in its practical aspects, its politics, arts, religion, morals; in the whole sources, and throughout the whole currents, of its spiritual, no less than its material activity.

Consider, for example, the state of Science generally, in Europe, at this period. It is admitted, on all sides, that the Metaphysical and Moral Sciences are falling into decay, while the Physical are engrossing, every day, more respect and attention. In most of the European nations there is now no such thing as a Science of Mind; only more or less advancement in the general science, or the special sciences, of matter. The French were the first to desert Metaphysics; and though they have lately affected to revive their school, it has yet no signs of vitality. The land of Malebranche, Pascal, Descartes and Fénelon, has now only its Cousins and Villemains;[13] while, in the department of

---

[13] Victor Cousin (1792–1867): French philosopher who taught that the function of philosophy was to explain the universal beliefs of mankind. Abel Francois Villemain (1790–1867): French man of letters. The comparison is meant to illustrate the decline in the quality of French thought.

Physics, it reckons far other names. Among ourselves, the Philosophy of Mind, after a rickety infancy, which never reached the vigour of manhood, fell suddenly into decay, languished and finally died out, with its last amiable cultivator, Professor Stewart.[14] In no nation but Germany has any decisive effort been made in psychological science; not to speak of any decisive result. The science of the age, in short, is physical, chemical, physiological; in all shapes mechanical. Our favourite Mathematics, the highly prized exponent of all these other sciences, has also become more and more mechanical. Excellence in what is called its higher departments depends less on natural genius than on acquired expertness in wielding its machinery. Without undervaluing the wonderful results which a Lagrange or Laplace[15] educes by means of it, we may remark, that their calculus, differential and integral, is little else than a more cunningly constructed arithmetical mill; where the factors being put in, are, as it were, ground into the true product, under cover, and without other effort on our part than steady turning the handle. We have more Mathematics than ever; but less Mathesis. Archimedes and Plato could not have read the *Mécanique Céleste*; but neither would the whole French Institute see aught in that saying, 'God geometrises!' but a sentimental rodomontade.

Nay, our whole Metaphysics itself, from Locke's[16] time downwards, has been physical; not a spiritual philosophy, but a material one. The singular estimation in which his Essay was so long held as a scientific work (an estimation grounded, indeed, on the estimable character of the man) will one day be thought a curious indication of the spirit of these times. His whole doctrine is mechanical, in its aim and origin, in its method and its results. It is not a philosophy of the mind: it is a mere discussion concerning the origin of our consciousness, or ideas, or what-

[14] Dugald Stewart (1753–1828), a Scottish philosopher and leader of the "Common Sense" school which argued that accurate and complete knowledge of reality can be achieved through the senses.

[15] Joseph Louis Lagrange (1736–1813) and Pierre Simon de Laplace (1749–1827): French mathematicians. Laplace wrote *Mécanique Céleste* (1799–1825).

[16] In this paragraph, Carlyle attacks John Locke's *Essay concerning Human Understanding* (1690) which asserts that the mind is a blank tablet that passively receives impressions of the external world.

ever else they are called; a genetic history of what we see *in* the mind. The grand secrets of Necessity and Freewill, of the Mind's vital or non-vital dependence on Matter, of our mysterious relations to Time and Space, to God, to the Universe, are not, in the faintest degree touched on in these inquiries; and seem not to have the smallest connexion with them.

The last class of our Scotch Metaphysicians had a dim notion that much of this was wrong; but they knew not how to right it. The school of Reid[17] had also from the first taken a mechanical course, not seeing any other. The singular conclusions at which Hume,[18] setting out from their admitted premises, was arriving, brought this school into being; they let loose Instinct, as an undiscriminating ban-dog, to guard them against these conclusions;—they tugged lustily at the logical chain by which Hume was so coldly towing them and the world into bottomless abysses of Atheism and Fatalism. But the chain somehow snapped between them; and the issue has been that nobody now cares about either,—any more than about Hartley's, Darwin's, or Priestley's[19] contemporaneous doings in England. Hartley's vibrations and vibratiuncles, one would think, were material and mechanical enough; but our Continental neighbours have gone still farther. One of their philosophers has lately discovered, that 'as the liver secretes bile, so does the brain secrete thought'; which astonishing discovery Dr. Cabanis, more lately still, in his *Rapports du Physique et du Morale de l'Homme,* has pushed into its minutest developments.

The metaphysical philosophy of this last inquirer is certainly no shadowy or unsubstantial one. He fairly lays open our moral structure with his dissecting-knives and real metal probes; and

---

[17] Thomas Reid (1710–1796), a Scottish philosopher of the "Common Sense" school.

[18] David Hume (1711–1776) argued that since knowledge consists only of single perceptions, knowledge of relationships in the external world is impossible of discovery.

[19] David Hartley (1705–1757), Erasmus Darwin (1731–1802) and Joseph Priestly (1733–1804) were all developers of a materialistic psychology based on the association of ideas. Hartley developed a materialistic psychological theory arguing that the "vibrations" created by perceived objects created corresponding material "vibratiuncles" in the nerves and brain.

exhibits it to the inspection of mankind, by Leuwenhoek microscopes, and inflation with the anatomical blowpipe. Thought, he is inclined to hold, is still secreted by the brain; but then Poetry and Religion (and it is really worth knowing) are 'a product of the smaller intestines'! We have the greatest admiration for this learned doctor: with what scientific stoicism he walks through the land of wonders, unwondering; like a wise man through some huge, gaudy, imposing Vauxhall,[20] whose fire-works, cascades and symphonies, the vulgar may enjoy and believe in,—but where he finds nothing real but the saltpetre, pasteboard and catgut. His book may be regarded as the ultimatum of mechanical metaphysics in our time; a remarkable realisation of what in Martinus Scriblerus[21] was still only an idea, that 'as the jack had a meat-roasting quality, so had the body a thinking quality,'—upon the strength of which the Nurembergers were to build a wood-and-leather man, 'who should reason as well as most country parsons.' Vaucanson did indeed make a wooden duck, that seemed to eat and digest; but that bold scheme of the Nurembergers remained for a more modern virtuoso.

This condition of the two great departments of knowledge, —the outward, cultivated exclusively on mechanical principles; the inward, finally abandoned, because, cultivated on such principles, it is found to yield no result,—sufficiently indicates the intellectual bias of our time, its all-pervading disposition towards that line of inquiry. In fact, an inward persuasion has long been diffusing itself, and now and then even comes to utterance, That, except the external, there are no true sciences; that to the inward world (if there be any) our only conceivable road is through the outward; that, in short, what cannot be investigated and understood mechanically, cannot be investigated and understood at all. We advert the more particularly to these intellectual propensities, as to prominent symptoms of our age, because Opinion is at all times doubly related to Action, first as

[20] A famous pleasure garden in London open to the public.
[21] *Memoirs of the Extraordinary Life, Works and Discoveries of Martinus Scriblerus* (1741), a satire on literature and learning by John Arbuthnot.

cause, then as effect; and the speculative tendency of any age will therefore give us, on the whole, the best indications of its practical tendency.

Nowhere, for example, is the deep, almost exclusive faith we have in Mechanism more visible than in the Politics of this time. Civil government does by its nature include much that is mechanical, and must be treated accordingly. We term it indeed, in ordinary language, the Machine of Society, and talk of it as the grand working wheel from which all private machines must derive, or to which they must adapt, their movements. Considered merely as a metaphor, all this is well enough; but here, as in so many other cases, the 'foam hardens itself into a shell,' and the shadow we have wantonly evoked stands terrible before us and will not depart at our bidding. Government includes much also that is not mechanical, and cannot be treated mechanically; of which latter truth, as appears to us, the political speculations and exertions of our time are taking less and less cognisance.

Nay, in the very outset, we might note the mighty interest taken in *mere political arrangements*, as itself the sign of a mechanical age. The whole discontent of Europe takes this direction. The deep, strong cry of all civilised nations,—a cry which, every one now sees, must and will be answered, is: Give us a reform of Government! A good structure of legislation, a proper check upon the executive, a wise arrangement of the judiciary, is *all* that is wanting for human happiness. The Philosopher of this age is not a Socrates, a Plato, a Hooker, or Taylor,[22] who inculcates on men the necessity and infinite worth of moral goodness, the great truth that our happiness depends on the mind which is within us, and not on the circumstances which are without us; but a Smith, a De Lolme,[23] a Bentham, who chiefly inculcates the reverse of this,—that our happiness

[22] Richard Hooker (1554–1600) and Jeremy Taylor (1613–1667) were theologians famous for their eloquent defense of the Church of England.
[23] Adam Smith (1723–1790): Scottish economist who argued that the economy will run according to the laws of supply and demand without the necessity of external regulation. Jean Louis de Lolme (1740–1806) was a Swiss commentator on English politics.

depends entirely on external circumstances; nay, that the strength and dignity of the mind within us is itself the creature and consequence of these. Were the laws, the government, in good order, all were well with us; the rest would care for itself! Dissentients from this opinion, expressed or implied, are now rarely to be met with; widely and angrily as men differ in its application, the principle is admitted by all.

Equally mechanical, and of equal simplicity, are the methods proposed by both parties for completing or securing this all-sufficient perfection of arrangement. It is no longer the moral, religious, spiritual condition of the people that is our concern, but their physical, practical, economical condition, as regulated by public laws. Thus is the Body-politic more than ever worshipped and tendered; but the Soul-politic less than ever. Love of country, in any high or generous sense, in any other than an almost animal sense, or mere habit, has little importance attached to it in such reforms, or in the opposition shown them. Men are to be guided only by their self-interests. Good government is a good balancing of these; and, except a keen eye and appetite for self-interest, requires no virtue in any quarter. To both parties it is emphatically a machine: to the discontented, a 'taxing-machine'; to the contented, a 'machine for securing property.' Its duties and its faults are not those of a father, but of an active parish-constable.

Thus it is by the mere condition of the machine, by preserving it untouched, or else by reconstructing it, and oiling it anew, that man's salvation as a social being is to be ensured and indefinitely promoted. Contrive the fabric of law aright, and without farther effort on your part, that divine spirit of Freedom, which all hearts venerate and long for, will of herself come to inhabit it; and under her healing wings every noxious influence will wither, every good and salutary one more and more expand. Nay, so devoted are we to this principle, and at the same time so curiously mechanical, that a new trade, specially grounded on it, has arisen among us, under the name of 'Codification,' or codemaking in the abstract; whereby any people, for a reasonable consideration, may be accommodated with a patent code;—more easily than curious individuals with patent breeches, for the people does *not* need to be measured first.

To us who live in the midst of all this, and see continually the faith, hope and practice of every one founded on Mechanism of one kind or other, it is apt to seem quite natural, and as if it could never have been otherwise. Nevertheless, if we recollect or reflect a little, we shall find both that it has been, and might again be otherwise. The domain of Mechanism,—meaning thereby political, ecclesiastical or other outward establishments,—was once considered as embracing, and we are persuaded can at any time embrace, but a limited portion of man's interests, and by no means the highest portion.

To speak a little pedantically, there is a science of *Dynamics* in man's fortunes and nature, as well as of *Mechanics*. There is a science which treats of, and practically addresses, the primary, unmodified forces and energies of man, the mysterious springs of Love, and Fear, and Wonder, of Enthusiasm, Poetry, Religion, all which have a truly vital and *infinite* character; as well as a science which practically addresses the finite, modified developments of these, when they take the shape of immediate 'motives,' as hope of reward, or as fear of punishment.

Now it is certain, that in former times the wise men, the enlightened lovers of their kind, who appeared generally as Moralists, Poets or Priests, did, without neglecting the Mechanical province, deal chiefly with the Dynamical; applying themselves chiefly to regulate, increase and purify the inward primary powers of man; and fancying that herein lay the main difficulty, and the best service they could undertake. But a wide difference is manifest in our age. For the wise men, who now appear as Political Philosophers, deal exclusively with the Mechanical province; and occupying themselves in counting-up and estimating men's motives, strive by curious checking and balancing, and other adjustments of Profit and Loss, to guide them to their true advantage: while, unfortunately, those same 'motives' are so innumerable, and so variable in every individual, that no really useful conclusion can ever be drawn from their enumeration. But though Mechanism, wisely contrived, has done much for man in a social and moral point of view, we cannot be persuaded that it has ever been the chief source of his worth or happiness. Consider the great elements of human enjoyment, the attainments and possessions that exalt man's life to its present height, and see what part of these he owes to institutions, to Mechanism of any kind; and what to the instinctive, unbounded force, which Nature herself lent him, and still continues to him. Shall we say, for example, that Science and Art are indebted principally to the founders of Schools and Universities? Did not Science originate rather, and gain advancement, in the obscure closets of the Roger Bacons, Keplers,[24] Newtons; in the workshops of the Fausts and the Watts; wherever, and in what guise soever Nature, from the first times downwards, had sent a gifted spirit upon the earth? Again, were Homer and Shakespeare members of any beneficed guild, or made Poets by means of it? Were Painting and Sculpture created by forethought, brought into the world by institutions for that end? No; Science and Art have, from first to last, been the free gift of Nature; an unsolicited, unexpected gift; often even a fatal one. These things rose up, as it were, by spontaneous growth, in the free soil and sunshine of Nature. They were not planted or grafted, nor even greatly multiplied or improved by the culture or manuring of institutions. Generally speaking, they have derived only partial help from these; often enough have suffered damage. They made constitutions for themselves. They originated in the Dynamical nature of man, not in his Mechanical nature.

Or, to take an infinitely higher instance, that of the Christian Religion, which, under every theory of it, in the believing or unbelieving mind, must ever be regarded as the crowning glory, or rather the life and soul, of our whole modern culture: How did Christianity arise and spread abroad among men? Was it by institutions, and establishments and well-arranged systems of mechanism? Not so; on the contrary, in all past and existing institutions for those ends, its divine spirit has invariably been

---

[24] Roger Bacon (c. 1214–1292): English monk noted for interest in science. Johannes Kepler (1571–1630): German astronomer who developed important laws of planetary motion.

found to languish and decay. It arose in the mystic deeps of man's soul; and was spread abroad by the 'preaching of the word,' by simple, altogether natural and individual efforts; and flew, like hallowed fire, from heart to heart, till all were purified and illuminated by it; and its heavenly light shone, as it still shines, and (as sun or star) will ever shine, through the whole dark destinies of man. Here again was no Mechanism; man's highest attainment was accomplished Dynamically, not Mechanically.

Nay, we will venture to say, that no high attainment, not even any far-extending movement among men, was ever accomplished otherwise. Strange as it may seem, if we read History with any degree of thoughtfulness, we shall find that the checks and balances of Profit and Loss have never been the grand agents with men; that they have never been roused into deep, thorough, all-pervading efforts by any computable prospect of Profit and Loss, for any visible, finite object; but always for some invisible and infinite one. The Crusades took their rise in Religion; their visible object was, commercially speaking, worth nothing. It was the boundless Invisible world that was laid bare in the imaginations of those men; and in its burning light, the visible shrunk as a scroll. Not mechanical, nor produced by mechanical means, was this vast movement. No dining at Freemasons' Tavern, with the other long train of modern machinery; no cunning reconciliation of 'vested interests,' was required here: only the passionate voice of one man, the rapt soul looking through the eyes of one man; and rugged, steel-clad Europe trembled beneath his words, and followed him whither he listed. In later ages it was still the same. The Reformation had an invisible, mystic and ideal aim; the result was indeed to be embodied in external things; but its spirit, its worth, was internal, invisible, infinite. Our English Revolution too originated in Religion. Men did battle, in those old days, not for Purse-sake, but for Conscience-sake. Nay, in our own days, it is no way different. The French Revolution itself had something higher in it than cheap bread and a Habeas-corpus act. Here too was an Idea; a Dynamic, not a Mechanic force. It was a struggle, though a blind and at last an insane one, for the infinite, divine nature of Right, of Freedom, of Country.

Thus does man, in every age, vindicate, consciously or unconsciously, his celestial birthright. Thus does Nature hold on her wondrous, unquestionable course; and all our systems and theories are but so many froth-eddies or sandbanks, which from time to time she casts up, and washes away. When we can drain the Ocean into mill-ponds, and bottle-up the Force of Gravity, to be sold by retail, in gas jars; then may we hope to comprehend the infinitudes of man's soul under formulas of Profit and Loss; and rule over this too, as over a patent engine, by checks, and valves, and balances.

Nay, even with regard to Government itself, can it be necessary to remind any one that Freedom, without which indeed all spiritual life is impossible, depends on infinitely more complex influences than either the extension or the curtailment of the 'democratic interest'? Who is there that, 'taking the high *priori* road,' shall point out what these influences are; what deep, subtle, inextricably entangled influences they have been and may be? For man is not the creature and product of Mechanism; but, in a far truer sense, its creator and producer: it is the noble People that makes the noble Government; rather than conversely. On the whole, Institutions are much; but they are not all. The freest and highest spirits of the world have often been found under strange outward circumstances: Saint Paul and his brother Apostles were politically slaves; Epictetus[25] was personally one. Again, forget the influences of Chivalry and Religion, and ask: What countries produced Columbus and Las Casas?[26] Or, descending from virtue and heroism to mere energy and spiritual talent: Cortes, Pizarro, Alba, Ximenes?[27]

[25] Greek Stoic philosopher of first century A.D.
[26] Bartolomé de Las Casas (1474–1566): Spanish missionary and historian of Spanish settlement of the New World.
[27] Hernando Cortes (1485–1547) and Francisco Pizarro (1470–1541): Spanish conquerors of Latin America. Duke of Alba (1508–1582): Spanish general responsible for bloody repression in Netherlands. Francisco Ximenes de Cisneros (1436–1517); Spanish soldier, statesman and cardinal.

The Spaniards of the sixteenth century were indisputably the noblest nation of Europe: yet they had the Inquisition and Philip II. They have the same government at this day; and are the lowest nation. The Dutch too have retained their old constitution; but no Siege of Leyden, no William the Silent, not even an Egmont or De Witt[28] any longer appears among them. With ourselves also, where much has changed, effect has nowise followed cause as it should have done: two centuries ago, the Commons Speaker addressed Queen Elizabeth on bended knees, happy that the virago's foot did not even smite him; yet the people were then governed, not by a Castlereagh, but by a Burghley;[29] they had their Shakspeare and Philip Sidney, where we have our Sheridan Knowles and Beau Brummel.[30]

These and the like facts are so familiar, the truths which they preach so obvious, and have in all past times been so universally believed and acted on, that we should almost feel ashamed for repeating them; were it not that, on every hand, the memory of them seems to have passed away, or at best died into a faint tradition, of no value as a practical principle. To judge by the loud clamour of our Constitution-builders, Statists, Economists, directors, creators, reformers of Public Societies; in a word, all manner of Mechanists, from the Cartwright up to the Code-maker; and by the nearly total silence of all Preachers and Teachers who should give a voice to Poetry, Religion and Morality, we might fancy either that man's Dynamical nature was, to all spiritual intents, extinct, or else so perfected that nothing more was to be made of it by the old means; and hence-

---

[28] Seige of Leyden: seige by Spanish was relieved when Dutch under William the Silent flooded surrounding lands enabling allied fleet to sail to rescue. Count of Egmont (1522–1568): Netherlands patriot executed by Duke of Alba for opposition to persecution of Protestants. Jan de Witt (1625–1672): Leader of the Dutch Republic.

[29] Viscount Castlereagh, Foreign Secretary (1812–1822), was instrumental in restoration of monarchical governments on European continent after defeat of Napoleon. Lord Burghley (1520–1598), chief advisor to Queen Elizabeth I.

[30] Philip Sidney (1554–1586), the Renaissance ideal of poet and soldier as compared to Sheridan Knowles (1784–1862), a contemporary minor playwright, and Beau Brummel (1778–1840), a contemporary man of fashion.

forth only in his Mechanical contrivances did any hope exist for him.

To define the limits of these two departments of man's activity, which work into one another, and by means of one another, so intricately and inseparably, were by its nature an impossible attempt. Their relative importance, even to the wisest mind, will vary in different times, according to the special wants and dispositions of those times. Meanwhile, it seems clear enough that only in the right coördination of the two, and the vigorous forwarding of *both*, does our true line of action lie. Undue cultivation of the inward or Dynamical province leads to idle, visionary, impracticable courses, and, especially in rude eras, to Superstition and Fanaticism, with their long train of baleful and well-known evils. Undue cultivation of the outward, again, though less immediately prejudicial, and even for the time productive of many palpable benefits, must, in the long-run, by destroying Moral Force, which is the parent of all other Force, prove not less certainly, and perhaps still more hopelessly, pernicious. This, we take it, is the grand characteristic of our age. By our skill in Mechanism, it has come to pass, that in the management of external things we excel all other ages; while in whatever respects the pure moral nature, in true dignity of soul and character, we are perhaps inferior to most civilised ages.

In fact, if we look deeper, we shall find that this faith in Mechanism has now struck its roots down into man's most intimate, primary sources of conviction; and is thence sending up, over his whole life and activity, innumerable stems,—fruit-bearing and poison-bearing. The truth is, men have lost their belief in the Invisible, and believe, and hope, and work only in the Visible; or, to speak it in other words: This is not a Religious age. Only the material, the immediately practical, not the divine and spiritual, is important to us. The infinite, absolute character of Virtue has passed into a finite, conditional one; it is no longer a worship of the Beautiful and Good; but a calculation of the Profitable. Worship, indeed, in any sense, is not recognised among us, or is mechanically explained into Fear of

21

pain, or Hope of pleasure. Our true Deity is Mechanism. It has subdued external Nature for us, and we think it will do all other things. We are Giants in physical power: in a deeper than metaphorical sense, we are Titans, that strive, by heaping mountain on mountain, to conquer Heaven also.

The strong Mechanical character, so visible in the spiritual pursuits and methods of this age, may be traced much farther into the condition and prevailing disposition of our spiritual nature itself. Consider, for example, the general fashion of Intellect in this era. Intellect, the power man has of knowing and believing, is now nearly synonymous with Logic, or the mere power of arranging and communicating. Its implement is not Meditation, but Argument. 'Cause and effect' is almost the only category under which we look at, and work with, all Nature. Our first question with regard to any object is not, What is it? but, How is it? We are no longer instinctively driven to apprehend, and lay to heart, what is Good and Lovely, but rather to inquire, as onlookers, how it is produced, whence it comes, whither it goes. Our favourite Philosophers have no love and no hatred; they stand among us not to do, nor to create anything, but as a sort of Logic-mills, to grind out the true causes and effects of all that is done and created. To the eye of a Smith, a Hume or a Constant,[31] all is well that works quietly. An Order of Ignatius Loyola, a Presbyterianism of John Knox, a Wickliffe or a Henry the Eighth,[32] are simply so many mechanical phenomena, caused or causing.

The *Euphuist* of our day differs much from his pleasant predecessors. An intellectual dapperling of these times boasts chiefly of his irresistible perspicacity, his 'dwelling in the daylight of truth,' and so forth; which, on examination, turns out to be a dwelling in the *rush*-light of 'closet-logic,' and a deep

[31] Benjamin Constant (1767–1830): French romantic novelist and political writer noted for his support of constitutional monarchy.
[32] Ignatius Loyola (1491–1556): soldier, priest, and mystic, founder of the Jesuit order. John Knox (1505–1572): the fanatical founder of Scottish Presbyterianism, the rigorous faith in which Carlyle was raised. John Wickliffe or Wyclif (c. 1328–1384): English religious reformer. Henry the Eighth (1491–1547) broke with the Roman Catholic Church to establish the separate Church of England.

unconsciousness that there is any other light to dwell in or any other objects to survey with it. Wonder, indeed, is, on all hands, dying out: it is the sign of uncultivation to wonder. Speak to any small man of a high, majestic Reformation, of a high majestic Luther; and forthwith he sets about 'accounting' for it; how the 'circumstances of the time' called for such a character, and found him, we suppose, standing girt and road-ready, to do its errand; how the 'circumstances of the time' created, fashioned, floated him quietly along into the result; how, in short, this small man, had he been there, could have performed the like himself! For it is the 'force of circumstances' that does everything; the force of one man can do nothing. Now all this is grounded on little more than a metaphor. We figure Society as a 'Machine,' and that mind is opposed to mind, as body is to body; whereby two, or at most ten, little minds must be stronger than one great mind. Notable absurdity! For the plain truth, very plain, we think is, that minds are opposed to minds in quite a different way; and *one* man that has a higher Wisdom, a hitherto unknown spiritual Truth in him, is stronger, not than ten men that have it not, or than ten thousand, but than *all* men that have it not; and stands among them with a quite ethereal, angelic power, as with a sword out of Heaven's own armory, sky-tempered, which no buckler, and no tower of brass, will finally withstand.

But to us, in these times, such considerations rarely occur. We enjoy, we see nothing by direct vision; but only by reflection, and in anatomical dismemberment. Like Sir Hudibras, for every Why we must have a Wherefore. We have our little *theory* on all human and divine things. Poetry, the workings of genius itself, which in all times, with one or another meaning, has been called Inspiration, and held to be mysterious and inscrutable, is no longer without its scientific exposition. The building of the lofty rhyme is like any other masonry or bricklaying: we have theories of its rise, height, decline and fall,—which latter, it would seem, is now near, among all people. Of our 'Theories of Taste,' as they are called, wherein the deep, infinite, unspeakable Love of Wisdom and Beauty, which dwells in all men, is 'explained,' made mechanically visible, from 'As-

23

sociation' and the like, why should we say anything? Hume has written us a 'Natural History of Religion'; in which one Natural History all the rest are included. Strangely too does the general feeling coincide with Hume's in this wonderful problem; for whether his 'Natural History' be the right one or not, that Religion must have a Natural History, all of us, cleric and laic, seem to be agreed. He indeed regards it as a Disease, we again as Health; so far there is a difference; but in our first principle we are at one.

To what extent theological Unbelief, we mean intellectual dissent from the Church, in its view of Holy writ, prevails at this day, would be a highly important, were it not, under any circumstances, an almost impossible inquiry. But the Unbelief, which is of a still more fundamental character, every man may see prevailing, with scarcely any but the faintest contradiction, all around him; even in the Pulpit itself. Religion in most countries, more or less in every country, is no longer what it was, and should be,—a thousand-voiced psalm from the heart of Man to his invisible Father, the fountain of all Goodness, Beauty, Truth, and revealed in every revelation of these; but for the most part, a wise prudential feeling grounded on mere calculation; a matter, as all others now are, of Expediency and Utility; whereby some smaller quantum of earthly enjoyment may be exchanged for a far larger quantum of celestial enjoyment. Thus Religion too is Profit, a working for wages; not Reverence, but vulgar Hope or Fear. Many, we know, very many we hope, are still religious in a far different sense; were it not so, our case were too desperate: but to witness that such is the temper of the times, we take any calm observant man, who agrees or disagrees in our feeling on the matter, and ask him whether our *view* of it is not in general well-founded.

Literature too, if we consider it, gives similar testimony. At no former era has Literature, the printed communication of Thought, been of such importance as it is now. We often hear that the Church is in danger; and truly so it is,—in a danger it seems not to know of: for, with its tithes in the most perfect safety, its functions are becoming more and more superseded. The true Church of England, at this moment, lies in the Editors of its Newspapers. These preach to the people daily, weekly; admonishing kings themselves; advising peace or war, with an authority which only the first Reformers, and a long-past class of Popes, were possessed of; inflicting moral censure; imparting moral encouragement, consolation, edification; in all ways diligently 'administering the Discipline of the Church.' It may be said too, that in private disposition the new Preachers somewhat resemble the Mendicant Friars of old times: outwardly full of holy zeal; inwardly not without stratagem, and hunger for terrestrial things. But omitting this class, and the boundless host of watery personages who pipe, as they are able, on so many scrannel straws, let us look at the higher regions of Literature, where, if anywhere, the pure melodies of Poesy and Wisdom should be heard. Of natural talent there is no deficiency: one or two richly-endowed individuals even give us a superiority in this respect. But what is the song they sing? Is it a tone of the Memnon Statue,[33] breathing music as the *light* first touches it? A 'liquid wisdom,' disclosing to our sense the deep, infinite harmonies of Nature and man's soul? Alas, no! It is not a matin or vesper hymn to the Spirit of Beauty, but a fierce clashing of cymbals, and shouting of multitudes, as children pass through the fire to Moloch! Poetry itself has no eye for the Invisible. Beauty is no longer the god it worships, but some brute image of Strength; which we may call an idol, for true Strength is one and the same with Beauty, and its worship also is a hymn. The meek, silent Light can mould, create and purify all Nature; but the loud Whirlwind, the sign and product of Disunion, of Weakness, passes on, and is forgotten. How widely this veneration for the physically Strongest has spread itself through Literature, any one may judge who reads either criticism or poem. We praise a work, not as 'true,' but as 'strong'; our highest praise is that it has 'affected' us, has 'terrified' us. All this, it has been well observed, is the 'maximum of the Barbarous,' the symptom, not of vigorous refinement, but of luxurious corruption. It speaks much, too, for men's indestructible love of truth, that nothing of this kind will abide with

---

[33] Legendary statue in Egypt said to utter musical tones when struck by the first light of dawn.

them; that even the talent of a Byron cannot permanently se-
duce us into idol-worship; that he too, with all his wild siren
charming, already begins to be disregarded and forgotten.

Again, with respect to our Moral condition: here also he who
runs may read that the same physical, mechanical influences are
everywhere busy. For the 'superior morality,' of which we hear
so much, we too would desire to be thankful: at the same time,
it were but blindness to deny that this 'superior morality' is
properly rather an 'inferior criminality,' produced not by greater
love of Virtue, but by greater perfection of Police; and of that
far subtler and stronger Police, called Public Opinion. This last
watches over us with its Argus eyes more keenly than ever; but
the 'inward eye' seems heavy with sleep. Of any belief in invisible, divine things, we find as few traces in our Morality as elsewhere. It is by tangible, material considerations that we are
guided, not by inward and spiritual. Self-denial, the parent of
all virtue, in any true sense of that word, has perhaps seldom
been rarer: so rare is it, that the most, even in their abstract
speculations, regard its existence as a chimera. Virtue is Pleasure, is Profit; no celestial, but an earthly thing. Virtuous men,
Philanthropists, Martyrs are happy accidents; their 'taste' lies
the right way! In all senses, we worship and follow after Power;
which may be called a physical pursuit. No man now loves
Truth, as Truth must be loved, with an infinite love; but only
with a finite love, and as it were *par amours*.[34] Nay, properly
speaking, he does not *believe* and know it, but only '*thinks*' it,
and that 'there is every probability!' He preaches it aloud, and
rushes courageously forth with it,—if there is a multitude huzzaing at his back; yet ever keeps looking over his shoulder, and
the instant the huzzaing languishes, he too stops short.

In fact, what morality we have takes the shape of Ambition,
of 'Honour': beyond money and money's worth, our only rational blessedness is Popularity. It were but a fool's trick to die
for conscience. Only for 'character,' by duel, or in case of
extremity, by suicide, is the wise man bound to die. By arguing
on the 'force of circumstances,' we have argued away all force

[34] "Through loves," with a play on paramour, one who loves or is
loved illicitly.

from ourselves; and stand leashed together, uniform in dress and movement, like the rowers of some boundless galley. This and that may be right and true; *but* we must not do it. Wonderful 'Force of Public Opinion'! We must act and walk in all points as it prescribes; follow the traffic it bids us, realise the sum of money, the degree of 'influence' it expects of us, *or* we shall be lightly esteemed; certain mouthfuls of articulate wind will be blown at us, and this what mortal courage can front? Thus, while civil liberty is more and more secured to us, our moral liberty is all but lost. Practically considered, our creed is Fatalism; and, free in hand and foot, we are shackled in heart and soul with far straiter than feudal chains. Truly may we say, with the Philosopher, 'the deep meaning of the Laws of Mechanism lies heavy on us'; and in the closet, in the marketplace, in the temple, by the social hearth, encumbers the whole movements of our mind, and over our noblest faculties is spreading a nightmare sleep.

These dark features, we are aware, belong more or less to other ages, as well as to ours. This faith in Mechanism, in the all-importance of physical things, is in every age the common refuge of Weakness and blind Discontent; of all who believe, as many will ever do, that man's true good lies without him, not within. We are aware also, that, as applied to ourselves in all their aggravation, they form but half a picture; that in the whole picture there are bright lights as well as gloomy shadows. If we here dwell chiefly on the latter, let us not be blamed: it is in general more profitable to reckon up our defects than to boast of our attainments.

Neither, with all these evils more or less clearly before us, have we at any time despaired of the fortunes of society. Despair, or even despondency, in that respect, appears to us, in all cases, a groundless feeling. We have a faith in the imperishable dignity of man; in the high vocation to which, throughout this his earthly history, he has been appointed. However it may be with individual nations, whatever melancholic speculators may assert, it seems a well-ascertained fact, that in all times, reckoning even from those of the Heraclides and Pelasgi, the happiness

27

and greatness of mankind at large have been continually progressive. Doubtless this age also is advancing. Its very unrest, its ceaseless activity, its discontent contains matter of promise. Knowledge, education are opening the eyes of the humblest; are increasing the number of thinking minds without limit. This is as it should be; for not in turning back, not in resisting, but only in resolutely struggling forward, does our life consist.

Nay, after all, our spiritual maladies are but of Opinion; we are but fettered by chains of our own forging, and which ourselves also can rend asunder. This deep, paralysed subjection to physical objects comes not from Nature, but from our own unwise mode of *viewing* Nature. Neither can we understand that man wants, at this hour, any faculty of heart, soul or body, that ever belonged to him. 'He, who has been born, has been a First Man'; has had lying before his young eyes, and as yet unhardened into scientific shapes, a world as plastic, infinite, divine, as lay before the eyes of Adam himself. If Mechanism, like some glass bell, encircles and imprisons us; if the soul looks forth on a fair heavenly country which it cannot reach, and pines, and in its scanty atmosphere is ready to perish,—yet the bell is but of glass; 'one bold stroke to break the bell in pieces, and thou art delivered!' Not the invisible world is wanting, for it dwells in man's soul, and this last is still here. Are the solemn temples, in which the Divinity was once visibly revealed among us, crumbling away? We can repair them, we can rebuild them. The wisdom, the heroic worth of our forefathers, which we have lost, we can recover. That admiration of old nobleness, which now so often shows itself as a faint *dilettantism*, will one day become a generous emulation, and man may again be all that he has been, and more than he has been. Nor are these the mere daydreams of fancy; they are clear possibilities; nay, in this time they are even assuming the character of hopes. Indications we do see in other countries and in our own, signs infinitely cheering to us, that Mechanism is not always to be our hard taskmaster, but one day to be our pliant, all-ministering servant; that a new and brighter spiritual era is slowly evolving itself for all men. But on these things our present course forbids us to enter.

Meanwhile, that great outward changes are in progress can be doubtful to no one. The time is sick and out of joint. Many things have reached their height; and it is a wise adage that tells us, 'the darkest hour is nearest the dawn.' Wherever we can gather indication of the public thought, whether from printed books, as in France or Germany, or from Carbonari[35] rebellions and other political tumults, as in Spain, Portugal, Italy and Greece, the voice it utters is the same. The thinking minds of all nations call for change. There is a deep-lying struggle in the whole fabric of society; a boundless grinding collision of the New with the Old. The French Revolution, as is now visible enough, was not the parent of this mighty movement, but its offspring. Those two hostile influences, which always exist in human things, and on the constant intercommunion of which depends their health and safety, had lain in separate masses, accumulating through generations, and France was the scene of their fiercest explosion; but the final issue was not unfolded in that country: nay, it is not yet anywhere unfolded. Political freedom is hitherto the object of these efforts; but they will not and cannot stop there. It is towards a higher freedom than mere freedom from oppression by his fellow-mortal, that man dimly aims. Of this higher, heavenly freedom, which is 'man's reasonable service,' all his noble institutions, his faithful endeavours and loftiest attainments, are but the body, and more and more approximated emblem.

On the whole, as this wondrous planet, Earth, is journeying with its fellows through infinite Space, so are the wondrous destinies embarked on it journeying through infinite Time, under a higher guidance than ours. For the present, as our astronomy informs us, its path lies towards *Hercules*, the constellation of *Physical Power*: but that is not our most pressing concern. Go where it will, the deep HEAVEN will be around it. Therein let us have hope and sure faith. To reform a world, to reform a nation, no wise man will undertake; and all but foolish men know, that the only solid, though a far slower reformation, is what each begins and perfects on *himself*.

[35] Secret revolutionary society active, especially in Italy, in early nineteenth century.

Sartor Resartus

The Life and Opinions of Herr Teufelsdröckh

Mein Vermächtniss, wie herrlich weit und breit!
Die Zeit ist mein Vermächtniss, mein Acker is die Zeit.

GOETHE

[My inheritance how wide and fair!
Time is my fair seed-field, of Time I'm heir.]

Sartor Resartus first appeared in serial form in
Fraser's Magazine from November 1833 to August 1834.
It was published in America in 1836, in an edition sponsored
by Carlyle's admirer, Ralph Waldo Emerson. The first
English edition appeared in 1838.

Book First

❧

Chapter I
Preliminary

No Philosophy of Clothes yet, notwithstanding all our Science.
Strangely forgotten that Man is by nature a *naked* animal. The
English mind all-too practically absorbed for any such in-
quiry. Not so, deep-thinking Germany. Advantage of Specu-
lation having free course. Editor receives from Professor
Teufelsdröckh his new Work on Clothes.

Considering our present advanced state of culture, and how
the Torch of Science has now been brandished and borne about,
with more or less effect, for five thousand years and upwards;
how, in these times especially, not only the Torch still burns,
and perhaps more fiercely than ever, but innumerable Rush-
lights, and Sulphur-matches, kindled thereat, are also glancing
in every direction, so that not the smallest cranny or doghole in
Nature or Art can remain unilluminated,—it might strike the
reflective mind with some surprise that hitherto little or nothing
of a fundamental character, whether in the way of Philosophy
or History, has been written on the subject of Clothes.

Our Theory of Gravitation is as good as perfect: Lagrange,
it is well known, has proved that the Planetary System, on
this scheme, will endure forever; Laplace, still more cunningly,

even guesses that it could not have been made on any other scheme. Whereby, at least, our nautical Logbooks can be better kept; and water-transport of all kinds has grown more commodious. Of Geology and Geognosy we know enough: what with the labours of our Werners and Huttons, what with the ardent genius of their disciples, it has come about that now, to many a Royal Society, the Creation of a World is little more mysterious than the cooking of a dumpling; concerning which last, indeed, there have been minds to whom the question, *How the apples were got in*, presented difficulties. Why mention our disquisitions on the Social Contract,[1] on the Standard of Taste,[2] on the Migrations of the Herring? Then, have we not a Doctrine of Rent, a Theory of Value,[3] Philosophies of Language, of History, of Pottery, of Apparitions, of Intoxicating Liquors? Man's whole life and environment have been laid open and elucidated; scarcely a fragment or fibre of his Soul, Body, and Possessions, but has been probed, dissected, distilled, desiccated, and scientifically decomposed: our spiritual Faculties, of which it appears there are not a few, have their Stewarts, Cousins, Royer Collards:[4] every cellular, vascular, muscular Tissue glories in its Lawrences, Majendies, Bichâts.[5]

How, then, comes it, may the reflective mind repeat, that the grand Tissue of all Tissues, the only real Tissue, should have been quite overlooked by Science,—the vestural Tissue, namely, of woollen or other cloth; which Man's Soul wears as its outmost wrappage and overall; wherein his whole other Tissues are in-

[1] *Le Contrat Social* (1762), the most famous work of Jean Jacques Rousseau (1712–1778).

[2] David Hume (1711–1776), Scottish philosopher, published *Of the Standard of Taste* in 1757.

[3] An ironic reference to writings of the political economists whom Carlyle constantly criticizes: Adam Smith (1723–1790), David Ricardo (1772–1823).

[4] Dugald Stewart, see "Signs of the Times," n. 14. Victor Cousin (1792–1867) and Pierre Royer-Collard (1763–1845) were French philosophers. For Cousin see "Signs of the Times," n. 13.

[5] Sir William Lawrence (1783–1867), François Magendie (1783–1855), and Maria François Xavier Bichât (1771–1802) were prominent in medical science.

cluded and screened, his whole Faculties work, his whole Self lives, moves, and has its being? For if, now and then, some straggling broken-winged thinker has cast an owl's-glance into this obscure region, the most have soared over it altogether heedless; regarding Clothes as a property, not an accident, as quite natural and spontaneous, like the leaves of trees, like the plumage of birds. In all speculations they have tacitly figured man as a *Clothed Animal*; whereas he is by nature a *Naked Animal*; and only in certain circumstances, by purpose and device, masks himself in Clothes. Shakespeare says, we are creatures that look before and after: the more surprising that we do not look round a little, and see what is passing under our very eyes.

But here, as in so many other cases, Germany, learned, indefatigable, deep-thinking Germany comes to our aid. It is, after all, a blessing that, in these revolutionary times, there should be one country where abstract Thought can still take shelter; that while the din and frenzy of Catholic Emancipations, and Rotten Boroughs, and Revolts of Paris,[6] deafen every French and every English ear, the German can stand peaceful on his scientific watch-tower; and, to the raging, struggling multitude here and elsewhere, solemnly, from hour to hour, with preparatory blast of cowhorn, emit his *Höret ihr Herren und lasset's Euch sagen*;[7] in other words, tell the Universe, which so often forgets that fact, what o'clock it really is. Not unfrequently the Germans have been blamed for an unprofitable diligence; as if they struck into devious courses, where nothing was to be had but the toil of a rough journey; as if, forsaking the gold-mines of finance and that political slaughter of fat oxen whereby a man himself grows fat, they were apt to run goose-hunting into

[6] Catholic Emancipation: a bitterly debated bill to give Catholics the right to hold most public offices was passed in 1829. Rotten Boroughs: electoral districts which, because of population shifts, contained few voters yet still had the right to send members to Parliament. Elimination of these districts was part of the demand for electoral reform leading up to the Reform Bill of 1832. Revolts of Paris: the revolution of 1830 which overthrew Charles X.
[7] "Listen, gentlemen, and let me tell you."

regions of bilberries and crowberries, and be swallowed up at last in remote peat-bogs. Of that unwise science, which, as our Humorist expresses it,[8]

'By geometric scale
Doth take the size of pots of ale;'

still more, of that altogether misdirected industry, which is seen virgorously thrashing mere straw, there can nothing defensive be said. In so far as the Germans are chargeable with such, let them take the consequence. Nevertheless be it remarked, that even a Russian steppe has tumuli and gold ornaments; also many a scene that looks desert and rock-bound from the distance, will unfold itself, when visited, into rare valleys. Nay, in any case, would Critisicm erect not only finger-posts and turnpikes, but spiked gates and impassable barriers, for the mind of man? It is written, 'Many shall run to and fro, and knowledge shall be increased.'[9] Surely the plain rule is, Let each considerate person have his way, and see what it will lead to. For not this man and that man, but all men make up mankind, and their united tasks the task of mankind. How often have we seen some such adventurous, and perhaps much-censured wanderer light on some out-lying, neglected, yet vitally momentous province; the hidden treasures of which he first discovered, and kept proclaiming till the general eye and effort were directed thither, and the conquest was completed;—thereby, in these his seemingly so aimless rambles, planting new standards, founding new habitable colonies, in the immeasurable circumambient realm of Nothingness and Night! Wise man was he who counselled that Speculation should have free course, and look fearlessly towards all the thirty-two points of the compass, whithersoever and howsoever it listed.

Perhaps it is proof of the stunted condition in which pure Science, especially pure moral Science, languishes among us English; and how our mercantile greatness, and invaluable

[8] Samuel Butler, *Hudibras*, I, i, 121–22.
[9] Daniel, xii, 4.

Constitution, impressing a political or other immediately practical tendency on all English culture and endeavour, cramps the free flight of Thoughts,—that this, not Philosophy of Clothes, but recognition even that we have no such Philosophy, stands here for the first time published in our language. What English intellect could have chosen such a topic, or by chance stumbled on it? But for that same unshackled, and even sequestered condition of the German Learned, which permits and induces them to fish in all manner of waters, with all manner of nets, it seems probable enough, this abstruse Inquiry might, in spite of the results it leads to, have continued dormant for indefinite periods. The Editor of these sheets, though otherwise boasting himself a man of confirmed speculative habits, and perhaps discursive enough, is free to confess, that never, till these last months, did the above very plain considerations, on our total want of a Philosophy of Clothes, occur to him; and then, by quite foreign suggestion. By the arrival, namely, of a new Book from Professor Teufelsdröckh of Weissnichtwo;[10] treating expressly of this subject, and in a style which, whether understood or not, could not even by the blindest be overlooked. In the present Editor's way of thought, this remarkable Treatise, with its Doctrines, whether as judicially acceded to, or judicially denied, has not remained without effect.

'*Die Kleider, ihr Werden und Wirken* (Clothes, their Origin and Influence): *von Diog. Teufelsdröckh, J.U.D. etc. Stillschweigen und Co*^{gnie}. *Weissnichtwo, 1831.*[11]

'Here,' says the *Weissnichtwo'sche Anzeiger*,[12] 'comes a Volume of that extensive, close-printed, close-meditated sort, which, be it spoken with pride, is seen only in Germany, perhaps only in Weissnichtwo. Issuing from the hitherto irreproachable Firm of Stillschweigen and Company, with every external furtherance, it is of such internal quality as to set Neglect at defiance.' * * * * 'A work,' concludes the well-nigh enthusiastic Reviewer,

[10] Teufelsdröckh: "Devil's dung." Weissnichtwo: "Know-not-where." His first name, Diogenes, means "born of God" and also alludes to the Greek Cynic philosopher (412–323 B.C.).
[11] "Clothes, their Origin and Influence: by Diogenes Teufelsdröckh, LL.D. etc. Silence and Company. Know-not-where, 1831."
[12] "Weissnichtwo Advertiser."

'interesting alike to the antiquary, the historian, and the philosophic thinker; a masterpiece of boldness, lynx-eyed acuteness, and rugged independent Germanism and Philanthropy (*derber Kerndeutschheit und Menschenliebe*); which will not, assuredly, pass current without opposition in high places; but must and will exalt the almost new name of Teufelsdröckh to the first ranks of Philosophy, in our German Temple of Honour.'

Mindful of old friendship, the distinguished Professor, in this the first blaze of his fame, which however does not dazzle him, sends hither a Presentation-copy of his Book; with compliments and encomiums which modesty forbids the present Editor to rehearse; yet without indicated wish or hope of any kind, except what may be implied in the concluding phrase: *Möchte es* (this remarkable Treatise) *auch im Brittischen Boden gedeihen!*[13]

Chapter II
Editorial Difficulties

How to make known Teufelsdröckh and his Book to English readers; especially *such* a book? Editor receives from the Hofrath Heuschrecke a letter promising Biographic Documents. Negotiations with Oliver Yorke. *Sartor Resartus* conceived. Editor's assurances and advice to his British reader.

If for a speculative man, 'whose seedfield,' in the sublime words of the Poet, 'is Time,'[1] no conquest is important but that of new ideas, then might the arrival of Professor Teufelsdröckh's Book be marked with chalk in the Editor's calendar. It is in-

---

[13] "May it also prosper on British soil."
[1] See motto on title page.

deed an 'extensive Volume,' of boundless, almost formless contents, a very Sea of Thought; neither calm nor clear, if you will; yet wherein the toughest pearl-diver may dive to his utmost depth, and return not only with sea-wreck but with true orients.

Directly on the first perusal, almost on the first deliberate inspection, it became apparent that here a quite new Branch of Philosophy, leading to as yet undescried ulterior results, was disclosed; farther, what seemed scarcely less interesting, a quite new human Individuality, an almost unexampled personal character, that, namely, of Professor Teufelsdröckh the Discloser. Of both which novelties, as far as might be possible, we resolved to master the significance. But as man is emphatically a proselytising creature, no sooner was such mastery even fairly attempted, than the new question arose: How might this acquired good be imparted to others, perhaps in equal need thereof: how could the philosophy of Clothes, and the Author of such Philosophy, be brought home, in any measure, to the business and bosoms of our own English Nation? For if new-got gold is said to burn the pockets till it be cast forth into circulation, much more may new truth.

Here, however, difficulties occurred. The first thought naturally was to publish Article after Article on this remarkable Volume, in such widely-circulating Critical Journals as the Editor might stand connected with, or by money or love procure access to. But, on the other hand, was it not clear that such matter as must here be revealed, and treated of, might endanger the circulation of any Journal extant? If, indeed, all party-divisions in the State, could have been abolished, Whig, Tory, and Radical, embracing in discrepant union; and all the Journals of the Nation could have been jumbled into one Journal, and the Philosophy of Clothes poured forth in incessant torrents therefrom, the attempt had seemed possible. But, alas, what vehicle of that sort have we, except *Fraser's Magazine*?[2] A vehicle all strewed (figuratively speaking) with the maddest Waterloo-Crackers,[3] exploding distractively and destructively, wheresoever the mystified passenger stands or sits; nay, in any

[2] *Sartor* appeared originally in serial form in *Fraser's Magazine.*
[3] Firecrackers.

case, understood to be, of late years, a vehicle full to overflowing, and inexorably shut! Besides, to state the Philosophy of Clothes without the Philosopher, the ideas of Teufelsdröckh without something of his personality, was it not to insure both of entire misapprehension? Now for Biography, had it been otherwise admissible, there were no adequate documents, no hope of obtaining such, but rather, owing to circumstances, a special despair. Thus did the Editor see himself, for the while, shut out from all public utterance of these extraordinary Doctrines, and constrained to revolve them, not without disquietude, in the dark depths of his own mind.

So had it lasted for some months; and now the Volume on Clothes, read and again read, was in several points becoming lucid and lucent; the personality of its Author more and more surprising, but, in spite of all that memory and conjecture could do, more and more enigmatic; whereby the old disquietude seemed fast settling into fixed discontent,—when altogether unexpectedly arrives a Letter from Herr Hofrath Heuschrecke,[4] our Professor's chief friend and associate in Weissnichtwo, with whom we had not previously corresponded. The Hofrath, after much quite extraneous matter, began dilating largely on the 'agitation and attention' which the Philosophy of Clothes was exciting in its own German Republic of Letters; on the deep significance and tendency of his Friend's Volume; and then, at length, with great circumlocution, hinted at the practicability of conveying 'some knowledge of it, and of him, to England, and through England to the distant West': a work on Professor Teufelsdröckh 'were undoubtedly welcome to the *Family*, the *National*, or any other of those patriotic *Libraries*,[5] at present the glory of British Literature'; might work revolutions in Thought; and so forth;—in conclusion, intimating not obscurely, that should the present Editor feel disposed to undertake a Biography of Teufelsdröckh, he, Hofrath Heuschrecke, had it in his power to furnish the requisite Documents.

As in some chemical mixture, that has stood long evaporat-

[4] "Councillor Grasshopper."
[5] An ironic reference to contemporary periodicals for popular education often called "libraries."

ing, but would not crystallize, instantly when the wire or other fixed substance is introduced, crystallisation commences, and rapidly proceeds till the whole is finished, so was it with the Editor's mind and this offer of Heuschrecke's. Form rose out of void solution and discontinuity; like united itself with like in definite arrangment: and soon either in actual vision and possession, or in fixed reasonable hope, the image of the whole Enterprise had shaped itself, so to speak, into a solid mass. Cautiously yet courageously, through the twopenny post, application to the famed redoubtable OLIVER YORKE[6] was now made: an interview, interviews with that singular man have taken place; with more of assurance on our side, with less of satire (at least of open satire) on his, than we anticipated;—for the rest, with such issue as is now visible. As to those same 'patriotic *Libraries*,' the Hofrath's counsel could only be viewed with silent amazement; but with his offer of Documents we joyfully and almost instantaneously closed. Thus, too, in the sure expectation of these, we already see our task begun; and this our *Sartor Resartus*, which is properly a 'Life and Opinions of Herr Teufelsdröckh,' hourly advancing.

Of our fitness for the Enterprise, to which we have such title and vocation, it were perhaps uninteresting to say more. Let the British reader study and enjoy, in simplicity of heart, what is here presented him, and with whatever metaphysical acumen and talent for meditation he is possessed of. Let him strive to keep a free, open sense; cleared from the mists of prejudice, above all from the paralysis of cant; and directed rather to the Book itself than to the Editor of the Book. Who or what such Editor may be, must remain conjectural, and even insignificant.[7] It is a voice publishing tidings of the Philosophy of Clothes; undoubtedly a Spirit addressing Spirits: whoso hath ears, let him hear.

On one other point the Editor thinks it needful to give warn-

[6] Pseudonym of William Maginn (1794–1842), editor of *Fraser's Magazine.*
[7] With us even he still communicates in some sort of mask, or muffler; and, we have reason to think, under a feigned name!—O.Y. [Carlyle's note.]

ing: namely, that he is animated with a true though perhaps a feeble attachment to the Institutions of our Ancestors; and minded to defend these, according to ability, at all hazards; nay, it was partly with a view to such defence that he engaged in this undertaking. To stem, or if that be impossible, profitably to divert the current of Innovation, such a Volume as Teufelsdröckh's, if cunningly planted down, were no despicable pile, or floodgate, in the logical wear.[8]

For the rest, be it nowise apprehended, that any personal connexion of ours with Teufelsdröckh, Heuschrecke, or this Philosophy of Clothes, can pervert our judgment, or sway us to extenuate or exaggerate. Powerless, we venture to promise, are those private Compliments themselves. Grateful they may well be; as generous illusions of friendship; as fair mementos of bygone unions, of those nights and suppers of the gods, when, lapped in the symphonies and harmonies of Philosophic Eloquence, though with baser accompaniments, the present Editor revelled in the feast of reason, never since vouchsafed him in so full measure! But what then? *Amicus Plato, magis amica veritas*;[9] Teufelsdröckh is our friend, Truth is our divinity. In our historical and critical capacity, we hope we are strangers to all the world; have feud or favour with no one,—save indeed the Devil, with whom, as with the Prince of Lies and Darkness, we do at all times wage internecine war. This assurance, at an epoch when puffery[10] and quackery have reached a height unexampled in the annals of mankind, and even English Editors, like Chinese Shopkeepers, must write on their door-lintels *No cheating here*,—we thought it good to premise.

---

[8] Weir, a dam for a mill.
[9] "Plato is my friend, but a greater friend is truth."
[10] Advertising.

Chapter III
Reminiscences

Teufelsdröckh at Weissnichtwo. Professor of Things in General at the University there: Outward aspect and character; memorable coffee-house utterances; domicile and watchtower: Sights thence of City-Life by day and by night; with reflections thereon. Old 'Liza and her ways. Character of Hofrath Heuschrecke, and his relation to Teufelsdröckh.

To the Author's private circle the appearance of this singular Work on Clothes must have occasioned little less surprise than it has to the rest of the world. For ourselves, at least, few things have been more unexpected. Professor Teufelsdröckh, at the period of our acquaintance with him, seemed to lead a quite still and self-contained life: a man devoted to the higher Philosophies, indeed; yet more likely, if he published at all, to publish a refutation of Hegel and Bardili,[1] both of whom, strangely enough, he included under a common ban; than to descend, as he has here done, into the angry noisy Forum, with an Argument that cannot but exasperate and divide. Not, that we can remember, was the Philosophy of Clothes once touched upon between us. If through the high, silent, meditative Transcendentalism of our Friend we detected any practical tendency whatever, it was at most Political, and towards a certain prospective, and for the present quite speculative, Radicalism; as indeed some correspondence, on his part, with Herr Oken of Jena[2]

[1] Georg Wilhelm Friedrich Hegel (1770–1831) and C. G. Bardili (1761–1808): German philosophers.
[2] Lorenz Oken (1779–1851), German philosopher, founder and editor of the *Isis*, a reforming magazine often suppressed in parts of Germany.

was now and then suspected; though his special contributions to the *Isis* could never be more than surmised at. But, at all events, nothing Moral, still less anything Didactico-Religious, was looked for from him.

Well do we recollect the last words he spoke in our hearing; which indeed, with the Night they were uttered in, are to be forever remembered. Lifting his huge tumbler of *Gukguk*,[3] and for a moment lowering his tobacco-pipe, he stood up in full coffeehouse (it was *Zur Grünen Gans*,[4] the largest in Weissnich-two, where all the Virtuosity, and nearly all the Intellect of the place assembled of an evening); and there, with low, soul-stirring tone, and the look truly of an angel, though whether of a white or of a black one might be dubious, proposed this toast: *Die Sache der Armen in Gottes und Teufels Namen* (The Cause of the Poor, in Heaven's name and——'s)! One full shout, breaking the leaden silence; then a gurgle of innumerable emptying bumpers, again followed by universal cheering, returned him loud acclaim. It was the finale of the night: resuming their pipes; in the highest enthusiasm, amid volumes of tobacco-smoke; triumphant, cloud-capt without and within, the assembly broke up, each to his thoughtful pillow. *Bleibt doch ein echter Spass- und Galgen-vogel*,[5] said several; meaning thereby that, one day, he would probably be hanged for his democratic sentiments. *Wo steckt doch der Schalk?*[6] added they, looking round: but Teufelsdröckh had retired by private alleys, and the Compiler of these pages beheld him no more.

In such scenes has it been our lot to live with this Philosopher, such estimate to form of his purposes and powers. And yet thou brave Teufelsdröckh, who could tell what lurked in thee? Under those thick locks of thine, so long and lank, overlappi roof-wise the gravest face we ever in this world saw, the dwelt a most busy brain. In thy eyes too, deep under the shaggy brows, and looking out so still and dreamy, have we not noticed gleams of an ethereal or else a diabolic fire, and half-

[3] Gukguk is unhappily only an academical—beer [Carlyle's note].
[4] "At the Green Goose."
[5] "He is a true joker and jail-bird."
[6] "Where is the rogue hiding?"

fancied that their stillness was but the rest of infinite motion, the *sleep* of a spinning-top? Thy little figure, there as, in loose ill-brushed threadbare habiliments, thou sattest, amid litter and lumber, whole days, to 'think and smoke tobacco,' held in it a mighty heart. The secrets of man's Life were laid open to thee; thou sawest into the mystery of the Universe, farther than another; thou hadst *in petto*[7] thy remarkable Volume on Clothes. Nay, was there not in that clear logically-founded Transcendentalism of thine; still more, in thy meek, silent, deep-seated Sansculottism,[8] combined with a true princely Courtesy of inward nature, the visible rudiments of such speculation? But great men are too often unknown, or what is worse, misknown. Already, when we dreamed not of it, the warp of thy remarkable Volume lay on the loom; and silently, mysterious shuttles were putting-in the woof!

How the Hofrath Heuschrecke is to furnish biographical data, in this case, may be a curious question; the answer of which, however, is happily not our concern, but his. To us it appeared, after repeated trial, that in Weissnichtwo, from the archives or memories of the best-informed classes, no Biography of Teufelsdröckh was to be gathered; not so much as a false one. He was a stranger there, wafted thither by what is called the course of circumstances; concerning whose parentage, birthplace, prospects, or pursuits, curiosity had indeed made inquiries, but satisfied herself with the most indistinct replies. For himself, he was a man so still and altogether unparticipating, that to question him even afar off on such particulars was a thing of more than usual delicacy: besides, in his sly way, he had ever some quaint turn, not without its satirical edge, wherewith to divert such intrusions, and deter you from the like. Wits spoke of him secretly as if he were a kind of Melchizedek, without father or mother of any kind; sometimes, with reference to his great his-

---

[7] In secret.
[8] Sansculottism: political radicalism, literally "without breeches," applied to the revolutionaries of the French Revolution of 1789 who rejected wearing knee-breeches, the fashion of the aristocracy, and wore trousers instead.

toric and statistic knowledge, and the vivid way he had of expressing himself like an eye-witness of distant transactions and scenes, they called him the *Ewige Jude*, Everlasting, or as we say, Wandering Jew.[9]

To the most, indeed, he had become not so much a Man as a Thing; which Thing doubtless they were accustomed to see, and with satisfaction; but no more thought of accounting for than for the fabrication of their daily *Allgemeine Zeitung*,[10] or the domestic habits of the Sun. Both were there and welcome; the world enjoyed what good was in them, and thought no more of the matter. The man Teufelsdröckh passed and repassed, in his little circle, as one of those originals and nondescripts, more frequent in German Universities than elsewhere; of whom, though you see them alive, and feel certain enough that they must have a History, no History seems to be discoverable; or only such as men give of mountain rocks and antediluvian ruins: That they have been created by unknown agencies, are in a state of gradual decay, and for the present reflect light and resist pressure; that is, are visible and tangible objects in this phantasm world, where so much other mystery is.

It was to be remarked that though, by title and diploma, *Professor der Allerley-Wissenschaft*, or as we should say in English, 'Professor of Things in General,' he had never delivered any Course; perhaps never been incited thereto by any public furtherance or requisition. To all appearance, the enlightened Government of Weissnichtwo, in founding their New University, imagined they had done enough, if 'in times like ours,' as the half-official Program expressed it, 'when all things are, rapidly or slowly, resolving themselves into Chaos, a Professorship of this kind had been established; whereby, as occasion called, the task of bodying somewhat forth again from such Chaos might be, even slightly, facilitated.' The actual Lectures should be held, and Public Classes for the 'Science of Things in General,' they doubtless considered premature; on which ground too they

[9] Legendary figure of the Jew who refused to allow Christ to rest at his house while bearing the Cross to Calvary and, as a result, was condemned to wander the earth until the Judgment Day.
[10] "Universal Newspaper."

had only established the Professorship, nowise endowed it; so that Teufelsdröckh, 'recommended by the highest Names,' had been promoted thereby to a Name merely.

Great, among the more enlightened classes, was the admiration of this new Professorship: how an enlightened Government had seen into the Want of the Age (*Zeitbedürfniss*); how at length, instead of Denial and Destruction, we were to have a science of Affirmation and Reconstruction; and Germany and Weissnichtwo were where they should be, in the vanguard of the world. Considerable also was the wonder at the new Professor, dropt opportunely enough into the nascent University; so able to lecture, should occasion call; so ready to hold his peace for indefinite periods, should an enlightened Government consider that occasion did not call. But such admiration and such wonder, being followed by no act to keep them living, could last only nine days; and, long before our visit to that scene, had quite died away. The more cunning heads thought it was all an expiring clutch at popularity, on the part of a Minister, whom domestic embarrassments, court intrigues, old age, and dropsy soon afterwards finally drove from the helm.

As for Teufelsdröckh, except by his nightly appearances at the *Grüne Gans*, Weissnichtwo saw little of him, felt little of him. Here, over his tumbler of Gukguk, he sat reading Journals; sometimes contemplatively looking into the clouds of his tobacco-pipe, without other visible employment: always, from his mild ways, an agreeable phenomenon there; more especially when he opened his lips for speech; on which occasions the whole Coffee-house would hush itself into silence, as if sure to hear something noteworthy. Nay, perhaps to hear a whole series and river of the most memorable utterances; such as, when once thawed, he would for hours indulge in, with fit audience: and the more memorable, as issuing from a head apparently not more interested in them, not more conscious of them, than is the sculptured stone head of some public fountain, which through its brass mouth-tube emits water to the worthy and the unworthy; careless whether it be for cooking victuals or quenching conflagrations; indeed, maintains the same earnest assiduous look, whether any water be flowing or not.

To the Editor of these sheets, as to a young enthusiastic Englishman, however unworthy, Teufelsdröckh opened himself perhaps more than to the most. Pity only that we could not then half guess his importance, and scrutinise him with due power of vision! We enjoyed, what not three men in Weissnichtwo could boast of, a certain degree of access to the Professor's private domicile. It was the attic floor of the highest house in the Wahngasse;[11] and might truly be called the pinnacle of Weissnichtwo, for it rose sheer up above the contiguous roofs, themselves rising from elevated ground. Moreover, with its windows it looked towards all the four *Orte*, or as the Scotch say, and we ought to say, *Airts*:[12] the sitting-room itself commanded three; another came to view in the *Schlafgemach* (Bed-room) at the opposite end; to say nothing of the kitchen, which offered two, as it were, *duplicates*, and showing nothing new. So that it was in fact the speculum or watch-tower of Teufelsdröckh; wherefrom, sitting at ease, he might see the whole life-circulation of that considerable City; the streets and lanes of which, with all their doing and driving (*Thun und Treiben*), were for the most part visible there.

'I look down into all that wasp-nest or bee-hive,' have we heard him say, 'and witness their wax-laying and honey-making, and poison-brewing, and choking by sulphur. From the Palace esplanade, where music plays while Serene Highness is pleased to eat his victuals, down to the low lane, where in her door-sill the aged widow, knitting for a thin livelihood, sits to feel the afternoon sun, I see it all; for, except the Schlosskirche[13] weathercock, no biped stands so high. Couriers arrive bestrapped and bebooted, bearing Joy and Sorrow bagged-up in pouches of leather; there, topladen, and with four swift horses, rolls-in the country Baron and his household; here, on timber-leg, the lamed Soldier hops painfully along, begging alms: a thousand carriages, and wains, and cars, come tumbling-in with Food, with young Rusticity, and other Raw Produce, inanimate or animate, and go tumbling out again with Produce manu-

---

[11] "Delusion-lane."
[12] Points of the compass.
[13] "Castle chapel."

factured. That living flood, pouring through these streets, of all qualities and ages, knowest thou whence it is coming, whither it is going? *Aus der Ewigkeit, zu der Ewigkeit hin*: From Eternity, onwards to Eternity! These are Apparitions: what else? Are they not Souls rendered visible: in Bodies, that took shape and will lose it, melting into air? Their solid Pavement is a Picture of the Sense; they walk on the bosom of Nothing, blank Time is behind them and before them. Or fanciest thou, the red and yellow Clothes-screen yonder, with spurs on its heels and feather in its crown, is but of Today, without a Yesterday or a Tomorrow; and had not rather its Ancestor alive when Hengst and Horsa overran thy Island?[14] Friend, thou seest here a living link in that Tissue of History, which inweaves all Being: watch well, or it will be past thee, and seen no more.

'*Ach, mein Lieber!*'[15] said he once, at midnight, when we had returned from the Coffee-house in rather earnest talk, 'it is a true sublimity to dwell here. These fringes of lamplight, struggling up through smoke and thousandfold exhalation, some fathoms into the ancient reign of Night, what thinks Boötes of them, as he leads his Hunting-dogs over the Zenith in their leash of sidereal fire? That stifled hum of Midnight, when Traffic has lain down to rest; and the chariot-wheels of Vanity, still rolling here and there through distant streets, are bearing her to Halls roofed-in, and lighted to the due pitch for her; and only Vice and Misery, to prowl or to moan like nightbirds, are abroad: that hum, I say, like the stertorous, unquiet slumber of sick Life, is heard in Heaven! Oh, under that hideous coverlet of vapours, and putrefactions, and unimaginable gases, what a Fermenting-vat lies simmering and hid! The joyful and the sorrowful are there; men are dying there, men are being born; men are praying,—on the other side of a brick partition, men are cursing; and around them all is the vast, void Night. The proud Grandee still lingers in his perfumed saloons, or reposes within damask curtains; Wretchedness cowers into truckle-beds, or shivers hunger-stricken into its lair of straw;

---

[14] Semi-legendary leaders of the Jutes, Germanic invaders of England in the fifth century.
[15] "Ah, my dear friend!"

in obscure cellars, *Rouge-et-Noir*[16] laguidly emits its voice-of-destiny to haggard hungry Villains; while Councillors of State sit plotting, and playing their high chess-game, whereof the pawns are Men. The Lover whispers his mistress that the coach is ready; and she, full of hope and fear, glides down, to fly with him over the borders: the Thief, still more silently, sets-to his picklocks and crowbars, or lurks in wait till the watchmen first snore in their boxes. Gay mansions, with supper-rooms, and dancing-rooms, are full of light and music and high-swelling hearts; but, in the Condemned Cells, the pulse of life beats tremulous and faint, and bloodshot eyes look-out through the darkness, which is around and within, for the light of a stern last morning. Six men are to be hanged on the morrow: comes no hammering from the *Rabenstein*?[17]—their gallows must even now be o' building. Upwards of five-hundred-thousand two-legged animals without feathers lie round us, in horizontal positions; their heads all in nightcaps, and full of the foolishest dreams. Riot cries aloud, and staggers and swaggers in his rank dens of shame; and the Mother, with streaming hair, kneels over her pallid dying infant, whose cracked lips only her tears now moisten.—All these heaped and huddled together, with nothing but a little carpentry and masonry between them;—crammed in, like salted fish in their barrel;—or weltering, shall I say, like an Egyptian pitcher of tamed vipers, each struggling to get its *head above* the others: *such* work goes on under that smoke-counterpane!—But I, *mein Werther*,[18] sit above it all; I am alone with the Stars.'

We looked in his face to see whether, in the utterance of such extraordinary Night-thoughts, no feeling might be traced there; but with the light we had, which indeed was only a single tallow-light, and far enough from the window, nothing save that old calmness and fixedness was visible.

These were the Professor's talking seasons: most commonly he spoke in mere monosyllables, or sat altogether silent and

---

[16] A gambling game.

[17] "Raven-stone" or gallows.

[18] "My sentimental young man." An allusion to Goethe's *Sorrows of Young Werther* (1774).

smoked; while the visitor had liberty either to say what he listed, receiving for answer an occasional grunt; or to look round for a space, and then take himself away. It was a strange apartment; full of books and tattered papers, and miscellaneous shreds of all conceivable substances, 'united in a common element of dust.' Books lay on tables, and below tables; here fluttered a sheet of manuscript, there a torn handkerchief, or nightcap hastily thrown aside; ink-bottles alternated with bread-crusts, coffee-pots, tobacco-boxes, Periodical Literature, and Blücher Boots. Old Lieschen (Lisekin, 'Liza), who was his bed-maker and stove-lighter, his washer and wringer, cook, errand-maid, and general lion's-provider, and for the rest a very orderly creature, had no sovereign authority in this last citadel of Teufelsdröckh; only some once in the month she half-forcibly made her way thither, with broom and duster, and (Teufelsdröckh hastily saving his manuscripts) effected a partial clearance, a jail-delivery of such lumber as was not Literary. These were her *Erdbeben* (earthquakes), which Teufelsdröckh dreaded worse than the pestilence; nevertheless, to such length he had been forced to comply. Glad would he have been to sit here philosophising forever, or till the litter by accumulation, drove him out of doors: but Lieschen was his right-arm, and spoon, and necessary of life, and would not be flatly gainsayed. We can still remember the ancient woman; so silent that some thought her dumb; deaf also you would often have supposed her; for Teufelsdröckh, and Teufelsdröckh only, would she serve or give heed to; and with him she seemed to communicate chiefly by signs; if it were not rather by some secret divination that she guessed all his wants, and supplied them. Assiduous old dame! she scoured, and sorted, and swept, in her kitchen, with the least possible violence to the ear; yet all was tight and right there: hot and black came the coffee ever at the due moment; and the speechless Lieschen herself looked out on you, from under her clean white coif with its lappets, through her clean withered face and wrinkles, with a look of helpful intelligence, almost of benevolence.

Few strangers, as above hinted, had admittance hither: the only one we ever saw there, ourselves excepted, was the Hofrath

Heuschrecke, already known, by name and expectation, to the readers of these pages. To us, at that period, Herr Heuschrecke seemed one of those purse-mouthed, crane-necked, clean-brushed, pacific individuals, perhaps sufficiently distinguished in society by this fact, that, in dry weather or in wet, 'they never appear without their umbrella.' Had we not known with what 'little wisdom' the world is governed; and how, in Germany as elsewhere, the ninety-and-nine Public Men can for most part be put mute train-bearers to the hundredth, perhaps but stalking-horses and willing or unwilling dupes,—it might have seemed wonderful how Herr Heuschrecke should be named a *Rath*, or Councillor, and Counsellor, even in Weissnichtwo. What counsel to any man, or to any woman, could this particular Hofrath give; in whose loose, zigzag figure; in whose thin visage, as it went jerking to and fro, in minute incessant fluctuation,—you traced rather confusion worse confounded; at most, Timidity and physical Cold? Some indeed said withal, he was 'the very Spirit of Love embodied': blue earnest eyes, full of sadness and kindness; purse ever open, and so forth; the whole of which, we shall now hope, for many reasons, was not quite groundless. Nevertheless friend Teufelsdröckh's outline, who indeed handled the burin like few in these cases, was probably the best: *Er hat Gemüth und Geist, hat wenigstens gehabt, doch ohne Organ, ohne Schicksals-Gunst; ist gegenwärtig aber halb-zerrüttet, halb-erstarrt*, 'He has heart and talent, at least has had such, yet without fit mode of utterance, or favour of Fortune; and so is now half-cracked, half-congealed.'—What the Hofrath shall think of this when he sees it, readers may wonder: we, safe in the stronghold of Historical Fidelity, are careless.

The main point, doubtless, for us all, is his love of Teufelsdröckh, which indeed was also by far the most decisive feature of Heuschrecke himself. We are enabled to assert that he hung on the Professor with the fondness of a Boswell for his Johnson. And perhaps with the like return; for Teufelsdröckh treated his gaunt admirer with little outward regard, as some half-rational or altogether irrational friend, and at best loved him out of gratitude and by habit. On the other hand, it was curious to observe with what reverent kindness, and a sort of fatherly protection, our Hofrath, being the elder, richer, and as he fondly imagined far more practically influential of the two, looked and tended on his little Sage, whom he seemed to consider as a living oracle. Let but Teufelsdröckh open his mouth, Heuschrecke's also unpuckered itself into a free doorway, besides his being all eye and all ear, so that nothing might be lost: and then, at every pause in the harangue, he gurgled-out his pursy chuckle of a cough-laugh (for the machinery of laughter took some time to get in motion, and seemed crank and slack), or else his twanging nasal, *Bravo! Das glaub' ich*;[19] in either case, by way of heartiest approval. In short, if Teufelsdröckh was Dalai-Lama, of which, except perhaps in his self-seclusion, and god-like indifference, there was no symptom, then might Heuschrecke pass for his chief Talapoin, to whom no dough-pill he could knead and publish was other than medicinal and sacred.

In such environment, social, domestic, physical, did Teufelsdröckh, at the time of our acquaintance, and most likely does he still, live and meditate. Here, perched-up in his high Wahngasse watch-tower, and often, in solitude, outwatching the Bear;[20] it was that the indomitable Inquirer fought all his battles with Dulness and Darkness; here, in all probability, that he wrote this surprising Volume on *Clothes*. Additional particulars: of his age, which was of that standing middle sort you could only guess at; of his wide surtout; the colour of his trousers, fashion of his broad-brimmed steeple-hat, and so forth, we might report, but do not. The Wisest truly is, in these times, the Greatest; so that an enlightened curiosity, leaving Kings and suchlike to rest very much on their own basis, turns more and more to the Philosophic Class: nevertheless, what reader expects that, with all our writing and reporting, Teufelsdröckh could be brought home to him, till once the Documents arrive? His Life, Fortunes, and Bodily Presence, are as yet hidden from us, or matter only of faint conjecture. But, on the other hand, does

---

[19] "That I believe."
[20] The constellation Ursa Major, or Great Bear, which never sets in the northern skies, *i.e.* Teufelsdröckh stayed up all night.

not his Soul lie enclosed in this remarkable Volume, much more truly than Pedro Garcia's did in the buried Bag of Doubloons?[21] To the soul of Diogenes Teufelsdröckh, to his opinions, namely, on the 'Origin and Influence of Clothes,' we for the present gladly return.

Chapter IV
Characteristics

Teufelsdröckh and his Work on Clothes: Strange freedom of speech; transcendentalism; force of insight and expression; multifarious learning: Style poetic, uncouth: Comprehensiveness of his humour and moral feeling. How the Editor once saw him laugh. Different kinds of Laughter and their significance.

It were a piece of vain flattery to pretend that this Work on Clothes entirely contents us; that it is not, like all works of genius, like the very Sun, which, though the highest published creation, or work of genius, has nevertheless black spots and troubled nebulosities amid its effulgence,—a mixture of insight, inspiration, with dulness, double-vision, and even utter blindness.

Without committing ourselves to those enthusiastic praises and prophesyings of the *Weissnichtwo'sche Anzeiger*, we admitted that the Book had in a high degree excited us to self-activity, which is the best effect of any book; that it had even operated changes in our way of thought; nay, that it promised

---

[21] A story in the Preface to Le Sage's *Gil Blas* tells of two men finding a tombstone with the inscription, "Here lies the soul of the licentiate Pedro Garcias." On searching, they found a purse of gold coins (doubloons).

to prove, as it were, the opening of a new mine-shaft, wherein the whole world of Speculation might henceforth dig to unknown depths. More especially it may now be declared that Professor Teufelsdröckh's acquirements, patience of research, philosophic and even poetic vigour, are here made indisputably manifest; and unhappily no less his prolixity and tortuosity and manifold ineptitude; that, on the whole, as in opening new mine-shafts is not unreasonable, there is much rubbish in his Book, though likewise specimens of almost invaluable ore. A paramount popularity in England we cannot promise him. Apart from the choice of such a topic as Clothes, too often the manner of treating it betokens in the Author a rusticity and academic seclusion, unblamable, indeed inevitable in a German, but fatal to his success with our public.

Of good society Teufelsdröckh appears to have seen little, or has mostly forgotten what he saw. He speaks-out with a strange plainness; calls many things by their mere dictionary names. To him the Upholsterer is no Pontiff, neither is any Drawing-room a Temple, were it never so begilt and overhung: 'a whole immensity of Brussels carpets, and pier-glasses, and or-molu,' as he himself expresses it, 'cannot hide from me that such Drawing-room is simply a section of Infinite Space, where so many God-created Souls do for the time meet together.' To Teufelsdröckh the highest Duchess is respectable, is venerable; but nowise for her pearl bracelets and Malines laces: in his eyes, the star of a Lord[1] is little less and little more than the broad button of Birmingham spelter in a Clown's smock; 'each is an implement,' he says, 'in its kind; a tag for *hooking-together*; and, for the rest, was dug from the earth, and hammered on a stithy before smith's fingers.' Thus does the Professor look in men's faces with a strange impartiality, a strange scientific freedom; like a man unversed in the higher circles, like a man dropped thither from the Moon. Rightly considered, it is in this peculiarity, running through his whole system of thought, that all these short-comings, over-shootings, and multiform perversities, take rise: if indeed they have not a second source also

[1] The star-shaped medallion given to members of the Order of the Bath, the Garter, etc.

55

natural enough, in his Transcendental Philosophies, and humour of looking at all Matter and Material things as Spirit; whereby truly his case were but the more hopeless, the more lamentable.

To the Thinkers of this nation, however, of which class it is firmly believed there are individuals yet extant, we can safely recommend the Work: nay, who knows but among the fashionable ranks too, if it be true, as Teufelsdröckh maintains, that 'within the most starched cravat there passes a windpipe and weasand, and under the thickliest embroidered waistcoat beats a heart,'—the force of that rapt earnestness may be felt, and here and there an arrow of the soul pierce through? In our wild Seer, shaggy, unkempt, like a Baptist living on locusts and wild honey,[2] there is an untutored energy, a silent, as it were unconscious, strength, which except in the higher walks of Literature, must be rare. Many a deep glance, and often with unspeakable precision, has he cast into mysterious Nature, and the still more mysterious Life of Man. Wonderful it is with what cutting words, now and then, he severs asunder the confusion; shears down, were it furlongs deep, into the true centre of the matter; and there not only hits the nail on the head, but with crushing force smites it home, and buries it.—On the other hand, let us be free to admit, he is the most unequal writer breathing. Often after some such feat, he will play truant for long pages, and go dawdling and dreaming, and mumbling and maundering the merest commonplaces, as if he were asleep with eyes open, which indeed he is.

Of his boundless Learning, and how all reading and literature in most known tongues, from *Sanchoniathon* to *Dr Lingard,* from your Oriental *Shasters,* and *Talmuds,* and *Korans,* with Cassini's *Siamese Tables,* and Laplace's *Mécanique Céleste,* down to *Robinson Crusoe* and the *Belfast Town and Country Almanack,*[3] are familiar to him,—we shall say nothing: for unexampled as it is with us, to the Germans such universality of

---

[2] Reference to St. John the Baptist, see Matthew, iii, 4.

[3] An anticlimactic catalogue including, respectively, a legendary Phoenician philosopher, an historian of England, the religious books of the Hindus, Jews and Moslems, an Italian and a French astronomical work, a famous novel and a provincial newspaper. Significantly, the learning is both scientific and religious.

study passes without wonder, as a thing commendable, indeed, but natural, indispensable, and there of course. A man that devotes his life to learning, shall he not be learned?

In respect of style our Author manifests the same genial capability, marred too often by the same rudeness, inequality, and apparent want of intercourse with the higher classes. Occasionally, as above hinted, we find consummate vigour, a true inspiration; his burning thoughts step forth in fit burning words, like so many full-formed Minervas, issuing amid flame and splendour from Jove's head; a rich, idiomatic diction, picturesque allusions, fiery poetic emphasis, or quaint tricksy turns; all the graces and terrors of a wild Imagination, wedded to the clearest Intellect, alternate in beautiful vicissitude. Were it not that sheer sleeping and soporific passages; circumlocutions, repetitions, touches even of pure doting jargon, so often intervene! On the whole, Professor Teufelsdröckh is not a cultivated writer. Of his sentences perhaps not more than nine-tenths stand straight on their legs; the remainder are in quite angular attitudes, buttressed-up by props (of parentheses and dashes), and ever with this or the other tagrag hanging from them; a few even sprawl-out helplessly on all sides, quite broken-backed and dismembered. Nevertheless, in almost his very worst moods, there lies in him a singular attraction. A wild tone pervades the whole utterance of the man, like its keynote and regulator; now screwing itself aloft as into the Song of Spirits, or else the shrill mockery of Fiends; now sinking in cadences, not without melodious heartiness, though sometimes abrupt enough, into the common pitch, when we hear it only as a monotonous hum; of which hum the true character is extremely difficult to fix. Up to this hour we have never fully satisfied ourselves whether it is a tone and hum of real Humour, which we reckon among the very highest qualities of genius, or some echo of mere Insanity and Inanity, which doubtless ranks below the very lowest.

Under a like difficulty, in spite even of our personal intercourse, do we still lie with regard to the Professor's moral feeling. Gleams of an ethereal love burst forth from him, soft wailings of infinite pity; he could clasp the whole Universe into his bosom, and keep it warm; it seems as if under that rude exterior there dwelt a very seraph. Then again he is so sly and still, so imperturbably saturnine; shows such indifference, malign coolness towards all that men strive after; and ever with some half-visible wrinkle of a bitter sardonic humour, if indeed it be not mere stolid callousness,—that you look on him almost with a shudder, as on some incarnate Mephistopheles, to whom this great terrestrial and celestial Round, after all, were but some huge foolish Whirligig, where kings and beggars, and angels and demons, and stars and street-sweepings, were chaotically whirled, in which only children could take interest. His look, as we mentioned, is probably the gravest ever seen: yet it is not of that cast-iron gravity frequent enough among our own Chancery[4] suitors; but rather the gravity as of some silent, high-encircled mountain-pool, perhaps the crater of an extinct volcano; into whose black deeps you fear to gaze: those eyes, those lights that sparkle in it, may indeed be reflexes of the heavenly Stars, but perhaps also glances from the region of Nether Fire!

Certainly a most involved, self-secluded, altogether enigmatic nature, this of Teufelsdröckh! Here, however, we gladly recall to mind that once we saw him *laugh*; once only, perhaps it was the first and last time in his life; but then such a peal of laughter, enough to have awakened the Seven Sleepers![5] It was of Jean Paul's[6] doing: some single billow in that vast World-Mahlstrom of Humour, with its heaven-kissing coruscations, which is now, alas, all congealed in the frost of death! The large-bodied Poet and the small, both large enough in soul, sat talking miscellaneously together, the present Editor being privileged to listen; and now Paul, in his serious way, was giving one of those inimitable 'Extra-harangues'; and, as it chanced, On the Proposal for a *Castmetal King*: gradually a light kindled in our Professor's eyes and face, a beaming, mantling, loveliest

---

[4] Highest division of the High Court of Justice in England. It was known for its long delays, see Dickens' *Bleak House*.
[5] Seven Christian youths of Ephesus who fled persecution (A.D. 250) by fleeing to a cave. According to the legend, they fell asleep and awoke after 230 years.
[6] Jean Paul Richter (1763–1825): German humorist. The style of *Sartor* closely follows Richter, who often included digressive chapters, or "Extra-harangues" in his work.

light; through those murky features, a radiant, ever-young Apollo looked; and he burst forth like the neighing of all Tattersall's,[7]—tears streaming down his cheeks, pipe held aloft, foot clutched into the air,—loud, long-continuing, uncontrollable; a laugh not of the face and diaphragm only, but of the whole man from head to heel. The present Editor, who laughed indeed, yet with measure, began to fear all was not right: however, Teufelsdröckh composed himself, and sank into his old stillness; on his inscrutable countenance there was, if anything, a slight look of shame; and Richter himself could not rouse him again. Readers who have any tincture of Psychology know how much is to be inferred from this; and that no man who has once heartily and wholly laughed can be altogether irreclaimably bad. How much lies in Laughter: the cipher-key, wherewith we decipher the whole man! Some men wear an everlasting barren simper; in the smile of others lies a cold glitter as of ice: the fewest are able to laugh, what can be called laughing, but only sniff and titter and snigger from the throat outwards; or at best, produce some whiffling husky cachinnation, as if they were laughing through wool: of none such comes good. The man who cannot laugh is not only fit for treasons, stratagems, and spoils; but his whole life is already a treason and a stratagem.

Considered as an Author, Herr Teufelsdröckh has one scarcely pardonable fault, doubtless his worst: an almost total want of arrangement. In this remarkable Volume, it is true, his adherence to the mere course of Time produces, through the Narrative portions, a certain show of outward method; but of true logical method and sequence there is too little. Apart from its multifarious sections and subdivisions, the Work naturally falls into two Parts; a Historical-Descriptive, and a Philosophical-Speculative: but falls, unhappily, by no firm line of demarcation; in that labyrinthic combination, each Part overlaps, and indents, and indeed runs quite through the other. Many sections are of a debatable rubric, or even quite nondescript and unnameable; whereby the Book not only loses in accessibility,

---

[7] Horse-market in London.

but too often distresses us like some mad banquet, wherein all courses had been confounded, and fish and flesh, soup and solid, oyster-sauce, lettuces, Rhine-wine and French mustard, were hurled into one huge tureen or trough, and the hungry Public invited to help itself. To bring what order we can out of this Chaos shall be part of our endeavour.

Chapter V
The World in Clothes

Futile cause-and-effect Philosophies. Teufelsdröckh's Orbis Vestitus. Clothes first invented for the sake of ornament. Picture of our progenitor, the Aboriginal Savage. Wonders of growth and progress in mankind's history. Man defined as a Tool-using Animal.

'As Montequieu wrote a *Spirit of Laws*,' observes our Professor, 'so could I write a *Spirit of Clothes*; thus, with an *Esprit des Lois*, properly an *Esprit de Coutumes*, we should have an *Esprit de Costumes*.[1] For neither in tailoring nor in legislating does man proceed by mere Accident, but the hand is ever guided on by mysterious operations of the mind. In all his Modes, and habilatory endeavours, an Architectural Idea will be found lurking; his Body and the Cloth are the site and materials whereon and whereby his beautified edifice, of a Person, is to be built. Whether he flow gracefully out in folded mantles, based or light sandals; tower-up in high headgear, from amid peaks, spangles and bell-girdles; swell-out in starched ruffs, buckram stuffings, and monstrous tuberosities; or girth himself into sepa-

---

[1] Carlyle's play on words can be translated, "Thus, with a 'Spirit of Laws,' properly a 'Spirit of Customs,' we should have a 'Spirit of Costumes.'"

rate sections, and front the world an Agglomeration of four limbs,—will depend on the nature of such Architectual Idea: whether Grecian, Gothic, Later-Gothic, or altogether Modern, and Parisian or Anglo-Dandiacal.[2] Again, what meaning lies in Colour! From the soberest drab to the high-flaming scarlet, spiritual idiosyncrasies unfold themselves in choice of Colour: if the Cut betoken Intellect and Talent, so does the Colour betoken Temper and Heart. In all which, among nations as among individuals, there is an incessant, indubitable, though infinitely complex working of Cause and Effect: every snip of the Scissors has been regulated and prescribed by ever-active Influences, which doubtless to Intelligences of a superior order are neither invisible nor illegible.

'For such superior Intelligences a Cause-and-Effect Philosophy of Clothes, as of Laws, were probably a comfortable winter-evening entertainment: nevertheless, for inferior Intelligences, like men, such Philosophies have always seemed to me uninstructive enough. Nay, what is your Montesquieu himself but a clever infant spelling Letters from a hieroglyphical prophetic Book, the lexicon of which lies in Eternity, in Heaven?—Let any Cause-and-Effect Philosopher explain, not why I wear such and such a Garment, obey such and such a Law; but even why *I* am *here*, to wear and obey anything!—Much, therefore, if not the whole, of that same *Spirit of Clothes* I shall suppress, as hypothetical, ineffectual, and even impertinent: naked Facts, and Deductions drawn therefrom in quite another than that omniscient style, are my humbler and proper province.'

Acting on which prudent restriction, Teufelsdröckh has nevertheless contrived to take-in a well-nigh boundless extent of field; at least, the boundaries too often lie quite beyond our horizon. Selection being indispensable, we shall here glance-over his First Part only in the most cursory manner.

This First Part is, no doubt, distinguished by omnivorous learning, and utmost patience and fairness: at the same time, in its results and delineations, it is much more likely to interest the Compilers of some *Library* of General, Entertaining, Useful, or

---

[2] A coined word referring to the vogue of the Dandy, or ostentatiously dressed man, in early nineteenth-century England.

even Useless Knowledge than the miscellaneous readers of these pages. Was it this Part of the Book which Heuschrecke had in view, when he recommended us to that joint-stock vehicle of publication, 'at present the glory of British Literature'? If so, the Library Editors are welcome to dig in it for their own behoof.

To the First Chapter, which turns on Paradise and Fig-leaves, and leads us into interminable disquisitions of a mythological, metaphorical, cabalistico-sartorial[3] and quite antediluvian cast, we shall content ourselves with giving an unconcerned approval. Still less have we to do with 'Lilis, Adam's first wife, whom, according to the Talmudists, he had before Eve, and who bore him, in that wedlock, the whole progeny of aerial, aquatic, and terrestrial Devils,'—very needlessly, we think. On this portion of the Work, with its profound glances into the *Adam-Kadmon*,[4] or Primeval Element, here strangely brought into relation with the *Nifl* and *Muspel* (Darkness and Light) of the antique North, it may be enough to say, that its correctness of deduction, and depth of Talmudic and Rabbinical lore have filled perhaps not the worst Hebraist in Britain with something like astonishment.

But, quitting this twilight region, Teufelsdröckh hastens from the Tower of Babel, to follow the dispersion of Mankind over the whole habitable and habilable globe. Walking by the light of Oriental, Pelasgic, Scandinavian, Egyptian, Otaheitean, Ancient and Modern researches of every conceivable kind, he strives to give us in compressed shape (as the Nürnbergers give an *Orbis Pictus*)[5] an *Orbis Vestitus*;[6] or view of the costumes of all mankind, in all countries, in all times. It is here that to the Antiquarian, to the Historian, we can triumphantly say: Fall to! Here is learning: an irregular Treasury, if you will; but inexhaustible as the Hoard of King Nibelung, which twelve

[3] Another of Carlyle's humorous coined words. It means mysteriously relating to clothes, from Cabala, a system of occult interpretation of the Scriptures used by certain Jewish sects.
[4] The "first man" in Cabalistic lore.
[5] "The World in Pictures" (1657), an illustrated school-book by Amos Comenius (1592–1671).
[6] "The World of Clothes," the title of this chapter.

wagons in twelve days, at the rate of three journeys a day, could not carry off. Sheepskin cloaks and wampum belts; phylacteries, stoles, albs; chlamydes, togas, Chinese silks, Afghaun shawls, trunk-hose, leather breeches, Celtic philibegs (though breeches, as the name *Gallia Braccata* indicates, are the more ancient), Hussar cloaks, Vandyke tippets, ruffs, fardingales, are brought vividly before us,—even the Kilmarnock nightcap is not forgotten.[7] For most part, too, we must admit that the Learning, heterogeneous as it is, and tumbled-down quite pell-mell, is true concentrated and purified Learning, the drossy parts smelted out and thrown aside.

Philosophical reflections intervene, and sometimes touching pictures of human life. Of this sort the following has surprised us. The first purpose of Clothes, as our Professor imagines, was not warmth or decency, but ornament. 'Miserable indeed,' says he, 'was the condition of the Aboriginal Savage, glaring fiercely from under his fleece of hair, which with the beard reached down to his loins, and hung round him like a matted cloak; the rest of his body sheeted in its thick natural fell. He loitered in the sunny glades of the forest, living on wild-fruits; or, as the ancient Caledonian,[8] squatted himself in morasses, lurking for his bestial or human prey; without implements, without arms, save the ball of heavy Flint, to which, that his sole possession and defence might not be lost, he had attached a long cord of plaited thongs; thereby recovering as well as hurling it with deadly unerring skill. Nevertheless, the pains of Hunger and Revenge once satisfied, his next care was not Comfort but Decoration (*Putz*). Warmth he found in the toils of the chase; or amid dried leaves, in his hollow tree, in his bark shed, or natural grotto: but for Decoration he must have Clothes. Nay, among wild people, we find tattooing and painting even prior to Clothes. The first spiritual want of a barbarous man is Decoration, as indeed we still see among the barbarous classes in civilised countries.

[7] A series illustrating the varied uses of clothing, as money (wampum), as aids to religion (phylacteries, stoles, albs) and as decoration. The Kilmarnock nightcap was a knitted woolen cap made in Scotland.
[8] Ancient Scot.

'Reader, the heaven-inspired melodious Singer; loftiest Serene Highness; nay they own amber-locked, snow-and-rose-bloom Maiden, worthy to glide sylphlike almost on air, whom thou lovest, worshippest as a divine Presence, which, indeed, symbolically taken, she is,—has descended, like thyself, from that same hair mantled, flint-hurling Aboriginal Anthropophagus![9] Out of the eater cometh forth meat; out of the strong cometh forth sweetness. What changes are wrought, not by Time, yet in Time! For not Mankind only, but all that Mankind does or beholds, is in continual growth, regenesis and self-perfecting vitality. Cast forth thy Act, thy Word, into the ever-living, ever-working Universe: it is a seed-grain that cannot die; unnoticed today (says one), it will be found flourishing as a Banyan-grove (perhaps, alas, as a Hemlock-forest!)[10] after a thousand years.

'He who first shortened the labour of Copyists by device of *Movable Types* was disbanding hired Armies, and cashiering most Kings and Senates, and creating a whole new Democratic world: he had invented the Art of Printing. The first ground handful of Nitre, Sulphur, and Charcoal drove Monk Schwartz's[11] pestle through the ceiling: what will the last do? Achieve the final undisputed prostration of Force under Thought, of Animal courage under Spiritual. A simple invention it was in the old-world Grazier,—sick of lugging his slow Ox about the country till he got it bartered for corn or oil,—to take a piece of Leather, and thereon scratch or stamp the mere Figure of an Ox (or *Pecus*); put it in his pocket, and call it *Pecunia*, Money. Yet hereby did Barter grow Sale, the Leather Money is now Golden and Paper, and all miracles have been out-miracled: for there are Rothschilds[12] and English National Debts; and whoso has sixpence is sovereign (to the length of sixpence) over all men; commands cooks to feed him, philosophers to teach him, kings to mount guard over him,—to the

[9] Man-eater, cannibal.

[10] Banyan-grove: an East Indian tree whose branches send out aerial roots that form additional trunks. Hemlock-forest: Carlyle confuses the hemlock pine with the poisonous hemlock herb.

[11] Monk Berthold Schwartz is said to have developed a process for granulating gunpowder in the fourteenth century.

[12] Prominent international banking family.

length of sixpence.—Clothes too, which began in foolishest love of Ornament, what have they not become! Increased Security and pleasurable Heat soon followed: but what of these? Shame, divine Shame, (*Schaam*, Modesty), as yet a stranger to the Anthropophagous bosom, arose there mysteriously under Clothes; a mystic grove-encircled shrine for the Holy in man. Clothes gave us individuality, distinctions, social polity; Clothes have made Men of us; they are threatening to make Clothes-screens of us.

'But, on the whole,' continues our eloquent Professor, 'Man is a Tool-using Animal (*Handthierendes Thier*). Weak in himself, and of small stature, he stands on a basis, at most for the flattest-soled, of some half-square foot, insecurely enough; has to straddle out his legs, lest the very wind supplant him. Feeblest of bipeds! Three quintals are a crushing load for him; the steer of the meadow tosses him aloft, like a waste rag. Nevertheless he can use Tools, can devise Tools: with these the granite mountain melts into light dust before him; he kneads glowing iron, as if it were soft paste; seas are his smooth highway, winds and fire his unwearying steeds. Nowhere do you find him without Tools: without Tools he is nothing, with Tools he is all.'

Here may we not, for a moment, interrupt the stream of Oratory with a remark, that this Definition of the Tool-using Animal appears to us, of all that Animal-sort, considerably the precisest and best? Man is called a Laughing Animal: but do not the apes also laugh, or attempt to do it; and is the manliest man the greatest and oftenest laugher? Teufelsdröckh himself, as we said, laughed only once. Still less do we make of that other French Definition of the Cooking Animal; which, indeed, for rigorous scientific purposes, is as good as useless. Can a Tartar be said to cook, when he only readies his steak by riding on it? Again, what Cookery does the Greenlander use, beyond stowing-up his whale-blubber, as a marmot, in the like case, might do? Or how would Monsieur Ude[13] prosper among those Orinocco Indians who, according to Humboldt,[14] lodge in crow-nests, on the branches of trees; and, for half the year, have no

[13] Famous French cook of the nineteenth century.
[14] Alexander von Humboldt (1769–1859), German naturalist and explorer of South America.

65

victuals but pipe-clay, the whole country being under water? But, on the other hand, show us the human being, of any period or climate, without his Tools: those very Caledonians, as we saw, had their Flintball, and Thong to it, such as no brute has or can have.

'Man is a Tool-using Animal,' concludes Teufelsdröckh in his abrupt way; 'of which truth Clothes are but one example: and surely if we consider the interval between the first wooden Dibble fashioned by man, and those Liverpool Steam-carriages,[15] or the British House of Commons, we shall note what progress he has made. He digs up certain black stones from the bosom of the earth, and says to them, *Transport me and this luggage at the rate of five-and-thirty miles an hour*; and they do it: he collects, apparently by lot, six-hundred and fifty-eight miscellaneous individuals, and says to them, *Make this nation toil for us, bleed for us, hunger and sorrow and sin for us*; and they do it.'

Chapter VI
Aprons

Divers Aprons in the world with divers uses. The Military and Police Establishment Society's working Apron. The Episcopal Apron with its corner tucked in. The Laystall. Journalists now our only Kings and Clergy.

One of the most unsatisfactory Sections in the whole Volume is that on *Aprons*. What though stout old Gao,[1] the Persian Blacksmith, 'whose Apron, now indeed hidden under jewels,

---

[15] The first English railway, between Liverpool and Manchester, had recently been opened (1830).
[1] A legendary figure who used his blacksmith's apron as the banner of rebellion against an early Persian ruler.

because raised in revolt which proved successful, is still the royal standard of that country'; what though John Knox's[2] Daughter, 'who threatened Sovereign Majesty that she would catch her husband's head in her Apron, rather than he should lie and be a bishop'; what though the Landgravine Elizabeth,[3] with many other Apron worthies,—figure here? An idle wire-drawing spirit, sometimes even a tone of levity, approaching to conventional satire, is too clearly discernible. What, for example, are we to make of such sentences as the following?

'Aprons are Defences; against injury to cleanliness, to safety, to modesty, sometimes to roguery. From the thin slip of notched silk (as it were, the emblem and beatified ghost of an Apron), which some highest-bred housewife, sitting at Nürnberg Workboxes and Toyboxes, has gracefully fastened on; to the thick-tanned hide, girt round him with thongs, wherein the Builder builds, and at evening sticks his trowel; or to those jingling sheet-iron Aprons, wherein your otherwise half-naked Vulcans hammer and smelt in their smelt-furnace,—is there not range enough in the fashion and uses of this Vestment? How much has been concealed, how much has been defended in Aprons! Nay, rightly considered, what is your whole Military and Police Establishment, charged at uncalculated millions, but a huge scarlet-coloured, iron-fastened Apron, wherein Society works (uneasily enough); guarding itself from some soil and stithy-sparks, in this Devil's-smithy (*Teufelsschmiede*) of a world? But of all Aprons the most puzzling to me hitherto has been the Episcopal or Cassock. Wherein consists the usefulness of this Apron? The Overseer (*Episcopus*) of Souls, I notice, has tucked in the corner of it, as if his day's work were done: what does he shadow forth thereby?' &c. &c.

[2] Elizabeth, youngest daughter of John Knox (1505–1572), Scottish religious reformer, married John Welsh, a minister. When told by King James that her banished husband might return if he would submit to the authority of the bishops, she raised her apron and said that she would rather carry his severed head there. Carlyle's wife Jane Welsh Carlyle, claimed descent from John Welsh.

[3] St. Elizabeth of Hungary (1207–1231) was surprised by her husband while carrying food to the poor against his wishes. She hid the basket under her apron and when he pulled the apron aside, the food had been miraculously changed to roses.

Or again, has it often been the lot of our readers to read and stuff as we shall now quote?

'I consider those printed Paper Aprons, worn by the Parisian Cooks, as a new vent, though a slight one, for Typography; therefore as an encouragement to modern Literature, and deserving of approval; nor is it without satisfaction that I hear of a celebrated London Firm having in view to introduce the same fashion, with important extensions, in England.'—We who are on the spot hear of no such thing; and indeed have reason to be thankful that hitherto there are other vents for our Literature, exuberant as it is.—Teufelsdröckh continues: "If such supply of printed Paper should rise so far as to choke-up the highways and public thoroughfares, new means must of necessity be had recourse to. In a world existing by Industry, we grudge to employ fire as a destroying element, and not as a creating one. However, Heaven is omnipotent, and will find us an outlet. In the mean while, is it not beautiful to see five-million quintals of Rags picked annually from the Laystall,[4] and annually, after being macerated, hot-pressed, printed-on, and sold,—returned thither; filling so many hungry mouths by the way? Thus is the Laystall, especially with its Rags or Clothes-rubbish, the grand Electric Battery, and Fountain-of-motion, from which and to which the Social Activities (like vitreous and resinous Electricities) circulate, in larger or smaller circles, through the mighty, billowy, stormtost Chaos of Life, which they keep alive!'—Such passages fill us, who love the man, and partly esteem him, with a very mixed feeling.

Farther down we meet with this: 'The Journalists are now the true Kings and Clergy: henceforth Historians, unless they are fools, must write not of Bourbon Dynasties, and Tudors and Hapsburgs; but of Stamped Broad-sheet Dynasties, and quite new successive Names, according as this or the other Able Editor, or Combination of Able Editors, gains the world's ear. Of the British Newspaper Press, perhaps the most important of all, and wonderful enough in its secret constitution and procedure, a valuable descriptive History already exists, in that lan-

[4] Rubbish heap.

guage, under the title of *Satan's Invisible World Displayed*;[5] which, however, by search in all the Weissnichtwo Libraries, I have not yet succeeded in procuring (*vermöchte nicht aufzutreiben*).'

Thus does the good Homer not only nod, but snore. Thus does Teufelsdröckh, wandering in regions where he had little business, confound the old authentic Presbyterian Witchfinder with a new, spurious, imaginary Historian of the *Brittische Journalistik*; and so stumble on perhaps the most egregious blunder in Modern Literature!

Chapter VII
Miscellaneous-Historical

How Men and Fashions come and go. German Costume in the fifteenth century. By what strange chances do we live in History! The costume of Bolivar's Cavalry.

Happier is our Professor, and more purely scientific and historic, when he reaches the Middle Ages in Europe, and down to the end of the Seventeenth Century; the true era of extravagance in Costume. It is here that the Antiquary and Student of Modes comes upon his richest harvest. Fantastic garbs, beggaring all fancy of a Teniers or a Callot,[1] succeeded each other, like monster devouring monster in a Dream. The whole too in brief authentic strokes, and touched not seldom with that breath of genius which makes even old raiment live. Indeed, so learned, precise, graphical, and everyway interesting have we

---

[5] The phrase is derived from the titles of various seventeenth and eighteenth century books on witchcraft, such as *The Wonders of the Invisible World,* by Cotton Mather (1663–1728).

[1] David Teniers (1610–1690): Flemish painter of genre scenes. Jacques Callot (1593–1635): French engraver.

found these Chapters, that it may be thrown-out as a pertinent question for parties concerned, Whether or not a good English translation thereof might henceforth be profitably incorporated with Mr. Merrick's valuable Work *On Ancient Armour*? Take, by way of example, the following sketch; as authority for which Paulinus's *Zeitkürzende Lust* (ii. 678)[2] is, with seeming confidence, referred to:

'Did we behold the German fashionable dress of the Fifteenth Century, we might smile; as perhaps those bygone Germans, were they to rise again, and see our haberdashery, would cross themselves, and invoke the Virgin. But happily no bygone German, or man, rises again; thus the Present is not needlessly trammelled with the Past; and only grows out of it, like a Tree, whose roots are not intertangled with its branches, but lie peaceably underground. Nay it is very mournful, yet not useless, to see and know, how the Greatest and Dearest, in a short while, would find his place quite filled-up here, and no room for him; the very Napoleon, the very Byron, in some seven years, has become obsolete, and were now a foreigner to his Europe. This is the law of Progress secured; and in Clothes, as in all other external things whatsoever, no fashion will continue.

'Of the military classes in those old times, whose buff-belts, complicated chains and gorgets, huge churn-boots, and other riding and fighting gear have been bepainted in modern Romance, till the whole has acquired somewhat of a signpost character,—I shall here say nothing: the civil and pacific classes, less touched upon, are wonderful enough for us.

'Rich men, I find, have *Teusinke*'[3] (a perhaps untranslateable article); 'also a silver girdle, whereat hang little bells; so that when a man walks, it is with continual jingling. Some few, of musical turn, have a whole chime of bells (*Glockenspiel*) fastened there; which, especially in sudden whirls, and the other accidents of walking, has a grateful effect. Observe too how fond they are of peaks, and Gothic-arch intersections. The male world wears peaked caps, an ell long, which hang bobbing

---

[2] Christian Franz Paullini (1643–1712). The following sections are a paraphrase of the cited work, with Carlyle's own interpolations.
[3] A bell-shaped girdle.

over the side (*schief*): their shoes are peaked in front, also to the length of an ell, and laced on the side with tags; even the wooden shoes have their ell-long noses: some also clap bells on the peak. Further, according to my authority, the men have breeches without seat (*ohne Gesäss*): these they fasten peakwise to their shirts; and the long round doublet must overlap them.

'Rich maidens, again, flit abroad in gowns scolloped out behind and before, so that back and breast are almost bare. Wives of quality, on the other hand, have train-gowns four or five ells in length; which trains there are boys to carry. Brave Cleopatras, sailing in their silk-cloth Galley, with a Cupid for steersman! Consider their welts, a handbreadth thick, which waver round them by way of hem; the long flood of silver buttons, or rather silver shells, from throat to shoe, wherewith these same welt-gowns are buttoned. The maidens have bound silver snoods about their hair, with gold spangles, and pendent flames (*Flammen*), that is sparkling hair-drops: but of their mother's headgear who shall speak? Neither in love of grace is comfort forgotten. In winter weather you behold the whole fair creation (that can afford it) in long mantles, with skirts wide below, and, for hem, not one but two sufficient hand-broad welts; all ending atop in a thick well-starched Ruff, some twenty inches broad: these are their Ruff-mantles (*Kragenmäntel*).

'As yet among the womankind hoop-petticoats are not; but the men have doublets of fustian, under which lie multiple ruffs of cloth, pasted together with batter (*mit Teig zusammen-gekleistert*), which create protuberance enough. Thus do the two sexes vie with each other in the art of Decoration; and as usual the stronger carries it.'

Our Professor, whether he have humour himself or not, manifests a certain feeling of the Ludicrous, a sly observance of it, which, could emotion of any kind be confidently predicated of so still a man, we might call a real love. None of those bell-girdles, bushel-breeches, cornuted shoes, or other the like phenomena, of which the History of Dress offers so many, escape him: more especially the mischances, or striking adventures, incident to the wearers of such, are noticed with due fidelity. Sir Walter Raleigh's fine mantle, which he spread in the mud

71

under Queen Elizabeth's feet, appears to provoke little enthusiasm in him; he merely asks, Whether at that period the Maiden Queen 'was red-painted on the nose, and white-painted on the cheeks, as her tirewomen, when from spleen and wrinkles she would no longer look in any glass, were wont to serve her?' We can answer that Sir Walter knew well what he was doing, and had the Maiden Queen been stuffed parchment dyed in verdigris, would have done the same.

Thus too, treating of those enormous habiliments, that were not only slashed and galooned, but artificially swollen-out on the broader parts of the body, by introduction of Bran,—our Professor fails not to comment on that luckless Courtier, who having seated himself on a chair with some projecting nail on it, and therefrom rising, to pay his *devoir* on the entrance of Majesty, instantaneously emitted several pecks of dry wheat-dust: and stood there dimished to a spindle, his galoons and slashes dangling sorrowful and flabby round him. Whereupon the Professor publishes this reflection:

'By what strange chances do we live in History? Erostratus by a torch; Milo by a bullock; Henry Darnley,[4] an unfledged booby and bustard, by his limbs; most Kings and Queens by being born under such and such a bed-tester; Boileau Despréaux (according to Helvetius) by the peck of a turkey;[5] and this ill-starred individual by a rent in his breeches,—for no Memorist of Kaiser Otto's Court omits him. Vain was the prayer of Themistocles for a talent of Forgetting: my Friends, yield cheerfully to Destiny, and read since it is written.'—Has Teufelsdröckh to be put in mind that, nearly related to the impossible talent of Forgetting, stands that talent of Silence, which even travelling Englishmen manifest?

---

[4] All figures who achieved fame by ludicrous or trivial actions. Erostratus: legendary figure said to have burnt the temple of Diana at Ephesus in fourth century B.C. in order to gain immortal fame. Milo: Greek athlete celebrated for carrying a young bullock for forty yards. Henry Darnley (1545–1567): second husband of Mary Queen of Scots and known for his attractive appearance.

[5] Nicolas Boileau (1636–1711): French critic. Helvétius attributed his lack of warmth as a writer to an injury he received as a youth from a turkey.

'The simplest costume,' observes our Professor, 'which I anywhere find alluded to in History, is that used as regimental, by Bolivar's Cavalry, in the late Columbian wars.[6] A square Blanket, twelve feet in diagonal, is provided (some were wont to cut-off the corners, and make it circular): in the centre a slit is effected eighteen inches long; through this the mother-naked Trooper introduces his head and neck; and so rides shielded from all weather, and in battle from many strokes (for he rolls it about his left arm); and not only dressed, but harnessed and draperied.'

With which picture of a State of Nature, affecting by its singularity, and Old-Roman contempt of the superfluous, we shall quit this part of our subject.

Chapter VIII
The World Out of Clothes

Teufelsdröckh's Theorem, 'Society founded upon Cloth'; his Method, Intuition quickened by Experience.—The mysterious question, Who am I? Philosophic systems all at fault: A deeper meditation has always taught, here and there an individual, that all visible things are appearances only; but also emblems and revelations of God. Teufelsdröckh first comes upon the question of Clothes: Baseness to which Clothing may bring us.

If in the Descriptive-Historical portion of this Volume, Teufelsdröckh, discussing merely the *Werden* (Origin and successive Improvement) of Clothes, has astonished many a reader, much more will he in the Speculative-Philosophical portion,

[6] Simon Bolivar (1783–1830) led rebellions against Spanish rule in South America.

which treats of their *Wirken*, or Influences. It is here that the present Editor first feels the pressure of his task; for here properly the higher and new Philosophy of Clothes commences: an untried, almost inconceivable region, or chaos; in venturing upon which, how difficult, yet how unspeakably important is it to know what course, of survey and conquest, is the true one; where the footing is firm substance and will bear us, where it is hollow, or mere cloud, and may engulf us! Teufelsdröckh undertakes no less than to expound the moral, political, even religious Influences of Clothes; he undertakes to make manifest, in its thousandfold bearings, this grand Proposition, that Man's earthly interests, 'are all hooked and buttoned together, and held up, by Clothes.' He says in so many words, 'Society is founded upon Cloth'; and again, 'Society sails through the Infinitude on Cloth, as on a Faust's Mantle, or rather like the Sheet of clean and unclean beasts in the Apostle's Dream; and without such Sheet or Mantle, would sink to endless depths, or mount to inane limboes, and in either case be no more.'

By what chains, or indeed infinitely completed tissues, of meditation this grand Theorem is here unfolded, and innumerable practical Corollaries are drawn therefrom, it were perhaps a mad ambition to attempt exhibiting. Our Professor's method is not, in any case, that of common school Logic, where the truths all stand in a row, each holding by the skirts of the other; but at best that of practical Reason, proceeding by large Intuition over whole systematic groups and kingdoms; whereby, we might say, a noble complexity, almost like that of Nature, reigns in his Philosophy, or spiritual Picture of Nature: a mighty maze, yet, as faith whispers, not without a plan. Nay we complained above, that a certain ignoble complexity, what we must call mere confusion, was also discernible. Often, also, we have to exclaim: Would to Heaven those same Biographical Documents were come! For it seems as if the demonstration lay much in the Author's individuality; as if it were not Argument that had taught him, but Experience. At present it is only in local glimpses, and by significant fragments, picked often at wide-enough intervals from the original Volume, and carefully collated, that we can hope to impart some outline or foreshadow of this Doctrine. Readers of any intelligence are once more invited to favour us with their most concentrated attention: let these, after intense consideration, and not till then, pronounce, Whether on the utmost verge of our actual horizon there is not a looming as of Land; a promise of new Fortunate Islands, perhaps whole undiscovered Americas, for such as have canvas to sail thither?—As exordium to the whole, stand here the following long citation:

'With men of a speculative turn,' writes Teufelsdröckh, there come seasons, meditative, sweet, yet awful hours, when in wonder and fear you ask yourself that unanswerable question: Who am *I*; the thing that can say "I" (*das Wesen das sich* ICH *nennt*)? The world, with its loud trafficking, retires into the distance; and, through the paper-hangings, and stone-walls, and thick-plied tissues of Commerce and Polity, and all the living and lifeless integuments (of Society and a Body), wherewith your Existence sits surrounded,—the sight reaches forth into the void Deep, and you are alone with the Universe, and silently commune with it, as one mysterious Presence with another.

'Who am I; what is this ME? A Voice, a Motion, an Appearance;—some embodied, visualised Idea in the Eternal Mind? *Cogito, ergo sum.*[1] Alas, poor Cogitator, this takes us but a little way. Sure enough, I am; and lately was not: but Whence? How? Whereto? The answer lies around, written in all colours and motions, uttered in all tones of jubilee and wail, in thousand-figured, thousand-voiced, harmonious Nature: but where is the cunning eye and ear to whom that God-written Apocalypse will yield articulate meaning? We sit as in a boundless Phantasmagoria and Dream-grotto; boundless, for the faintest star, the remotest century, lies not even nearer the verge thereof: sounds and many-coloured visions flit round our sense; but Him, the Unslumbering, whose work both Dream and Dreamer are, we see not; except in rare half-waking moments, suspect not. Creation, says one, lies before us, like a glorious Rainbow; but the Sun that made it lies behind us, hidden from us. Then, in that strange Dream, how we clutch at shadows as

---

[1] "I think, therefore I am," famous statement of Descartes.

if they were substances; and sleep deepest while fancying ourselves most awake! Which of your Philosophical Systems is other than a dream-theorem; a net quotient, confidently given out, where divisor and dividend are both unknown? What are all your national Wars, with their Moscow Retreats,[2] and sanguinary hate-filled Revolutions, but the Somnambulism of uneasy Sleepers? This Dreaming, this Somnambulism is what we on Earth call Life; wherein the most indeed undoubtedly wander, as if they knew right hand from left; yet they only are wise who know that they know nothing.

'Pity that all Metaphysics had hitherto proved so inexpressibly unproductive! The secret of Man's Being is still like the Sphinx's secret: a riddle that he cannot rede; and for ignorance of which he suffers death, the worst death, a spiritual. What are your Axioms, and Categories, and Systems, and Aphorisms? Words, words. High Air-castles are cunningly built of Words, the Words well bedded also in good Logic-mortar; wherein, however, no Knowledge will come to lodge. *The whole is greater than the part*: how exceedingly true! *Nature abhors a vacuum*: how exceedingly false and calumnious! Again, *Nothing can act but where it is*:[3] with all my heart; only, WHERE IS it? Be not the slave of Words: is not the Distant, the Dead, while I love it, and long for it, and mourn for it, Here, in the genuine sense, as truly as the floor I stand on? But that same WHERE, with its brother WHEN, are from the first the master-colours of our Dream-grotto; say rather, the Canvas (the warp and woof thereof) whereon all our Dreams and Life-visions are painted. Nevertheless, has not a deeper meditation taught certain of every climate and age, that the WHERE and WHEN, so mysteriously inseparable from all our thoughts, are but superficial terrestrial adhesions to thought; that the Seer may discern them where they mount up out of the celestial EVERYWHERE and FOREVER: have not all nations conceived their God as Omnipresent and Eternal; as existing in a universal HERE, an ever-

[2] Winter retreat of Napoleon from Moscow in 1812, in which thousands died.
[3] Carlyle is suggesting the limitations of these axioms of Euclidean geometry and Newtonian science.

lasting Now? Think well, thou too wilt find that Space is but a mode of our human Sense, so likewise Time; there *is* no Space and no Time: WE are—we know not what;—light-sparkles floating in the æther of Deity!

'So that this so solid-seeming World, after all, were but an air-image, our ME the only reality: and Nature, with its thousandfold production and destruction, but the reflex of our own inward Force, the "phantasy of our Dream"; or what the Earth-Spirit in *Faust* names it, *the living visible Garment of God*:

> ' "In Being's floods, in Action's storm,
>   I walk and work, above, beneath,
>   Work and weave in endless motion!
>   Birth and Death,
>   An infinite ocean;
>   A seizing and giving
>   The fire of Living:
>   'Tis thus at the roaring Loom of Time I ply,
>   And weave for God the Garment thou seest Him by."[4]

Of twenty millions that have read and spouted this thunder-speech of the *Erdgeist*, are there yet twenty units of us that have learned the meaning thereof?

'It was in some such mood, when wearied and fordone with these high speculations, that I first came upon the question of Clothes. Strange enough, it strikes me, is this same fact of there being Tailors and Tailored. The Horse I ride has his own whole fell: strip him of the girths and flaps and extraneous tags I have fastened round him, and the noble creature is his own sempster and weaver and spinner; nay his own bootmaker, jeweler, and man-milliner; he bounds free through the valleys, with a perennial rainproof court-suit on his body; wherein warmth and easiness of fit have reached perfection; nay, the graces also have been considered, and frills and fringes, with gay variety of colour, featly appended, and ever in the right place, are not

---

[4] This passage, an important source of *Sartor*, is from Goethe's *Faust*, I, scene i.

wanting. While I—good Heaven!—have thatched myself over with the dead fleeces of sheep, the bark of vegetables, the entrails of worms, the hides of oxen or seals, the felt of furred beasts; and walk abroad a moving Rag-screen, overheaped with shreds and tatters raked from the Charnel-house of Nature, where they would have rotted, to rot on me more slowly! Day after day, I must thatch myself anew; day after day, this despicable thatch must lose some film of its thickness; some film of it, frayed away by tear and wear, must be brushed-off into the Ashpit, into the Laystall; till by degrees the whole has been brushed thither, and I, the dust-making, patent Rag-grinder, get new material to grind down. O subter-brutish! vile! most vile! For have not I too a compact all-enclosing Skin, whiter or dingier? Am I a botched mass of tailors' and cobblers' shreds, then; or a tightly-articulated, homogeneous little Figure, automatic, nay alive?

'Strange enough how creatures of the human-kind shut their eyes to plainest facts; and by the mere inertia of Oblivion and Stupidity, live at ease in the midst of Wonders and Terrors. But indeed man is, and was always, a blockhead and dullard; much readier to feel and digest, than to think and consider. Prejudice, which he pretends to hate, is his absolute lawgiver; mere use-and-wont everywhere leads him by the nose; thus let but a Rising of the Sun, let but a Creation of the World happen *twice*, and it ceases to be marvellous, to be noteworthy, or noticeable. Perhaps not once in a lifetime does it occur to your ordinary biped, of any country or generation, be he gold-mantled Prince, or russet-jerkined Peasant, that his Vestments and his Self are not one and indivisible; that *he* is naked, without vestments, till he buy or steal such, and by forethought sew and button them.

'For my own part, these considerations, of our Clothes-thatch, and how, reaching inwards even to our heart of hearts, it tailorises and demoralises us, fill me with a certain horror at myself and mankind; almost as one feels at those Dutch Cows, which, during the wet season, you see grazing deliberately with jackets and petticoats (of striped sacking), in the meadows of Gouda. Nevertheless there is something great in the moment when a man first strips himself of adventitious wrappages; and sees indeed that he is naked, and, as Swift has it, "a forked straddling animal with bandy legs"; yet also a Spirit, and unutterable Mystery of Mysteries.'

Chapter IX
Adamitism

The universal utility of Clothes, and their higher mystic virtue, illustrated. Conception of Mankind stripped naked; and immediate consequent dissolution of civilised Society.

Let no courteous reader take offence at the opinions broached in the conclusion of the last Chapter. The Editor himself, on first glancing over that singular passage, was inclined to exclaim: What, have we got not only a Sansculottist, but an enemy to Clothes in the abstract? A new Adamite,[1] in this century, which flatters itself that it is the Nineteenth, and destructive both to Superstition and Enthusiasm?

Consider, thou foolish Teufelsdröckh, what benefits unspeakable all ages and sexes derive from Clothes. For example, when thou thyself, a watery, pulpy, slobbery fresh-man and newcomer in this Planet, sattest muling and puking in thy nurse's arms; sucking thy coral, and looking forth into the world in the blankest manner, what hadst thou been without thy blankets, and bibs, and other nameless hulls? A terror to thyself and mankind! Or hast thou forgotten the day when thou first receivedst breeches, and thy long clothes became short? The village where thou livedst was all apprised of the fact; and neighbour after neighbour kissed thy pudding-cheek, and gave thee, as handsel, silver or copper coins, on that the first gala-day of

[1] A heretical religious sect, the members of which went naked in imitation of the innocent Adam.

thy existence. Again, wert not thou, at one period of life, a Buck, or Blood, or Macaroni, or Incroyable, or Dandy,[2] or by whatever name, according to year and place, such phenomenon is distinguished? In that one word lie included mysterious volumes. Nay, now when the reign of folly is over, or altered, and thy clothes are not for triumph but for defence, hast thou always worn them perforce, and as a consequence of Man's Fall; never rejoiced in them as in a warm movable House, a Body round thy Body, wherein that strange THEE of thine sat snug, defying all variations of Climate? Girt with thick double-milled kerseys; half-buried under shawls and broadbrims, and overalls and mud-boots, thy very fingers cased in doeskin and mittens, thou hast bestrode that 'Horse I ride'; and, though it were in wild winter, dashed through the world, glorying in it as if thou wert its lord. In vain did the sleet beat round thy temples; it lighted only on thy impenetrable, felted or woven, case of wool. In vain did the winds howl,—forests sounding and creaking, deep calling unto deep,—and the storms heap themselves together into one huge Arctic whirlpool: thou flewest through the middle thereof, striking fire from the highway; wild music hummed in thy ears, thou too wert as a 'sailor of the air'; the wreck of matter and the crash of worlds was thy element and propitiously wafting tide. Without Clothes, without bit or saddle, what hadst thou been; what had thy fleet quadruped been?—Nature is good, but she is not the best: here truly was the victory of Art over Nature. A thunderbolt indeed might have pierced thee; all short of this thou couldst defy.

Or, cries the courteous reader, has your Teufelsdröckh forgotten what he said lately about 'Aboriginal Savages,' and their 'condition miserable indeed'? Would he have all this unsaid; and us betake ourselves again to the 'matted cloak,' and go sheeted in a 'thick natural fell'?

Nowise, courteous reader! The Professor knows full well what he is saying; and both thou and we, in our haste, do him wrong. If Clothes, in these times, 'so tailorise and demoralise us,' have they no redeeming value; can they not be altered to serve better; must they of necessity be thrown to the dogs? The truth is,

---

[2] All terms for fashionable young men.

Teufelsdröckh, though a Sansculottist, is no Adamite; and much perhaps as he might wish to go forth before this degenerate age 'as a Sign,' would nowise wish to do it, as those old Adamites did, in a state of Nakedness. The utility of Clothes is altogether apparent to him: nay perhaps he has an insight into their more recondite, and almost mystic qualities, what we might call the omnipotent virtue of Clothes, such as was never before vouchsafed to any man. For example:

'You see two individuals,' he writes, 'one dressed in fine Red, the other in coarse threadbare Blue: Red says to Blue, "Be hanged and anatomised"; Blue hears with a shudder, and (O wonder of wonders!) marches sorrowfully to the gallows; is there noosed-up, vibrates his hour, and the surgeons dissect him, and fit his bones into a skeleton for medical purposes. How is this; or what make ye of your *Nothing can act but where it is?* Red has no physical hold of Blue, no *clutch* of him, is nowise in *contact* with him: neither are those ministering Sheriffs and Lord-Lieutenants and Hangmen and Tipstaves so related to commanding Red, that he can tug them hither and thither; but each stands distinct within his own skin. Nevertheless, as it is spoken, so is it done: the articulated Word sets all hands in Action; and Rope and Improved-drop perform their work.

'Thinking reader, the reason seems to me twofold: First, that *Man is a Spirit*, and bound by invisible bonds to *All Men*; secondly, that *he wears Clothes*, which are the visible emblems of that fact. Has not your Red hanging-individual a horsehair wig, squirrel-skins, and a plush-gown; whereby all mortals know that he is a JUDGE?—Society, which the more I think of it astonishes me the more, is founded upon Cloth.

'Often in my atrabiliar moods, when I read of pompous ceremonials, Frankfort Coronations, Royal Drawing-rooms, Levees, Couchees; and how the ushers and macers and pursuivants are all in waiting; how Duke this is presented by Arch-duke that, and Colonel A by General B, and innumerable Bishops, Admirals, and miscellaneous Functionaries, and advancing gallantly to the Anointed Presence; and I strive, in my remote privacy, to form a clear picture of that solemnity,—on a sudden, as by some enchanter's wand, the—shall I speak it?—the Clothes fly-off the whole dramatic corps; and Dukes,

Grandees, Bishops, Generals, Anointed Presence itself, every mother's son of them, stand straddling there, not a shirt on them; and I know not whether to laugh or weep. This physical or psychical infirmity, in which perhaps I am not singular, I have, after hesitation, thought right to publish, for the solace of those afflicted with the like.'

Would to Heaven, say we, thou hadst thought right to keep it secret! Who is there now that can read the five columns of Presentations in his Morning Newspaper without a shudder? Hypochondriac men, and all men are to a certain extent hypochondriac, should be more gently treated. With what readiness our fancy, in this shattered state of the nerves, follows out the consequences which Teufelsdröckh, with a devilish coolness, goes on to draw:

'What would Majesty do, could such an accident befall in reality; should the buttons all simultaneously start, and the solid wool evaporate, in very Deed, as here in Dream? *Ach Gott!* How each skulks into the nearest hiding-place; their high State Tragedy. (*Haupt- und Staats-Action*) becomes a Pickleherring-Farce to weep at, which is the worst kind of Farce; *the tables* (according to Horace), and with them, the whole fabric of Government, Legislation, Property, Police, and Civilized Society, *are dissolved*, in wails and howls.'

Lives the man that can figure a naked Duke of Windlestraw addressing a naked House of Lords? Imagination, choked as in mephitic air, recoils on itself, and will not forward with the picture. The Woolsack,[3] the Ministerial, the Opposition Benches —*infandum! infandum!*[4] And yet why is the thing impossible? Was not every soul, or rather every body, of these Guardians of our Liberties, naked, or nearly so, last night; 'a forked Radish with a head fantastically carved'? And why might be not, did our stern fate so order it, walk out to St. Stephen's,[5] as well as into bed, in that no-fashion; and there, with other similar Radishes, hold a Bed of Justice? 'Solace of those afflicted with the like!' Unhappy Teufelsdröckh, had man ever such a 'physical

[3] The chair of the Lord Chancellor in the English House of Lords.
[4] "Terrible!"
[5] Houses of Parliament.

or psychical infirmity' before? And now how many, perhaps, may thy unparalleled confession (which we, even to the sounder British world, and goaded-on by Criticial and Biographical duty, grudge to reimpart) incurably infect therewith! Art thou the malignest of Sansculottists, or only the maddest?

'It will remain to be examined,' adds the inexorable Teufelsdröckh, in how far the SCARECROW, as a Clothed Person, is not also entitled to benefit of clergy, and English trial by jury: nay perhaps, considering his high function (for is not he too a Defender of Property, and Sovereign armed with the *terrors* of the Law?), to a certain royal Immunity and Inviolability; which, however, misers and the meaner class of persons are not always voluntarily disposed to grant him.' * * * * 'O my friends, we are (in Yorick Sterne's words) but as "turkeys driven with a stick and red clout, to the market":[6] or if some drivers, as they do in Norfolk, take a dried bladder and put peas in it, the rattle thereof terrifies the boldest!'

Chapter X
Pure Reason[1]

A Naked World possible, nay actually exists, under the clothed one. Man, in the eye of Pure Reason, a visible God's Presence. The beginning of all wisdom, to look fixedly on Clothes till they become transparent. Wonder, the basis of Worship: Perennial in man. Modern Sciolists who cannot wonder: Teufelsdröckh's contempt for, and advice to them.

It must now be apparent enough that our Professor, as above hinted, is a speculative Radical, and of the very darkest tinge;

[6] Laurence Sterne, *Tristram Shandy*, V, vii.
[1] The chapter title is taken from Immanuel Kant's *Critique of Pure Reason* (1781).

acknowledging, for most part, in the solemnities and paraphernalia of civilised Life, which we make so much of, nothing but so many Cloth-rags, turkey-poles, and 'bladders with dried peas.' To linger among such speculations, longer than mere Science requires, a discerning public can have no wish. For our purposes the simple fact that such a *Naked World* is possible, nay actually exists (under the Clothed one), will be sufficient. Much, therefore, we omit about 'Kings wrestling naked on the green with Carmen,' and the Kings being thrown: 'dissect them with scalpels,' says Teufelsdröckh; 'the same viscera, tissues, livers, lights, and other life-tackle, are there: examine their spiritual mechanism; the same great Need, great Greed, and little Faculty; nay ten to one but the Carman, who understands draught-cattle, the rimming of wheels, something of the laws of unstable and stable equilibrium, with other branches of wagon-science, and has actually put forth his hand and operated on Nature, is the more cunningly gifted of the two. Whence, then, their so unspeakable difference? From Clothes.' Much also we shall omit about confusion of Ranks, and Joan and My Lady, and how it would be everywhere 'Hail fellow well met,' and Chaos were come again: all which to any one that has once fairly pictured-out the grand mother-idea, *Society in a state of Nakedness*, will spontaneously suggest itself. Should some sceptical individual still entertain doubts whether in a world without Clothes, the smallest Politeness, Polity, or even Police, could exist, let him turn to the original Volume, and view. There the boundless Serbonian Bog of Sansculottism, stretching sour and pestilential: over which we have lightly flown; where not only whole armies but whole nations might sink! If indeed the following argument, in its brief riveting emphasis, be not of itself incontrovertible and final:

'Are we Opossums; have we natural Pouches, like the Kangaroo? Or how, without Clothes, could we possess the master-organ, soul's seat, and true pineal gland[2] of the Body Social: I mean, a PURSE?'

---

[2] A small gland near the brain, once thought to contain the soul.

Nevertheless it is impossible to hate Professor Teufelsdröckh; at worst, one knows not whether to hate or to love him. For though, in looking at the fair tapestry of human Life, with its royal and even sacred figures, he dwells not on the obverse alone, but here chiefly on the reverse; and indeed turns out the rough seams, tatters, and manifold thrums of that unsightly wrong-side, with an almost diabolic patience and indifference, which must have sunk him in the estimation of most readers,— there is that within which unspeakably distinguishes him from all other past and present Sansculottists. The grand unparalleled peculiarity of Teufelsdröckh is, that with all this Descendental-ism, he combines a Transcendentalism, no less superlative; whereby if on the one hand he degrade man below most ani-mals, except those jacketed Gouda Cows, he, on the other, exalts him beyond the visible Heavens, almost to an equality with the Gods.

'To the eye of vulgar Logic,' says he, 'what is man? An omnivorous Biped that wears Breeches. To the eye of Pure Reason what is he? A Soul, a Spirit, and divine Apparition. Round his mysterious ME, there lies, under all those woolrags, a Garment of Flesh (or of Senses), contextured in the Loom of Heaven; whereby he is revealed to his like, and dwells with them in UNION and DIVISION; and sees and fashions for himself a Universe, with azure Starry Spaces, and long Thousands of Years. Deep-hidden is he under that strange Garment; amid Sounds and Colours and Forms, as it were, swathed-in, and inextricably over-shrouded: yet it is sky-woven, and worthy of a God. Stands he not thereby in the centre of Immensities, in the conflux of Eternities? He feels; power has been given him to know, to believe; nay does not the spirit of Love, free in its celestial primeval brightness, even here, though but for mo-ments, look through? Well said Saint Chrysostom, with his lips of gold, "the true SHEKINAH[3] is Man": where else is the GOD's-PRESENCE manifested not to our eyes only, but to our hearts, as in our fellow-man?'

[3] Hebrew term meaning the symbol or dwelling place of the Divine Presence.

In such passages, unhappily too rare, the high Platonic Mysticism of our Author, which is perhaps the fundamental element of his nature, bursts forth, as it were, in full flood: and, through all the vapour and tarnish of what is often so perverse, so mean in his exterior and environment, we seem to look into a whole inward Sea of Light and Love;—though, alas, the grim coppery clouds soon roll together again, and hide it from view.

Such tendency to Mysticism is everywhere traceable in this man; and indeed, to attentive readers, must have been long ago apparent. Nothing that he sees but has more than a common meaning, but has two meanings: thus, if in the highest Imperial Sceptre and Charlemagne-Mantle, as well as in the poorest Ox-goad and Gipsy-Blanket, he finds Prose, Decay, Contempti-bility; there is in each sort Poetry also, and a reverend Worth. For Matter, were it never so despicable, in Spirit, the manifesta-tion of Spirit: were it never so honourable, can it be more? The thing Visible, nay the thing Imagined, the thing in any way conceived as Visible, what is it but a Garment, a Clothing of the higher, celestial Invisible, 'unimaginable, formless, dark with excess of bright'? Under which point of view the following pas-sage, so strange in purport, so strange in phrase, seems char-acteristic enough:

'The beginning of all Wisdom is to look fixedly on Clothes, or even with armed eyesight, till they become *transparent*. "The Philosopher," says the wisest of this age, "must station himself in the middle": how true! The Philosopher is he to whom the Highest has descended, and the Lowest has mounted up; who is the equal and kindly brother of all.

'Shall we tremble before clothwebs and cobwebs, whether woven in Arkwright[4] looms, or by the silent Arachnes[5] that weave unrestingly in our imagination? Or, on the other hand, what is there that we cannot love; since all was created by God?

'Happy he who can look through the Clothes of a Man (the

---

[4] Richard Arkwright (1732–1792), inventor of the spinning Jenny and early industrialist.
[5] In Greek mythology a Lydian girl who was changed into a spider for challenging Athena to a weaving contest.

86

woollen, and fleshly, and official Bank-paper and State-paper
Clothes) into the Man himself; and discern, it may be, in this
or the other Dread Potentate, a more or less incompetent
Digestive-apparatus; yet also an inscrutable venerable Mystery,
in the meanest Tinker that sees with eyes!'

For the rest, as is natural to a man of this kind, he deals
much in the feeling of Wonder; insists on the necessity and high
worth of universal Wonder; which he holds to be the only
reasonable temper for the denizen of so singular a Planet as
ours. 'Wonder,' says he, 'is the basis of Worship: the reign of
wonder is perennial, indestructible in Man; only at certain stages
(as the present), it is, for some short season, a reign *in partibus
infidelium.*'[6] That progress of Science, which is to destroy Wonder, and in its stead substitute Mensuration and Numeration,
finds small favour with Teufelsdröckh, much as he otherwise
venerates these two latter processes.

'Shall your Science,' exclaims he, 'proceed in the small chink-
lighted, or even oil-lighted, underground workshop of Logic
alone; and man's mind become an Arithmetical Mill, whereof
Memory is the Hopper, and mere Tables of Sines and Tangents,
Codification, and Treatises of what you call Political Economy,
are the Meal? And what is that Science, which the scientific
head alone, were it screwed off, and (like the Doctor's in the
Arabian Tale) set in a basin to keep it alive, could prosecute
without shadow of a heart,—but one other of the mechanical
and menial handicrafts, for which the Scientific Head (having a
Soul in it) is too noble an organ? I mean that Thought without
Reverence is barren, perhaps poisonous; at best, dies like cookery with the day that called it forth; does not live, like sowing,
in successive tilths and wider-spreading harvests, bringing food
and plenteous increase to all Time.'

In such wise does Teufelsdröckh deal hits, harder or softer,
according to ability; yet ever, as we would fain persuade ourselves, with charitable intent. Above all, that class of 'Logic-
choppers, and treble-pipe Scoffers, and professed Enemies to

[6] "In the lands of unbelievers." Term applied by Roman Catholic
Church to bishops holding sees which are no longer Roman Catholic.

Wonder; who, in these days, so numerously patrol as night-constables about the Mechanics' Institute[7] of Science, and cackle like true Old-Roman geese and goslings round their Capitol, on any alarm, or on none; nay who often, as illuminated Sceptics, walk abroad into peaceable society, in full day-light, with rattle and lantern, and insist on guiding you and guarding you therewith, though the Sun is shining, and the street populous with mere justice-loving men:' that whole class is inexpressibly wearisome to him. Hear with what uncommon animation he perorates:

'The man who cannot wonder, who does not habitually wonder (and worship), were he President of innumerable Royal Societies, and carried the whole *Mécaniqué Céleste* and *Hegel's Philosophy*, and the epitome of all Laboratories and Observatories with their results, in his single head,—is but a Pair of Spectacles behind which there is no Eye. Let those who have Eyes look through him, then he may be useful.

'Thou wilt have no Mystery and Mysticism; wilt walk through thy world by the sunshine of what thou callest Truth, or even by the hand-lamp of what I call Attorney-Logic; and "explain" all, "account" for all, or believe nothing of it? Nay, thou wilt attempt laughter; whoso recognises the unfathomable, all-pervading domain of Mystery, which is everywhere under our feet and among our hands; to whom the Universe is an Oracle and Temple, as well as a Kitchen and Cattlestall,—he shall be a delirious Mystic; to him thou, with sniffing charity, wilt protrusively proffer thy hand-lamp, and shriek, as one injured, when he kicks his foot through it?—*Armer Teufel!*[8] Doth not thy cow calve, doth not thy bull gender? Thou thyself, wert thou not born, wilt thou not die? "Explain" me all this, or do one of two things: Retire into private places with thy foolish cackle; or, what were better, give it up, and weep, not that the reign of wonder is done, and God's world all disembellished and prosaic, but that thou hitherto art a Dilettante and sand-blind Pedant.'

[7] Workingmen's colleges developed in early nineteenth century.
[8] "Poor Devil."

Chapter XI
Prospective

Nature not an Aggregate, but a Whole. All visible things are emblems, Clothes; and exist for a time only. The grand scope of the Philosophy of Clothes.—Biographic Documents arrive. Letter from Heuschrecke on the importance of Biography. Heterogeneous character of the documents: Editor sorely perplexed; but desperately grapples with his work.

The Philosophy of Clothes is now to all readers, as we predicted it would do, unfolding itself into new boundless expansions, of a cloudcapt, almost chimerical aspect, yet not without azure loomings in the far distance, and streaks as of an Elysian brightness; the highly questionable purport and promise of which it is becoming more and more important for us to ascertain. Is that a real Elysian brightness, cries many a timid wayfarer, or the reflex of Pandemonian lava? Is it of a truth leading us into beatific Asphodel meadows, or the yellow-burning marl of a Hell-on-Earth?

Our Professor, like other Mystics, whether delirious or inspired, gives an Editor enough to do. Ever higher and dizzier are the heights he leads us to; more piercing, all-comprehending, all-confounding are his views and glances. For example, this of Nature being not an Aggregate but a Whole:

'Well sang the Hebrew Psalmist: "If I take the wings of the morning and dwell in the uttermost parts of the universe, God is there."[1] Thou thyself, O cultivated reader, who too probably art no Psalmist, but a Prosaist, knowing GOD only by tradition,

---

[1] Psalms, cxxix, 9–10.

knowest thou any corner of the world where at least FORCE is not? The drop which thou shakest from thy wet hand, rests not where it falls, but tomorrow thou findest it swept away; already on the wings of the Northwind, it is nearing the Tropic of Cancer. How came it to evaporate, and not lie motionless? Thinkest thou there is ought motionless; without Force, and utterly dead?

'As I rode through the Schwarzwald, I said to myself: That little fire which grows star-like across the dark-growing (*nach-tende*) moor, where the sooty smith bends over his anvil, and thou hopest to replace thy lost horse-shoe,—is it a detached, separated speck, cut-off from the whole Universe; or indissolubly joined to the whole? Thou fool, that smithy-fire was (primarily) kindled at the Sun; is fed by air that circulates from before Noah's Deluge, from beyond the Dogstar; therein, with Iron Force, and Coal Force, and the far stranger Force of Man, are cunning affinities and battles and victories of Force brought about; it is a little ganglion, or nervous centre, in the great vital system of Immensity. Call it, if thou wilt, an unconscious Altar, kindled on the bosom of the All; whose iron sacrifice, whose iron smoke and influence reach quite through the All; whose dingy Priest, not by word, yet by brain and sinew, preaches forth the mystery of Force; nay preaches forth (exoterically enough) one little textlet from the Gospel of Freedom, the Gospel of Man's Force, commanding, and one day to be all-commanding.

'Detached, separated! I say there is no such separation: nothing hitherto was ever stranded, cast aside; but all, were it only a withered leaf, works together with all; is borne forward on the bottomless, shoreless flood of Action, and lives through perpetual metamorphoses. The withered leaf is not dead and lost, there are Forces in it and around it, though working in inverse order; else how could it *rot*? Despise not the rag from which man makes Paper, or the litter from which the earth makes Corn. Rightly viewed no meanest object is insignificant; all objects are as windows, through which the philosophic eye looks into Infinitude itself.'

Again, leaving that wondrous Schwarzwald Smithy-Altar,

what vacant, high-sailing air-ships are these, and whither will they sail with us?

'All visible things are emblems; what thou seest is not there on its own account; strictly taken, is not there at all: Matter exists only spiritually, and to represent some Idea, and *body* it forth. Hence Clothes, as despicable as we think them, are so unspeakably significant. Clothes, from the King's mantle downwards, are emblematic, not of want only, but of a manifold cunning Victory over Want. On the other hand, all Emblematic things are properly Clothes, thought-woven or hand-woven: must not the Imagination weave Garments, visible Bodies, wherein the else invisible creations and inspirations of our Reason are, like Spirits, revealed, and first become all-powerful;— the rather if, as we often see, the Hand too aid her, and (by wool Clothes or otherwise) reveal such even to the outward eye?

'Men are properly said to be clothed with Authority, clothed with Beauty, with Curses, and the like. Nay, if you consider it, what is Man himself, and his whole terrestrial Life, but an Emblem; a Clothing or visible Garment for that divine ME of his, cast hither, like a light-particle, down from Heaven? Thus is he said also to be clothed with a Body.

'Language is called the Garment of Thought: however, it should rather be, Language is the Flesh-Garment, the Body, of Thought. I said that Imagination wove this Flesh-Garment; and does not she? Metaphors are her stuff: examine Language; what, if you except some few primitive elements (of natural sound), what is it all but Metaphors, recognised as such, or no longer recognised; still fluid and florid, or now solid-grown and colourless? If those same primitive elements are the osseous fixtures in the Flesh-Garment, Language,—then are Metaphors its muscles and tissues and living integuments. An unmetaphorical style you shall in vain seek for: is not your very *Attention* a *Stretching-to*? The difference lies here: some styles are lean, adust, wiry, the muscle itself seems osseous; some are even quite pallid, hunger-bitten and dead-looking; while others again glow in the flush of health and vigorous self-growth, sometimes (as in my own case) not without an apoplectic tendency. Moreover, there are sham Metaphors, which overhanging that same

Thought's-Body (best naked), and deceptively bedizening, or bolstering it out, may be called its false stuffings, superfluous show-cloaks (*Putz-Mäntel*), and tawdry woollen rags: whereof he that runs and reads may gather whole hampers,—and burn them.'

Than which paragraph on Metaphors did the reader ever chance to see a more surprisingly metaphorical? However, that is not our chief grievance; the Professor continues:

'Why multiply instances? It is written, the Heavens and the Earth shall fade away like a Vesture; which indeed they are: the Time-vesture of the Eternal. Whatsoever sensibly exists, whatsoever represents Spirit to Spirit, is properly a Clothing, a suit of Raiment, put on for a season, and to be laid off. Thus in this one pregnant subject of CLOTHES, rightly understood, is included all that men have thought, dreamed, done, and been: the whole External Universe and what it holds is but Clothing; and the essence of all Science lies in the PHILOSOPHY OF CLOTHES.'

Towards these dim infinitely-expanded regions, close-bordering on the impalpable Inane, it is not without apprehension, and perpetual difficulties, that the Editor sees himself journeying and struggling. Till lately a cheerful daystar of hope hung before him, in the expected Aid of Hofrath Heuschrecke; which daystar, however, melts now, not into the red of morning, but into a vague, gray half-light, uncertain whether dawn of day or dusk of utter darkness. For the last week, these so-called Biographical Documents are in his hand. By the kindness of a Scottish Hamburg Merchant, whose name, known to the whole mercantile world, he must not mention; but whose honourable courtesy, now and often before spontaneously manifested to him, a mere literary stranger, he cannot soon forget,—the bulky Weissnichtwo Packet, with all its Customhouse seals, foreign hieroglyphs, and miscellaneous tokens of Travel, arrived here in perfect safety, and free of cost. The reader shall now fancy with what hot haste it was broken up, with what breathless expectation glanced over; and, alas, with what unquiet disappointment it has, since then, been often thrown down, and again taken up.

Hofrath Heuschrecke, in a too long-winded Letter, full of

compliments, Weissnichtwo politics, dinners, dining repartees, and other ephemeral trivialities, proceeds to remind us of what we knew well already: that however it may be with Metaphysics, and other abstract Science originating in the Head (*Verstand*) alone, no Life-Philosophy (*Lebensphilosophie*), such as this of Clothes pretends to be, which originates equally in the Character (*Gemüth*), and equally speaks thereto, can attain its significance till the Character itself is known and seen; 'till the Author's View of the World (*Weltansicht*), and how he actively and passively came by such view, are clear: in short till a Biography of him has been philosophico-poetically written, and philosophico-poetically read.' 'Nay,' adds he, 'were the speculative scientific Truth even known, you still, in this inquiring age, ask yourself, Whence came it, and Why, and How?—and rest not, till, if no better may be, Fancy have shaped-out an answer; and either in the authentic lineaments of Fact, or the forged ones of Fiction, a complete picture and Genetical History of the Man and his spiritual Endeavour lies before you. But why,' says the Hofrath, and indeed say we, 'do I dilate on the uses of our Teufelsdröckh's Biography? The great Herr Minister von Goethe has penetratingly remarked that "Man is properly the *only* object that interests man": thus I too have noted, that in Weissnichtwo our whole conversation is little or nothing else but Biography or Auto-Biography; ever humano-anecdotical (*menschlich-anek-dotisch*). Biography is by nature the most universally profitable, universally pleasant of all things: especially Biography of distinguished individuals.

'By this time, *mein Verehrtester* (my Most Esteemed),' continues he, with an eloquence which, unless the words be purloined from Teufelsdröckh, or some trick of his, as we suspect, is well-nigh unaccountable, 'by this time you are fairly plunged (*vertieft*) in that mighty forest of Clothes-Philosophy; and looking round, as all readers do, with astonishment enough. Such portions and passages as you have already mastered, and brought to paper, could not but awaken a strange curiosity touching the mind they issued from; the perhaps unparalleled psychical mechanism, which manufactured such matter, and emitted it to the light of day. Had Teufelsdröckh also a father and mother; did he, at one time, wear drivel-bibs, and live on spoon-meat? Did he ever, in rapture and tears, clasp a friend's bosom to his; looks he also wistfully into the long burial-aisle of the Past, where only winds, and their low harsh moan, give inarticulate answer? Has he fought duels; —good Heaven! how did he comport himself when in Love? By what singular stair-steps, in short, and subterranean passages, and sloughs of Despair, and steep Pisgah[2] hills, has he reached this wonderful prophetic Hebron[3] (a true Old-Clothes Jewry)[4] where he now dwells?

'To all these natural questions the voice of public History is as yet silent. Certain only that he has been, and is, a Pilgrim, and a Traveller from a far Country; more or less footsore and travel-soiled; has parted with road-companions; fallen among thieves, been poisoned by bad cookery, blistered with bugbites; nevertheless, at every stage (for they have let him pass), has had the Bill to discharge. But the whole particulars of his Route, his Weather-observations, the picturesque Sketches he took, though all regularly jotted down (in indelible sympathetic-ink by an invisible interior Penman), are these nowhere forthcoming? Perhaps quite lost: one other leaf of that mighty Volume (of human Memory) left to fly abroad, unprinted, unpublished, unbound up, as waste paper; and to rot, the sport of rainy winds?

'No, *verehrtester Herr Herausgeber,*[5] in no wise! I here, by the unexampled favour you stand in with our Sage, send not a Biography only, but an Autobiography: at least the materials for such; wherefrom, if I misreckon not, your perspicacity will draw fullest insight: and so the whole Philosophy and Philosopher of Clothes will stand clear to the wondering eyes of England, nay thence, through America, through Hindostan, and the antipodal New Holland, finally conquer (*einnehmen*) great part of this terrestrial Planet!'

And now let the sympathising reader judge of our feeling

[2] The mountain from which Moses viewed the Promised Land.
[3] Hebron was the residence of King David.
[4] A play on Old Jewry, a former ghetto that had become a place of residence of lawyers.
[5] "Most respected Editor."

when, in place of this same Autobiography with 'fullest insight,' we find—Six considerable PAPER-BAGS, carefully sealed, and marked successively, in gilt China-ink, with the symbols of the Six southern Zodiacal Signs, beginning at Libra; in the inside of which sealed Bags lie miscellaneous masses of Sheets, and oftener Shreds and Snips, written in Professor Teufelsdröckh's scarce legible *cursiv-schrift*;[6] and treating of all imaginable things under the Zodiac and above it, but of his own personal history only at rare intervals, and then in the most enigmatic manner.

Whole fascicles there are, wherein the Professor, or, as he here, speaking in the third person, calls himself, 'the Wanderer,' is not once named. Then again, amidst what seems to be a Metaphysico-theological Disquisition, 'Detached Thoughts on the Steam-engine,' or, 'The continued Possibility of Prophecy,' we shall meet with some quite private, not unimportant Bio-graphical fact. On certain sheets stand Dreams, authentic or not, while the circumjacent waking Actions are omitted. Anecdotes, oftenest without date of place or time, fly loosely on separate slips, like Sibylline leaves.[7] Interspersed also are long purely Autobiographical delineations; yet without con-nexion, without recognisable coherence; so unimportant, so superfluously minute, they almost remind us of 'P.P. Clerk of this Parish.'[8] Thus does famine of intelligence alternate with waste. Selection, order, appears to be unknown to the Profes-sor. In all Bags the same imbroglio; only perhaps in the Bag *Capricorn*, and those near it, the confusion a little worse con-founded. Close by a rather eloquent Oration, 'On receiving the Doctor's-Hat,' lie wash-bills, marked *bezahlt* (settled). His Travels are indicated by the Street-Advertisements of the various cities he has visited; of which Street-Advertisements, in most living tongues, here is perhaps the completest collection extant.

So that if the Clothes-Volume itself was too like a Chaos, we

---

[6] Handwriting in which the letters are joined.

[7] The Sibyl, a legendary prophetess, would leave her prophecies out-side her cave on leaves, which would be scattered by the wind and thus become incomprehensible.

[8] *Memoirs of P. P., Clerk of this Parish*, a book attributed to John Arbuthnot (1667–1735).

have now instead of the solar Luminary that should still it, the airy Limbo which by intermixture will farther volatilise and discompose it! As we shall perhaps see it our duty ultimately to deposit these Six Paper-Bags in the British Museum, farther description, and all vituperation of them, may be spared. Biography or Autobiography of Teufelsdröckh there is, clearly enough, none to be gleaned here: at most some sketchy, shadowy fugitive likeness of him may, by unheard-of efforts, partly of intellect, partly of imagination, on the side of Editor and of Reader, rise up between them. Only as a gaseous-chaotic Appendix to that aqueous-chaotic Volume can the contents of the Six Bags hover round us, and portions thereof be incorporated with our delineation of it.

Daily and nightly does the Editor sit (with green spectacles) deciphering these unimaginable Documents from their perplexed *cursiv-schrift*; collating them with the almost equally unimaginable Volume, which stands in legible print. Over such a universal medley of high and low, of hot, cold, moist and dry, is he here struggling (by union of like with like, which is Method) to build a firm Bridge for British travellers. Never perhaps since our first Bridge-builders, Sin and Death, built that stupendous Arch from Hell-gate to the Earth, did any Pontifex, or Pontiff,[9] undertake such a task as the present Editor. For in this Arch too, leading, as we humbly presume, far otherwards than that grand primeval one, the materials are to be fished-up from the weltering deep, and down from the simmering air, here one mass, there another, and cunningly cemented, while the elements boil beneath: nor is there any supernatural force to do it with; but simply the Diligence and feeble thinking Faculty of an English Editor, endeavouring to evolve printed Creation out of a German printed and written Chaos, wherein, as he shoots to and fro in it, gathering, clutching, piecing the Why to the far-distant Wherefore, his whole Faculty and Self are like to be swallowed up.

Patiently, under these incessant toils and agitations, does the Editor, dismissing all anger, see his otherwise robust health

---

[9] Pontifex: title of ancient Roman official in charge of maintaining bridges. The title was assumed by the Pope, or Pontiff.

declining; some fraction of his allotted natural sleep nightly leaving him, and little but an inflamed nervous-system to be looked for. What is the use of health, or of life, if not to do some work therewith? And what work nobler than transplanting foreign Thought into the barren domestic soil; except indeed planting Thought of your own, which the fewest are privileged to do? Wild as it looks, this Philosophy of Clothes, can we ever reach its real meaning, promises to reveal new-coming Eras, the first dim rudiments and already-budding germs of a nobler Era, in Universal History. Is not such a prize worth some striving? Forward with us, courageous reader; be it towards failure, or towards success! The latter thou sharest with us; the former also is not all our own.

Book Second

Chapter I
Genesis

Old Andreas Futteral and Gretchen his wife: their quiet
home. Advent of a mysterious stranger, who deposits with
them a young infant, the future Herr Diogenes Teufelsdröckh.
After-yearnings of the youth for his unknown Father. Sovereign power of Names and Naming. Diogenes a flourishing
Infant.

In a psychological point of view, it is perhaps questionable
whether from birth and genealogy, how closely scrutinised soever, much insight is to be gained. Nevertheless, as in every
phenomenon the Beginning remains always the most notable
moment; so, with regard to any great man, we rest not till, for
our scientific profit or not, the whole circumstances of his first
appearance in this Planet, and what manner of Public Entry he
made, are with utmost completeness rendered manifest. To the
Genesis of our Clothes-Philosopher, then, be this First Chapter
consecrated. Unhappily, indeed, he seems to be of quite obscure
extraction; uncertain, we might almost say, whether of any: so
that this Genesis of his can properly be nothing but an Exodus
(or transit out of Invisibility into Visibility); where of the
preliminary portion is nowhere forthcoming.

'In the village of Entepfuhl,'[1] thus writes he, in the Bag *Libra*, on various Papers, which we arrange with difficulty, 'dwelt Andreas Futteral and his wife; childless, in still seclusion and cheerful though now verging towards old age. Andreas had been grenadier Sergeant, and even regimental Schoolmaster under Frederick the Great; but now, quitting the halbert and ferule for the spade and pruning-hook, cultivated a little Orchard, on the produce of which he, Cincinnatus-like,[2] lived not without dignity. Fruits, the peach, the apple, the grape, with other varieties came in their season; all which Andreas knew how to sell: on evenings he smoked largely, or read (as beseemed a regmental Schoolmaster), and talked to neighbours that would listen about the Victory of Rossbach, and how Fritz the Only (*der Einzige*) had once with his own royal lips spoken to him, had been pleased to say, when Andreas as camp-sentinel demanded the pass-word, "*Schweig Hund* (Peace, hound)!" before any of his staff-adjutants could answer. "*Das nenn' ich mir einen König*, There is what I call a King," would Andreas exclaim: "but the smoke of Kunersderf was still smarting his eyes."

'Gretchen, the housewife, won like Desdemona by the deeds rather than the looks of her now veteran Othello, lived not in altogether military subordination; for, as Andreas said, "the womankind will not drill (*wer kann die Weiberchen dressiren*): nevertheless she at heart loved him both for valour and wisdom; to her a Prussian grenadier Sergeant and Regiment's Schoolmaster was little other than a Cicero and Cid: what you see, yet cannot see over, is as good as infinite. Nay, was not Andreas in very deed a man of order, courage, downrightness (*Geradheit*); that understood Büsching's *Geography*, had been in the victory of Rossbach, and left for dead in the camisade of Hochkirch? The good Gretchen, for all her fretting, watched over him and hovered round him as only a true housemother can: assiduously she cooked and sewed and scoured for him; so

---

[1] These chapters are based upon Carlyle's own childhood in the little Scottish village of Ecclefechan.
[2] Legendary Roman hero who was called from his farming to become Dictator. After leading his country in war, he returned to his farm.

that not only his old regimental sword and grenadier-cap, but the whole habitation and environment, where on pegs of honour they hung, looked ever trim and gay: a roomy painted Cottage, embowered in fruit-trees and forest-trees, evergreens and honey-suckles; rising many-coloured from amid shaven grass-plots, flowers struggling-in through the very windows; under its long projecting eaves nothing but garden-tools in methodic piles (to screen them from rain), and seats where, especially on summer nights, a King might have wished to sit and smoke, and call it his. Such a *Bauergut* (Copyhold) had Gretchen given her veteran; whose sinewy arms, and long-disused gardening talent, had made it what you saw.

'Into this umbrageous Man's-nest, one meek yellow evening or dusk, when the Sun, hidden indeed from terrestrial Entepfuhl, did nevertheless journey visible and radiant along the celestial Balance (*Libra*), it was that a Stranger of reverend aspect entered; and, with grave salutation, stood before the two rather astonished housemates. He was close-muffled in a wide mantle; which without farther parley unfolding, he deposited therefrom what seemed some Basket, overhung with green Persian silk; saying only: *Ihr lieben Leute, hier bringe ein unschätzbares Verleihen; nehmet es in aller Acht, sorgfältigst benützt es: mit hohem Lohn, oder wohl mit schweren Zinsen, wird's einst zurückgefordert.* "Good Christian people, here lies for you an invaluable Loan; take all heed thereof, in all carefulness employ it: with high recompense, or else with heavy penalty, will it one day be required back." Uttering which singular words, in a clear, bell-like, forever memorable tone, the Stranger gracefully withdrew; and before Andreas or his wife, gazing in expectant wonder, had time to fashion either question or answer, was clean gone. Neither out of doors could aught of him be seen or heard; he had vanished in the thickets, in the dusk; the Orchard-gate stood quietly closed: the Stranger was gone once and always. So sudden had the whole transaction been, in the autumn stillness and twilight, so gentle, noiseless, that the Futterals could have fancied it all a trick of Imagination, or some visit from an authentic Spirit. Only that the green-silk Basket, such as neither Imagination nor authentic Spirits are wont to carry, still stood visible and tangible on their little parlour-table. Towards this the astonished couple, now with lit candle, hastily turned their attention. Lifting the green veil, to see what invaluable it hid, they descried there, amid down and rich white wrappages, no Pitt Diamond or Hapsburg Regalia, but, in the softest sleep, a little red-coloured Infant! Beside it, lay a roll of gold Friedrichs, the exact amount of which was never publicly known; also a *Taufschein* (baptismal certificate), wherein unfortunately nothing but the Name was decipherable; other document or indication none whatever.

'To wonder and conjecture was unavailing, then and always thenceforth. Nowhere in Entepfuhl, on the morrow or next day, did tidings transpire of any such figure as the Stranger; nor could the Traveller, who had passed through the neighbouring Town in coach-and-four, be connected with this Apparition, except in the way of gratuitous surmise. Meanwhile, for Andreas and his wife, the grand practical problem was: What to do with this little sleeping red-coloured Infant? Amid amazements and curiosities, which had to die away without external satisfying, they resolved, as in such circumstances charitable prudent people needs must, on nursing it, though with spoon-meat, into whiteness, and if possible into manhood. The Heavens smiled on their endeavour: thus has that same mysterious Individual ever since had a status for himself in this visible Universe, some modicum of victual and lodging and parade-ground; and now expanded in bulk, faculty and knowledge of good and evil, he, as HERR DIOGENES TEUFELSDRÖCKH, professes or is ready to profess, perhaps not altogether without effect, in the New University of Weissnichtwo, the new Science of Things in General.'

Our Philosopher declares here, as indeed we should think he well might, that these facts, first communicated, by the good Gretchen Futteral, in his twelfth year, 'produced on the boyish heart and fancy a quite indelible impression. Who this reverend Personage,' he says, 'that glided into the Orchard Cottage when the Sun was in Libra, and then, as on spirit's wings, glided out again, might be? An inexpressible desire, full of love and of sadness, has often since struggled within me to shape an answer. Ever, in my distresses and my loneliness, has Fantasy turned, full of longing (*sehnsuchtsvoll*), to that unknown Father, who perhaps far from me, perhaps near, either way invisible, might have taken me to his paternal bosom, there to lie screened from many a woe. Thou beloved Father, dost thou still, shut out from me only by thin penetrable curtains of earthly Space, wend to and fro among the crowd of the living? Or art thou hidden by those far thicker curtains of the Everlasting Night, or rather of the Everlasting Day, through which my mortal eye and out-stretched arms need not strive to reach? Alas, I know not, and in vain vex myself to know. More than once, heart-deluded, have I taken for thee this and the other noble-looking Stranger; and approached him wistfully, with infinite regard; but he too had to repel me, he too was not thou.

'And yet, O Man born of Woman,' cries the Autobiographer, with one of his sudden whirls, 'wherein is my case peculiar? Hadst thou, any more than I, a Father whom thou knowest? The Andreas and Gretchen, or the Adam and Eve, who led thee into Life, and for a time suckled and pap-fed thee there, whom thou namest Father and Mother; these were, like mine, but thy nursing-father and nursing-mother: thy true Beginning and Father is in Heaven, whom with the bodily eye thou shalt never behold, but only with the spiritual.'

'The little green veil,' adds he, among much similar moralis-ing, and embroiled discoursing, 'I yet keep; still more insepa-rably the Name, Diogenes Teufelsdröckh. From the veil can nothing be inferred: a piece of now quite faded Persian silk, like thousands of others. On the Name I have many times medi-tated and conjectured; but neither in this lay there any clue. That it was my unknown Father's name I must hesitate to believe. To no purpose have I searched through all the Herald's Books, in and without the German Empire, and through all manner of Subscriber-Lists (*Pränumeranten*), Militia-Rolls, and other Name-catalogues; extraordinary names as we have in Germany, the name Teufelsdröckh, except as appended to my own person, nowhere occurs. Again, what may the unchristian rather than Christian "Diogenes" mean? Did that reverend Basket-bearer intend, by such designation, to shadow-forth my future destiny, or his own present malign humour? Perhaps the latter, perhaps both. Thou ill-starred Parent, who like an Ostrich hadst to leave thy ill-starred off-spring to be hatched into self-support by the mere sky-influences of Chance, can thy pilgrimage have been a smooth one? Beset by Misfortune thou doubtless hast been; or indeed by the worst figure of Misfortune, by Misconduct. Often have I fancied how, in thy hard life-battle, thou wert shot at, and slung at, wounded, hand-fettered, hamstrung, browbeaten and bedevilled by the Time-Spirit (*Zeitgeist*) in thyself and others, till the good soul first given thee was seared into grim rage; and thou hadst nothing for it but to leave in me an indignant appeal to the Future, and living speaking Protest against the Devil, as that same Spirit not of the Time only, but of Time itself, is well named! Which Appeal and Protest, may I now modestly add, was not perhaps quite lost in air.

'For indeed, as Walter Shandy[3] often insisted, there is much, nay almost all, in Names. The Name is the earliest Garment you wrap round the earth-visiting ME; to which it thenceforth cleaves, more tenaciously (for there are Names that have lasted nigh thirty centuries) than the very skin. And now from without, what mystic influences does it not send inwards, even to the centre; especially in those plastic first-times, when the whole soul is yet infantine, soft, and the invisible seedgrain will grow to be an all overshadowing tree! Names? Could I unfold the influence of Names, which are the most important of all Clothings, I were a second greater Trismegistus.[4] Not only all common Speech, but Science, Poetry itself is no other, if thou consider it, than a right *Naming*. Adam's first task was giving names to natural Appearances: what is ours still but a continuation of the same; be the Appearances exotic-vegetable, organic, mechanic, stars, or starry movements (as in Science); or (as in Poetry) passions, virtues, calamities, God-attributes, Gods?—In a very plain sense the Proverb says, *Call one a thief, and he*

---

[3] Pedantic father of hero in Laurence Sterne's *Tristram Shandy*.
[4] Hermes Trismegistus: supposed author of sacred writings of ancient Egyptians. Trismegistus is praised by Walter Shandy in *Tristram Shandy*, IV, xi.

will steal; in an almost similar sense may we not perhaps say, *Call one Diogenes Teufelsdröckh, and he will open the Philosophy of Clothes?*'

'Meanwhile the incipient Diogenes, like others, all ignorant of his Why, his How or Whereabout, was opening his eyes to the kind Light; sprawling-out his ten fingers and toes; listening, tasting, feeling; in a word, by all his Five Senses, still more by his Sixth Sense of Hunger, and a whole infinitude of inward, spiritual, half-awakened Senses, endeavouring daily to acquire for himself some knowledge of this strange Universe where he had arrived, be his task therein what it might. Infinite was his progress; thus in some fifteen months, he could perform the miracle of—Speech! To breed a fresh Soul, is it not like brooding a fresh (celestial) Egg; wherein as yet all is formless, powerless; yet by degrees organic elements and fibres shoot through the watery albumen; and out of vague Sensation grows Thought, grows Fantasy and Force, and we have Philosophies, Dynasties, nay Poetries and Religions!

'Young Diogenes, or rather young Gneschen, for by such diminutive had they in their fondness named him, travelled forward to those high consummations, by quick yet easy stages. The Futterals, to avoid vain talk, and moreover keep the roll of gold Friedrichs safe, gave-out that he was a grandnephew; the orphan of some sister's daughter, suddenly deceased, in Andreas's distant Prussian birthland; of whom, as of her indigent sorrowing widower, little enough was known at Entepfuhl. Heedless of all which, the Nurseling took to his spoon-meat, and throve. I have heard him noted as a still infant, that kept his mind much to himself; above all, that seldom or never cried. He already felt that time was precious; that he had other work cut-out for him than whimpering.'

Such, after utmost painful search and collation among these miscellaneous Paper-masses, is all the notice we can gather of Herr Teufelsdröckh's genealogy. More imperfect, more enigmatic it can seem to few readers than to us. The Professor, in whom truly we more and more discern a certain satirical turn, and deep under-currents of roguish whim, for the present stands pledged in honour, so we will not doubt him: but seems it not conceivable that, by the 'good Gretchen Futteral,' or some other perhaps interested party, he has himself been deceived? Should these sheets, translated or not, ever reach the Entepfuhl Circulating Library, some cultivated native of that district might feel called to afford explanation. Nay, since Books, like invisible scouts, permeate the whole habitable globe, and Timbuctoo itself is not safe from British Literature, may not some Copy find out even the mysterious basket-bearing Stranger, who in a state of extreme senility perhaps still exists; and gently force even him to disclose himself; to claim openly a son, in whom any father may feel pride?

Chapter II
Idyllic

Happy Childhood! Entepfuhl: Sights, hearings and experiences of the boy Teufelsdröckh; their manifold teaching. Education; what it can do, what cannot. Obedience our universal duty and destiny. Gneschen sees the good Gretchen pray.

'Happy season of Childhood!' exclaims Teufelsdröckh: 'Kind Nature, that art to all a bountiful mother; that visitest the poor man's hut with auroral radiance; and for thy Nurseling hast provided a soft swathing of Love and infinite Hope, wherein he waxes and slumbers, danced-round (*umgaukelt*) by sweetest Dreams! If the paternal Cottage still shuts us in, its roof still screens us; with a Father we have as yet a prophet, priest and king, and an Obedience that makes us free. The young spirit has awakened out of Eternity, and knows not what we mean by Time; as yet Time is no fast-hurrying stream, but a sportful sunlit ocean; years to the child are as ages: ah! the secret of Vicissitude, of that slower or quicker decay and ceaseless down-rushing of the universal World-fabric, from the granite mountain to the man or day-moth, is yet unknown; and in a motionless Universe, we taste, what afterwards in this quick-whirling Universe, is forever denied us, the balm of Rest. Sleep on, thou fair Child, for thy long rough journey is at hand! A little while, and thou too shalt sleep no more, but thy very dreams shall be mimic battles; thou too, with old Arnauld, wilt have to say in stern patience: "Rest? Rest? Shall I not have all Eternity to rest in?" Celestial Nepenthe! though a Pyrrhus conquer empires, and an Alexander sack the world, he finds thee not; and thou hast once fallen gently, of thy own accord, on the eyelids, on the heart of every mother's child. For as yet, sleep and waking are one: the fair Life-garden rustles infinite around, and everywhere is dewy fragrance, and the budding of Hope; which budding, if in youth, too frostnipt, it grow to flowers, will in manhood yield no fruit, but a prickly, bitter-rinded stone-fruit, of which the fewest can find the kernel.'

In such rose-coloured light does our Professor, as Poets are wont, look back on his childhood; the historical details of which (to say nothing of much other vague oratorical matter) he accordingly dwells on with an almost wearisome minuteness. We hear of Entepfuhl standing 'in trustful derangement' among the woody slopes; the paternal Orchard flanking it as extreme outpost from below; the little Kuhbach gushing kindly by, among beech-rows, through river after river, into the Donau, into the Black Sea, into the Atmosphere and Universe; and how 'the brave old Linden,' stretching like a parasol of twenty ells in radius, overtopping all other rows and clumps, towered-up from the central *Agora* and *Campus Martius*[1] of the Village, like its Sacred Tree; and how the old men sat talking under its shadow (Gneschen often greedily listening), and the wearied labourers reclined, and the unwearied children sported, and the young men and maidens often danced to flute-music. 'Glorious summer twilights,' cries Teufelsdröckh, 'when the Sun, like a proud Conqueror and Imperial Taskmaster, turned his back,

---

[1] Agora: Marketplace in Greek cities. Camps Martius: Field of Mars, public gathering place outside Rome.

with his gold-purple emblazonry, and all his fireclad body-guard (of Prismatic Colours); and the tired brickmakers of this clay Earth might steal a little frolic, and those few meek Stars would not tell of them!'

Then we have long details of the *Weinlesen* (Vintage), the Harvest-Home, Christmas, and so forth; with a whole cycle of the Entepfuhl Children's-games, differing apparently by mere superficial shades from those of other countries. Concerning all which, we shall here, for obvious reasons, say nothing. What cares the world for our as yet miniature Philosopher's achievements under that 'brave old Linden'? Or even where is the use of such practical reflections as the following? 'In all the sports of Children, were it only in their wanton breakages and defacements, you shall discern a creative instinct (*schaffenden Trieb*): the Mankin feels that he is a born Man, that his vocation is to work. The choicest present you can make him is a Tool; be it knife or pen-gun, for construction or for destruction; either way it is for Work, for Change. In gregarious sports of skill or strength, the Boy trains himself to Coöperation, for war or peace, as governor or governed: the little Maid again, provident of her domestic destiny, takes with preference to Dolls.'

Perhaps, however, we may give this anecdote, considering who it is that relates it: 'My first short-clothes were of yellow serge; or rather, I should say, my first short-cloth, for the vesture was one and indivisible, reaching from neck to ankle, a mere body with four limbs: of which fashion how little could I then divine the architectural, how much less the moral significance!'

More graceful is the following little picture: 'On fine evenings I was wont to carry-forth my supper (bread-crumb boiled in milk), and eat it out-of-doors. On the coping of the Orchard-wall, which I could reach by climbing, or still more easily if Father Andreas would set-up the pruning-ladder, my porringer was placed: there, many a sunset, have I, looking at the distant western Mountains, consumed, not without relish, my evening meal. Those hues of gold and azure, that hush of World's expectation as Day died, were still a Hebrew Speech for me; nevertheless I was looking at the fair illuminated Letters, and had an eye for their gilding.'

With 'the little one's friendship for cattle and poultry' we

107

shall not much intermeddle. It may be that hereby he acquired a 'certain deeper sympathy with animated Nature': but when, we would ask, saw any man, in a collection of Biographical Documents, such a piece as this: 'Impressive enough (*bedeutungsvoll*) was it to hear, in early morning, the Swine-herd's horn; and know that so many hungry happy quadrupeds were, on all sides, starting in hot haste to join him, for breakfast on the Heath. Or to see them at eventide, all marching-in again, with short squeak, almost in military order; and each, topo-graphically correct, trotting-off in succession to the right or left, through its own lane, to its own dwelling; till old Kunz, at the Village-head, now left alone, blew his last blast, and retired for the night. We are wont to love the Hog chiefly in the form of Ham; yet did not these bristly thick-skinned beings here mani-fest intelligence, perhaps humour of character; at any rate, a touching trustful submissiveness to Man,—who, were he but a Swineherd, in darned gabardine, and leather breeches more resembling slate or discoloured-tin breeches, is still the Hierarch of this lower world?'

It is maintained, by Helvetius[2] and his set, that an infant of genius is quite the same as any other infant, only that certain surprisingly favourable influences accompany him through life, especially through childhood, and expand him, while others lie closefolded and continue dunces. Herein, say they, consists the whole difference between an inspired Prophet and a double-barrelled Game-preserver:[3] the inner man of the one has been fostered into generous development; that of the other, crushed-down perhaps by vigour of animal digestion, and the like, has exuded and evaporated, or at best sleeps now irresuscitably stagnant at the bottom of his stomach. 'With which opinion,' cries Teufelsdröckh, 'I should as soon agree as with this other, that an acorn might, by favourable or unfavourable influences of soil and climate, be nursed into a cabbage, or the cabbage-seed into an oak.

---

[2] Claude Adrien Helvétius (1715–1771): French materialist philoso-pher.
[3] Carlyle's term for the English aristocracy. See *Past and Present*, "Democracy," n. 11.

'Nevertheless,' continues he, 'I too acknowledge the all-but omnipotence of early culture and nurture: hereby we have either a doddered dwarf bush, or a high-towering, wide-shadowing tree; either a sick yellow cabbage, or an edible luxuriant green one. Of a truth, it is the duty of all men, especially of all philosophers, to note-down with accuracy the characteristic circumstances of their Education, what furthered, what hindered, what in any way modified it: to which duty, nowadays so pressing for many a German Autobiographer, I also zealously address myself.'—Thou rogue! Is it by short-clothes of yellow serge, and swineherd horns, that an infant of genius is educated? And yet, as usual, it ever remains doubtful whether he is laughing in his sleeve at these Autobiographical times of ours, or writing from the abundance of his own fond ineptitude. For he continues: 'If among the ever-streaming currents of Sights, Hearings, Feelings for Pain or Pleasure, whereby, as in a Magic Hall, young Gneschen went about environed, I might venture to select and specify, perhaps these following were also of the number:

'Doubtless, as childish sports call forth Intellect, Activity, so the young creature's Imagination was stirred up, and a Historical tendency given him by the narrative habits of Father Andreas; who, with his battle-reminiscences, and gray austere yet hearty patriarchal aspect, could not but appear another Ulysses and "much-enduring Man." Eagerly I hung upon his tales, when listening neighbours enlivened the hearth; from these perils and these travels, wild and far almost as Hades itself, a dim world of Adventure expanded itself within me. Incalculable also was the knowledge I acquired in standing by the Old Men under the Linden-tree: the whole of Immensity was yet new to me; and had not these reverend seniors, talkative enough, been employed in partial surveys thereof for nigh fourscore years? With amazement I began to discover that Entepfuhl stood in the middle of a Country, of a World; that there was such a thing as History, as Biography; to which I also, one day, by hand and tongue, might contribute.

'In a like sense worked the *Postwagen* (Stage-coach), which, slow-rolling under its mountains of men and luggage, wended through our Village: northwards, truly, in the dead of night; yet southwards visibly at eventide. Not till my eighth year did I reflect that this Postwagen could be other than some terrestrial Moon, rising and setting by mere Law of Nature, like the heavenly one; that it came on made highways, from far cities towards far cities; weaving them like a monstrous shuttle into closer and closer union. It was then that, independently of Schiller's *Wilhelm Tell*, I made this not quite insignificant reflection (so true also in spiritual things): *Any road, this simple Entepfuhl road, will lead you to the end of the World!*

'Why mention our Swallows, which, out of far Africa, as I learned, threading their way over seas and mountains, corporate cities and belligerent nations, yearly found themselves, with the month of May, snug-lodged in our Cottage Lobby? The hospitable Father (for cleanliness' sake) had fixed a little bracket plumb under their nest: there they built, and caught flies, and twittered, and bred; and all, I chiefly, from the heart loved them. Bright, nimble creatures, who taught *you* the mason-craft; nay, stranger still, gave you a masonic incorporation, almost social police? For if, by ill chance, and when time pressed, your House fell, have I not seen five neighbourly Helpers appear next day; and swashing to and fro, with animated, loud, long-drawn chirpings, and activity almost super-hirundine, complete it again before nightfall?

'But undoubtedly the grand summary of Entepfuhl child's-culture, where as in a funnel its manifold influences were concentrated and simultaneously poured-down on us, was the annual Cattle-fair. Here, assembling from all the four winds, came the elements of an unspeakable hurlyburly. Nutbrown maids and nutbrown men, all clear-washed, loud-laughing, bedizened and beribanded; who came for dancing, for treating, and if possible, for happiness. Topbooted Graziers from the North; Swiss Brokers, Italian Drovers, also topbooted, from the South; these with their subalterns in leather jerkins, leather skull-caps, and long oxgoads; shouting in half-articulate speech, amid the inarticulate barking and bellowing. Apart stood Potters from far Saxony, with their crockery in fair rows; Nürnberg Pedlars, in booths that to me seemed richer than Ormuz bazaars; Showmen from the Lago Maggiore; detachments of the *Wiener Schub* (Offscourings of Vienna) vociferously superintending games of chance. Ballad-singers brayed, Auctioneers grew hoarse; cheap New Wine (*heuriger*) flowed like water, still worse confounding the confusion; and high over all, vaulted, in ground-and-lofty tumbling, a particoloured Merry-Andrew, like the genius of the place and of Life itself.

'Thus encircled by the mystery of Existence; under the deep heavenly Firmament; waited-on by the four golden Seasons, with their vicissitudes of contribution, for even grim Winter brought its skating-matches and shooting-matches, its snow-storms and Christmas-carols,—did the Child sit and learn. These things were the Alphabet, whereby in aftertime he was to syllable and partly read the grand Volume of the World: what matters it whether such Alphabet be in large gilt letters or in small ungilt ones, so you have an eye to read it? For Gneschen, eager to learn, the very act of looking thereon was a blessedness that gilded all: his existence was a bright, soft element of Joy; out of which, as in Prospero's Island,[4] wonder after wonder bodied itself forth, to teach by charming.

'Nevertheless, I were but a vain dreamer to say, that even then my felicity was perfect. I had, once for all, come down from Heaven into the Earth. Among the rainbow colours that glowed on my horizon, lay even in childhood a dark ring of Care, as yet no thicker than a thread, and often quite overshone; yet always it reappeared, nay ever waxing broader and broader; till in after-years it almost over-shadowed my whole canopy, and threatened to engulf me in final night. It was the ring of Necessity whereby we are all begirt; happy he for whom a kind heavenly Sun brightens it into a ring of Duty, and plays round it with beautiful prismatic diffractions; yet ever, as basis and as bourne for our whole being, it is there.

'For the first few years of our terrestrial Apprenticeship, we have not much work to do; but, boarded and lodged gratis, are set down mostly to look about us over the workshop, and see

4 Scene of Shakespeare's *The Tempest*.

others work, till we have understood the tools a little, and can handle this and that. If good Passivity alone, and not good Passivity and good Activity together, were the thing wanted, then was my early position favourable beyond the most. In all that respects openness of Sense, affectionate Temper, ingenuous Curiosity, and the fostering of these, what more could I have wished? On the other side, however, things went not so well. My Active Power (*Thatkraft*) was unfavourably hemmed-in; of which misfortune how many traces yet abide with me! In an orderly house, where the litter of children's sports is hateful enough, your training is too stoical; rather to bear and forbear than to make and do. I was forbid much: wishes in any measure bold I had to renounce; everywhere a strait bond of Obedience inflexibly held me down. Thus already Freewill often came in painful collision with Necessity; so that my tears flowed, and at seasons the Child itself might taste that root of bitterness, where-with the whole fruitage of our life is mingled and tempered.

'In which habituation to Obedience, truly, it was beyond measure safer to err by excess than by defect. Obedience is our universal duty and destiny; wherein whoso will not bend must break: too early and too thoroughly we cannot be trained to know that Would, in this world of ours, is as mere zero to Should, and for most part as the smallest of fractions even to Shall. Hereby was laid for me the basis of worldly Discretion, nay of Morality itself. Let me not quarrel with my upbringing. It was rigorous, too frugal, compressively secluded, everyway unscientific: yet in that very strictness and domestic solitude might there not lie the root of deeper earnestness, of the stem from which all noble fruit must grow? Above all, how unskil-ful soever, it was loving, it was well-meant, honest; whereby every deficiency was helped. My kind Mother, for as such I must ever love the good Gretchen, did me one altogether invaluable service: she taught me, less indeed by word than by act and daily reverent look and habitude, her own simple version of the Christian Faith. Andreas too attended Church; yet more like a parade-duty, for which he in the other world expected pay with arrears,—as, I trust, he has received; but my Mother, with a true woman's heart, and fine though uncultivated sense, was in the strictest acceptation Religious. How indestructibly the Good grows, and propagates itself, even among the weedy entanglements of Evil! The highest whom I knew on Earth I here saw bowed down, with awe unspeakable, before a Higher in Heaven: such things, especially in infancy, reach inwards to the very core of your being; mysteriously does a Holy of Holies build itself into visibility in the mysterious deeps, and Reverence, the divinest in man, springs forth undying from its mean envelopment of Fear. Wouldst thou rather be a peasant's son that knew, were it never so rudely, there was a God in Heaven and in Man; or a duke's son that only knew there were two-and-thirty quarters[5] on the family-coach?'

To which last question we must answer: Beware, O Teufelsdröckh, of spiritual pride!

Chapter III
Pedagogy

Teufelsdröckh's School. His Education. How the ever-flowing Kuhbach speaks of Time and Eternity. The Hinterschlag Gymnasium: rude Boys; and pedant Professors. The need of true Teachers, and their due recognition. Father Andreas dies; and Teufelsdröckh learns the secret of his birth: His reflections thereon. The Nameless University. Statistics of Imposture much wanted. Bitter fruits of Rationalism: Teufelsdröckh's religious difficulties. The young Englishman Herr Towgood. Modern Friendship.

Hitherto we see young Gneschen, in his indivisible case of yellow serge, borne forward mostly on the arms of kind Nature

---

[5] The division of panels in the family insignia painted on the coach would indicate a distinguished ancestry.

alone; seated, indeed, and much to his mind, in the terrestrial workshop, but (except his soft hazel eyes, which we doubt not already gleamed with a still intelligence) called upon for little voluntary movement there. Hitherto, accordingly, his aspect is rather generic, that of an incipient Philosopher and Poet in the abstract; perhaps it would puzzle Herr Heuschrecke himself to say wherein the special Doctrine of Clothes is as yet fore-shadowed or betokened. For with Gneschen, as with others, the Man may indeed stand pictured in the Boy (at least all the pigments are there); yet only some half of the Man stands in the Child, or young Boy, namely, his Passive endowment, not his Active. The more impatient are we to discover what figure he cuts in this latter capacity; how, when, to use his own words, 'he understands the tools a little, and can handle this or that,' he will proceed to handle it.

Here, however, may be the place to state that, in much of our Philosopher's history, there is something of an almost Hindoo character: nay perhaps in that so well-fostered and every-way excellent 'Passivity' of his, which, with no free development of the antagonist Activity, distinguished his childhood, we may detect the rudiments of much that, in after days, and still in these present days, astonishes the world. For the shallow-sighted, Teufelsdröckh is oftenest a man without Activity of any kind, a No-man; for the deep-sighted, again, a man with Activity almost superabundant, yet so spiritual, close-hidden, enigmatic, that no mortal can foresee its explosions, or even when it has exploded, so much as ascertain its significance. A dangerous, difficult temper for the modern European; above all, disadvantageous in the hero of a Biography! Now as hereto-fore it will behove the Editor of these pages, were it never so unsuccessfully, to do his endeavour.

Among the earliest tools of any complicacy which a man, especially a man of letters, gets to handle, are his Class-books. On this portion of his History, Teufelsdröckh looks down pro-fessedly as indifferent. Reading he 'cannot remember ever to have learned'; so perhaps had it by nature. He says generally: 'Of the insignificant portion of my Education, which depended on Schools, there need almost no notice be taken. I learned what others learn; and kept it stored-by in a corner of my head, seeing as yet no manner of use in it. My Schoolmaster, a downbent, brokenhearted, underfoot martyr, as others of that guild are, did little for me, except discover that he could do little: he, good soul, pronounced me a genius, fit for the learned professions; and that I must be sent to the Gymnasium,[1] and one day to the University. Meanwhile, what printed thing soever I could meet with I read. My very copper pocket-money I laid-out on stall-literature;[2] which, as it accumulated, I with my own hands sewed into volumes. By this means was the young head furnished with a considerable miscellany of things and shadows of things: History in authentic fragments lay mingled with Fabulous chimeras, wherein also was reality; and the whole not as dead stuff, but as living pabulum, tolerably nutritive for a mind as yet so peptic.'

That the Entepfuhl Schoolmaster judged well, we now know. Indeed, already in the youthful Gneschen, with all his outward stillness, there may have been manifest an inward vivacity that promised much; symptoms of a spirit singularly open, thoughtful almost poetical. Thus, to say nothing of his suppers on the Orchard-wall, and other phenomena of that earlier period, have many readers of these pages stumbled, in their twelfth year, on such reflections as the following? 'It struck me much, as I sat by the Kuhbach, one silent noontide, and watched it flowing, gurgling, to think how this same streamlet had flowed and gurgled, through all changes of weather and of fortune, from beyond the earliest date of History. Yes, probably on the morning when Joshua forded Jordan; even as at the mid-day when Cæsar, doubtless with difficulty, swam the Nile, yet kept his *Commentaries* dry,—this little Kuhbach, assiduous as Tiber, Eurotas or Siloa, was murmuring on across the wilderness, as yet unnamed, unseen: here, too, as in the Euphrates and the Ganges, is a vein or veinlet of the grand World-circulation of Waters, which, with its atmospheric arteries, has lasted and lasts simply with the World. Thou fool! Nature alone is antique, and the oldest art a mushroom; that idle crag thou sittest on is six-

---

[1] German secondary school preparing students for the university.

[2] Inexpensive pamphlets sold at bookseller's "stall" or outside tables.

thousand years of age.' In which little thought, as in a little fountain, may there not lie the beginning of those well-nigh unutterable meditations on the grandeur and mystery of TIME, and its relation to ETERNITY, which play such a part in this Philosophy of Clothes?

Over his Gymnasic and Academic years the Professor by no means lingers so lyrical and joyful as over his childhood. Green sunny tracts there are still; but intersected by bitter rivulets of tears, here and there stagnating, into sour marches of discontent. 'With my first view of the Hinterschlag[3] Gymnasium,' writes he, 'my evil days began. Well do I still remember the red sunny Whitsuntide morning, when, trotting full of hope by the side of Father Andreas, I entered the main street of the place, and saw its steeple-clock (then striking Eight) and *Schuldthurm* (Jail), and the aproned or disaproned Burghers moving-in to breakfast: a little dog, in mad terror, was rushing past; for some human imps had tied a tin-kettle to its tail; thus did the agonised creature, loud-jingling, career through the whole length of the Borough, and become notable enough. Fit emblem of many a Conquering Hero, to whom Fate (wedding Fantasy to Sense, as it often elsewhere does) has milignantly appended a tin-kettle of Ambition, to chase him on; which the faster he runs, urges him the faster, the more loudly and more foolishly! Fit emblem also of much that awaited myself, in that mischievous Den; as in the World, whereof it was a portion and epitome!

'Alas, the kind beech-rows of Entepfuhl were hidden in the distance: I was among strangers, harshly, at best indifferently, disposed towards me; the young heart felt, for the first time, quite orphaned and alone.' His schoolfellows, as is usual persecuted him: 'They were Boys,' he says, 'mostly rude Boys, and obeyed the impulse of rude Nature, which bids the deerherd fall upon any stricken hart, the duck-flock put to death any broken-winged brother or sister, and on all hands the strong tyrannise over the weak.' He admits that though 'perhaps in an unusual degree morally courageous,' he succeeded ill in battle, and

---

[3] "Strike-behind." This paragraph describes Carlyle's own experience on entering Annan Academy.

would fain have avoided it; a result, as would appear, owing less to his small personal stature (for in passionate seasons he was 'incredibly nimble'), than to his 'virtuous principles': 'if it was disgraceful to be beaten,' says he, 'it was only a shade less disgraceful to have so much as fought; thus was I drawn two ways at once, and in this important element of school-history, the war-element, had little but sorrow.' On the whole, that same excellent 'Passivity,' so notable in Teufelsdröckh's childhood, is here visibly enough again getting nourishment. 'He wept often; indeed to such a degree that he was nicknamed *Der Weinende* (the Tearful), which epithet, till towards his thirteenth year, was indeed not quite unmerited. Only at rare intervals did the young soul burst-forth into fire-eyed rage, and, with a stormfulness (*Ungestüm*) under which the boldest quailed, assert that he too had Rights of Man, or at least of Mankin.' In all which, who does not discern a fine flower-tree and cinnamon-tree (of genius) nigh choked among pumpkins, reed-grass and ignoble shrubs; and forced if it would live, to struggle upwards only, and not outwards; into a *height* quite sickly, and disproportioned to its *breadth*?

We find, moreover, that his Greek and Latin were 'mechanically' taught; Hebrew scarce even mechanically; much else which they called History, Cosmography, Philosophy, and so forth, not better than not at all. So that, except inasmuch as Nature was still busy; and he himself 'went about, as was of old his wont, among the Craftsmen's workshops, there learning many things'; and farther lighted on some small store of curious reading, in Hans Wachtel the Cooper's house, where he lodged, —his time, it would appear, was utterly wasted. Which facts the Professor has not yet learned to look upon with any contentment. Indeed, throughout the whole of this Bag *Scorpio*, where we now are, and often in the following Bag, he shows himself unusually animated on the matter of Education, and not without some touch of what we might presume to be anger.

'My Teachers,' says he, 'were hide-bound Pedants, without knowledge of man's nature, or of boy's; or of aught save their lexicons and quarterly account-books. Innumerable dead Vocables (no dead Language, for they themselves knew no Language) they crammed into us, and called it fostering the growth of mind. How can an inanimate, mechanical Gerund grinder,[4] the like of whom will, in a subsequent century, be manufactured at Nürnberg out of wood and leather, foster the growth of anything; much more of Mind, which grows, not like a vegetable (by having its roots littered with etymological compost), but like a spirit, by mysterious contact of Spirit; Thought kindling itself at the fire of living Thought? How shall *he* give kindling, in whose own inward man there is no live coal, but all is burnt-out to a dead grammatical cinder? The Hinterschlag Professors knew syntax enough; and of the human soul thus much: that it had a faculty called Memory, and could be acted-on through the muscular integument by appliance of birch-rods.

'Alas, so is it everywhere, so will it ever be; till the Hodman is discharged, or reduced to hodbearing; and an Architect is hired, and on all hands fitly encouraged: till communities and individuals discover, not without surprise, that fashioning the souls of a generation by Knowledge can rank on a level with blowing their bodies to pieces by Gunpowder; that with Generals and Fieldmarshals for killing, there should be world-honoured Dignitaries, and were it possible, true God-ordained Priests, for teaching. But as yet, though the Soldier wears openly, and even parades, his butchering-tool, nowhere, far as I have travelled, did the Schoolmaster make show of his instructing-tool: nay, were he to walk abroad with birch girt on thigh, as if he therefrom expected honour, would there not, among the idler class, perhaps a certain levity be excited?'

In the third year of this Gymnasic period, Father Andreas seems to have died: the young Scholar, otherwise so maltreated, saw himself for the first time clad outwardly in sables, and inwardly in quite inexpressible melancholy. 'The dark bottomless Abyss, that lies under our feet, had yawned open; the pale kingdoms of Death, with all their innumerable silent nations and generations, stood before him; the inexorable word, NEVER! now first showed its meaning. My Mother wept, and her sorrow got vent; but in my heart there lay a whole lake of tears, pent-up

---

[4] Carlyle's term for pedantic teacher of grammar.

in silent desolation. Nevertheless the unworn Spirit is strong; Life is so healthful that it even finds nourishment in Death: these stern experiences, planted down by Memory in my Imagination, rose there to a whole cypress-forest, sad but beautiful; waving, with not unmelodious sighs, in dark luxuriance, in the hottest sunshine, through long years of youth:—as in manhood also it does, and will do; for I have now pitched my tent under a Cypress-tree; the Tomb is now my inexpugnable Fortress, ever close by the gate of which I look upon the hostile armaments, and pains and penalties of tyrannous Life placidly enough, and listen to its loudest threatenings with a still smile. O ye loved ones, that already sleep in the noiseless Bed of Rest, whom in life I could only weep for and never help; and ye, who wide-scattered still toil lonely in the monster-bearing Desert, dyeing the flinty ground with your blood,—yet a little while, and we shall all meet THERE, and our Mother's bosom will screen us all; and Oppression's harness, and Sorrow's fire-whip, and all the Gehenna Bailiffs[5] that patrol and inhabit ever-vexed Time, cannot thenceforth harm us any more!'

Close by which rather beautiful apostrophe, lies a laboured Character of the deceased Andreas Futteral; of his natural ability, his deserts in life (as Prussian Sergeant); with long historical inquiries into the genealogy of the Futteral Family, here traced back as far as Henry the Fowler:[6] the whole of which we pass over, not without astonishment. It only concerns us to add, that now was the time when Mother Gretchen revealed to her foster-son that he was not at all of this kindred; or indeed of any kindred, having come into historical existence in the way already known to us. 'Thus was I doubly orphaned,' says he; 'bereft not only of Possession, but even of Remembrance. Sorrow and Wonder, here suddenly united, could not but produce abundant fruit. Such a disclosure, in such a season, struck its roots through my whole nature: ever till the years of mature manhood, it mingled with my whole thoughts, was as the stem whereon all my day-dreams and night-dreams grew. A certain poetic elevation, yet also a corresponding civic depres-

---

[5] Officers of Hell.
[6] Henry I, Emperor of Germany (876–936).

sion, it naturally imparted: *I was like no other*; in which fixed-idea, leading sometimes to highest, and oftener to frightfullest results, may there not lie the first spring of tendencies, which in my Life have become remarkable enough? As in birth, so in action, speculation, and social position, my fellows are perhaps not numerous.'

In the Bag *Sagittarius*, as we at length discover, Teufelsdröckh has become a University man; though how, when, or of what quality, will nowhere disclose itself with the smallest certainty. Few things, in the way of confusion and capricious indistinctness, can now surprise our readers; not even the total want of dates, almost without parallel in a Biographical work. So enigmatic, so chaotic we have always found, and must always look to find, these scattered Leaves. In *Sagittarius*, however, Teufelsdröckh begins to show himself even more than usually Sibylline:[7] fragments of all sorts; scraps of regular Memoir, College-Exercises, Programs, Professional Testimoniums, Milkscores, torn Billets, sometimes to appearance of an amatory cast; all blown together as if by merest chance, henceforth bewilder the sane Historian. To combine any picture of these University, and the subsequent, years; much more, to decipher therein any illustrative primordial elements of the Clothes-Philosophy, becomes such a problem as the reader may imagine.

So much we can see; darkly, as through the foliage of some wavering thicket: a youth of no common endowment, who has passed happily through Childhood, less happily yet still vigorously through Boyhood, now at length perfect in 'dead vocables,' and set down, as he hopes, by the living Fountain, there to superadd Ideas and Capabilities. From such Fountain he draws, diligently, thirstily, yet never or seldom with his whole heart, for the water nowise suits his palate; discouragements, entanglements, aberrations are discoverable or supposable. Nor perhaps are even pecuniary distresses wanting; for 'the good Gretchen, who in spite of advices from not disinterested rela-

[7] See *Sartor*, Book I, Chapter 11, n. 7.

tives has sent him hither, must after a time withdraw her willing but too feeble hand.' Nevertheless in an atmosphere of Poverty and manifold Chagrin, the Humour of that young Soul, what character is in him, first decisively reveals itself; and, like strong sunshine in weeping skies, gives out variety of colours, some of which are prismatic. Thus, with the aid of Time and of what Time brings, has the stripling Diogenes Teufelsdröckh waxed into manly stature; and into so questionable an aspect, that we ask with new eagerness, How he specially came by it, and regret anew that there is no more explicit answer. Certain of the intelligible and partially significant fragments, which are few in number, shall be extracted from that Limbo of a Paper-bag, and presented with the usual preparation.

As if, in the Bag *Scorpio*, Teufelsdröckh had not already expectorated his antipedagogic spleen; as if, from the name *Sagittarius*, he had thought himself called upon to shoot arrows, we here again fall-in with such matter as this:[8] 'The University where I was educated still stands vivid enough in my remembrance, and I know its name well; which name, however, I, from tenderness to existing interests and persons, shall in nowise divulge. It is my painful duty to say that, out of England and Spain, ours was the worst of all hitherto discovered Universities. This is indeed a time when right Education is, as nearly as may be, impossible: however, in degrees of wrongness there is no limit: nay, I can conceive a worse system than that of the Nameless itself; as poisoned victual may be worse than absolute hunger.

'It is written, When the blind lead the blind, both shall fall into the ditch: wherefore, in such circumstances, may it not sometimes be safer, if both leader and lead simply—sit still? Had you, anywhere in Crim Tartary, walled-in a square enclosure; furnished it with a small, ill-chosen Library; and then turned loose into it eleven-hundred Christian striplings, to tumble about as they listed, from three to seven years: certain persons, under the title of Professors, being stationed at the gates, to declare aloud that it was a University, and exact considerable

[8] The following account corresponds closely to Carlyle's experiences at Edinburgh University, which he attended from 1809–1814.

admission-fees,—you had, not indeed in mechanical structure, yet in spirit and result, some imperfect resemblance of our High Seminary. I say, imperfect; for if our mechanical structure was quite other, so neither was our result altogether the same: unhappily, we were not in Crim Tartary, but in a corrupt European city, full of smoke and sin; moreover, in the middle of a Public, which, without far costlier apparatus than that of the Square Enclosure, and Declaration aloud, you could not be sure of gulling.

'Gullible, however, by fit apparatus, all Publics are; and gulled, with the most surprising profit. Towards anything like a *Statistics of Imposture*, indeed, little as yet has been done: with a strange indifference, our Economists, nigh buried under Tables for minor Branches of Industry, have altogether overlooked the grand all-overtopping Hypocrisy Branch; as if our whole arts of Puffery, of Quackery, Priestcraft, Kingcraft, and the innumerable other crafts and mysteries of that genus, had not ranked in Productive Industry at all! Can any one, for example, so much as say, What moneys, in Literature and Shoeblacking, are realised by actual instruction and actual jet Polish; what by fictitious-persuasive Proclamation of such; specifying, in distinct items, the distributions, circulations, disbursements, incomings of said moneys, with the smallest approach to accuracy? But to ask, How far, in all the several infinitely-complected departments of social business, in government, education, in manual, commercial, intellectual fabrication of every sort, man's Want is supplied by true Ware; how far by the mere Appearance of true Ware:—in other words, To what extent, by what methods, with what effects, in various times and countries, Deception takes the place of wages of Performance: here truly is an Inquiry big with results for the future time, but to which hitherto only the vaguest answer can be given. If for the present, in our Europe, we estimate the ratio of Ware to Appearance of Ware so high even as at One to a Hundred (which, considering the Wages of a Pope, Russian Autocrat, or English Game-Preserver, is probably not far from the mark),—what almost prodigious saving may there not be anticipated, as the *Statistics of Imposture* advances, and so the manufacturing of Shams (that of Realities rising into clearer and clearer distinction therefrom) gradually declines, and at length becomes all but wholly unnecessary!

'This for the coming golden ages. What I had to remark, for the present brazen one, is, that in several provinces, as in Education, Polity, Religion, where so much is wanted and indispensable, and so little can as yet be furnished, probably Imposture is of sanative, anodyne nature, and man's Gullibility not his worst blessing. Suppose your sinews of war quite broken; I mean your military chest insolvent, forage all but exhausted; and that the whole army is about to mutiny, disband, and cut your and each other's throat,—then were it not well could you, as if by miracle, pay them in any sort of fairy-money, feed them on coagulated water, or mere imagination of meat; whereby, till the real supply came up, they might be kept together and quiet? Such perhaps was the aim of Nature, who does nothing without aim, in furnishing her favourite, Man, with this his so omnipotent or rather omnipatient Talent of being Gulled.

'How beautifully it works, with a little mechanism; nay, almost makes mechanism for itself! These Professors in the Nameless lived with ease, with safety, by a mere Reputation, constructed in past times, and then too with no great effort, by quite another class of persons. Which Reputation, like a strong, brisk-going undershot wheel, sunk into the general current, bade fair, with only a little annual repainting on their part, to hold long together, and of its own accord assiduously grind for them. Happy that it was so, for the Millers! They themselves needed not to work; their attempts at working, at what they called Educating, now when I look back on it, fill me with a certain mute admiration.

'Besides all this, we boasted ourselves a Rational University; in the highest degree hostile to Mysticism; thus was the young vacant mind furnished with much talk about Progress of the Species, Dark Ages, Prejudice,[9] and the like; so that all were quickly enough blown out into a state of windy argumentativeness; whereby the better sort had soon to end in sick, impotent

[9] Favorite catch-phrases of believers in rationalism and progress.

Scepticism; the worser sort explode (*crepiren*) in finished Self-conceit, and to all spiritual intents become dead.—But this too is portion of mankind's lot. If our era is the Era of Unbelief, why murmur under it; is there not a better coming, nay come? As in long-drawn systole and long-drawn diastole, must the period of Faith alternate with the period of Denial; must the vernal growth, the summer luxuriance of all Opinions, Spiritual Representations and Creations, be followed by, and again follow, the autumnal decay, the winter dissolution. For man lives in Time, has his whole earthly being, endeavour and destiny shaped for him by Time: only in the transitory Time-Symbol is the ever-motionless Eternity we stand on made manifest. And yet, in such winter-seasons of Denial, it is for the nobler-minded perhaps a comparative misery to have been born, and to be awake and work; and for the duller a felicity, if, like hibernating animals, safe-lodged in some Salamanca University, or Sybaris city, or other superstitious or voluptuous Castle of Indolence,[10] they can slumber-through in stupid dreams, and only awaken when the loud-roaring hailstorms have all done their work, and to our prayers and martyrdoms the new Spring has been vouchsafed.'

That in the environment, here mysteriously enough shadowed forth Teufelsdröckh must have felt ill at ease, cannot be doubtful. 'The hungry young,' he says, 'looked up to their spiritual Nurses; and, for food, were bidden eat the east-wind. What vain jargon of controversial Metaphysic, Etymology, and mechanical Manipulation falsely named Science, was current there, I indeed learned, better perhaps than the most. Among eleven-hundred Christian youths, there will not be wanting some eleven eager to learn. By collision with such, a certain warmth, a certain polish was communicated; by instinct and happy accident, I took less to rioting (*renommiren*), than to thinking and reading, which latter also I was free to do. Nay from the chaos of that Library. I succeeded in fishing-up more books perhaps than had been known to the very keepers thereof. The founda-

[10] Salamanca University: famous medieval university in Spain. Sybaris City: Greek colony in Italy famous for its luxury. Castle of Indolence: poem by James Thomson (1700–1748).

tion of a Literary Life was hereby laid. I learned, on my own strength, to read fluently in almost all cultivated languages, on almost all subjects and sciences; farther, as man is ever the prime object to man, already it was my favourite employment to read character in speculation, and from the Writing to construe the Writer. A certain groundplan of Human Nature and Life began to fashion itself in me; wondrous enough, now when I look back on it; for my whole Universe, physical and spiritual, was as yet a Machine! However, such a conscious, recognised groundplan, the truest I had, *was* beginning to be there, and by additional experiments might be corrected and indefinitely extended.'

Thus from poverty does the strong educe nobler wealth; thus in the destitution of the wild desert does our young Ishmael acquire for himself the highest of all possessions, that of Self-help. Nevertheless a desert this was, waste, and howling with savage monsters. Teufelsdröckh gives us long details of his 'fever-paroxysms of Doubt'; his Inquiries concerning Miracles, and the Evidences of religious Faith; and how 'in the silent night-watches, still darker in his heart than over sky and earth, he has cast himself before the All-seeing, and with audible prayers cried vehemently for Light, for deliverance from Death and the Grave. Not till after long years, and unspeakable agonies, did the believing heart surrender; sink into spell-bound sleep, under the nightmare, Unbelief; and, in this hag-ridden dream, mistake God's fair living world for a pallid, vacant Hades and extinct Pandemonium. But through such Purgatory pain,' continues he, 'it is appointed us to pass; first must the dead Letter of Religion own itself dead, and drop piecemeal into dust, if the living Spirit of Religion, freed from this its charnel-house, is to arise on us, newborn of Heaven, and with new healing under its wings.'

To which Purgatory pains, seemingly severe enough, if we add a liberal measure of Earthly distresses, want of practical guidance, want of sympathy, want of money, want of hope; and all this in the fervid season of youth, so exaggerated in imagining, so boundless in desires, yet here so poor in means,—do we not see a strong incipient spirit oppressed and overloaded from without and from within; the fire of genius struggling-up among fuel-wood of the greenest, and as yet with more of bitter vapour than of clear flame?

From various fragments of Letters and other documentary scraps, it is to be inferred that Teufelsdröckh, isolated, shy, retiring as he was, had not altogether escaped notice: certain established men are aware of his existence; and, if stretching-out no helpful hand, have at least their eyes on him. He appears, though in dreary enough humour, to be addressing himself to the Profession of Law;—whereof, indeed, the world has since seen him a public graduate. But omitting these broken, unsatisfactory thrums of Economical relation, let us present rather the following small thread of Moral relation; and therewith, the reader for himself weaving it in at the right place, conclude our dim arras-picture of these University years.

'Here also it was that I formed acquaintance with Herr Towgood, or, as it is perhaps better written, Herr Toughgut; a young person of quality (*von Adel*), from the interior parts of England. He stood connected, by blood and hospitality, with the Counts von Zähdarm,[11] in this quarter of Germany; to which noble Family I likewise was, by his means, with all friendliness, brought near. Towgood had a fair talent, unspeakably ill-cultivated; with considerable humour of character: and, bating his total ignorance, for he knew nothing except Boxing and a little Grammar, showed less of that aristocratic impassivity, and silent fury, than for most part belongs to Travellers of his nation. To him I owe my first practical knowledge of the English and their ways; perhaps also something of the partiality with which I have ever since regarded that singular people. Towgood was not without an eye, could he have come at any light. Invited doubtless by the presence of the Zähdarm Family, he had travelled hither, in the almost frantic hope of perfecting his studies; he, whose studies had as yet been those of infancy, hither to a University where so much as the notion of perfection, not to say the effort after it, no longer existed! Often we would condole over the hard destiny of the Young in this era: how, after all our toil, we were to be turned-out into the world,

---

[11] "Toughgut."

with beards on our chins indeed, but with few other attributes of manhood; no existing thing that we were trained to Act on, nothing that we could so much as Believe. "How has our head on the outside a polished Hat," would Towgood exclaim, "and in the inside Vacancy, or a froth of Vocables and Attorney-Logic! At a small cost men are educated to make leather into shoes; but at a great cost, what am I educated to make? By Heaven, Brother! what I have already eaten and worn, as I came thus far, would endow a considerable Hospital of Incurables." —"Man, indeed," I would answer, "has a Digestive Faculty, which must be kept working, were it even partly by stealth. But as for our Mis-education, make not bad worse; waste not the time yet ours, in trampling on thistles because they have yielded us no figs. *Frisch zu, Bruder!*[12] Here are Books, and we have brains to read them; here is a whole Earth and a whole Heaven, and we have eyes to look on them: *Frisch zu!*"

'Often also our talk was gay; not without brilliancy, and even fire. We looked-out on Life, with its strange scaffolding, where all at once harlequins dance, and men are beheaded and quartered: motley, not unterrific was the aspect; but we looked on it like brave youths. For myself, these were perhaps my most genial hours. Towards this young warmhearted, strongheaded and wrongheaded Herr Towgood I was even near experiencing the now obsolete sentiment of Friendship. Yes, foolish Heathen that I was, I felt that, under certain conditions, I could have loved this man, and taken him to my bosom, and been his brother once and always. By degrees, however, I understood the new time, and its wants. If man's *Soul* is indeed, as in the Finnish Language, and Utilitarian Philosophy, a kind of *Stomach*, what else is the true meaning of Spiritual Union but an Eating together? Thus we, instead of Friends, are Dinner-guests; and here as elsewhere have cast away chimeras.'

So ends, abruptly as is usual, and enigmatically, this little incipient romance. What henceforth becomes of the brave Herr Towgood, or Toughgut? He has dived-under, in the Autobiographical Chaos, and swims we see not where. Does any reader 'in the interior parts of England' know of such a man?

[12] "Get to work, Brother!"

Chapter IV
Getting under Way

The grand thaumaturgic Art of Thought. Difficulty in fitting Capability to Opportunity, or of getting under way. The advantage of Hunger and Bread-Studies. Teufelsdröckh has to enact the stern monodrama of *No object and no rest*. Sufferings as Auscultator. Given up as a man of genius. Zähdarm House. Intolerable presumption of young men. Irony and its consequences. Teufelsdröckh's Epitaph on Count Zähdarm.

'Thus nevertheless,' writes our Autobiographer, apparently as quitting College, 'was there realised Somewhat; namely, I, Diogenes Teufelsdröckh: a visible Temporary Figure (*Zeitbild*), occupying some cubic feet of Space, and containing within it Forces both physical and spiritual; hopes, passions, thoughts; the whole wondrous furniture, in more or less perfection, belonging to that mystery, a Man. Capabilities there were in me to give battle, in some small degree, against the great Empire of Darkness: does not the very Ditcher and Delver, with his spade, extinguish many a thistle and puddle; and so leave a little Order, where he found the opposite? Nay your very Daymoth has capabilities in this kind; and ever organises something (into its own Body, if no otherwise), which was before Inorganic; and of mute dead air makes living music, though only of the faintest, by humming.

'How much more, one whose capabilities are spiritual; who has learned, or begun learning, the grand thaumaturgic art of Thought! Thaumaturgic I name it; for hitherto all Miracles have been wrought thereby, and henceforth innumerable will be wrought; whereof we, even in these days, witness some. Of the Poet's and Prophet's inspired Message, and how it makes and

128

unmakes whole worlds, I shall forbear mention: but cannot the dullest hear Steam-Engines clanking around him? Has he not seen the Scottish Brassmith's IDEA (and this but a mechanical one) travelling on fire-wings round the Cape, and across two Oceans,[1] and stronger than any other Enchanter's familiar, on all hands unweariedly fetching and carrying: at home, not only weaving Cloth; but rapidly enough overturning the whole old system of Society; and, for Feudalism and Preservation of the Game, preparing us, by indirect but sure methods, Industrialism and the Government of the Wisest? Truly a Thinking Man is the worst enemy the Prince of Darkness can have; every time such a one announces himself, I doubt not, there runs a shudder through the Nether Empire; and new Emissaries are trained, with new tactics, to, if possible, entrap him, and hoodwink and handcuff him.

'With such high vocation had I too, as denizen of the Universe, been called. Unhappy it is, however, that though born to the amplest Sovereignty, in this way, with no less than sovereign right of Peace and War against the Time-Prince (*Zeitfürst*), or Devil, and all his Dominions, your coronation-ceremony costs such trouble, your sceptre is so difficult to get at, or even to get eye on!'

By which last wiredrawn similitude does Teufelsdröckh mean no more than that young men find obstacles in what we call 'getting under way'? 'Not what I Have,' continues he, 'but what I Do is my Kingdom. To each is given a certain inward Talent, a certain outward Environment of Fortune; to each, by wisest combination of these two, a certain maximum of Capability. But the hardest problem were ever this first: To find by study of yourself, and of the ground you stand on, what your combined inward and outward Capability specially is. For, alas, our young soul is all budding with Capabilities, and we see not yet which is the main and true one. Always too the new man is in a new time, under new conditions; his course can be the *fac-simile* of no prior one, but is by its nature original. And then how seldom will the outward Capability fit the inward: though

---

[1] James Watt's steam engine. See "Signs of the Times," n. 5.

talented wonderfully enough, we are poor, unfriended, dyspeptical, bashful; nay what is worse than all, we are foolish. Thus, in a whole imbroglio of Capabilities, we go stupidly groping about, to grope which is ours, and often clutch the wrong one: in this mad work must several years of our small term be spent, till the purblind Youth, by practice, acquire notions of distance, and become a seeing Man. Nay, many so spend their whole term, and in ever-new expectation, ever-new disappointment, shift from enterprise to enterprise, and from side to side: till at length, as exasperated striplings of threescore-and-ten, they shift into their last enterprise, that of getting buried.

'Such, since the most of us are too ophthalmic, would be the general fate; were it not that one thing saves us: our Hunger. For on this ground, as the prompt nature of Hunger is well known, must a prompt choice be made: hence have we, with wise foresight, Indentures and Apprenticeships for our irrational young; whereby, in due season, the vague universality of a Man shall find himself ready-moulded into a specific Craftsman; and so thenceforth work, with much or with little waste of Capability as it may be; yet not with the worst waste, that of time. Nay even in matters spiritual, since the spiritual artist too is born blind, and does not, like certain other creatures, receive sight in nine days, but far later, sometimes never,—is it not well that there should be what we call Professions, or Bread-studies (*Brodzwecke*), preappointed us? Here, circling like the gin-horse, for whom partial or total blindness is no evil, the Bread-artist can travel contentedly round and round, still fancying that it is forward and forward; and realise much: for himself victual; for the world an additional horse's power in the grand corn-mill or hemp-mill of Economic Society. For me too had such a leading-string been provided; only that it proved a neck-halter, and had nigh throttled me, till I broke it off. Then, in the words of Ancient Pistol, did the world generally become mine oyster, which I, by strength or cunning, was to open, as I would and could. Almost had I deceased (*fast wär ich umgekommen*), so obstinately did it continue shut.'

We see here, significantly foreshadowed, the spirit of much that was to befall our Autobiographer; the historical embodiment of which, as it painfully takes shape in his Life, lies scattered, in dim disastrous details, through this Bag *Pisces*, and those that follow. A young man of high talent, and high though still temper, like a young mettled colt, 'breaks-off his neckhalter,' and bounds forth, from his peculiar manger, into the wide world; which, alas, he finds all rigorously fenced-in. Richest clover-fields tempt his eye; but to him they are forbidden pasture: either pining in progressive starvation, he must stand; or, in mad exasperation, must rush to and fro, leaping against sheer stone-walls, which he cannot leap over, which only lacerate and lame him; till at last, after thousand attempts and endurances, he, as if by miracle, clears his way; not indeed into luxuriant and luxurious clover, yet into a certain bosky wilderness where existence is still possible, and Freedom, though waited on by Scarcity, is not without sweetness. In a word, Teufelsdröckh having thrown-up his legal Profession, finds himself without landmark of outward guidance; whereby his previous want of decided Belief, or inward guidance, is frightfully aggravated. Necessity urges him on; Time will not stop, neither can he, a Son of Time; wild passions without solacement, wild faculties without employment, ever vex and agitate him. He too must enact that stern Monodrama, *No Object and no Rest*; must front its successive destinies, work through to its catastrophe, and deduce therefrom what moral he can.

Yet let us be just to him, let us admit that his 'neck-halter' sat nowise easy on him; that he was in some degree forced to break it off. If we look at the young man's civic position, in this Nameless capital, as he emerges from its Nameless University, we can discern well that it was far from enviable. His first Law-Examination he has come through triumphantly; and can even boast that the *Examen Rigorosum* need not have frightened him: but though he is hereby 'an *Auscultator*[2] of respectability,' what avails it? There is next to no employment to be had. Neither, for a youth without connexions, is the process of Expectation very hopeful in itself; nor for one of his disposition much cheered from without. 'My fellow Auscultators,' he says,

[2] *Examen Rigorosum:* final law examination in German university. *Auscultator:* "lawyers assistant."

'were Auscultators: they dressed, and digested, and talked articulate words; other vitality showed they almost none. Small speculation in those eyes, that they did glare withal! Sense neither for the high nor for the deep, nor for aught human or divine, save only for the faintest scent of coming Preferment.' In which words, indicating a total estrangement on the part of Teufelsdröckh, may there not also lurk traces of a bitterness as from wounded vanity? Doubtless these prosaic Auscultators may have sniffed at him, with his strange ways; and tried to hate, and what was much more impossible, to despise him. Friendly communion, in any case, there could not be: already has the young Teufelsdröckh left the other young geese; and swims apart, through as yet uncertain whether he himself is cygnet or gosling.

Perhaps, too, what little employment he had was performed ill, at best unpleasantly. 'Great practical method and expertness' he may brag of; but is there not also great practical pride, though deep-hidden, only the deeper-seated? So shy a man can never have been popular. We figure to ourselves, how in those days he may have played strange freaks with his independence, and so forth: do not his own words betoken as much? 'Like a very young person, I imagined it was with Work alone, and not also with Folly and Sin, in myself and others, that I had been appointed to struggle.' Be this as it may, his progress from the passive Auscultatorship, towards any active Assessorship, is evidently of the slowest. By degrees, those same established men, once partially inclined to patronise him, seem to withdraw their countenance, and give him up as 'a man of genius': against which procedure he, in these Papers, loudly protests. 'As if,' says he, 'the higher did not presuppose the lower; as if he who can fly into heaven, could not also walk post if he resolved on it! But the world is an old woman, and mistakes any gilt farthing for a gold coin; whereby being often cheated, she will thenceforth trust nothing but the common copper.'

How our winged sky-messenger, unaccepted as a terrestrial runner, contrived, in the mean while, to keep himself from flying skyward without return, is not too clear from these Documents. Good old Gretchen seems to have vanished from the scene, perhaps from the Earth; other Horn of Plenty, or even of Parsimony, nowhere flows for him; so that 'the prompt nature of Hunger being well known,' we are not without our anxiety. From private Tuition, in never so many languages and sciences, the aid derivable is small; neither, to use his own words, 'does the young Adventurer hitherto suspect in himself any literary gift; but at best earns bread-and-water wages, by his wide faculty of Translation.[3] Nevertheless,' continues he, 'that I subsisted is clear, for you find me even now alive.' Which fact, however, except upon the principle of our true-hearted, kind old Proverb, that 'there is always life for a living one,' we must profess ourselves unable to explain.

Certain Landlords' Bills, and other economic Documents, bearing the mark of Settlement, indicate that he was not without money; but, like an independent Hearth-holder, if not House-holder, paid his way. Here also occur, among many others, two little mutilated Notes, which perhaps throw light on his condition. The first has now no date, or writer's name, but a huge Blot; and runs to this effect: 'The (*Inkblot*), tied-down by previous promise, cannot, except by best wishes, forward the Herr Teufelsdröckh's views on the Assessorship in question; and sees himself under the cruel necessity of forbearing, for the present, what were otherwise his duty and joy, to assist in opening the career for a man of genius, on whom far higher triumphs are yet waiting.' The other is on gilt paper; and interests us like a sort of epistolary mummy now dead, yet which once lived and beneficently worked. We give it in the original: '*Herr Teufelsdröckh wird von der Frau Gräfinn, auf Donnerstag, zum* ÆSTHETISCHEN THEE *schönstens eingeladen.*'[4]

Thus, in answer to a cry for solid pudding, whereof there is the most urgent need, comes, epigrammatically enough, the invitation to a wash of quite fluid *Æsthetic Tea*! How Teufelsdröckh, now at actual handgrips with Destiny herself, may have comported himself among these Musical and Literary Dilettanti

[3] After graduation from the University, Carlyle supported himself as a teacher and by translating German romances and scientific works.
[4] "Her Ladyship requests the pleasure of the company of Herr Teufelsdröckh at an AESTHETIC TEA on Thursday."

of both sexes, like a hungry lion invited to a feast of chicken-weed, we can only conjecture. Perhaps in expressive silence, and abstinence: otherwise if the lion, in such case, is to feast at all, it cannot be on the chickenweed, but only on the chickens. For the rest, as this Frau Gräfinn dates from the *Zähdarm House*, she can be no other than the Countess and mistress of the same; whose intellectual tendencies, and good-will to Teufelsdröckh, whether on the footing of Herr Towgood, or on his own footing, are hereby manifest. That some sort of rela-tion, indeed, continued, for a time, to connect our Autobio-grapher, though perhaps feebly enough, with this noble House, we have elsewhere express evidence. Doubtless, if he expected patronage, it was in vain; enough for him if he here obtained occasional glimpses of the great world, from which we at one time fancied him to have been always excluded. 'The Zähdarms,' says he, 'lived in the soft, sumptuous garniture of Aristocracy; whereto Literature and Art, attracted and attached from with-out, were to serve as the handsomest fringing. It was to the *Gnädigen Frau* (her Ladyship) that this latter improvement was due: assiduously she gathered, dextrously she fitted-on, what fringing was to be had; lace or cobweb, as the place yielded.' Was Teufelsdröckh also a fringe, of lace or cobweb; or promis-ing to be such? 'With his *Excellenz* (the Count),' continues he, 'I have more than once had the honour to converse; chiefly on general affairs, and the aspect of the world, which he, though now past middle life, viewed in no unfavourable light; finding indeed, except the Outrooting of Journalism (*die auszurottende Journalistik*), little to desiderate therein. On some points, as his *Excellenz* was not uncholeric, I found it more pleasant to keep silence. Besides, his occupation being that of Owning Land, there might be faculties enough, which, as superfluous for such use, were little developed in him.'

That to Teufelsdröckh the aspect of the world was nowise so faultless, and many things besides 'the Outrooting of Journal-ism' might have seemed improvements, we can readily conjec-ture. With nothing but a barren Auscultatorship from without, and so many mutinous thoughts and wishes from within, his position was no easy one. 'The Universe,' he says, 'was as a mighty Sphinx-riddle, which I knew so little of, yet must rede, or be devoured. In red streaks of unspeakable grandeur, yet also in the blackness of darkness, was Life, to my too-unfurnished Thought, unfolding itself. A strange contradiction lay in me; and I as yet knew not the solution of it; knew not that spiritual music can spring only from discords set in harmony; that but for Evil there were no Good, as victory is only possible by battle.'

'I have heard affirmed (surely in jest),' observes he else-where, 'by not unphilanthropic persons, that it were a real in-crease of human happiness, could all young men from the age of nineteen be covered under barrels, or rendered otherwise invisi-ble; and there left to follow their lawful studies and callings, till they emerged, sadder and wiser, at the age of twenty-five. With which suggestion, at least as considered in the light of a prac-tical scheme, I need scarcely say that I nowise coincide. Never-theless it is plausibly urged that, as young ladies (*Mädchen*) are, to mankind, precisely the most delightful in those years; so young gentlemen (*Bübchen*) do then attain their maximum of detestability. Such gawks (*Gecken*) are they, and foolish peacocks, and yet with such a vulturous hunger for self-indul-gence; so obstinate, obstreperous, vain-glorious; in all senses, so froward and so forward. No mortal's endeavour or attainment will, in the smallest, content the as yet unendeavouring, un-attaining young gentleman; but he could make it all infinitely better, were it worthy of him. Life everywhere is the most man-ageable matter, simple as a question in the Rule-of-Three: multiply your second and third term together, divide the prod-uct by the first, and your quotient will be the answer,—which you are but an ass if you cannot come at. The booby has not yet found-out, by any trial, that, do what one will, there is ever a cursed fraction, oftenest a decimal repeater, and no net integer quotient so much as to be thought of.'

In which passage does not there lie an implied confession that Teufelsdröckh himself, besides his outward obstructions, had an inward, still greater, to contend with; namely, a certain temporary, youthful, yet still afflictive derangement of head? Alas, on the former side alone, his case was hard enough. 'It continues ever true,' says he, 'that Saturn, or Chronos, or what we call TIME, devours all his Children:[5] only by incessant Running, by incessant Working, may you (for some threescore-and-ten years) escape him; and you too he devours at last. Can any Sovereign, or Holy Alliance[6] of Sovereigns, bid Time stand still; even in thought, shake themselves free of Time? Our whole terrestrial being is based on Time, and built of Time; it is wholly a Movement, a Time-impulse; Time is the author of it, the material of it. Hence also our Whole Duty, which is to move, to work,—in the right direction. Are not our Bodies and our Souls in continual movement, whether we will or not; in a continual Waste, requiring a continual Repair? Utmost satisfaction of our whole outward and inward Wants were but satisfaction for a space of Time; thus, whatso we have done, is done, and for us annihilated, and ever must we go and do anew. O Time-Spirit, how hast thou environed and imprisoned us, and sunk us so deep in thy troublous dim Time-Element, that only in lucid moments can so much as glimpses of our upper Azure Home be revealed to us! Me, however, as a Son of Time, un-happier than some others, was Time threatening to eat quite prematurely; for, strive as I might, there was no good Running, so obstructed was the path, so gyved were the feet.' That is to say, we presume, speaking in the dialect of this lower world, that Teufelsdröckh's whole duty and necessity was, like other men's, 'to work,—in the right direction,' and that no work was to be had; whereby he became wretched enough. As was natural: with haggard Scarcity threatening him in the distance; and so vehement a soul languishing in restless inaction, and forced thereby, like Sir Hudibras's sword by rust,

> To eat into itself, for lack
> Of something else to hew and hack!

But on the whole, that same 'excellent Passivity,' as it has all along done, is here again vigorously flourishing; in which

[5] In classical mythology, the Roman god Saturn, identified with the Greek god Chronos, the god of Time, devoured his children.
[6] Compact signed in 1815 by Russia, Austria and Prussia to maintain the existing dynasties.

circumstance may we not trace the beginnings of much that now characterises our Professor; and perhaps, in faint rudiments, the origin of the Clothes-Philosophy itself? Already the attitude he has assumed towards the World is too defensive; not, as would have been desirable, a bold attitude of attack. 'So far hitherto,' he says, 'as I had mingled with mankind, I was notable, if for anything, for a certain stillness of manner, which, as my friends often rebukingly declared, did but ill express the keen ardour of my feelings. I, in truth, regarded men with an excess both of love and of fear. The mystery of a Person, indeed, is ever divine to him that has a sense for the Godlike. Often, notwithstanding, was I blamed, and by half-strangers hated, for my so-called Hardness (*Härte*), my Indifferentism towards men; and the seemingly ironic tone I had adopted, as my favourite dialect in conversation. Alas, the panoply of Sarcasm was but as a buckram case, wherein I had striven to envelope myself; that so my own poor Person might live safe there, and in all friendliness, being no longer exasperated by wounds. Sarcasm I now see to be, in general, the language of the Devil; for which reason I have long since as good as renounced it. But how many individuals did I, in those days, provoke into some degree of hostility thereby! An ironic man, with his sly stillness, and ambuscading ways, more especially an ironic young man, from whom it is least expected, may be viewed as a pest to society. Have we not seen persons of weight and name coming forward, with gentlest indifference, to tread such a one out of sight, as an insignificancy and worm, start ceiling-high (*balkenhoch*), and thence fall shattered and supine, to be born home on shutters, not without indignation, when he proved electric and a torpedo!'

Alas, how can a man with this devilishness of temper make way for himself in Life; where the first problem, as Teufelsdröckh too admits, is 'to unite yourself with some one and with somewhat (*sich anzushliessen*)'? Division, not union, is written on most part of his procedure. Let us add too that, in no great length of time, the only important connexion he had ever succeeded in forming, his connexion with the Zähdarm Family, seems to have been paralysed, for all practical uses, by the death of the 'not uncholeric' old Count. This fact stands recorded, quite incidentally, in a certain *Discourse on Epitaphs,* huddled into the present Bag, among so much else; of which Essay the learning and curious penetration are more to be approved of than the spirit. His grand principle is, that lapidary inscriptions, of what sort soever, should be Historical rather than Lyrical. 'By request of that worthy Nobleman's survivors,' says he, 'I undertook to compose his Epitaph; and not unmindful of my own rules, produced the following; which however, for an alleged defect of Latinity, a defect never yet fully visible to myself, still remains unengraven;'—wherein, we may predict, there is more than the Latinity that will surprise an English reader:

HIC JACET

PHILIPPUS ZAEHDARM, COGNOMINE MAGNUS,

ZAEHDARMI COMES,

EX IMPERII CONCILIO,

VELLERIS AUREI, PERISCELIDIS, NECNON VULTURIS NIGRI

EQUES.

QUI DUM SUB LUNA AGEBAT,

QUINQUIES MILLE PERDICES

PLUMBO CONFECIT:

VARII CIBI

CENTUMPONDIA MILLIES CENTENA MILLIA,

PER SE, PERQUE SERVOS QUADRUPEDES BIPEDESVE,

HAUD SINE TUMULTU DEVOLVENS,

IN STERCUS

PALAM CONVERTIT.

NUNC A LABORE REQUIESCENTEM

OPERA SEQUUNTUR.

SI MONUMENTUM QUÆRIS,

FIMETUM ADSPICE.

PRIMUM IN ORBE DEJECIT [*sub dato*]; POSTREMUM[*sub dato*].[7]

---

[7] "Here lies Philip Zaehdarm, called the Great, Count of Zaehdarm, of the Imperial Council, Knight of the Golden Fleece, Garter, and of the Black Vulture. Who, while on earth, shot five thousand partridges: a hundred million hundredweight of various foods he, and his servants both four-legged and two-legged, not without noise in the process, converted into manure. Now resting from labor, his works follow him. If you seek his monument, look at this heap. Begun (as given); finished (as given)."

Chapter V
Romance

Teufelsdröckh gives up his Profession. The heavenly mystery
of Love. Teufelsdröckh's feeling of worship towards women.
First and only love. Blumine. Happy hearts and free tongues.
The infinite nature of Fantasy. Love's joyful progress; sudden
dissolution; and final catastrophe.

'For long years,' writes Teufelsdröckh, 'had the poor Hebrew,
in this Egypt of an Auscultatorship, painfully toiled, baking
bricks without stubble, before ever the question once struck
him with entire force: For what?—*Beym Himmel!* For Food
and Warmth! And are Food and Warmth nowhere else, in the
whole wide Universe, discoverable?—Come of it what might, I
resolved to try.'

Thus then are we to see him in a new independent capacity,
though perhaps far from an improved one. Teufelsdröckh is
now a man without Profession. Quitting the common Fleet of
herring-busses[1] and whalers, where indeed his leeward, laggard
condition was painful enough, he desperately steers off, on a
course of his own, by sextant and compass of his own. Unhappy
Teufelsdröckh! Though neither Fleet, nor Traffic, nor Commo-
dores pleased thee, still was it not *a Fleet*, sailing in prescribed
track, for fixed objects; above all, in combination, wherein, by
mutual guidance, by all manner of loans and borrowings, each
could manifoldly aid the other? How wilt thou sail in unknown
seas; and for thyself find that shorter North-west Passage to thy
fair Spice-country of a Nowhere?—A solitary rover, on such a
voyage, with such nautical tactics, will meet with adventures.

[1] Fishing boats.

Nay, as we forthwith discover, a certain Calypso-Island[2] detains him at the very outset; and as it were falsifies and oversets his whole reckoning.

'If in youth,' writes he once, 'the Universe is majestically unveiling, and everywhere Heaven revealing itself on Earth, nowhere to the Young Man does this Heaven on Earth so immediately reveal itself as in the Young Maiden. Strangely enough, in this strange life of ours, it has been so appointed. On the whole, as I have often said, a Person (*Persönlichkeit*) is ever holy to us; a certain orthodox Anthropomorphism connects my *Me* with all *Thees* in bonds of Love: but it is in this approximation of the Like and Unlike, that such heavenly attraction, as between Negative and Positive, first burns-out into a flame. Is the pitifullest mortal Person, think you, indifferent to us? Is it not rather our heartfelt wish to be made one with him; to unite him to us, by gratitude, by admiration, even by fear; or failing all these, unite ourselves to him? But how much more, in this case of the Like-Unlike! Here is conceded us the higher mystic possibility of such a union, the highest in our Earth; thus, in the conducting medium of Fantasy, flames-forth that *fire*-development of the universal Spiritual Electricity, which, as unfolded between man and woman, we first emphatically denominate LOVE.

'In every well-conditioned stripling, as I conjecture, there already blooms a certain prospective Paradise, cheered by some fairest Eve; nor, in the stately vistas, and flowerage and foliage of that Garden, is a Tree of Knowledge, beautiful and awful in the midst thereof, wanting. Perhaps too the whole is but the lovelier, if Cherubim and a Flaming Sword divide it from all footsteps of men; and grant him, the imaginative stripling, only the view, not the entrance. Happy season of virtuous youth, when shame is still an impassable celestial barrier; and the sacred air-cities of Hope have not shrunk into the mean clay-hamlets of Reality; and man, by his nature, is yet infinite and free!

'As for our young Forlorn,' continues Teufelsdröckh, evidently meaning himself, 'in his secluded way of life, and with his glowing Fantasy, the more fiery that it burnt under cover, as

[2] Island on which Ulysses was detained by the nymph Calypso for seven years.

in a reverberating furnace, his feeling towards the Queens of this Earth was, and indeed is, altogether unspeakable. A visible Divinity dwelt in them; to our young Friend all women were holy, were heavenly. As yet he but saw them flitting past, in their many-coloured angel-plumage; or hovering mute and inaccessible on the outskirts of *Æsthetic Tea*: all of air they were, all Soul and Form; so lovely, like mysterious priestesses, in whose hand was the invisible Jacob's-ladder, whereby man might mount into very Heaven. That he, our poor Friend, should ever win for himself one of these Gracefuls (*Holden*)— *Ach Gott*! how could he hope it; should he not have died under it? There was a certain delirious vertigo in the thought.

'Thus was the young man, if all-sceptical of Demons and Angels such as the vulgar had once believed in, nevertheless not unvisited by hosts of true Sky-born, who visibly and audibly hovered round him wheresoever he went; and they had that religious worship in his thought, though as yet it was by their mere earthly and trivial name that he named them. But now, if on a soul so circumscribed, some actual Air-maiden, incorporated into tangibility and reality, should cast any electric glance of kind eyes, saying thereby, "Thou too mayst love and be loved"; and so kindle him,—good Heaven, what a volcanic, earthquake-bringing, all-consuming fire were probably kindled!'

Such a fire, it afterwards appears, did actually burst-forth, with explosions more or less Vesuvian, in the inner man of Herr Diogenes; as indeed how could it fail? A nature, which, in his own figurative style, we might say, had now not a little carbonised tinder, of Irritability; with so much nitre of latent Passion, and sulphurous Humour enough; the whole lying in such hot neighbourhood, close by 'a reverberating furnace of Fantasy': have we not here the components of driest Gunpowder, ready, on occasion of the smallest spark, to blaze-up? Neither, in this our Life-element, are sparks anywhere wanting. Without doubt, some Angel, whereof so many hovered round, would one day, leaving 'the outskirts of *Æesthetic Tea*,' flit nigher; and, by electric Promethean glance, kindle no despicable firework. Happy, if it indeed proved a Firework, and flamed-off rocket-wise, in successive beautiful bursts of splendour, each growing naturally from the other, through the several stages of a happy

Youthful Love; till the whole were safely burnt-out; and the young soul relieved with little damage! Happy, if it did not rather prove a Conflagration and mad Explosion; painfully lacerating the heart itself; nay perhaps bursting the heart in pieces (which were Death); or at best, bursting the thin walls of your 'reverberating furnace,' so that it rage thenceforth all unchecked among the contiguous combustibles (which were Madness): till of the so fair and manifold internal world of our Diogenes, there remained Nothing, or only the 'crater of an extinct volcano'!

From multifarious Documents in this Bag *Capricornus*, and in the adjacent ones on both sides thereof, it becomes manifest that our philosopher, as stoical and cynical as he now looks, was heartily and even frantically in Love: here therefore may our old doubts whether his heart were of stone or of flesh give way. He loved once; not wisely but too well. And once only: for as your Congreve needs a new case or wrappage for every new rocket,[3] so each human heart can properly exhibit but one Love, if even one; the 'First Love which is infinite' can be followed by no second like unto it. In more recent years, accordingly, the Editor of these Sheets was led to regard Teufelsdröckh as a man not only who would never wed, but who would never even flirt; whom the grand-climacteric itself, and *St Martin's Summer*[4] of incipient Dotage, would crown with no new myrtle-garland.[5] To the Professor, women are henceforth Pieces of Art; of Celestial Art, indeed; which celestial pieces he glories to survey in galleries, but has lost thought of purchasing.

Psychological readers are not without curiosity to see how Teufelsdröckh, in this for him unexampled predicament, demeans himself; with what specialities of successive configuration, splendour and colour, his Firework blazes-off. Small, as usual, is the satisfaction that such can meet with here. From amid these confused masses of Eulogy and Elegy, with their mad Petrarchan and Werterean[6] ware lying madly scattered among

---

[3] Congreve rocket: a type of rocket used in warfare.
[4] Term applied to warm weather in autumn, Indian summer.
[5] The myrtle was considered sacred to Venus.
[6] Allusion to Petrarch's love-sonnets to Laura and to Goethe's novel of unhappy young love, *The Sorrows of Young Werther* (1774).

all sorts of quite extraneous matter, not so much as the fair one's name can be deciphered. For, without doubt, the title *Blumine*,[7] whereby she is here designated, and which means simply Goddess of Flowers, must be fictitious. Was her real name Flora, then? But what was her surname, or had she none? Of what station in Life was she; of what parentage, fortune, aspect? Specially, by what Preëstablished Harmony of occurrences did the Lover and the Loved meet one another in so wide a world; how did they behave in such a meeting? To all which questions, not unessential in a Biographic work, mere Conjecture must for most part return answer. 'It was appointed,' says our Philosopher, 'that the high celestial orbit of Blumine should intersect the low sublunary one of our Forlorn; that he, looking in her empyrean eyes, should fancy the upper Sphere of Light was come down into this nether sphere of Shadows; and finding himself mistaken, make noise enough.'

We seem to gather that she was young, hazel-eyed, beautiful, and some one's Cousin; highborn, and of high spirit; but unhappily dependent and insolvent; living, perhaps, on the not too gracious bounty of moneyed relatives. But how came 'the Wanderer' into her circle? Was it by the humid vehicle of *Æsthetic Tea*, or by the arid one of mere Business? Was it on the hand of Herr Towgood; or of the Gnädige Frau, who, as an ornamental Artist, might sometimes like to promote flirtation, especially for young cynical Nondescripts? To all appearance, it was chiefly by Accident, and the grace of Nature.

'Thou fair Waldschloss,'[8] writes our Autobiographer, 'what stranger ever saw thee, were it even an absolved Auscultator, officially bearing in his pocket the last *Relatio ex Actis*[9] he would ever write, but must have paused to wonder! Noble Mansion! There stoodest thou, in deep Mountain Amphitheatre, on umbrageous lawns, in thy serene solitude; stately, massive, all of granite; glittering in the western sunbeams, like a palace of El Dorado, overlaid with precious metal. Beautiful rose up,

[7] The figure of Blumine combines the qualities of several women Carlyle knew in his youth, as well as those of his wife, Jane Welsh Carlyle.
[8] "Castle in the Woods."
[9] "Official reports."

in wavy curvature, the slope of thy guardian Hills; of the greenest was their sward, embossed with its dark-brown frets of crag, or spotted by some spreading solitary Tree and its shadow. To the unconscious Wayfarer thou wert also as an Ammon's Temple,[10] in the Libyan Waste; where, for joy and woe, the tablet of his Destiny lay written. Well might he pause and gaze: in that glance of his were prophecy and nameless forebodings.'

Put now let us conjecture that the so presentient Auscultator has handed-in his *Relatio ex Actis*; been invited to a glass of Rhine-wine; and so, instead of returning dispirited and athirst to his dusty Town-home, is ushered into the Gardenhouse, where sit the choicest party of dames and cavaliers: if not engaged in Æsthetic Tea, yet in trustful evening conversation, and perhaps Musical Coffee, for we hear of 'harps and pure voices making the stillness live.' Scarcely, it would seem, is the Gardenhouse inferior in respectability to the noble mansion itself. 'Embowered amid rich foliage, rose-clusters, and the hues and odours of thousand flowers, here sat that brave company; in front, from the wide-opened doors, fair outlook over blossom and bush, over grove and velvet green, stretching, undulating onwards to the remote Mountain peaks: so bright, so mild, and everywhere the melody of birds and happy creatures: it was all as if man had stolen a shelter from the Sun in the bosom-vesture of Summer herself. How came it that the Wanderer advanced thither with such forecasting heart (*ahndungsvoll*), by the side of his gay host? Did he feel that to these soft influences his hard bosom ought to be shut; that here, once more, Fate had it in view to try him; to mock him, and see whether there were Humour in him?

'Next moment he finds himself presented to the party; and especially by name to—Blumine! Peculiar among all dames and damosels glanced Blumine, there in her modesty, like a star among earthly lights. Noblest maiden! whom he bent to, in body and in soul; yet scarcely dared look at, for the presence filled him with painful yet sweetest embarrassment.

'Blumine's was a name well known to him; far and wide was

[10] Legendary shrine of an oracle, located in an oasis in Libyan desert.

the fair one heard of, for her gifts, her graces, her caprices: from all which vague colourings of Rumour, from the censures no less than from the praises, had our friend painted for himself a certain imperious Queen of Hearts, and blooming warm Earth-angel, much more enchanting than your mere white Heaven-angels of women, in whose placid veins circulates too little naphtha-fire. Herself also he had seen in public places; that light yet so stately form; those dark tresses, shading a face where smiles and sunlight played over earnest deeps: but all this he had seen only as a magic vision, for him inaccessible, almost without reality. Her sphere was too far from his; how should she ever think of him; O Heaven! how should they so much as once meet together? And now that Rose-goddess sits in the same circle with him; the light of *her* eyes has smiled on him; if he speak, she will hear it! Nay, who knows, since the heavenly Sun looks into lowest valleys, but Blumine herself might have aforetime noted the so unnotable; perhaps, from his very gainsayers, as he had from hers, gathered wonder, gathered favour for him? Was the attraction, the agitation mutual, then; pole and pole trembling towards contact, when once brought into neighbourhood? Say rather, heart swelling in presence of the Queen of Hearts; like the Sea swelling when once near its Moon! With the Wanderer it was even so: as in heavenward gravitation, suddenly as at the touch of a Seraph's wand, his whole soul is roused from its deepest recesses; and all that was painful and that was blissful there, dim images, vague feelings of a whole Past and a whole Future, are heaving in unquiet eddies within him.

'Often, in far less agitating scenes, had our still Friend shrunk forcibly together; and shrouded-up his tremors and flutterings, of what sort soever, in a safe cover of Silence, and perhaps of seeming Stolidity. How was it, then, that here, when trembling to the core of his heart, he did not sink into swoons, but rose into strength, into fearlessness and clearness? It was his guiding Genius (*Dämon*) that inspired him; he must go forth and meet his Destiny. Show thyself now, whispered it, or be forever hid. Thus sometimes it is even when your anxiety becomes transcendental, that the soul first feels herself able to transcend it;

that she rises above it, in fiery victory; and borne on new-found wings of victory, moves so calmly, even because so rapidly, so irresistibly. Always must the Wanderer remember, with a certain satisfaction and surprise, how in this case he sat not silent, but struck adroitly into the stream of conversation; which thenceforth, to speak with an apparent not a real vanity, he may say that he continued to lead. Surely, in those hours, a certain inspiration was imparted him, such inspiration as is still possible in our late era. The self-secluded unfolds himself in noble thoughts, in free, glowing words; his soul is as one sea of light, the peculiar home of Truth and Intellect; wherein also Fantasy bodies-forth form after form, radiant with all prismatic hues.'

It appears, in this otherwise so happy meeting, there talked one 'Philistine';[11] who even now, to the general weariness, was dominantly pouring-forth Philistinism (*Philistriositäten*); little witting what hero was here entering to demolish him! We omit the series of Socratic, or rather Diogenic utterances, not unhappy in their way, whereby the monster, 'persuaded into silence,' seems soon after to have withdrawn for the night. 'Of which dialectic marauder,' writes our hero, 'the discomfiture was visibly felt as a benefit by most: but what were all applauses to the glad smile, threatening every moment to become a laugh, wherewith Blumine herself repaid the victor? He ventured to address her, she answered with attention: nay what if there were a slight tremor in that silver voice; what if the red glow of evening were hiding a transient blush!

'The conversation took a higher tone, one fine thought called forth another: it was one of those rare seasons, when the soul expands with full freedom, and man feels himself brought near to man. Gaily in light, graceful abandonment, the friendly talk played round that circle; for the burden was rolled from every heart; the barriers of Ceremony, which are indeed the laws of polite living, had melted as into vapour; and the poor claims of *Me* and *Thee*, no longer parted by rigid fences, now flowed softly into one another; and Life lay all harmonious, many-tinted, like some fair royal champaign, the sovereign and owner of which were Love only. Such music springs from kind

---

[11] Narrow, prosaic person opposed to the spirit of art.

hearts, in a kind environment of place and time. And yet as the light grew more aërial on the mountaintops, and the shadows fell longer over the valley, some faint tone of sadness may have breathed through the heart; and, in whispers more or less audible, reminded every one that as this bright day was drawing towards its close, so likewise must the Day of Man's Existence decline into dust and darkness; and with all its sick toilings, and joyful and mournful noises, sink in the still Eternity.

'To our Friend the hours seemed moments; holy was he and happy: the words from those sweetest lips came over him like dew on thirsty grass; all better feelings in his soul seemed to whisper, It is good for us to be here. At parting, the Blumine's hand was in his: in the balmy twilight, with the kind stars above them, he spoke something of meeting again, which was not contradicted; he pressed gently those small soft fingers, and it seemed as if they were not hastily, not angrily withdrawn.'

Poor Teufelsdröckh! it is clear to demonstration thou art smit: the Queen of Hearts would see a 'man of genius' also sigh for her; and there, by art-magic, in that preternatural hour, has she bound and spell-bound thee. 'Love is not altogether a Delirium,' says he elsewhere; 'yet has it many points in common therewith. I call it rather a discerning of the Infinite in the Finite, of the Idea made Real; which discerning again may be either true or false, either seraphic or demoniac, Inspiration or Insanity. But in the former case too, as in common Madness, it is Fantasy that superadds itself to sight; on the so petty domain of the Actual plants its Archimedes-lever,[12] whereby to move at will the infinite Spiritual. Fantasy I might call the true Heaven-gate and Hell-gate of man: his sensuous life is but the small temporary stage (*Zeitbühne*), whereon thick-streaming influences from both these far yet near regions meet visibly, and act tragedy and melodrama. Sense can support herself handsomely, in most countries, for some eighteen-pence a day; but for Fantasy planets and solar-systems will not suffice. Witness your Pyrrhus conquering the world, yet drinking no better red wine than he had before.' Alas! witness also your Diogenes, flame-clad, scal-

---

[12] Archimedes, third-century Greek philosopher to whom the discovery of the principle of the lever is attributed, is reputed to have said, "Give me a place to stand on and I shall move the world."

ing the upper Heaven, and verging towards Insanity, for prize of a 'high-souled Brunette,' as if the earth held but one and not several of these!

He says that, in Town, they met again: 'day after day, like his heart's sun, the blooming Blumine shone on him. Ah! a little while ago, and he was yet in all darkness: him what Graceful (*Holde*) would ever love? Disbelieving all things, the poor youth had never learned to believe in himself. Withdrawn, in proud timidity, within his own fastnesses; solitary from men, yet baited by night-spectres enough, he saw himself, with a sad indignation, constrained to renounce the fairest hopes of existence. And now, O now! "She looks on thee," cried he: "she the fairest, noblest; do not her dark eyes tell thee, thou art not despised? The Heaven's-Messenger! All Heaven's blessings be hers!" Thus did soft melodies flow through his heart; tones of an infinite gratitude; sweetest intimations that he also was a man, that for him also unutterable joys had been provided.

'In free speech, earnest or gay, amid lambent glances, laughter, tears, and often with the inarticulate mystic speech of Music: such was the element they now lived in; in such a many-tinted, radiant Aurora, and by this fairest of Orient Light-bringers must our Friend be blandished, and the new Apocalypse of Nature unrolled to him. Fairest Blumine! And, even as a Star, all Fire and humid Softness, a very Light-ray incarnate! Was there so much as a fault, a "caprice," he could have dispensed with? Was she not to him in very deed a Morning-Star; did not her presence bring with it airs from Heaven? As from Æolian Harps in the breath of dawn, as from the Memnon's Statue struck by the rosy finger of Aurora, unearthly music was around him, and lapped him into untried balmy Rest. Pale Doubt fled away to the distance; Life bloomed-up with happiness and hope. The past, then, was all a haggard dream; he had been in the Garden of Eden, then, and could not discern it! But lo now! the black walls of his prison melt away; the captive is alive, is free. If he loved his Disenchantress? *Ach Gott!* His whole heart and soul and life were hers, but never had he named it Love: existence was all a Feeling, not yet shaped into a Thought.'

Nevertheless, into a Thought, nay into an Action, it must be shaped; for neither Disenchanter nor Disenchantress, mere 'Children of Time,' can abide by Feeling alone. The Professor knows not, to this day, 'how in her soft, fervid bosom the Lovely found determination, even on hest of Necessity, to cut asunder these so blissful bonds.' He even appears surprised at the 'Duenna Cousin,' whoever she may have been, 'in whose meagre, hunger-bitten philosophy, the religion of young hearts was, from the first, faintly approved of.' We, even at such distance, can explain it without necromancy. Let the Philosopher answer this one question. What figure, at that period, was a Mrs Teufelsdröckh likely to make in polished society? Could she have driven so much as a brassbound Gig,[13] or even a simple iron-spring one? Thou foolish 'absolved Auscultator,' before whom lies no prospect of capital, will any yet known 'religion of young hearts' keep the human kitchen warm? Pshaw! thy divine Blumine, when she 'resigned herself to wed some richer,' shows more philosophy, through but 'a woman of genius,' than thou, a pretended man.

Our readers have witnessed the origin of this Love-mania, and with what royal splendour it waxes, and rises. Let no one ask us to unfold the glories of its dominant state; much less the horrors of its almost instantaneous dissolution. How from such inorganic masses, henceforth madder than ever, as lie in these Bags, can even fragments of a living delineation be organised? Besides, of what profit were it? We view, with a lively pleasure, the gay silk Montgolfier[14] start from the ground, and shoot upwards, cleaving the liquid deeps, till it dwindle to a luminous star: but what is there to look longer on, when once, by natural elasticity, or accident of fire, it has exploded? A hapless air-navigator, plunging, amid torn parachutes, sand-bags, and confused wreck, fast enough into the jaws of the Devil! Suffice it to know that Teufelsdröckh rose into the highest regions of the Empyrean, by a natural parabolic track, and returned thence in a quick perpendicular one. For the rest, let any feeling reader, who has been unhappy enough to do the like, paint it out for himself: considering only that if he, for his perhaps comparatively insignificant mistress, underwent such agonies and fren-

---

[13] See *Past and Present,* "Captains of Industry," n. 9.
[14] Type of hot-air balloon.

zies, what must Teufelsdröckh's have been, with a fire-heart, and for a nonpareil Blumine! We glance merely at the final scene:

'One morning, he found his Morning-star all dimmed and dusky-red; the fair creature was silent, absent, she seemed to have been weeping. Alas, no longer a Morning-star, but a troublous skyey Portent, announcing that the Doomsday had dawned! She said, in a tremulous voice, They were to meet no more.' The thunderstruck Air-sailor is not wanting to himself in this dread hour: but what avails it? We omit the passionate expostulations, entreaties, indignations, since all was vain, and not even an explanation was conceded him; and hasten to the catastrophe. ' "Farewell, then, Madam!" said he, not without sternness, for his stung pride helped him. She put her hand in his, she looked in his face, tears started to her eyes; in wild audacity he clasped her to his bosom; their lips were joined, their two souls, like two dew-drops, rushed into one,—for the first time, and for the last!' Thus was Teufelsdröckh made immortal by a kiss. And then? Why, then—'thick curtains of Night rushed over his soul, as rose the immeasurable Crash of Doom; and through the ruins as of a shivered Universe was he falling, falling, towards the Abyss.'

Chapter VI
Sorrows of Teufelsdröckh

Teufelsdröckh's demeanour thereupon. Turns pilgrim. A last wistful look on native Entepfuhl: Sunset amongst primitive Mountains. Basilisk-glance of the Barouche-and-four. Thoughts on View-hunting. Wanderings and Sorrowings.

We have long felt that, with a man like our Professor, matters must often be expected to take a course of their own; that in so multiplex, intricate a nature, there might be channels, both for admitting and emitting, such as the Psychologist had seldom noted; in short, that on no grand occasion and convulsion, neither in the joy-storm nor in the woe-storm, could you predict his demeanour.

To our less philosophical readers, for example, it is now clear that the so passionate Teufelsdröckh, precipitated through 'a shivered Universe' in this extraordinary way has only one of three things which he can next do: Establish himself in Bedlam; begin writing Santanic Poetry;[1] or blow-out his brains. In the progress towards any of which consummations, do not such readers anticipate extravagance enough; breast-beating, brow-beating (against walls), lion-bellowings of blasphemy and the like, stampings, smitings, breakages of furniture, if not arson itself?

Nowise so does Teufelsdröckh deport him. He quietly lifts his *Pilgerstab* (Pilgrim-staff), 'old business being soon wound-up'; and begins a perambulation and circumambulation of the terraqueous Globe! Curious it is, indeed, how with such vivacity of conception, such intensity of feeling, above all, with these unconscionable habits of Exaggeration in speech, he combines that wonderful stillness of his, that stoicism in external procedure. Thus, if his sudden bereavement, in this matter of the Flower-goddess, is talked of as a real Doomsday and Dissolution of Nature, in which light doubtless it partly appeared to himself, his own nature is nowise dissolved thereby; but rather is compressed closer. For once, as we might say, a Blumine by magic appliances has unlocked that shut heart of his, and its hidden things rush-out tumultuous, bondless, like genii enfranchised from their glass phial: but no sooner are your magic appliances withdrawn, than the strange casket of a heart springs-to again; and perhaps there is now no key extant that will open it; for a Teufelsdröckh, as we remarked, will not love a second time. Singular Diogenes! No sooner has that heart-rending occurrence fairly taken place, than he affects to regard it as a thing natural, of which there is nothing more to be said.

[1] Contemporary term for Byron and his followers.

'One highest hope, seemingly legible in the eyes of an Angel, had recalled him as out of Death-shadows into celestial Life: but a gleam of Tophet passed over the face of his Angel; he was rapt away in whirlwinds, and heard the laughter of Demons. It was a Calenture,[2] adds he, 'whereby the Youth saw green Paradise-groves in the waste Ocean-waters: a lying vision, yet not wholly a lie, for *he* saw it.' But what things soever passed in him, when he ceased to see it; what ragings and despairings so-ever Teufelsdröckh's soul was the scene of, he has the goodness to conceal under a quite opaque cover of Silence. We know it well; the first mad paroxysm past, our brave Gneschen collected his dismembered philosophies, and buttoned himself together; he was meek, silent, or spoke of the weather and the Journals: only by a transient knitting of those shaggy brows, by some deep flash of those eyes, glancing one knew not whether with tear-dew or with fierce fire,—might you have guessed what a Gehenna was within; that a whole Satanic School were spouting, though inaudibly, there. To consume your own choler, as some chimneys consume their own smoke; to keep a whole Satanic School spouting, if it must spout, inaudibly, is a negative yet no slight virtue, nor one of the commonest in these times.

Nevertheless, we will not take upon us to say, that in the strange measure he fell upon, there was not a touch of latent Insanity; whereof indeed the actual condition of these Docu-ments in *Capricornus* and *Aquarius* is no bad emblem. His so unlimited Wanderings, toilsome enough, are without assigned or perhaps assignable aim; internal Unrest seems his sole guid-ance; he wanders, wanders, as if that curse of the Prophet had fallen on him, and he were 'made like unto a wheel.' Doubtless, too, the chaotic nature of these Paper-bags aggravates our obscurity. Quite without note of preparation, for example, we come upon the following slip: 'A peculiar feeling it is that will rise in the Traveller, when turning some hill-range in his desert road, he descries lying far below, embosomed among its groves and green natural bulwarks, and all diminished to a toybox, the

---

[2] A fever said to be common to sailors, in which they imagine the sea to be green fields.

fair Town, where so many souls, as it were seen and yet unseen, are driving their multifarious traffic. Its white steeple is then truly a starward-pointing finger; the canopy of blue smoke seems like a sort of Life-breath: for always, of its own unity, the soul gives unity to whatsoever it looks on with love; thus does the little Dwellingplace of men, in itself a congeries of houses and huts, become for us an individual, almost a person. But what thousand other thoughts unite thereto, if the place has to ourselves been the arena of joyous or mournful experiences; if perhaps the cradle we were rocked in still stands there, if our Loving ones still dwell there, if our Buried ones there slumber!' Does Teufelsdröckh, as the wounded eagle is said to make for its own eyrie, and indeed military deserters, and all hunted outcast creatures, turn as if by instinct in the direction of their birthland,—fly first, in this extremity, towards his native Entepfuhl; but reflecting that there no help awaits him, take only one wistful look from the distance, and then wend elsewhither?

Little happier seems to be his next flight: into the wilds of Nature; as if in her mother-bosom he would seek healing. So at least we incline to interpret the following Notice, separated from the former by some considerable space, wherein, however, is nothing noteworthy:

'Mountains were not new to him; but rarely are Mountains seen in such combined majesty and grace as here. The rocks are of that sort called Primitive by the mineralogists, which always arrange themselves in masses of a rugged, gigantic character; which ruggedness, however, is here tempered by a singular airiness of form, and softness of environment: in a climate favourable to vegetation, the gray cliff, itself covered with lichens, shoots-up through a garment of foliage or verdure; and white, bright cottages, tree-shaded, cluster round the everlasting granite. In fine vicissitude, Beauty alternates with Grandeur: you ride through stony hollows, along strait passes, traversed by torrents, overhung by high walls of rock; now winding amid broken shaggy chasms, and huge fragments; now suddenly emerging into some emerald valley, where the streamlet collects itself into a Lake, and man has again found a fair dwelling, and it seems as if Peace had established herself in the bosom of Strength.

'To Peace, however, in this vortex of existence, can the Son of Time not pretend: still less if some Spectre haunt him from the Past; and the Future is wholly a Stygian Darkness, spectre-bearing. Reasonably might the Wanderer exclaim to himself: Are not the gates of this world's Happiness inexorably shut against thee; hast thou a hope that is not mad? Nevertheless, one may still murmur audibly, or in the original Greek if that suit thee better: "Whoso can look on Death will start at no shadows."

'From such meditations is the Wanderer's attention called outwards; for now the Valley closes-in abruptly, intersected by a huge mountain mass, the stony water-worn ascent of which is not to be accomplished on horseback. Arrived aloft, he finds himself again lifted into the evening sunset light; and cannot but pause, and gaze round him, some moments there. An upland irregular expanse of wold, where valleys in complex branchings are suddenly or slowly arranging their descent towards every quarter of the sky. The mountain-ranges are beneath your feet, and folded together: only the loftier summits look down here and there as on a second plain; lakes also lie clear and earnest in their solitude. No trace of man now visible; unless indeed it were he who fashioned that little visible link of Highway, here, as would seem, scaling the inaccessible, to unite Province with Province. But sun-wards lo you! how it towers sheer up, a world of Mountains, the diadem and centre of the mountain region! A hundred and a hundred savage peaks, in the last light of Day; all glowing, of gold and amethyst, like giant spirits of the wilderness; there in their silence, in their solitude, even as on the night when Noah's Deluge first dried! Beautiful, nay solemn, was the sudden aspect to our Wanderer. He gazed over those stupendous masses with wonder, almost with longing desire; never till this hour had he known Nature, that she was One, that she was his Mother and divine. And as the ruddy glow was fading into clearness in the sky, and the Sun had now departed, a murmur of Eternity and Immensity, of Death and of Life, stole through his soul; and he felt as if Death and Life were one, as if the Earth were not dead, as if the Spirit of the Earth had its throne in that splendour, and his own spirit were therewith holding communion.

'The spell was broken by a sound of carriage-wheels. Emerging from the hidden Northward, to sink soon into the hidden Southward, came a gay Barouche-and-four: it was open; servants and postillions wore wedding-favours: that happy pair, then, had found each other, it was their marriage evening! Few moments brought them near: *Du Himmel!*[3] It was Herr Towgood and——Blumine! With slight unrecognising salutation they passed me; plunged down amid the neighbouring thickets, onwards, to Heaven, and to England; and I, in my friend Richter's words, *I remained alone, behind them, with the Night.*'

Were it not cruel in these circumstances, here might be the place to insert an observation, gleaned long ago from the great *Clothes-Volume*, where it stands with quite other intent: 'Some time before Small-pox was extirpated,' says the Professor, there came a new malady of the spiritual sort on Europe: I mean the epidemic, now endemical, of View-hunting. Poets of old date, being privileged with Senses, had also enjoyed external Nature; but chiefly as we enjoy the crystal cup which holds good or bad liquor for us; that is to say, in silence, or with slight incidental commentary: never, as I compute, till after the *Sorrows of Werter*, was there man found who would say: Come let us make a Description! Having drunk the liquor, come let us eat the glass! Of which endemic the Jenner[4] is unhappily still to seek.' Too true!

We reckon it more important to remark that the Professor's Wanderings, so far as his stoical and cynical envelopment admits us to clear insight, here first take their permanent character, fatuous or not. That Basilisk-glance[5] of the Barouche-and-four seems to have withered-up what little remnant of a purpose may have still lurked in him: Life has become wholly a dark

[3] "Good Heavens!"
[4] Edward Jenner (1749–1823): developed vaccination against small-pox.
[5] A fabulous monster whose very glance was fatal.

labyrinth; wherein, through long years, our Friend, flying from spectres, has to stumble about at random, and naturally with more haste than progress.

Foolish were it in us to attempt following him, even from afar, in this extraordinary world-pilgrimage of his; the simplest record of which, were clear record possible, would fill volumes. Hopeless is the obscurity, unspeakable the confusion. He glides from country to country, from condition to condition; vanishing and re-appearing, no man can calculate how or where. Through all quarters of the world he wanders, and apparently through all circles of society. If in any scene, perhaps difficult to fix geographically, he settles for a time, and forms connexions, be sure he will snap them abruptly asunder. Let him sink out of sight as Private Scholar (*Privatisirender*), living by the grace of God in some European capital, you may next find him as Hadjee[6] in the neighbourhood of Mecca. It is an inexplicable Phantasmagoria, capricious, quick-changing; as if our Traveller, instead of limbs and highways, had transported himself by some wishing-carpet, or Fortunatus' Hat.[7] The whole, too, imparted emblematically, in dim multifarious tokens (as that collection of Street-Advertisements); with only some touch of direct historical notice sparingly interspersed: little light-islets in the world of haze! So that, from this point, the Professor is more of an enigma than ever. In figurative language, we might say he becomes, not indeed a spirit, yet spiritualised, vaporised. Fact unparalleled in Biography: The river of his History, which we have traced from its tiniest fountains, and hoped to see flow onward, with increasing current, into the ocean, here dashes itself over that terrific Lover's Leap; and, as a mad-foaming cataract, flies wholly into tumultuous clouds of spray! Low down it indeed collects again into pools and plashes; yet only at a great distance, and with difficulty, if at all, into a general stream. To cast a glance into certain of those pools and plashes, and trace whither they run, must, for a chapter or two, form the limit of our endeavour.

[6] A Moslem pilgrim.
[7] Allusion to popular folktale in which the hero, Fortunatus, receives a magical cap which takes him to any place he wishes.

For which end doubtless those direct historical Notices, where they can be met with, are the best. Nevertheless, of this sort too there occurs much, which, with our present light, it were questionable to emit. Teufelsdröckh, vibrating everywhere between the highest and the lowest levels, comes into contact with public History itself. For example, those conversations and relations with illustrious Persons, as Sultan Mahmoud, the Emperor Napoleon, and others, are they not as yet rather of a diplomatic character than of a biographic? The Editor, appreciating the sacredness of crowned heads, nay perhaps suspecting the possible trickeries of a Clothes-Philosopher, will eschew this province for the present; a new time may bring new insight and a different duty.

If we ask now, not indeed with what ulterior Purpose, for there was none, yet with what immediate outlooks; at all events, in what mood of mind, the Professor undertook and prosecuted this world-pilgrimage,—the answer is more distinct than favourable. 'A nameless Unrest,' says he, 'urged me forward; to which the outward motion was some momentary lying solace. Whither should I go? My Loadstars were blotted out; in that canopy of grim fire shone no star. Yet forward must I; the ground burnt under me; there was no rest for the sole of my foot. I was alone, alone! Ever too the strong inward longing shaped Fantasms for itself: towards these, one after the other, must I fruitlessly wander. A feeling I had, that for my fever-thirst there was and must be somewhere a healing Fountain. To many fondly imagined Fountains, the Saints' Wells of these days, did I pilgrim; to great Men, to great Cities, to great Events: but found there no healing. In strange countries, as in the well-known; in savage deserts, as in the press of corrupt civilisation, it was ever the same: how could your Wanderer escape from—*his own Shadow*? Nevertheless still Forward! I felt as if in great haste; to do I saw not what. From the depths of my own heart, it called to me, Forwards! The winds and the streams, and all Nature sounded to me, Forwards! *Ach Gott*, I was even, once for all, a Son of Time.'

From which is it not clear that the internal Satanic School was still active enough? He says elsewhere: 'The *Enchiridion of*

Epictetus[8] I had ever with me, often as my sole rational companion; and regret to mention that the nourishment it yielded was trifling.' Thou foolish Teufelsdröckh! How could it else? Hadst thou not Greek enough to understand thus much: *The end of Man is an Action, and not a Thought, though it were the noblest?*

'How I lived?' writes he once: 'Friend, hast thou considered the "rugged all-nourishing Earth," as Sophocles well names her; how she feeds the sparrow on the house-top much more her darling, man? While thou stirrest and livest, thou hast a probability of victual. My breakfast of tea has been cooked by a Tartar woman, with water of the Amur, who wiped her earthen kettle with a horse-tail. I have roasted wild-eggs in the sand of Sahara; I have awakened in Paris *Estrapades* and Vienna *Malzleins,*[9] with no prospect of breakfast beyond elemental liquid. That I had my Living to seek saved me from Dying,— by suicide. In our busy Europe, is there not an everlasting demand for Intellect, in the chemical, mechanical, political, religious, educational, commercial departments? In Pagan countries, cannot one write Fetishes?[10] Living! Little knowest thou what alchemy is in an inventive Soul; how, as with its little finger, it can create provision enough for the body (of a Philosopher); and then, as with both hands, create quite other than provision; namely, spectres to torment itself withal.'

Poor Teufelsdröckh! Flying with Hunger always parallel to him; and a whole Infernal Chase in his rear; so that the countenance of Hunger is comparatively a friend's! Thus must he, in the temper of ancient Cain, or of the modern Wandering Jew,[11]—save only that he feels himself not guilty and but suffering the pains of guilt,—wend to and fro with aimless speed. Thus must he, over the whole surface of the Earth (by footprints), write his *Sorrows of Teufelsdröckh*; even as the great Goethe, in passionate words, had to write his *Sorrows of Werter,* before the spirit freed herself, and he could become a Man. Vain

[8] Maxims of Epictetus, Greek Stoic philosopher of first century A.D.
[9] Estrapade: street in Paris. Malzlein: suburb of Vienna.
[10] An object supposed to have magical properties.
[11] See Book I, Chapter 3, n. 9.

truly is the hope of your swiftest Runner to escape 'from his own Shadow'! Nevertheless, in these sick days, when the Born of Heaven first descries himself (about the age of twenty) in a world such as ours, richer than usual in two things, in Truths grown obsolete, and Trades grown obsolete,—what can the fool think but that it is all a Den of Lies, wherein whoso will not speak Lies and act Lies, must stand idle and despair? Whereby it happens that, for your nobler minds, the publishing of some such Work of Art, in one or the other dialect, becomes almost a necessity. For what is it properly but an Altercation with the Devil, before you begin honestly Fighting him? Your Byron publishes his *Sorrows of Lord George*, in verse and in prose, and copiously otherwise: your Bonaparte represents his *Sorrows of Napoleon* Opera, in an all-too stupendous style; with music of cannon-volleys, and murder-shrieks of a world; his stage-lights are the fires of Conflagration; his rhyme and recitative are the tramp of embattled Hosts and the sound of falling Cities.— Happier is he who, like our Clothes-Philosopher, can write such matter, since it must be written, on the insensible Earth, with his shoe-soles only; and also survive the writing thereof!

Chapter VII
The Everlasting No

Loss of Hope, and of Belief. Profit-and-Loss Philosophy. Teufelsdröckh in his darkness and despair still clings to Truth and follows Duty. Inexpressible pains and fears of Unbelief. Fever-crisis: Protest against the Everlasting No: Baphometic Fire-Baptism.

Under the strange nebulous envelopment, wherein our Professor has now shrouded himself, no doubt but his spiritual nature is nevertheless progressive, and growing: for how can the 'Son of Time,' in any case, stand still? We behold him, through those dim years, in a state of crisis, of transition: his mad Pilgrimings, and general solution into aimless Discontinuity, what is all this but a mad Fermentation; wherefrom, the fiercer it is, the clearer product will one day evolve itself?

Such transitions are ever full of pain: thus the Eagle when he moults is sickly; and, to attain his new beak, must harshly dash-off the old one upon rocks. What Stoicism soever our Wanderer, in his individual acts and motions, may affect, it is clear that there is a hot fever of anarchy and misery raging within; coruscations of which flash out: as, indeed, how could there be other? Have we not seen him disappointed, bemocked of Destiny, through long years? All that the young heart might desire and pray for has been denied; nay, as in the last worst instance, offered and then snatched away. Ever an 'excellent Passivity'; but of useful, reasonable Activity, essential to the former as Food to Hunger, nothing granted: till at length, in this wild Pilgrimage, he must forcibly seize for himself an Activity, though useless, unreasonable. Alas, his cup of bitterness, which had been filling drop by drop, ever since that first 'ruddy morning' in the Hinterschlag Gymnasium, was at the very lip; and then with that poison-drop, of the Towgood-and-Blumine business, it runs over, and even hisses over in a deluge of foam.

He himself says once, with more justice than originality: 'Man is, properly speaking, based upon Hope, he has no other possession but Hope; this world of his is emphatically the Place of Hope.' What, then, was our Professor's possession? We see him, for the present, quite shut-out from Hope; looking not into the golden orient, but vaguely all round into a dim copper firmament, pregnant with earthquake and tornado.

Alas, shut-out from Hope, in a deeper sense than we yet dream of! For, as he wanders wearisomely through this world, he has now lost all tidings of another and higher. Full of religion, or at least of religiosity, as our Friend has since exhibited himself, he hides not that, in those days, he was wholly irreligious: 'Doubt had darkened into Unbelief,' says he; 'shade after shade goes grimly over your soul, till you have the fixed, starless,

Tartarean black.' To such readers as have reflected, what can be called reflecting, on man's life, and happily discovered, in contradiction to much Profit-and-Loss Philosophy,[1] speculative and practical, that Soul is *not* synonymous with Stomach; who understand, therefore, in our Friend's words, 'that, for man's well-being, Faith is properly the one thing needful; how, with it, Martyrs, otherwise weak, can cheerfully endure the shame and the cross; and without it, Worldlings puke-up their sick existence, by suicide, in the midst of luxury': to such it will be clear that, for a pure moral nature, the loss of his religious Belief was the loss of everything. Unhappy young man! All wounds, the crush of long-continued Destitution, the stab of false Friendship and of false Love, all wounds in thy so genial heart, would have healed again, had not its life-warmth been withdrawn. Well might he exclaim, in his wild way: 'Is there no God, then; but at best an absentee God, sitting idle, ever since the first Sabbath, at the outside of his Universe, and *see*ing it go? Has the word Duty no meaning; is what we call Duty no divine Messenger and Guide, but a false earthly Fantasm, made-up of Desire and Fear, of emanations from the Gallows and from Doctor Graham's Celestial-Bed?[2] Happiness of an approving Conscience! Did not Paul of Tarsus, whom admiring men have since named Saint, feel that *he* was "the chief of sinners"; and Nero of Rome, jocund in spirit (*wohlgemuth*), spend much of his time in fiddling? Foolish Wordmonger and Motive-grinder, who in thy Logic-mill hast an earthly mechanism for the Godlike itself, and wouldst fain grind me out Virtue from the husks of Pleasure,[3]—I tell thee, Nay! To the unregenerate Prometheus Vinctus[4] of a man, it is ever the bitterest aggravation of his wretchedness that he is conscious of Virtue, that he feels himself

[1] Carlyle's term for Utilitarianism.
[2] Dr. James Graham (1745–1794) was a famous quack doctor who employed a bed supposed to cure married people of sterility.
[3] Allusion to the Benthamite philosophy which judged the moral value of a law by the amount of pleasure that it produced. With a possible pun on name of James Mill.
[4] *Prometheus Bound*, drama by Aeschylus. Prometheus, who stole fire from heaven and was punished by Zeus, was a favorite romantic hero.

the victim not of suffering only, but of injustice. What then?
Is the heroic inspiration we name Virtue but some Passion; some
bubble of the blood, bubbling in the direction others *profit* by?
I know not: only this I know, If what thou namest Happiness
be our true aim, then are we all astray. With Stupidity and sound
Digestion man may front much. But what, in these dull unima-
ginative days, are the terrors of Conscience to the diseases of the
Liver! Not on Morality, but on Cookery, let us build our stronghold: there brandishing our frying-pan, as censer, let us offer
sweet incense to the Devil, and live at ease on the fat things *he*
has provided for his Elect!'

Thus has the bewildered Wanderer to stand, as so many have
done, shouting question after question into the Sibyl-cave of
Destiny, and receive no Answer but an Echo. It is all a grim
Desert, this once-fair world of his; wherein is heard only the
howling of wild-beasts, or the shrieks of despairing, hate-filled
men; and no Pillar of Cloud by day, and no Pillar of Fire by
night, any longer guides the Pilgrim. To such length has the
spirit of Inquiry carried him. 'But what boots it (*was thut's*)?'
cries he: 'it is but the common lot in this era. Not having come
to spiritual majority prior to the *Siècle de Louis Quinze*,[5] and
not being born purely a Loghead (*Dummkopf*), thou hadst no
other outlook. The whole world is, like thee, sold to Unbelief;
their old Temples of the Godhead, which for long have not been
rainproof, crumble down; and men ask now: Where is the Godhead; our eyes never saw him?'

Pitiful enough were it, for all these wild utterances, to call
our Diogenes wicked. Unprofitable servants as we all are, perhaps at no era of his life was he more decisively the Servant of
Goodness, the Servant of God, than even now when doubting
God's existence. 'One circumstance I note,' says he: 'after all
the nameless woe that Inquiry, which for me, what it is not
always, was genuine Love of Truth, had wrought me, I nevertheless still loved Truth, and would bate no jot of my allegiance
to her. "Truth!" I cried, "though the Heavens crush me for fol-

---

[5] "Century of Louis XV," title of a history by Voltaire and used by
Carlyle to represent the age of rationalism.

lowing her: no Falsehood! though a whole celestial Lubber-land[6] were the price of Apostasy." In conduct it was the same. Had a divine Messenger from the clouds, or miraculous Hand-writing on the wall, convincingly proclaimed to me *This thou shalt do*, with what passionate readiness, as I often thought, would I have done it, had it been leaping into the infernal Fire. Thus, in spite of all Motive-grinders, and Mechanical Profit-and-Loss Philosophies, with the sick ophthalmia and halluci-nation they had brought on, was the Infinite nature of Duty still dimly present to me: living without God in the world, of God's light I was not utterly bereft; if my as yet sealed eyes, with their unspeakable longing, could nowhere see Him, nevertheless in my heart He was present, and His heaven-written Law still stood legible and sacred there.'

Meanwhile, under all these tribulations, and temporal and spiritual destitutions, what must the Wanderer, in his silent soul, have endured! 'The painfullest feeling,' writes he, 'is that of your own Feebleness (*Unkraft*); ever, as the English Milton says, to be weak is the true misery. And yet of your Strength there is and can be no clear feeling, save by what you have prospered in, by what you have done. Between vague wavering Capability and fixed indubitable Performance, what a differ-ence! A certain inarticulate Self-consciousness dwells dimly in us; which only our Works can render articulate and decisively discernible. Our Works are the mirror wherein the spirit first sees its natural lineaments. Hence, too, the folly of that impossi-ble Precept, *Know thyself*; till it be translated into this partially possible one, *Know what thou canst work at*.

'But for me, so strangely unprosperous had I been, the net-result of my Workings amounted as yet simply to—Nothing. How then could I believe in my Strength, when there was as yet no mirror to see it in? Ever did this agitating, yet, as I now perceive, quite frivolous question, remain to me insoluble: Hast thou a certain Faculty, a certain Worth, such even as the most have not; or art thou the completest Dullard of these mod-

---

[6] Land of plenty and luxury.

ern times? Alas, the fearful Unbelief is unbelief in yourself; and how could I believe? Had not my first, last Faith in myself, when even to me the Heavens seemed laid open, and I dared to love, been all-too cruelly belied? The speculative Mystery of Life grew ever more mysterious to me: neither in the practical Mystery had I made the slightest progress, but been everywhere buffeted, foiled, and contemptuously cast out. A feeble unit in the middle of a threatening Infinitude, I seemed to have nothing given me but eyes, whereby to discern my own wretchedness. Invisible yet impenetrable walls, as of Enchantment, divided me from all living: was there, in the wide world, any true bosom I could press trustfully to mine? O Heaven, No, there was none! I kept a lock upon my lips: why should I speak much with that shifting variety of so-called Friends, in whose withered, vain and too-hungry souls Friendship was but an incredible tradition? In such cases, your resource is to talk little, and that little mostly from the Newspapers. Now when I look back, it was a strange isolation I then lived in. The men and women around me, even speaking with me, were but Figures; I had, practically, forgotten that they were alive that they were not merely automatic. In the midst of their crowded streets and assemblages, I walked solitary; and (except as it was my own heart, not another's, that I kept devouring) savage also, as the tiger in his jungle. Some comfort it would have been, could I, like a Faust, have fancied myself tempted and tormented of the Devil; for a Hell, as I imagine, without Life, though only diabolic Life, were more frightful: but in our age of Down-pulling and Disbelief, the very Devil has been pulled down, you cannot so much as believe in a Devil. To me the Universe was all void of Life, of Purpose, of Volition, even of Hostility: it was one huge, dead, immeasurable Steam-engine, rolling on, in its dead indifference, to grind me limb from limb. O, the vast, gloomy, solitary Golgotha, and Mill of Death! Why was the Living banished thither companionless, conscious? Why, if there is no Devil; nay, unless the Devil is your God?'

A prey incessantly to such corrosions, might not, moreover, as the worst aggravation to them, the iron constitution even of a

Teufelsdröckh threaten to fail? We conjecture that he has known sickness; and, in spite of his locomotive habits, perhaps sickness of the chronic sort. Hear this, for example: 'How beautiful to die of broken-heart, on Paper! Quite another thing in practice; every window of your Feeling, even of your Intellect, as it were, begrimed and mud-bespattered, so that no pure ray can enter; a whole Drugshop in your inwards; the fordone soul drowning slowly in quagmires of Disgust!'

Putting all which external and internal miseries together, may we not find in the following sentences, quite in our Professor's still vein, significance enough?[7] 'From Suicide a certain aftershine (*Nachschein*) of Christianity withheld me: perhaps also a certain indolence of character; for, was not that a remedy I had at any time within reach? Often, however, was there a question present to me: Should some one now, at the turning of that corner, blow thee suddenly out of Space, into the other World, or other No-world, by pistol-shot,—how were it? On which ground, too, I often, in sea-storms and sieged cities and other death-scenes, exhibited an imperturbability, which passed, falsely enough, for courage.'

'So had it lasted,' concludes the Wanderer, 'so had it lasted, as in bitter protracted Death-agony, through long years. The heart within me, unvisited by any heavenly dew-drop was smouldering in sulphurous, slow-consuming fire. Almost since earliest memory I had shed no tear; or once only when I, murmuring half-audibly, recited Faust's Death-song, that wild *Selig der den er im Siegesglanze findet* (Happy whom *he* finds in Battle's splendour), and thought that of this last Friend even I was not forsaken, that Destiny itself could not doom me not to die. Having no hope, neither had I any definite fear, were it of Man or of Devil: nay, I often felt as if it might be solacing, could the Arch-Devil himself, though in Tartarean terrors, but rise to me, that I might tell him a little of my mind. And yet, strangely enough, I lived in a continual, indefinite, pining fear; tremulous, pusillanimous, apprehensive of I knew not what; it

---

[7] Carlyle had contemplated suicide at times during the difficult years after leaving the university.

seemed as if all things in the Heavens above and the Earth beneath would hurt me; as if the Heavens and the Earth were but boundless jaws of a devouring monster, wherein I, palpitating, waited to be devoured.

'Full of such humour, and perhaps the miserablest man in the whole French Capital or Suburbs, was I, one sultry Dogday, after much perambulation, toiling along the dirty little *Rue Saint-Thomas de l'Enfer*,[8] among civic rubbish enough, in a close atmosphere, and over pavements hot as Nebuchadnezzar's Furnace; whereby doubtless my spirits were little cheered; when, all at once, there rose a Thought in me, and I asked myself: "What *art* thou afraid of? Wherefore, like a coward, dost thou forever pip and whimper, and go cowering and trembling? Despicable biped! what is the sum-total of the worst that lies before thee? Death? Well, Death; and say the pangs of Tophet too, and all that the Devil and Man may, will or can do against thee! Hast thou not a heart; canst thou not suffer whatsoever it be; and, as a Child of Freedom, though outcast, trample Tophet itself under thy feet, while it consumes thee? Let it come, then; I will meet it and defy it!" And as I so thought, there rushed like a stream of fire over my whole soul; and I shook base Fear away from me forever. I was strong, of unknown strength; a spirit, almost a god. Ever from that time, the temper of my misery was changed: not Fear or whining Sorrow was it, but Indignation and grim fire-eyed Defiance.

'Thus had the EVERLASTING NO (*das ewige Nein*)[9] pealed authoritatively through all the recesses of my Being, of my ME; and then was it that my whole ME stood up, in native God-created majesty, and with emphasis recorded its Protest. Such a Protest, the most important transaction in Life, may that same Indignation and Defiance, in a psychological point of view, be fitly called. The Everlasting No had said: "Behold, thou art

---

[8] Carlyle said that *Sartor* is "symbolical myth all, except that of the incident in the Rue St. Thomas de l'Enfer, which occured quite literally to myself in Leith Walk [Edinburgh], during three weeks of total sleeplessness." Thomas was the doubting disciple. Enfer: "Hell."
[9] In this central passage, the Everlasting No is the amoral, mechanistic universe, not the act of protest by the hero.

fatherless, outcast, and the Universe is mine (the Devil's)"; to which my whole Me now made answer: "*I* am not thine, but Free, and forever hate thee!"

'It is from this hour that I incline to date my Spiritual New-birth, or Baphometic[10] Fire-baptism; perhaps I directly thereupon began to be a Man.'

Chapter VIII
Centre of Indifference

Teufelsdröckh turns now outwardly to the *Not-me*; and finds wholesomer food. Ancient Cities: Mystery of their origin and growth: Invisible inheritances and possessions. Power and virtue of a true Book. Wagram Battlefield: War. Great Scenes beheld by the Pilgrim: Great Events, and Great Men. Napoleon, a divine missionary, preaching *La carrière ouverte aux talens*. Teufelsdröckh at the North Cape: Modern means of self-defence. Gunpowder and duelling. The Pilgrim, despising his miseries, reaches the Centre of Indifference.

Though, after this 'Baphometic Fire-baptism' of his, our Wanderer signifies that his Unrest was but increased; as, indeed, 'Indignation and Defiance,' especially against things in general, are not the most peaceable inmates; yet can the Psychologist surmise that it was no longer a quite hopeless Unrest; that henceforth it had at least a fixed centre to revolve round. For the fire-baptised soul, long so scathed and thunder-riven, here feels its own Freedom, which feeling is its Baphometic Baptism: the citadel of its whole kingdom it has thus gained by assault,

---

[10] Sudden spiritual illumination. A word created by Carlyle from various sources.

and will keep inexpugnable; outwards from which the remaining dominions, not indeed without hard battling, will doubtless by degrees be conquered and pacificated. Under another figure, we might say, if in that great moment, in the *Rue Saint-Thomas de l'Enfer*, the old inward Satanic School was not yet thrown out of doors, it received peremptory judicial notice to quit;— whereby, for the rest, its howl-chantings, Ernulphus-cursings, and rebellious gnashings of teeth, might, in the meanwhile, become only the more tumultuous, and difficult to keep secret.

Accordingly, if we scrutinise these Pilgrimings well, there is perhaps discernible henceforth a certain incipient method in their madness. Not wholly as a Spectre does Teufelsdröckh now storm through the world; at worst as a spectre-fighting Man, nay who will one day be a Spectre-queller. If pilgriming restlessly to so many 'Saints' Wells,' and ever without quenching of his thirst, he nevertheless finds little secular wells, whereby from time to time some alleviation is ministered. In a word, he is now, if not ceasing, yet intermitting to 'eat his own heart'; and clutches round him outwardly on the NOT-ME[1] for wholesomer food. Does not the following glimpse exhibit him in a much more natural state?

'Towns also and Cities, especially the ancient, I failed not to look upon with interest. How beautiful to see thereby, as through a long vista, into the remote Time; to have as it were, an actual section of almost the earliest Past brought safe into the Present, and set before your eyes! There, in that old City, was a live ember of Culinary Fire put down, say only two-thousand years ago; and there, burning more or less triumphantly, with such fuel as the region yielded, it has burnt, and still burns, and thou thyself seest the very smoke thereof. Ah! and the far more mysterious live ember of Vital Fire was then also put down there; and still miraculously burns and spreads; and the smoke and ashes thereof (in these Judgment-Halls and Churchyards), and its bellows-engines (in these Churches), thou still seest; and its flame, looking out from every kind countenance, and every hateful one, still warms thee or scorches thee.

[1] Translation of German transcendentalist term for external world, all that is not mind.

'Of Man's Activity and Attainment the chief results are aeriform, mystic, and preserved in Tradition only: such are his Forms of Government, with the Authority they rest on; his Customs, or Fashions both of Cloth-habits and of Soul-habits; much more his collective stock of Handicrafts, the whole Faculty he has acquired of manipulating Nature: all these things, as indispensable and priceless as they are, cannot in any way be fixed under lock and key, but must flit, spirit-like, on impalpable vehicles, from Father to Son; if you demand sight of them, they are nowhere to be met with. Visible Ploughmen and Hammermen there have been, ever from Cain and Tubalcain downwards: but where does your accumulated Agricultural, Metallurgic, and other Manufacturing SKILL lie warehoused? It transmits itself on the atmospheric air, on the sun's rays (by Hearing and by Vision); it is a thing aeriform, impalpable, of quite spiritual sort. In like manner, ask me not, Where are the LAWS; where is the GOVERNMENT? In vain wilt thou go to Schönbrunn, to Downing Street, to the Palais Bourbon:[2] thou findest nothing there but brick or stone houses, and some bundles of Papers tied with tape. Where, then, is that same cunningly-devised almighty GOVERNMENT of theirs to be laid hands on? Everywhere, yet nowhere: seen only in its works, this too is a thing aeriform, invisible; or if you will, mystic and miraculous. So spiritual (*geistig*) is our whole daily Life: all that we do springs out of Mystery, Spirit, invisible Force; only like a little Cloud-image, or Armida's Palace, air-built, does the Actual body itself forth from the great mystic Deep.

'Visible and tangible products of the Past, again, I reckon-up to the extent of three: Cities, with their Cabinets and Arsenals; then tilled Fields, to either or to both of which divisions Roads with their Bridges, may belong; and thirdly——Books. In which third truly, the last invented, lies a worth far surpassing that of the two others. Wondrous indeed is the virtue of a true Book. Not like a dead city of stones, yearly crumbling, yearly needing repair; more like a tilled field, but then a spiritual field: like a spiritual tree, let me rather say, it stands from year

---

[2] Seats, respectively, of Austrian, English and French governments.

to year, and from age to age (we have Books that already number some hundred-and-fifty human ages); and yearly comes its new produce of leaves (Commentaries, Deductions, Philosophical, Political Systems; or were it only Sermons, Pamphlets, Journalistic Essays), every one of which is talismanic and thaumaturgic, for it can persuade men. O thou who art able to write a Book, which once in the two centuries or oftener there is a man gifted to do, envy not him whom they name City-builder, and inexpressibly pity him whom they name Conqueror or City-burner! Thou too art a Conqueror and Victor; but of the true sort, namely over the Devil: thou too hast built what will outlast all marble and metal, and be a wonder-bringing City of the Mind, a Temple and Seminary and Prophetic Mount, whereto all kindreds of the Earth will pilgrim.—Fool! why journeyest thou wearisomely, in thy antiquarian fervour, to gaze on the stone pyramids of Geeza, or the clay ones of Sacchara? These stand there, as I can tell thee, idle and inert, looking over the Desert, foolishly enough, for the last three-thousand years: but canst thou not open thy Hebrew BIBLE, then, or even Luther's Version thereof?'

No less satisfactory is his sudden appearance not in Battle, yet on some Battle-field; which, we soon gather, must be that of Wagram,[3] so that here, for once, is a certain approximation to distinctiveness of date. Omitting much, let us impart what follows:

'Horrible enough! A whole Marchfeld strewed with shell-splinters, cannon-shot, ruined tumbrils, and dead men and horses; stragglers still remaining not so much as buried. And those red mould heaps: ay, there lie the Shells of Men, out of which all the Life and Virtue has been blown; and now are they swept together and crammed-down out of sight, like blown Egg-shells!—Did Nature, when she bade the Donau bring down his mould-cargoes from the Carinthian and Carpathian Heights, and spread them out here into the softest, richest level,—intend

---

[3] Site of battle in which Napoleon defeated the Hapsburgs (July, 1809). The village of Wagram is located on a plain called the Marchfeld, site of a thirteenth century battle in which Ottocar of Bohemia was slain by Rudolf of Hapsburg.

thee, O Marchfeld, for a corn-bearing Nursery, whereon her children might be nursed; or for a Cockpit, wherein they might the more commodiously be throttled and tattered? Were thy three broad Highways, meeting here from the ends of Europe, made for Ammunition-wagons, then? Were thy Wagrams and Stillfrieds but so many ready-built Casemates, wherein the house of Hapsburg might batter with artillery, and with artillery be battered? König Ottokar, amid younder hillocks, dies under Rodolf's truncheon; here Kaiser Franz falls a-swoon under Napoleon's: within which five centuries, to omit the others, how has thy breast, fair Plain, been defaced and defiled! The greensward is torn-up and trampled-down; man's fond care of it, his fruit-trees, hedge-rows, and pleasant dwellings, blown away with gunpowder; and the kind seedfield lies a desolate, hideous Place of Sculls.—Nevertheless, Nature is at work; neither shall these Powder-Devilkins with their utmost devilry gainsay her: but all that gore and carnage will be shrouded-in, absorbed into manure; and next year the Marchfeld will be green, nay greener. Thrifty unwearied Nature, ever out of our great waste educing some little profit of thy own,—how dost thou, from the very carcass of the Killer, bring Life for the Living!

'What, speaking in quite unofficial language, is the net-purport and upshot of war? To my own knowledge, for example, there dwell and toil, in the British village of Dumdrudge,[4] usually some five-hundred souls. From these, by certain "Natural Enemies" of the French, there are successively selected, during the French war, say thirty able-bodied men: Dumdrudge, at her own expense, has suckled and nursed them: she has, not without difficulty and sorrow, fed them up to manhood, and even trained them to crafts, so that one can weave, another build, another hammer, and the weakest can stand under thirty stone avoirdupois. Nevertheless, amid much weeping and swearing, they are selected; all dressed in red; and shipped away, at the public charges, some two-thousand miles, or say only to the south of Spain,[5] and fed there till wanted. And now to that same

---

[4] "Dumb-drudge," Carlyle's term for the oppressed rural population.
[5] Site of Peninsular War (1808–1814) in which the British and Spanish fought against Napoleon.

spot, in the south of Spain, are thirty similar French artisans, from a French Dumdrudge, in like manner wending: till at length, after infinite effort, the two parties come into actual juxtaposition; and Thirty stands fronting Thirty, each with a gun in his hand. Straightway the word "Fire!" is given; and they blow the souls out of one another; and in place of sixty brisk useful craftsmen, the world has sixty dead carcasses, which it must bury, and anew shed tears for. Had these men any quarrel? Busy as the Devil is, not the smallest! They lived far enough apart; were the entirest strangers; nay, in so wide a Universe, there was even, unconsciously, by Commerce, some mutual helpfulness between them. How then? Simpleton! their Governors had fallen-out; and, instead of shooting one another, had the cunning to make these poor blockheads shoot.—Alas, so is it in Deutschland, and hitherto in all other lands; still as of old, "what devilry soever Kings do, the Greeks must pay the piper!"—In that fiction of the English Smollet, it is true, the final Cessation of War is perhaps prophetically shadowed forth; where the two Natural Enemies, in person, take each a Tobacco-pipe, filled with Brimstone; light the same, and smoke in one another's faces, till the weaker gives in: but from such predicted Peace-Era, what blood-filled trenches, and contentious centuries, may still divide us!'

Thus can the Professor, at least in lucid intervals, look away from his own sorrows, over the many-coloured world, and pertinently enough note what is passing there. We may remark, indeed, that for the matter of spiritual culture, if for nothing else, perhaps few periods of his life were richer than this. Internally, there is the most momentous instructive Course of Practical Philosophy, with Experiments, going on; towards the right comprehension of which his Peripatetic habits, favourable to Meditation, might help him rather than hinder. Externally, again, as he wanders to and fro, there are, if for the longing heart little substance, yet for the seeing eye sights enough: in these so boundless Travels of his, granting that the Satanic School was even partially kept down, what an incredible knowledge of our Planet, and its Inhabitants and their Works, that is to say, of all knowable things, might not Teufelsdröckh acquire!

'I have read in most Public Libraries,' says he, 'including those of Constantinople and Samarcand: in most Colleges, except the Chinese Mandarin ones, I have studied, or seen that there was no studying. Unknown Languages have I oftenest gathered from their natural repertory, the Air, by my organ of Hearing; Statistics, Geographics, Topographics came, through the Eye, almost of their own accord. The ways of Man, how he seeks food, and warmth, and protection for himself, in most regions, are ocularly known to me. Like the great Hadrian,[6] I meted-out much of the terraqueous Globe with a pair of Compasses that belonged to myself only.

'Of great Scenes why speak? Three summer days, I lingered reflecting, and even composing (*dichtete*), by the Pine-chasms of Vaucluse; and in that clear Lakelet moistened my bread. I have sat under the Palm-trees of Tadmor; smoked a pipe among the ruins of Babylon. The great Wall of China I have seen; and can testify that it is of gray brick, coped and covered with granite, and shows only second-rate masonry.—Great Events, also, have not I witnessed? Kings sweated-down (*ausgemergelt*) into Berlin-and-Milan Customhouse-Officers;[7] the World well won, and the World well lost; oftener than once a hundred-thousand individuals shot (by each other) in one day. All kindreds and peoples and nations dashed together, and shifted and shovelled into heaps, that they might ferment there, and in time unite. The birth-pangs of Democracy, wherewith convulsed Europe was groaning in cries that reached Heaven, could not escape me.

'For great Men I have ever had the warmest predilection; and can perhaps boast that few such in this era have wholly escaped me. Great Men are the inspired (speaking and acting) Texts of that divine BOOK OF REVELATIONS, where of a Chapter is

---

[6] This Roman Emperor traveled extensively through his dominions.
[7] In 1806 Napoleon issued the Berlin and Milan decrees ordering the seizure of British exports. The kings of Europe were compelled to enforce these trade restrictions.

completed from epoch to epoch, and by some named HISTORY; to which inspired Texts your numerous talented men, and your innumerable untalented men, are the better or worse exegetic Commentaries, and wagonload of too-stupid, heretical or orthodox, weekly Sermons. For my study, the inspired Texts themselves! Thus did not I, in very early days, having disguised me as tavern-waiter, stand behind the field-chairs, under that shady Tree at Treisnitz by the Jena Highway; waiting upon the great Schiller and greater Goethe; and hearing what I have not forgotten. For——'

——But at this point the Editor recalls his principle of caution, some time ago laid down, and must suppress much. Let not the sacredness of Laurelled, still more, of Crowned Heads, be tampered with. Should we, at a future day, find circumstances altered, and the time come for Publication, then may these glimpses into the privacy of the Illustrious be conceded; which for the present were little better than treacherous, perhaps traitorous Eavesdroppings. Of Lord Byron, therefore, of Pope Pius, Emperor Tarakwang, and the 'White Water-roses' (Chinese Carbonari) with their mysteries, no notice here! Of Napoleon himself we shall only, glancing from afar, remark that Teufelsdröckh's relation to him seems to have been of very varied character. At first we find our poor Professor on the point of being shot as a spy; then taken into private conversation, even pinched on the ear, yet presented with no money; at last indignantly dismissed, almost thrown out of doors, as an 'Ideologist.' 'He himself,' says the Professor, 'was among the completest Ideologists, at least Ideopraxists: in the Idea (*in der Idee*) he lived, moved and fought. The man was a Divine Missionary, though unconscious of it; and preached, through the cannon's throat, that great doctrine, *La carrière ouverte aux talens* (The Tools to him that can handle them), which is our ultimate Political Evangel, wherein alone can liberty lie. Madly enough he preached, it is true, as Enthusiasts and first Missionaries are wont, with imperfect utterance, amid much frothy rant; yet as articulately perhaps as the case admitted. Or call him, if you will, an American Backwoodsman, who had to fell unpenetrated forests, and battle with innumerable wolves, and did not entirely forbear strong liquor, rioting, and even theft; whom, notwithstanding, the peaceful Sower will follow, and, as he cuts the boundless harvest, bless.'

More legitimate and decisively authentic is Teufelsdröckh's appearance and emergence (we know not well whence) in the solitude of the North Cape, on that June Midnight. He has a 'light-blue Spanish cloak' hanging round him, as his 'most commodious, principal, indeed sole upper-garment'; and stands there, on the World-promontory, looking over the infinite Brine, like a little blue Belfry (as we figure), now motionless indeed, yet ready, if stirred, to ring quaintest changes.

'Silence as of death,' writes he; 'for Midnight, even in the Arctic latitudes, has its character: nothing but the granite cliffs ruddy-tinged, the peaceable gurgle of that slow-heaving Polar Ocean, over which in the utmost North the great Sun hangs low and lazy, as if he too were slumbering. Yet is his cloud-couch wrought of crimson and cloth-of-gold; yet does his light stream over the mirror of waters, like a tremulous fire-pillar, shooting downwards to the abyss, and hide itself under my feet. In such moments, Solitude also is invaluable; for who would speak, or be looked on, when behind him lies all Europe and Africa, fast asleep, except the watchmen; and before him the silent Immensity, and Palace of the Eternal, whereof our Sun is but a porch-lamp?

'Nevertheless, in this solemn moment comes a man, or monster, scrambling from among the rock-hollows; and, shaggy, huge as the Hyperborean Bear, hails me in Russian speech: most probably, therefore, a Russian Smuggler. With courteous brevity, I signify my indifference to contraband trade, my humane intentions, yet strong wish to be private. In vain: the monster, counting doubtless on his superior stature, and minded to make sport for himself, or perhaps profit, were it with murder, continues to advance; ever assailing me with his importunate train-oil breath; and now has advanced, till we stand both on the verge of the rock, the deep Sea rippling greedily down below. What argument will avail? On the thick Hyperborean, cherubic reasoning, seraphic eloquence were lost. Prepared for such extremity, I, deftly enough, whisk aside one step; draw out, from my interior reservoirs, a sufficient Birmingham Horse-pistol, and say, "Be so obliging as retire, Friend (*Er ziehe sich zurück, Freund*), and with promptitude!" This logic even the Hyperborean understands: fast enough, with apologetic, petitionary growl, he sidles off; and, except for suicidal as well as homicidal purposes, need not return.

'Such I hold to be the genuine use of Gunpowder: that it makes all men alike tall. Nay, if thou be cooler, cleverer than I, if thou have more *Mind*, though all but no *Body* whatever, then canst thou kill me first, and art the taller. Hereby, at last, is the Goliath powerless, and the David resistless; savage Animalism is nothing, inventive Spiritualism is all.

'With respect to Duels, indeed, I have my own ideas. Few things, in this so surprising world, strike me with more surprise. Two little visual Spectra of men, hovering with insecure enough cohesion in the midst of the UNFATHOMABLE, and to dissolve therein, at any rate, very soon,—make pause at the distance of twelve paces asunder; whirl round; and, simultaneously by the cunningest mechanism, explode one another into Dissolution; and off-hand become Air, and Non-extant! Deuce on it (*verdammt*), the little spitfires!—Nay, I think with old Hugo von Trimberg: "God must needs laugh outright, could such a thing be, to see his wondrous Manikins here below." '

But amid these specialties, let us not forget the great generality, which is our chief quest here: How prospered the inner man of Teufelsdröckh under so much outward shifting? Does Legion still lurk in him, though repressed; or has he exorcised that Devil's Brood? We can answer that the symptoms continue promising. Experience is the grand spiritual Doctor; and with him Teufelsdröckh has been long a patient, swallowing many a bitter bolus. Unless our poor Friend belong to the numerous class of Incurables, which seems not likely, some cure will doubtless be effected. We should rather say that Legion, or the Satanic School, was now pretty well extirpated and cast out, but next to nothing introduced in its room; whereby the heart remains, for the while, in a quiet but no comfortable state.

'At length, after so much roasting,' thus writes our Auto-biographer, 'I was what you might name calcined. Pray only that it be not rather, as is the more frequent issue, reduced to a *caput-mortuum*![8] But in any case, by mere dint of practice, I had grown familiar with many things. Wretchedness was still wretched; but I could now partly see through it, and despise it. Which highest mortal, in this inane Existence, had I not found a Shadow-hunter, or Shadow-hunted; and, when I looked through his brave garnitures, miserable enough? Thy wishes have all been sniffed aside, thought I: but what, had they even been all granted! Did not the Boy Alexander weep because he had not two Planets to conquer; or a whole Solar System; or after that, a whole Universe? *Ach Gott*, when I gazed into these Stars, have they not looked-down on me as if with pity, from their serene spaces; like Eyes glistening with heavenly tears over the little lot of man! Thousands of human generations, all as noisy as our own, have been swallowed-up of Time, and there remains no wreck of them any more; and Arcturus and Orion and Sirius and the Pleiades are still shining in their courses, clear and young, as when the Shepherd first noted them in the plain of Shinar. Pshaw! what is this paltry little Dog-cage[9] of an Earth; what are thou that sittest whining there? Thou art still Nothing, Nobody: true; but who, then, is Something, Some-body? For thee the Family of Man has no use; it rejects thee; thou art wholly as a dissevered limb: so be it; perhaps it is better so!'

Too-heavy-laden Teufelsdröckh! Yet surely his bands are loosening; one day he will hurl the burden far from him, and bound forth free and with a second youth.

'This,' says our Professor, 'was the CENTRE OF INDIFFER-ENCE I had now reached; through which whoso travels from the Negative Pole to the Positive must necessarily pass.'[10]

[8] "Death's head," term for worthless residue left after a chemical process.
[9] A wheel-like cage into which a dog was put to turn the spit for roasting meat.
[10] The Centre of Indifference is the midpoint of a magnet at which the attractive force of each pole is balanced.

Chapter IX
The Everlasting Yea

Temptations in the Wilderness: Victory over the Tempter.
Annihilation of Self. Belief in God, and love to Man. The
Origin of Evil, a problem ever requiring to be solved anew:
Teufelsdröckh's solution. Love of Happiness a vain whim:
A Higher in man than Love of Happiness. The Everlasting
Yea. Worship of Sorrow. Voltaire: his task now finished.
Conviction worthless, impossible, without Conduct. The true
Ideal, the Actual: Up and work!

'Temptations in the Wilderness!' exclaims Teufelsdröckh:
'Have we not all to be tried with such? Not so easily can the old
Adam, lodged in us by birth, be dispossessed. Our Life is com-
passed round with Necessity; yet is the meaning of Life itself
no other than freedom, than Voluntary Force: thus have we a
warfare; in the beginning, especially, a hard-fought battle. For
the God-given mandate, *Work thou in Welldoing*, lies mysteriously written, in Promethean Prophetic Characters, in our
hearts; and leaves us no rest, night or day, till it be deciphered
and obeyed; till it burn forth, in our conduct, a visible, acted
Gospel of Freedom. And as the clay-given mandate, *Eat thou
and be filled*, at the same time persuasively proclaims itself
through every nerve,—must not there be a confusion, a contest,
before the better Influence can become the upper?

To me nothing seems more natural than that the Son of Man,
when such God-given mandate first prophetically stirs within
him, and the Clay must now be vanquished or vanquish,—
should be carried of the spirit into grim Solitudes, and there
fronting the Tempter do grimmest battle with him; defiantly

setting him at naught, till he yield and fly. Name it as we choose: with or without visible Devil, whether in the natural Desert of rocks and sands, or in the populous moral Desert of selfishness and baseness,—to such Temptation are we all called. Unhappy if we are not! Unhappy if we are but Half-men, in whom that divine handwriting has never blazed forth, all-subduing, in true sun-splendour; but quivers dubiously amid meaner lights: or smoulders, in dull pain, in darkness, under earthly vapours!—Our Wilderness is the wide World in an Atheistic Century; our Forty Days are long years of suffering and fasting: nevertheless, to these also comes an end. Yes, to me also was given, if not Victory, yet the consciousness of Battle, and the resolve to persevere therein while life or faculty is left. To me also, entangled in the enchanted forests, demon-peopled, doleful of sight and of sound, it was given after weariest wanderings, to work out my way into the higher sunlight slopes—of that Mountain which has no summit, or whose summit is in Heaven only!'

He says elsewhere, under a less ambitious figure; as figures are, once for all, natural to him: 'Has not thy Life been that of most sufficient men (*tüchtigen Männer*) thou hast known in this generation? An outflush of foolish young Enthusiasm, like the first fallow-crop, wherein are as many weeds as valuable herbs: this all parched away, under the Droughts of practical and spiritual Unbelief, as Disappointment, in thought and act, often-repeated gave rise to Doubt, and Doubt gradually settled into Denial! If I have had a second-crop, and now see the perennial greensward, and sit under umbrageous cedars, which defy all Drought (and Doubt); herein too, be the Heavens praised, I am not without examples, and even exemplars.'

So that, for Teufelsdröckh also, there has been a 'glorious revolution': these mad shadow-hunting and shadow-hunted Pilgrimings of his were but some purifying 'Temptation in the Wilderness,' before his apostolic work (such as it was) could begin; which Temptation is now happily over, and the Devil once more worsted! Was 'that high moment in the *Rue de l'Enfer*,' then, properly the turning-point of the battle; when the

179

Fiend said, *Worship me, or be torn in shreds*; and was answered valiantly with an *Apage Satana?*[1]—Singular Teufelsdröckh, would thou hadst told thy singular story in plain words! But it is fruitless to look there, in those Paper-bags, for such. Nothing but innuendoes, figurative crotchets: a typical Shadow, fitfully wavering prophetico-satiric; no clear logical Picture. 'How paint to the sensual eye,' asks he once, 'what passes in the Holy-of-Holies of Man's Soul; in what words, known to these profane times, speak even afar-off of the unspeakable?' We ask in turn: Why perplex these times, profane as they are, with needless obscurity, by omission and by commission? Not mystical only is our Professor, but whimsical; and involves himself, now more than ever, in eye-bewildering *chiaroscuro*. Successive glimpses, here faithfully imparted, our more gifted readers must endeavour to combine for their own behoof.

He says: 'The hot Harmattan wind had raged itself out; its howl went silent within me; and the long-deafened soul could now hear. I paused in my wild wanderings; and sat me down to wait, and consider; for it was as if the hour of change drew nigh. I seemed to surrender, to renounce utterly, and say: Fly, then, false shadows of Hope; I will chase you no more, I will believe you no more. And ye too, haggard spectres of Fear, I care not for you; ye too are all shadows and a lie. Let me rest here: for I am way-weary and life-weary; I will rest here, were it but to die: to die or to live is alike to me; alike insignificant.'—And again: 'Here, then, as I lay in that CENTRE OF INDIFFERENCE; cast, doubtless by benignant upper Influence, into a healing sleep, the heavy dreams rolled gradually away, and I awoke to a new Heaven and a new Earth. The first preliminary moral Act, Annihilation of Self (*Selbst-tödtung*), had been happily accomplished; and my mind's eyes were now unsealed, and its hands ungyved.'

Might we not also conjecture that the following passage refers to his Locality, during this same 'healing sleep'; that his Pilgrim-staff lies cast aside here, on 'the high table-land'; and indeed that the repose is already taking wholesome effect on him? If it

[1] "Get thee hence, Satan." Matthew, iv, 10.

180

were not that the tone, in some parts, has more of riancy, even of levity, than we could have expected! However, in Teufelsdröckh, there is always the strangest Dualism: light dancing, with guitar-music, will be going on in the fore-court, while by fits from within comes the faint whimpering of woe and wail. We transcribe the piece entire.

'Beautiful it was to sit there, as in my skyey Tent, musing and meditating; on the high table-land, in front of the Mountains; over me, as roof, the azure Dome, and around me, for walls, four azure-flowing curtains,—namely, of the Four azure Winds, on whose bottom-fringes also I have seen gilding. And then to fancy the fair Castles that stood sheltered in these Mountain hollows; with their green flower-lawns, and white dames and damosels, lovely enough: or better still, the straw-roofed Cottages, wherein stood many a Mother baking bread, with her children round her:—all hidden and protectingly folded-up in the valley-folds; yet there and alive, as sure as if I beheld them. Or to see, as well as fancy, the nine Towns and Villages, that lay round my mountain-seat, which, in still weather, were wont to speak to me (by their steeple-bells) with metal tongue; and, in almost all weather, proclaimed their vitality by repeated Smoke-clouds; whereon, as on a culinary horologe, I might read the hour of the day. For it was the smoke of cookery, as kind housewives at morning, midday, eventide, were boiling their husbands' kettles; and ever a blue pillar rose up into the air, successively or simultaneously, from each of the nine, saying, as plainly as smoke could say: Such and such a meal is getting ready here. Not uninteresting! For you have the whole Borough, with all its love-makings and scandal-mongeries, contentions and contentments, as in miniature, and could cover it all with your hat.—If, in my wide Wayfarings, I had learned to look into the business of the World in its details, here perhaps was the place for combining it into general propositions, and deducing inferences therefrom.

'Often also could I see the black Tempest marching in anger through the Distance: round some Schreckhorn, as yet grim-blue, would the eddying vapour gather, and there tumultuously eddy, and flow down like a mad witch's hair; till, after a space, it vanished, and, in the clear sunbeam, your Schreckhorn stood smiling grim-white, for the vapour had held snow. How thou fermentest and elaboratest, in thy great fermenting-vat and laboratory of an Atmosphere, of a World, O Nature!—Or what is Nature? Ha! why do I not name thee GOD? Art not thou the "Living Garment of God"? O Heavens, is it, in very deed, HE, then, that ever speaks through thee; that lives and loves in thee, that lives and loves in me?

'Fore-shadows, call them rather fore-splendours, of that Truth, and Beginning of Truths, fell mysteriously over my soul. Sweeter than Dayspring to the Shipwrecked in Nova Zembla; ah, like the mother's voice to her little child that strays bewildered, weeping, in unknown tumults; like soft streamings of celestial music to my too-exasperated heart, came that Evangel. The Universe is not dead and demoniacal, a charnel-house with spectres; but godlike, and my Father's!

'With other eyes, too, could I now look upon my fellow man: with an infinite Love, an infinite Pity. Poor, wandering, wayward man! Art thou not tried, and beaten with stripes, even as I am? Ever, whether thou bear the royal mantle or the beggar's gabardine, art thou not so weary, so heavy-laden; and thy Bed of Rest is but a Grave. O my Brother, my Brother, why cannot I shelter thee in my bosom, and wipe away all tears from thy eyes!—Truly, the din of many-voiced Life, which, in this solitude, with the mind's organ, I could hear, was no longer a maddening discord, but a melting one; like inarticulate cries, and sobbings of a dumb creature, which in the ear of Heaven are prayers. The poor Earth, with her poor joys, was now my needy Mother, not my cruel Stepdame; Man, with his so mad Wants and so mean Endeavours, had become the dearer to me; and even for his sufferings and his sins, I now first named him Brother. Thus was I standing in the porch of that "*Sanctuary of Sorrow*"; by strange, steep ways had I too been guided thither; and ere long its sacred gates would open, and the "*Divine Depth of Sorrow*" lie disclosed to me.'

The Professor says, he here first got eye on the Knot that had been strangling him, and straightway could unfasten it, and was free. 'A vain interminable controversy,' writes he, 'touching what is at present called Origin of Evil, or some such thing, arises in every soul, since the beginning of the world; and in every soul, that would pass from idle Suffering into actual Endeavouring, must first be put an end to. The most, in our time, have to go content with a simple, incomplete enough Suppression of this controversy; to a few some Solution of it is indispensable. In every new era, too, such Solution comes-out in different terms; and ever the Solution of the last era has become obsolete, and is found unserviceable. For it is man's nature to change his Dialect from century to century; he cannot help it though he would. The authentic *Church-Catechism* of our present century has not yet fallen into my hands: meanwhile, for my own private behoof, I attempt to elucidate the matter so. Man's Unhappiness as I construe, comes of his Greatness; it is because there is an Infinite in him, which with all his cunning he cannot quite bury under the Finite. Will the whole Finance Ministers and Upholsterers and Confectioners of modern Europe undertake, in joint-stock company, to make one Shoeblack HAPPY? They cannot accomplish it, above an hour or two: for the Shoeblack also has a Soul quite other than his Stomach; and would require, if you consider it, for his permanent satisfaction and saturation, simply this allotment, no more, and no less: *God's infinite Universe altogether to himself,* therein to enjoy infinitely, and fill every wish as fast as it rose Oceans of Hochheimer,[2] a Throat like that of Ophiuchus:[3] speak not of them; to the infinite Shoeblack they are as nothing. No sooner is your ocean filled, than he grumbles that it might have been of better vintage. Try him with half of a Universe, of an Omnipotence, he sets to quarrelling with the proprietor of the other half, and declares himself the most maltreated of men.——Always there is a black spot in our sunshine: it is even, as I said, the *Shadow of Ourselves.*

'But the whim we have of Happiness is somewhat thus. By certain valuations, and averages, of our own striking, we come upon some sort of average terrestrial lot; this we fancy belongs to us by nature, and of indefeasible right. It is simple payment of our wages, of our deserts; requires neither thanks nor complaint; only such *overplus* as there may be do we account Hap-

[2] A German wine.
[3] The serpent in the constellation known as Serpentarius.

piness; any *deficit* again is Misery. Now consider that we have the valuation of our own deserts ourselves, and what a fund of Self-conceit there is in each of us,—do you wonder that the balance should so often dip the wrong way, and many a Blockhead cry: See there, what a payment; was ever worthy gentlemen so used!—I tell thee, Blockhead, it all comes of thy Vanity; of what thou *fanciest* those same deserts of thine to be. Fancy that thou deservest to be hanged (as is most likely), thou wilt feel it happiness to be only shot: fancy that thou deservest to be hanged in a hair-halter, it will be a luxury to die in hemp.

'So true is it, what I then said, that *the Fraction of Life can be increased in value not so much by increasing your Numerator as by lessening your Denominator.* Nay, unless my Algebra deceive me, *Unity* itself divided by *Zero* will give *Infinity.* Make thy claim of wages a zero, then; thou hast the world under thy feet. Well did the Wisest of our time[4] write: "It is only with Renunciation (*Entsagen*) that Life, properly speaking, can be said to begin."

'I asked myself: What is this that, ever since earliest years, thou hast been fretting and fuming, and lamenting and self-tormenting, on account of? Say it in a word: is it not because thou art not HAPPY? Because the THOU (sweet gentleman) is not sufficiently honoured, nourished, soft-bedded, and lovingly cared-for? Foolish soul! What Act of Legislature was there that *thou* shouldst be Happy? A little while ago thou hadst no right to *be* at all. What if thou wert born and predestined not to be Happy, but to be Unhappy! Art thou nothing other than a Vulture, then, that fliest through the Universe seeking after somewhat to *eat*; and shrieking dolefully because carrion enough is not given thee? Close thy *Byron*; open thy *Goethe*.'

'*Es leuchtet mir ein*, I see a glimpse of it!' cries he elsewhere: 'there is in man a HIGHER than Love of Happiness: he can do without Happiness, and instead thereof find Blessedness! Was it not to preach-forth this same HIGHER that sages and martyrs, the Poet and the Priest, in all times, have spoken and suffered; bearing testimony, through life and through death, of the Godlike that is in Man, and how in the Godlike only has he Strength

4 Goethe, in *Wilhelm Meister*.

and Freedom? Which God-inspired Doctrine art thou also honoured to be taught; O Heavens! and broken with manifold merciful Afflictions, even till thou become contrite, and learn it! O, thank thy Destiny for these; thankfully bear what yet remain: thou hadst need of them; the Self in thee needed to be annihilated. By benignant fever-paroxysms is Life rooting out the deep-seated chronic Disease, and triumphs over Death. On the roaring billows of Time, thou art not engulfed, but borne aloft into the azure of Eternity. Love not Pleasure; love God. This is the EVERLASTING YEA, wherein all contradiction is solved: wherein whoso walks and works, it is well with him.'

And again: 'Small is it that thou canst trample the Earth with its injuries under thy feet, as old Greek Zeno[5] trained thee; thou canst love the Earth while it injures thee, and even because it injures thee; for this a Greater than Zeno was needed, and he too was sent. Knowest thou that "*Worship of Sorrow*"? The Temple thereof, founded some eighteen centuries ago, now lies in ruins, overgrown with jungle, the habitation of doleful creatures: nevertheless, venture forward; in a low crypt, arched out of falling fragments, thou findest the Altar still there, and its sacred Lamp perennially burning.'

Without pretending to comment on which strange utterances, the Editor will only remark, that there lies beside them much of a still more questionable character; unsuited to the general apprehension; nay wherein he himself does not see his way. Nebulous disquisitions on Religion, yet not without bursts of splendour; on the 'perennial continuance of Inspiration'; on Prophecy; that there are 'true Priests, as well as Baal-Priests,[6] in our own day': with more of the like sort. We select some fractions, by way of finish to this farrago.

'Cease, my much-respected Herr von Voltaire,' thus apostrophises the Professor: 'shut thy sweet voice; for the task appointed thee seems finished. Sufficiently hast thou demonstrated this proposition, considerable or otherwise: That the Mythus of the Christian Religion looks not in the eighteenth century as it did in the eighth. Alas, were thy six-and-thirty quartos, and the six-and-thirty thousand other quartos and folios, and flying

[5] Greek Stoic philosopher of third century B.C.
[6] False priests.

sheets or reams, printed before and since on the same subject, all
needed to convince us of so little! But what next? Wilt thou
help us to embody the divine Spirit of that Religion in a new
Mythus, in a new vehicle and vesture, that our Souls, otherwise too like perishing, may live? What! thou hast no faculty in
that kind? Only a torch for burning, no hammer for building?
Take our thanks, then, and——thyself away.

Meanwhile what are antiquated Mythuses to me? Or is the
God present, felt in my own heart, a thing which Herr von
Voltaire will dispute out of me; or dispute into me? To the
"*Worship of Sorrow*" ascribe what origin and genesis thou
pleasest, *has* not that Worship originated, and been generated;
is it not *here*? Feel it in thy heart, and then say whether it is of
God! This is Belief; all else is Opinion,—for which latter whoso
will, let him worry and be worried.'

'Neither,' observes he elsewhere, 'shall ye tear-out one another's eyes, struggling over "Plenary Inspiration," and suchlike: try rather to get a little even Partial Inspiration, each of
you for himself. One BIBLE I know, of whose Plenary Inspiration doubt is not so much as possible; nay with my own eyes I
saw the God's-Hand writing it: thereof all other Bibles are but
Leaves,—say, in Picture-Writing to assist the weaker faculty.'

Or, to give the wearied reader relief, and bring it to an end,
let him take the following perhaps more intelligible passage:

'To me, in this our life,' says the Professor, 'which is an
internecine warfare with the Time-spirit, other warfare seems
questionable. Hast thou in any way a Contention with thy
brother, I advise thee, think well what the meaning thereof is.
If thou gauge it to the bottom, it is simply this: "Fellow, see!
thou art taking more than thy share of Happiness in the world,
something from *my* share: which, by the Heavens, thou shalt
not; nay I will fight three rather."—Alas, and the whole lot to
be divided is such a beggarly matter, truly a "feast of shells,"
for the substance has been spilled out: not enough to quench
one Appetite; and the collective human species clutching at
them!—Can we not, in all such cases, rather say: "Take it, thou
too-ravenous individual; take that pitiful additional fraction of a
share, which I reckoned mine, but which thou so wantest; take
it with a blessing: would to Heaven I had enough for thee!"—

If Fichte's *Wissenschaftslehre*[7] be, "to a certain extent, Applied Christianity," surely to a still greater extent, so is this. We have here not a Whole Duty of Man, yet a Half Duty, namely the Passive half: could we but do it, as we can demonstrate it!

'But indeed Conviction, were it never so excellent, is worthless till it convert itself into Conduct. Nay properly Conviction is not possible till then; inasmuch as all Speculation is by nature endless, formless, a vortex amid vortices: only by a felt indubitable certainty of Experience does it find any centre to revolve round, and so fashion itself into a system. Most true is it, as a wise man teaches us, that "Doubt of any sort cannot be removed except by Action." On which ground, too, let him who gropes painfully in darkness or uncertain light, and prays vehemently that the dawn may ripen into day, lay this other precept well to heart, which to me was of invaluable service: *"Do the Duty which lies nearest thee,"* which thou knowest to be a Duty! Thy second Duty will already have become clearer.

'May we not say, however, that the hour of Spiritual Enfranchisement is even this: When your Ideal World, wherein the whole man has been dimly struggling and inexpressibly languishing to work, becomes revealed, and thrown open; and you discover, with amazement enough, like the Lothario in *Wilhelm Meister*, that your "America is here or nowhere"? The Situation that has not its Duty, its Ideal, was never yet occupied by man. Yes here, in this poor, miserable, hampered, despicable Actual, wherein thou even now standest, here or nowhere is thy Ideal: work it out therefrom; and working, believe, live be free. Fool! the Ideal is in thyself, the impediment too is in thyself: thy Condition is but the stuff thou art to shape that same Ideal out of: what matters whether such stuff be of this sort or that, so the Form thou give it be heroic, be poetic? O thou that pinest in the imprisonment of the Actual, and criest bitterly to the gods for a kingdom wherein to rule and create, know this of a truth: the thing thou seekest is already with thee, "here or nowhere," couldst thou only see!

'But it is with man's Soul as it was with Nature: the beginning of Creation is—Light. Till the eye have vision, the whole mem-

---

[7] Johann Fichte (1762–1814), German transcendentalist, wrote the *Wissenschaftslehre* (Principles of Knowledge) in 1794.

bers are in bonds. Divine moment, when over the tempest-tost Soul, as once over the wild-weltering Chaos, it is spoken: Let there be Light! Ever to the greatest that has felt such moment, is it not miraculous and God-announcing; even as, under simpler figures, to the simplest and least. The mad primeval Discord is hushed; the rudely-jumbled conflicting elements bind themselves into separate Firmaments: deep silent rock-foundations are built beneath; and the skyey vault with its everlasting Luminaries above: instead of a dark wasteful Chaos, we have a blooming, fertile, heaven-encompassed World.

'I too could now say to myself: Be no longer a Chaos, but a World, or even Worldkin. Produce! Produce! Were it but the pitifullest infinitesimal fraction of a Product, produce it, in God's name! 'Tis the utmost thou hast in thee: out with it, then. Up, up! Whatsoever thy hand findeth to do, do it with thy whole might. Work while it is called Today; for the Night cometh, wherein no man can work.'[8]

Chapter X
Pause

Conversion; a spiritual attainment peculiar to the modern Era. Teufelsdröckh accepts Authorship as his divine calling. The scope of the command *Thou shalt not steal*.—Editor begins to suspect the authenticity of the Biographical documents; and abandons them for the great Clothes volume. Result of the preceding ten Chapters: Insight into the character of Teufelsdröckh: His fundamental beliefs, and how he was forced to seek and find them.

Thus have we, as closely and perhaps satisfactorily as, in such circumstances, might be, followed Teufelsdröckh through the

Ecclesiastes, ix, 10; John, ix, 4.

various successive states and stages of Growth, Entanglement, Unbelief, and almost Reprobation, into a certain clearer state of what he himself seems to consider as Conversion. 'Blame not the word,' says he; 'rejoice rather that such a word, signifying such a thing, has come to light in our modern Era, though hidden from the wisest Ancients. The old World knew nothing of Conversion; instead of an *Ecce Homo*,[1] they had only some *Choice of Hercules*.[2] It was a new-attained progress in the Moral Development of man: hereby has the Highest come home to the bosoms of the most Limited; what to Plato was but a hallucination, and to Socrates a chimera, is now clear and certain to your Zinzendorfs, your Wesleys, and the poorest of their Pietists and Methodists.'[3]

It is here, then, that the spiritual majority of Teufelsdröckh commences: we are henceforth to see him 'work in well-doing,' with the spirit and clear aims of a Man. He has discovered that the Ideal Workshop he so panted for is even this same Actual ill-furnished Workshop he has so long been stumbling in. He can say to himself: 'Tools? Thou hast no Tools? Why, there is not a Man, or a Thing, now alive but has tools. The basest of created animalcules, the Spider itself, has a spinning-jenny, and warping-mill, and power-loom within its head: the stupidest of Oysters has a Papin's-Digester,[4] with stone-and-lime house to hold it in: every being that can live can do something: this let him *do*.—Tools? Hast thou not a Brain, furnished, furnishable with some glimmerings of Light; and three fingers to hold a Pen withal? Never since Aaron's rod[5] went out of practice, or even before it, was there such a wonder-working Tool: greater than all recorded miracles have been performed by Pens. For strangely in this so solid-seeming World, which nevertheless is in continual restless flux, it is appointed that *Sound*, to ap-

---

[1] "Behold the Man," Christ (John, xix, 5).

[2] Choice between vice and virtue, as opposed to deep religious conversion.

[3] Count Nicolaus Ludwig von Zinzendorf (1700–1760): founder of strict religious sect, the Moravian Brethren. John Wesley (1703–1791): founder of Methodism.

[4] Device for cooking by steam.

[5] See "Signs of the Times," n. 1.

pearance the most fleeting, should be the most continuing of all things. The WORD is well said to be omnipotent in this world; man, thereby divine, can create as by a *Fiat.* Awake, arise! Speak forth what is in thee; what God has given thee, what the Devil shall not take away. Higher task than that of Priesthood was allotted to no man: wert thou but the meanest in that sacred Hierarchy, is it not honour enough therein to spend and be spent?

'By this Art, which whoso will may sacrilegiously degrade into a handicraft,' adds Teufelsdröckh, 'have I thenceforth abidden. Writings of mine, not indeed known as mine (for what am *I*?), have fallen perhaps not altogether void, into the mighty seed-field of Opinion; fruits of my unseen sowing gratifyingly meet me here and there. I thank the Heavens that I have now found my Calling; wherein, with or without perceptible result, I am minded diligently to persevere.

'Nay how knowest thou,' cries he, 'but this and the other pregnant Device, now grown to be a world-renowed far-working Institution; like a grain of right mustard-seed once cast into the right soil, and now stretching-out strong boughs to the four winds, for the birds of the air to lodge in,—may have been properly my doing? Some one's doing, it without doubt was; from some Idea, in some single Head, it did first of all take beginning: why not from some Idea in mine?' Does Teufelsdröckh here glance at that 'SOCIETY FOR THE CONSERVATION OF PROPERTY (*Eigenthums-conservirende Gesellschaft*),' of which so many ambiguous notices glide spectre-like through these inexpressible Paper-bags? 'An Institution,' hints he, 'not unsuitable to the wants of the time; as indeed such sudden extension proves: for already can the Society number, among its office-bearers or corresponding members, the highest Names, if not the highest Persons, in Germany, England, France; and contributions, both of money and of meditation, pour in from all quarters; to, if possible, enlist the remaining Integrity of the world, and, defensively and with forethought, marshal it round this Palladium.' Does Teufelsdröckh mean, then, to give himself out as the originator of that so notable *Eigenthums-conservirende* ('Owndom-conserving') *Gesellschaft*; and if so, what, in the

Devil's name, is it? He again hints: 'at a time when the divine Commandment, *Thou shalt not steal*, wherein truly, if well understood, is comprised the whole Hebrew Decalogue, with Solon's and Lycurgus's Constitutions, Justinian's Pandects, the Code Napoléon, and all Codes, Catechisms, Divinities, Moralities whatsoever, that man has hitherto devised (and enforced with Altar-fire and Gallows-ropes) for his social guidance: at a time, I say, when this divine Commandment has all-but faded away from the general remembrance; and, with little disguise, a new opposite Commandment, *Thou shalt steal*, is everywhere promulgated,—it perhaps behoved, in this universal dotage and deliration, the sound portion of mankind to bestir themselves and rally. When the widest and wildest violations of that divine right of Property, the only divine right now extant or conceivable, are sanctioned and recommended by a vicious Press, and the world has lived to hear it asserted that *we have no Property in our very Bodies, but only an accidental Possession and Life-rent*, what is the issue to be looked for? Hangmen and Catch-poles may, by their noose-gins and baited fall-traps, keep down the smaller sort of vermin; but what, except perhaps some such Universal Association, can protect us against whole meat-devouring and man-devouring hosts of Boa-constrictors? If, therefore, the more sequestered Thinker have wondered, in his privacy, from what hand that perhaps not ill-written *Program* in the Public Journals, with its high *Prize-Questions* and so liberal *Prizes*, could have proceeded,—let him now cease such wonder; and, with undivided faculty, betake himself to the *Concurrenz* (Competition).'

We ask: Has this same 'perhaps not ill-written *Program*,' or any other authentic Transaction of that Property-conserving Society, fallen under the eye of the British Reader, in any Journal foreign or domestic? If so, what are those *Prize-Questions*; what are the terms of Competition, and when and where? No printed Newspaper-leaf, no farther light of any sort, to be met with in these Paper-bags! Or is the whole business one other of those whimsicalities and perverse inexplicabilities, whereby Herr Teufelsdröckh, meaning much or nothing, is pleased so often to play fast-and-loose with us?

Thomas Carlyle

Here, indeed, at length, must the Editor give utterance to a painful suspicion, which, through late Chapters, has begun to haunt him; paralysing any little enthusiasm that might still have rendered his thorny Biographical task a labour of love. It is a suspicion grounded perhaps on trifles, yet confirmed almost into certainty by the more and more discernible humoristico-satirical tendency of Teufelsdröckh, in whom underground humours and intricate sardonic rogueries, wheel within wheel, defy all reckoning: a suspicion, in one word, that these Auto-biographical Documents are partly a mystification! What if many a so-called Fact were little better than a Fiction; if here we had no direct Camera-obscura Picture of the Professor's History; but only some more or less fantastic Adumbration, symbolically, perhaps significantly enough, shadowing-forth the same! Our theory begins to be that, in receiving as literally authentic what was but hieroglyphically so, Hofrath Heuschrecke, whom in that case we scruple not to name Hofrath Nose-of-Wax, was made a fool of, and set adrift to make fools of others. Could it be expected, indeed, that a man so known for impenetrable reticence as Teufelsdröckh, would all at once frankly unlock his private citadel to an English Editor and a German Hofrath; and not rather deceptively *in*lock both Editor and Hofrath in the labyrinthic tortuosities and covered-ways of said citadel (having enticed them thither), to see, in his half-devilish way, how the fools would look?

Of one fool, however, the Herr Professor will perhaps find himself short. On a small slip, formerly thrown aside as blank, the ink being all-but invisible, we lately notice, and with effort decipher, the following: 'What are your historical Facts; still more your biographical? Wilt thou know a Man, above all a Mankind, by stringing-together beadrolls of what thou namest Facts? The Man is the spirit he worked in; not what he did, but what he became. Facts are engraved Hierograms, for which the fewest have the key. And then how your Block-head (*Dummkopf*) studies not their Meaning; but simply whether they are well or ill cut, what he calls Moral or Immoral! Still worse is it with your Bungler (*Pfuscher*): such I have seen reading some Rousseau, with pretences of interpretation; and mistaking the

192

ill-cut Serpent-of-Eternity[6] for a common poisonous reptile.'
Was the Professor apprehensive lest an Editor, selected as the
present boasts himself, might mistake the Teufelsdröckh
Serpent-of-Eternity in like manner? For which reason it was to
be altered, not without underhand satire, into a plainer Symbol?
Or is this merely one of his half-sophisms, half-truisms, which
if he can but set on the back of a Figure, he cares not whither
it gallop? We say not with certainty; and indeed, so strange is
the Professor, can never say. If our suspicion be wholly un-
founded, let his own questionable ways, not our necessary cir-
cumspectness, bear the blame.

But be this as it will, the somewhat exasperated and indeed
exhausted Editor determines here to shut these Paper-bags for
the present. Let it suffice that we know of Teufelsdröckh, so far,
if 'not what he did, yet what he became': the rather, as his
character has now taken its ultimate bent, and no new revolution, of importance, is to be looked for. The imprisoned
Chrysalis is now a winged Psyche[7]: and such, wheresoever be
its flight, it will continue. To trace by what complex gyrations
(flights or involuntary waftings) through the mere external
Life-element, Teufelsdröckh reaches his University Professorship, and the Psyche clothes herself in civic Titles, without
altering her now fixed nature,—would be comparatively an unproductive task, were we even unsuspicious of its being, for us at
least, a false and impossible one. His outward Biography, therefore, which, at the Blumine Lover's-Leap, we saw churned
utterly into spray-vapour, may hover in that condition, for aught
that concerns us here. Enough that by survey of certain 'pools
and plashes,' we have ascertained its general direction; do we
not already know that, by one way and other, it *has* long since
rained-down again into a stream; and even now, as Weissnichtwo, flows deep and still, fraught with the *Philosophy of
Clothes*, and visible to whoso will cast eye thereon? Over much
invaluable matter, that lies scattered, like jewels among quarry-

---

[6] The serpent with its tail in its mouth, traditional symbol of eternity,
was adopted by Carlyle as his personal seal.
[7] Psyche is the Greek personification of the soul, her emblem is the
butterfly.

rubbish, in those Paper-catacombs, we may have occasion to glance back, and somewhat will demand insertion at the right place: meanwhile be our tiresome diggings therein suspended.

If now, before reopening the great *Clothes-Volume*, we ask what our degree of progress, during these Ten Chapters, has been, towards right understanding of the *Clothes-Philosophy*, let not our discouragement become total. To speak in that old figure of the Hell-gate Bridge over Chaos, a few flying pontoons have perhaps been added, though as yet they drift straggling on the Flood; how far they will reach, when once the chains are straightened and fastened, can, at present, only be matter of conjecture.

So much we already calculate: Through many a little loop-hole, we have had glimpses into the internal world of Teufelsdröckh; his strange mystic, almost magic Diagram of the Universe, and how it was gradually drawn, is not henceforth altogether dark to us. Those mysterious ideas on TIME, which merit consideration, and are not wholly unintelligible with such, may by and by prove significant. Still more may his somewhat peculiar view of Nature, the decisive Oneness he ascribes to Nature. How all Nature and Life are but one *Garment*, a 'Living Garment,' woven and ever aweaving in the 'Loom of Time';[8] is not here, indeed, the outline of a whole *Clothes-Philosophy*; at least the arena it is to work in? Remark, too, that the Character of the Man, nowise without meaning in such a matter, becomes less enigmatic: amid so much tumultuous obscurity, almost like diluted madness, do not a certain indomitable Defiance and yet a boundless Reverence seem to loom forth, as the two mountain-summits, on whose rock-strata all the rest were based and built?

Nay further, may we not say that Teufelsdröckh's Biography, allowing it even, as suspected, only a hieroglyphical truth, exhibits a man, as it were preappointed for Clothes-Philosophy? To look through the Shows of things into Things themselves he is led and compelled. The 'Passivity' given him by birth is fostered by all turns of his fortune. Everywhere cast out, like oil out of water, from mingling in any Employment, in any public

[8] See Book I, Chapter 8, n. 4.

Communion, he has no portion but Solitude, and a life of Meditation. The whole energy of his existence is directed, through long years, on one task: that of enduring pain, if he cannot cure it. Thus everywhere do the Shows of things oppress him, withstand him, threaten him with fearfullest destruction: only by victoriously penetrating into Things themselves can he find peace and a stronghold. But is not this same looking-through the Shows, or Vestures, into the Things, even the first preliminary to a *Philosophy of Clothes*? Do we not, in all this, discern some beckonings towards the true higher purport of such a Philosophy; and what shape it must assume with such a man, in such an era?

Perhaps in entering on Book Third, the courteous Reader is not utterly without guess whither he is bound: nor, let us hope, for all the fantastic Dream-Grottoes through which, as is our lot with Teufelsdröckh, he must wander, will there be wanting between whiles some twinkling of a steady Polar Star.

Book Third

Chapter I
Incident in Modern History

Story of George Fox the Quaker; and his perennial suit of Leather. A man God-possessed, witnessing for spiritual freedom and manhood.

As a wonder-loving and wonder-seeking man, Teufelsdröckh, from an early part of this Clothes-Volume, has more and more exhibited himself. Striking it was, amid all his perverse cloudiness, with what force of vision and of heart he pierced into the mystery of the World; recognising in the highest sensible phenomena, so far as Sense went, only fresh or faded Raiment; yet ever, under this, a celestial Essence thereby rendered visible: and while, on the one hand, he trod the old rags of Matter, with their tinsels, into the mire, he on the other everywhere exalted Spirit above all earthly principalities and powers, and worshipped it, though under the meanest shapes, with a true Platonic mysticism. What the man ultimately purposed by thus casting his Greek-fire[1] into the general Wardrobe of the Universe; what such, more or less complete, rending and burning of Garments throughout the whole compass of Civilised Life

---

[1] An incendiary mixture said to take fire on wetting.

and Speculation, should lead to; the rather as he was no Adamite, in any sense, and could not, like Rousseau, recommend
either bodily or intellectual Nudity, and a return to the savage
state: all this our readers are now bent to discover; this is, in
fact, properly the gist and purport of Professor Teufelsdröckh's
Philosophy of Clothes.

Be it remembered, however, that such purport is here not so
much evolved, as detected to lie ready for evolving. We are to
guide our British Friends into the new Gold-country, and show
them the mines; nowise to dig-out and exhaust its wealth, which
indeed remains for all time inexhaustible. Once there, let each
dig for his own behoof, and enrich himself.

Neither, is so capricious inexpressible a Work as this of the
Professor's, can our course now more than formerly be straightforward, step by step, but at best leap by leap. Significant
Indications stand-out here and there; which for the critical eye,
that looks both widely and narrowly, shape themselves into
some ground-scheme of a Whole: to select these with judgment,
so that a leap from one to the other be possible, and (in our old
figure) by chaining them together, a passable Bridge be
effected: this, as heretofore, continues our only method. Among
such light-spots, the following, floating in much wild matter
about *Perfectibility*, has seemed worth clutching at:

'Perhaps the most remarkable incident in Modern History,'
says Teufelsdröckh, 'is not the Diet of Worms,[2] still less the
Battle of Austerlitz, Waterloo, Peterloo,[3] or any other Battle;
but an incident passed carelessly over by most Historians, and
treated with some degree of ridicule by others: namely, George
Fox's[4] making to himself a suit of Leather. This man, the first
of the Quakers, and by trade a Shoemaker, was one of those,
to whom, under ruder or purer form, the Divine Idea of the
Universe is pleased to manifest itself; and, across all the hulls

[2] The convocation in Worms, Germany, which condemned Martin
Luther in 1521.
[3] Austerlitz: site of battle (1805) in which Napoleon defeated the
Austrians and Russians. Peterloo: name given to attack by military
on protesting workers at St. Peter's Field, Manchester in 1819. Name
is suggested by Waterloo.
[4] George Fox (1624–1691), founder of Society of Friends (Quakers).

of Ignorance and earthly Degradation, shine through, in unspeakable Awfulness, unspeakable Beauty, on their souls: who therefore are rightly accounted Prophets, God-possessed; or even Gods, as in some periods it has chanced. Sitting in his stall; working on tanned hides, amid pincers, paste-horns, rosin, swine-bristles, and a nameless flood of rubbish, this youth had, nevertheless, a Living Spirit belonging to him; also an antique Inspired Volume, through which, as through a window, it could look upwards, and discern its celestial Home. The task of a daily pair of shoes, coupled even with some prospect of victuals, and an honourable Mastership in Cordwainery, and perhaps the post of Thirdborough in his hundred, as the crown of long faithful sewing,—was nowise satisfaction enough to such a mind: but ever amid the boring and hammering came tones from that far country, came Splendours and Terrors; for this poor Cordwainer, as we said, was a Man; and the Temple of Immensity, wherein as Man he had been sent to minister, was full of holy mystery to him.

'The Clergy of the neighbourhood, the ordained Watchers and Interpreters of that same holy mystery, listened with unaffected tedium to his consultations, and advised him, as the solution of such doubts, to "drink beer and dance with the girls." Blind leaders of the blind! For what end were their tithes levied and eaten; for what were their shovel-hats scooped-out, and their surplices and cassock-aprons girt-on; and such a church-repairing, and chaffering, and organing, and other racketing, held over that spot of God's Earth,—if Man were but a Patent Digester,[5] and the Belly with its adjuncts the grand Reality? Fox turned from them, with tears and a sacred scorn, back to his Leather-parings and his Bible. Mountains of encumbrance, higher than Ætna, had been heaped out over that Spirit: but it was a Spirit, and would not lie buried there. Through long days and nights of silent agony, it struggled and wrestled with a man's force, to be free: how its prison-mountains heaved and swayed tumultuously, as the giant spirit shook them to this hand and that, and emerged into the light of

[5] See Book II, Chapter 10, n. 4.

Heaven! That Leicester shoe-shop, had men known it, was a holier place than any Vatican or Loretto-shrine.—"So bandaged, and hampered, and hemmed in," groaned he, "with thousand requisitions, obligations, straps, tatters, and tagrags, I can neither see nor move: not my own am I, but the World's; and Time flies fast, and Heaven is high, and Hell is deep: Man! bethink thee, if thou hast power of Thought! Why not; what binds me here? Want, want!—Ha, of what? Will all the shoe-wages under the Moon ferry me across into that far Land of Light? Only Meditation can, and devout Prayer to God. I will to the woods: the hollow of a tree will lodge me, wildberries feed me; and for Clothes, cannot I stitch myself one perennial suit of Leather!"

'Historical Oil-painting,' continues Teufelsdröckh, 'is one of the Arts I never practised; therefore shall I not decide whether this subject were easy of execution on the canvas. Yet often has it seemed to me as if such first outflashing of man's Freewill, to lighten, more and more into Day, the Chaotic Night that threatened to engulf him in its hindrances and its horrors, were properly the only grandeur there is in History. Let some living Angelo or Rosa,[6] with seeing eye and understanding heart, picture George Fox on that morning, when he spreads-out his cutting-board for the last time, and cuts cowhides by unwonted patterns, and stitches them together into one continuous all-including Case, the farewell service of his awl! Stitch away, thou noble Fox: every prick of that little instrument is pricking into the heart of Slavery, and World-worship, and the Mammon-god. Thy elbows jerk, as in strong swimmer-strokes, and every stroke is bearing thee across the Prison-ditch, within which Vanity holds her Workhouse and Ragfair, into lands of true Liberty; were the work done, there is in broad Europe one Free Man, and thou art he!

'Thus from the lowest depth there is a path to the loftiest height; and for the Poor also a Gospel has been published. Surely if, as D'Alembert asserts, my illustrious namesake, Diogenes, was the greatest man of Antiquity, only that he wanted

---

[6] Michelangelo (1475–1564) and Salvator Rosa (1615–1673): Italian artists.

Decency, then by stronger reason is George Fox the greatest of the Moderns, and greater than Diogenes himself: for he too stands on the adamantine basis of his Manhood, casting aside all props and shoars; yet not, in half-savage Pride, undervaluing the Earth; valuing it rather, as a place to yield him warmth and food, he looks Heavenward from his Earth, and dwells in an element of Mercy and Worship, with a still Strength, such as the Cynic's Tub[7] did nowise witness. Great, truly, was that Tub; a temple from which man's dignity and divinity was scornfully preached abroad: but greater is the Leather Hull, for the same sermon was preached there, and not in Scorn but in Love.'

George Fox's 'perennial suit,' with all that it held, has been worn quite into ashes for nigh two centuries: why, in a discussion on the *Perfectibility of Society*, reproduce it now? Not out of blind sectarian partisanship: Teufelsdröckh himself is no Quaker; with all his pacific tendencies, did not we see him, in that scene at the North Cape, with the Archangel Smuggler, exhibit fire-arms?

For us, aware of his deep Sansculottism, there is more meant in this passage than meets the ear. At the same time, who can avoid smiling at the earnestness and Bœotian simplicity (if indeed there be not an underhand satire in it), with which that 'Incident' is here brought forward; and, in the Professor's ambiguous way, as clearly perhaps as he durst in Weissnichtwo, recommended to imitation! Does Teufelsdröckh anticipate that, in this age of refinement, any considerable class of the community, by way of testifying against the 'Mammon-god,' and escaping from what he calls 'Vanity's Workhouse and Ragfair,' where doubtless some of them are toiled and whipped and hoodwinked sufficiently,—will sheathe themselves in close-fitting cases of Leather? The idea is ridiculous in the extreme. Will Majesty lay aside its robes of state, and Beauty its frills and train-gowns, for a second-skin of tanned hide? By which change Huddersfield and Manchester, and Coventry and Paisley,[8] and the Fancy-Bazaar, were reduced to hungry solitudes; and only

[7] Diogenes, the Cynic philosopher, is said to have lived in a tub.
[8] Textile-manufacturing cities in England.

Day and Martin[9] could profit. For neither would Teufels-dröckh's mad day-dream, here as we presume covertly intended, of levelling Society (*levelling* it indeed with a vengeance, into one huge drowned marsh!), and so attaining the political effects of Nudity without its frigorific or other consequences,—be thereby realised. Would not the rich man purchase a waterproof suit of Russia Leather; and the high-born Belle step-forth in red or azure morocco, lined with shamoy: the black cowhide being left to the Drudges and Gibeonites[10] of the world; and so all the old Distinctions be reëstablished?

Or has the Professor his own deeper intention; and laughs in his sleeve at our strictures and glosses, which indeed are but a part thereof?

Chapter II
Church-Clothes

Church-Clothes defined; the Forms under which the Religious Principle is temporarily embodied. Outward Religion originates by Society: Society becomes possible by Religion. The condition of Church-Clothes in our time.

Not less questionable in his Chapter on *Church-Clothes*, which has the farther distinction of being the shortest in the Volume. We here translate it entire:

'By Church-Clothes, it need not be premised that I mean infinitely more than Cassocks and Surplices; and do not at all mean the mere haberdasher Sunday Clothes that men go to Church in. Far from it! Church-Clothes, are, in our vocabulary,

[9] London manufacturers of shoe-polish.
[10] People condemned to be hewers of wood and drawers of water (Joshua, ix, 3–27).

the Forms, the *Vestures*, under which men have at various periods embodied and represented for themselves the Religious Principle; that is to say, invested the Divine Idea of the World with a sensible and practically active Body, so that it might dwell among them as a living and life-giving WORD.

'These are unspeakably the most important of all the vestures and garnitures of Human Existence. They are first spun and woven, I may say, by that wonder of wonders, SOCIETY; for it is still only when "two or three are gathered together," that Religion, spiritually existent, and indeed indestructible, however latent, in each, first outwardly manifests itself (as with "cloven tongues of fire"), and seeks to be embodied in a visible Communion and Church Militant. Mystical, more than magical, is that Communing of Soul with Soul, both looking heavenward: here properly Soul first speaks with Soul; for only in looking heavenward, take it in what sense you may, not in looking earthward, does what we can call Union, mutual Love, Society, begin to be possible. How true is that of Novalis:[1] "It is certain, my Belief gains quite *infinitely* the moment I can convince another mind thereof"! Gaze thou in the face of thy Brother, in those eyes where plays the lambent fire of Kindness, or in those where rages the lurid conflagration of Anger; feel how thy own so quiet Soul is straightway involuntarily kindled with the like, and ye blaze and reverberate on each other, till it is all one limitless confluent flame (of embracing Love, or of deadly-grappling Hate); and then say what miraculous virtue goes out of man into man. But if so, through all the thickplied hulls of our Earthly Life; how much more when it is of the Divine Life we speak, and inmost ME is, as it were, brought into contact with inmost ME!

'Thus was it that I said, the Church-Clothes are first spun and woven by Society; outward Religion originates by Society, Society becomes possible by Religion. Nay, perhaps, every conceivable Society, past and present, may well be figured as properly and wholly a Church, in one or other of these three predicaments: an audibly preaching and prophesying Church, which is the best; second, a Church that struggles to preach and

---

[1] Pseudonym of Friedrich von Hardenberg (1772–1801), German romantic poet and mystic.

prophesy, but cannot as yet, till its Pentecost come; and third and worst, a Church gone dumb with old age, or which only mumbles delirium prior to dissolution. Whoso fancies that by Church is here meant Chapterhouses and Cathedrals, or by preaching and prophesying, mere speech and chanting, let him,' says the oracular Professor, 'read on, light of heart (*getrosten Muthes*).

'But with regard to your Church proper, and the Church-Clothes specially recognised as Church-Clothes, I remark, fearlessly enough, that without such Vestures and sacred Tissues Society has not existed, and will not exist. For if Government is, so to speak, the outward SKIN of the Body Politic, holding the whole together and protecting it; and all your Craft-Guilds, and Associations for Industry, of hand or of head, are the Fleshly Clothes, the muscular and osseous Tissues (lying *under* such SKIN), whereby Society stands and works;—then is Religion the inmost Pericardial and Nervous Tissue, which ministers Life and warm Circulation to the whole. Without which Pericardial Tissue the Bones and Muscles (of Industry) were inert, or animated only by a Galvanic vitality; the SKIN would become a shrivelled pelt, or fast-rotting raw-hide; and Society itself a dead carcass,—deserving to be buried. Men were no longer Social, but Gregarious; which latter state also could not continue, but must gradually issue in universal selfish discord, hatred, savage isolation, and dispersion;—whereby, as we might continue to say, the very dust and dead body of Society would have evaporated and become abolished. Such, and so all-important, all-sustaining, are the Church-Clothes to civilised or even to rational men.

'Meanwhile, in our era of the World, those same Church-Clothes have gone sorrowfully out-at-elbows: nay, far worse, many of them have become mere hollow Shapes, or Masks, under which no living Figure or Spirit any longer dwells; but only spiders and unclean beetles, in horrid accumulation, drive their trade; and the mask still glares on you with its glass-eyes, in ghastly affectation of Life,—some generation-and-half after Religion has quite withdrawn from it, and in unnoticed nooks is weaving for herself new Vestures, wherewith to reappear, and bless us, or our sons or grandsons. As a Priest, or Interpreter of the Holy, is the noblest and highest of all men, so is a Sham-priest (*Schein-priester*) the falsest and basest; neither is it doubtful that his Canonicals, were they Popes' Tiaras, will one day be torn from him, to make bandages for the wounds of mankind; or even to burn into tinder, for general scientific or culinary purposes.

'All which, as out of place here, falls to be handled in my Second Volume, *On the Palingenesia, or Newbirth of Society*; which volume, as treating practically of the Wear, Destruction, and Retexture of Spiritual Tissues, or Garments, forms, properly speaking, the Transcendental or ultimate Portion of this my work *on Clothes*, and is already in a state of forwardness.'[2]

And herewith, no farther exposition, note, or commentary being added, does Teufelsdröckh, and must his Editor now, terminate the singular chapter on Church-Clothes!

Chapter III
Symbols

The benignant efficacies of Silence and Secrecy. Symbols; revelations of the Infinite in the Finite: Man everywhere encompassed by them; lives and works by them. Theory of Motive-millwrights, a false account of human nature. Symbols of an extrinsic value; as Banners, Standards: Of intrinsic value; as Works of Art, Lives and Deaths of Heroic men. Religious Symbols; Christianity. Symbols hallowed by Time; but finally defaced and desecrated. Many superannuated Symbols in our time, needing removal.

Probably it will elucidate the drift of these foregoing obscure utterances, if we here insert somewhat of our Professor's specu-

[2] See Book III, Chapter 5.

lations on *Symbols*. To state his whole doctrine, indeed, were beyond our compass: nowhere is he more mysterious, impalpable, than in this of 'Fantasy being the organ of the Godlike'; and how 'Man thereby, though based, to all seeming, on the small Visible, does nevertheless extend down into the infinite deeps of the Invisible, of which Invisible, indeed, his Life is properly the bodying forth.' Let us, omitting these high transcendental aspects of the matter, study to glean (whether from the Paper-bags or the Printed Volume) what little seems logical and practical, and cunningly arrange it into such degree of coherence as it will assume. By way of proem, take the following not injudicious remarks:

'The benignant efficacies of Concealment,' cries our Professor, 'who shall speak or sing? SILENCE and SECRECY! Altars might still be raised to them (were this an altar-building time) for universal worship. Silence is the element in which great things fashion themselves together; that at length they may emerge, full-formed and majestic, into the daylight of Life, which they are thenceforth to rule. Not William the Silent[1] only, but all the considerable men I have known, and the most undiplomatic and unstrategic of these, forbore to babble of what they were creating and projecting. Nay, in thy own mean perplexities, do thou thyself but *hold thy tongue for one day*: on the morrow, how much clearer are thy purposes and duties; that wreck and rubbish have those mute workmen within thee swept away, when intrusive noises were shut out! Speech is too often not, as the Frenchman defined it, the art of concealing Thought; but of quite stifling and suspending Thought, so that there is none to conceal. Speech too is great, but not the greatest. As the Swiss Inscription says: *Sprechen ist silbern, Schweigen ist golden* (Speech is silvern, Silence is golden); or as I might rather express it: Speech is of Time, Silence is of Eternity.

'Bees will not work except in darkness; Thought will not work except in Silence: neither will Virtue work except in Secrecy. Let not thy left hand know what thy right hand doeth!

[1] William of Orange (1533–1584), leader in Dutch struggle against Spain, often used silence as an effective method in diplomacy.

Neither shalt thou prate even to thy own heart of "those secrets known to all." Is not Shame (*Schaam*) the soil of all Virtue, of all good manners and good morals? Like other plants, Virtue will not grow unless its root be hidden, buried from the eye of the sun. Let the sun shine on it, nay do but look at it privily thyself, the root withers, and no flowers will glad thee. O my Friends, when we view the fair clustering flowers that over-wreathe, for example, the Marriage-bower, and encircle man's life with the fragrance and hues of Heaven, what hand will not smite the foul plunderer that grubs them up by the roots, and with grinning, grunting satisfaction, shows us the dung they flourish in! Men speak much of the Printing-Press with its Newspapers: *du Himmel!* what are these to Clothes and the Tailor's Goose?'[2]

'Of kin to the so incalculable influences of Concealment, and connected with still greater things, is the wondrous agency of *Symbols*. In a Symbol there is concealment and yet revelation: here therefore, by Silence and by Speech acting together, comes a double significance. And if both the Speech be itself high, and the Silence fit and noble, how expressive will their union be! Thus in many a painted Device, or simple Seal-emblem, the commonest Truth stands out to us proclaimed with quite new emphasis.

'For it is here that Fantasy with her mystic wonderland plays into the small prose domain of Sense, and becomes incorporated therewith. In the Symbol proper, what we can call a Symbol, there is ever, more or less distinctly and directly, some embodiment and revelation of the Infinite; the Infinite is made to blend itself with the Finite, to stand visible, and as it were, attainable there. By Symbols, accordingly, is man guided and commanded, made happy, made wretched. He everywhere finds himself encompassed with Symbols, recognised as such or not recognised: the Universe is but one vast Symbol of God; nay if thou wilt have it, what is man himself but a Symbol of God; is not all that he does symbolical; a revelation to Sense of the mystic god-given force that is in him; a "Gospel of Freedom,"

[2] Tailor's iron.

206

which he, the "Messias of Nature,"[3] preaches, as he can, by act and word? Not a Hut he builds but is the visible embodiment of a Thought; but bears visible record of invisible things; but is, in the transcendental sense, symbolical as well as real.'

'Man,' says the Professor elsewhere, in quite antipodal contrast with these high-soaring delineations, which we have here cut-short on the verge of the inane, 'Man is by birth somewhat of an owl. Perhaps, too, of all the owleries that ever possessed him, the most owlish, if we consider it, is that of your actually existing Motive-Millwrights.[4] Fantastic tricks enough man has played, in his time; has fancied himself to be most things, down even to an animated heap of Glass: but to fancy himself a dead Iron-Balance for weighing Pains and Pleasures on, was reserved for this his latter era. There stands he, his Universe one huge Manger, filled with hay and thistles to be weighed against each other; and looks long-eared enough. Alas, poor devil! spectres are appointed to haunt him: one age he is hagridden, bewitched; the next, priestridden, befooled; in all ages, bedevilled. And now the Genius of Mechanism smothers him worse than any Nightmare did; till the Soul is nigh choked out of him, and only a kind of Digestive, Mechanic life remains. In Earth and in Heaven he can see nothing but Mechanism; has fear for nothing else, hope in nothing else: the world would indeed grind him to pieces; but cannot he fathom the Doctrine of Motives, and cunningly compute these, and mechanise them to grind the other way?

'Were he not, as has been said, purblinded by enchantment, you had but to bid him open his eyes and look. In which country, in which time, was it hitherto that man's history, or the history of any man, went-on by calculated or calculable "Motives"? What make ye of your Christianities, and Chivalries, and Reformations, and Marseillese Hymns, and Reigns of Terror? Nay, has not perhaps the Motive-grinder himself been *in Love*? Did he never stand so much as a contested Election? Leave him to Time, and the medicating virtue of Nature."

---

[3] The actions of man are signs of his "natural" or inherent freedom of will, much as Christ's acts are signs of supernatural truths.

[4] Another of Carlyle's terms for Benthamites.

Thomas Carlyle

'Yes, Friends,' elsewhere observes the Professor, 'not our Logical, Mensurative faculty, but our Imaginative one is King over us; I might say, Priest and Prophet to lead us heavenward; or Magician and Wizard to lead us hellward. Nay, even for the basest Sensualist, what is Sense but the implement of Fantasy; the vessel it drinks out of? Ever in the dullest existence there is a sheen either of Inspiration or of Madness (thou partly hast it in thy choice, which of the two), that gleams-in from the circumambient Eternity, and colours with its own hues our little islet of Time. The Understanding is indeed thy window, too clear thou canst not make it; but Fantasy is thy eye, with its colour-giving retina, healthy or diseased.[5] Have not I myself known five-hundred living soldiers sabred into crows'-meat for a piece of glazed cotton, which they called their Flag; which, had you sold it at any market-cross, would not have brought above three groschen? Did not the whole Hungarian Nation rise, like some tumultuous moon-stirred Atlantic, when Kaiser Joseph pocketed their Iron Crown;[6] an implement, as was sagaciously observed, in size and commercial value little differing from a horse-shoe? It is in and through *Symbols* that man, consciously or unconsciously, lives, works, and has his being: those ages, moreover, are accounted the noblest which can the best recognise symbolical worth, and prize it the highest. For is not a Symbol ever, to him who has eyes for it, some dimmer or clearer revelation of the Godlike?

'Of Symbols, however, I remark farther, that they have both an extrinsic and intrinsic value; oftenest the former only. What, for instance, was in that clouted Shoe, which the Peasants bore aloft with them as ensign in their *Bauernkrieg* (Peasants' War)? Or in the Wallet-and-staff round which the Netherland *Gueux*,[7]

---

[5] Carlyle is here using the Kantian distinction between "Understanding," or the lower rationalistic powers, and the higher reason that transcends the categories of time and space. He calls this higher reason "fantasy" throughout this chapter.

[6] Joseph II of Austria refused to be crowned King of Hungary with the traditional iron crown of that country and instead removed the crown to Vienna.

[7] "Beggars." Name given to the nobles in the Netherlands who in 1566 opposed the rule of Philip II of Spain.

glorying in that nickname of Beggars, heroically rallied and prevailed, though against King Philip himself? Intrinsic significance these had none; only extrinsic; as the accidental Standards of multitudes more or less sacredly uniting together; in which union itself, as above noted, there is ever something mystical and borrowing of the Godlike. Under a like category, too, stand, or stood, the stupidest heraldic Coats-of-arms; military Banners everywhere; and generally all national or other sectarian Costumes and Customs: they have no intrinsic, necessary divineness, or even worth; but have acquired an extrinsic one. Nevertheless through all these there glimmers something of a Divine Idea; as through military Banners themselves, the Divine Idea of Duty, of heroic Daring; in some instances of Freedom, of Right. Nay the highest ensign that men ever met and embraced under, the Cross itself, had no meaning save an accidental extrinsic one.

'Another matter it is, however, when your Symbol has intrinsic meaning, and is of itself *fit* that men should unite round it. Let but the Godlike manifest itself to Sense; let but Eternity look, more or less visibly, through the Time-Figure (*Zeitbild*)! Then is it fit that men unite there; and worship together before such Symbol; and so from day to day, and from age to age, superadd to it new divineness.

'Of this latter sort are all true Works of Art: in them (if thou know a Work of Art from a Daub of Artifice) wilt thou discern Eternity looking though Time; the Godlike rendered visible. Here too may an extrinsic value gradually superadd itself: thus certain *Iliads*, and the like, have, in three-thousand years, attained quite new significance. But nobler than all in this kind are the Lives of heroic god-inspired Men; for what other Work of Art is so divine? In Death too, in the Death of the Just, as the last perfection of a Work of Art, may we not discern symbolic meaning? In that divinely transfigured Sleep, as of Victory, resting over the beloved face which now knows thee no more, read (if thou canst for tears) the confluence of Time with Eternity, and some gleam of the latter peering through.

'Highest of all Symbols are those wherein the Artist or Poet has risen into Prophet, and all men can recognise a present God, and worship the same: I mean religious Symbols. Various enough have been such religious Symbols, what we call *Religions*; as men stood in this stage of culture or the other, and could worse or better body-forth the Godlike: some Symbols with a transient intrinsic worth; many with only an extrinsic. If thou ask to what height man has carried it in this manner, look on our divinest Symbol: on Jesus of Nazareth, and his Life, and his Biography, and what followed therefrom. Higher has the human Thought not yet reached: this is Christianity and Christendom; a Symbol of quite perennial, infinite character; whose significance will ever demand to be anew inquired into, and anew made manifest.

'But on the whole, as Time adds much to the sacredness of Symbols, so likewise in his progress he at length defaces, or even desecrates them; and Symbols, like all terrestrial Garments, wax old. Homer's Epos has not ceased to be true; yet it is no longer *our* Epos, but shines in the distance, if clearer and clearer, yet also smaller and smaller, like a receding Star. It needs a scientific telescope, it needs to be reinterpreted and artificially brought near us, before we can so much as know that it *was* a Sun. So likewise a day comes when the Runic Thor, with his Eddas, must withdraw into dimness; and many an African Mumbo-Jumbo and Indian Pawaw be utterly abolished. For all things, even Celestial Luminaries, much more atmospheric meteors, have their rise, their culmination, their decline.'

'Small is this which thou tellest me, that the Royal Sceptre is but a piece of gilt-wood; that the Pyx has become a most foolish box, and truly, as Ancient Pistol thought, "of little price." A right Conjuror might I name thee, couldst thou conjure back into these wooden tools the divine virtue they once held.'

'Of this thing, however, be certain: wouldst thou plant for Eternity, then plant into the deep infinite faculties of man, his Fantasy and Heart; wouldst thou plant for Year and Day, then plant into his shallow superficial faculties, his Self-love and Arithmetical Understanding, what will grow there. A Hierarch, therefore, and Pontiff of the World will we call him, the Poet and inspired Maker; who, Prometheus-like, can shape new Symbols, and bring new Fire from Heaven to fix it there. Such too will not always be wanting; neither perhaps now are. Meanwhile, as the average of matters goes, we account him Legislator and wise who can so much as tell when a Symbol has grown old, and gently remove it.

'When, as the last English Coronation was preparing,' concludes this wonderful Professor, 'I read in their Newspapers that the "Champion of England," he who has to offer battle to the Universe for his new King, had brought it so far that he could now "mount his horse with little assistance,"[8] I said to myself: Here also we have a Symbol well-nigh superannuated. Alas, move whithersoever you may, are not the tatters and rags of superannuated worn-out Symbols (in this Ragfair of a World) dropping off everywhere, to hoodwink, to halter, to tether you; nay, if you shake them not aside, threatening to accumulate, and perhaps produce suffocation?'

Chapter IV
Helotage

Heuschrecke's Malthusian Tract, and Teufelsdröckh's marginal notes thereon. The true workman, for daily bread, or spiritual bread, to be honoured; and no other. The real privation of the Poor not poverty or toil, but ignorance. Overpopulation: With a world like ours and wide as ours, can there be too many men? Emigration.

At this point we determine on adverting shortly, or rather reverting, to a certain Tract of Hofrath Heuschrecke's, entitled *Institute for the Repression of Population*; which lies, dishonourably enough (with torn leaves, and a perceptible smell of aloetic drugs), stuffed into the Bag *Pisces*. Not indeed for the

---

[8] This official appears in full armor at the coronation. The reference is to the coronation of George IV in 1821.

sake of the Tract itself, which we admire little; but of the marginal Notes, evidently in Teufelsdröckh's hand, which rather copiously fringe it. A few of these may be in their right place here.

Into the Hofrath's *Institute*, with its extraordinary schemes, and machinery of Corresponding Boards and the like, we shall not so much as glance. Enough for us to understand that Heuschrecke is a disciple of Malthus;[1] and so zealous for the doctrine, that his zeal almost literally eats him up. A deadly fear of Population possesses the Hofrath; something like a fixed-idea; undoubtedly akin to the more diluted forms of Madness. Nowhere, in that quarter of his intellectual world, is there light; nothing but a grim shadow of Hunger; open mouths opening wider and wider; a world to terminate by the frightfullest consummation: by its too dense inhabitants, famished into delirium, universally eating one another. To make air for himself in which strangulation, choking enough to a benevolent heart, the Hofrath founds, or proposes to found, this *Institute* of his, as the best he can do. It is only with our Professor's comments thereon that we concern ourselves.

First, then, remark that Teufelsdröckh, as a speculative Radical, has his own notions about human dignity; that the Zähdarm palaces and courtesies have not made him forgetful of the Futteral cottages. On the blank cover of Heuschrecke's Tract we find the following indistinctly engrossed:

'Two men I honour, and no third. First, the toilworn Craftsman that with earth-made Implement laboriously conquers the Earth, and makes her man's. Venerable to me is the hard Hand; crooked, coarse; wherein notwithstanding lies a cunning virtue, indefeasibly royal, as of the Sceptre of this Planet. Venerable too is the rugged face, all weather-tanned, besoiled, with its rude intelligence; for it is the face of a Man living manlike. O, but the more venerable for thy rudeness, and even because we must pity as well as love thee! Hardly-entreated Brother! For us was

---

[1] Thomas Malthus (1766–1834) set forth the theory that population increases geometrically while the means of subsistence increases only arithmetically. This theory was often used in the nineteenth century as an argument to prove that the poverty of the working classes was natural and therefore irremediable.

thy back so bent, for us were thy straight limbs and fingers so deformed: thou wert our Conscript, on whom the lot fell, and fighting our battles wert so marred. For in thee too lay a god-created Form, but it was not to be unfolded; encrusted must it stand with the thick adhesions and defacements of Labour; and thy body, like thy soul, was not to know freedom. Yet toil on, toil on: *thou* art in thy duty, be out of it who may; thou toilest for the altogether indispensable, for daily bread.

'A second man I honour, and still more highly: Him who is seen toiling for the spiritually indispensable; not daily bread, but the bread of Life. Is not he too in his duty; endeavouring towards inward Harmony; revealing this, by act or by word, through all his outward endeavours, be they high or low? Highest of all, when his outward and his inward endeavour are one: when we can name him Artist; not earthly Craftsman only, but inspired Thinker, who with heaven-made Implement conquers Heaven for us! If the poor and humble toil that we have Food, must not the high and glorious toil for him in return, that he have Light, have Guidance, Freedom, Immortality?—These two, in all their degrees, I honour: all else is chaff and dust, which let the wind blow whither it listeth.

'Unspeakably touching is it, however, when I find both dignities united; and he that must toil outwardly for the lowest of man's wants, is also toiling inwardly for the highest. Sublimer in this world know I nothing than a Peasant Saint, could such now anywhere be met with. Such a one will take thee back to Nazareth itself; thou wilt see the splendour of Heaven spring forth from the humblest depths of Earth, like a light shining in great darkness.'

And again: 'It is not because of his toils that I lament for the poor: we must all toil, or steal (howsoever we name our stealing), which is worse; no faithful workman finds his task a pastime. The poor is hungry and athirst; but for him also there is food and drink: he is heavy-laden and weary; but for him also the Heavens send Sleep, and of the deepest; in his smoky cribs, a clear dewy heaven of Rest envelops him, and fitful glitterings of cloud-skirted Dreams. But what I do mourn over is, that the lamp of his soul should go out; that no ray of heavenly, or even of earthly knowledge, should visit him; but only, in the haggard darkness, like two spectres, Fear and Indignation bear him company. Alas, while the body stands so broad and brawny, must the Soul lie blinded, dwarfed, stupefied, almost annihilated! Alas, was this too a Breath of God; bestowed in Heaven, but on earth never to be unfolded!—That there should one Man die ignorant who had capacity for Knowledge, this I call a tragedy, were it to happen more than twenty times in the minute, as by some computations it does. The miserable fraction of Science which our united Mankind, in a wide Universe of Nescience, has acquired, why is not this, with all diligence, imparted to all?'

Quite in an opposite strain is the following: 'The old Spartans had a wiser method; and went out and hunted-down their Helots,[2] and speared and spitted them, when they grew too numerous. With our improved fashions of hunting, Herr Hofrath, now after the invention of fire-arms, and standing-armies, how much easier were such a hunt! Perhaps in the most thickly-peopled country, some three days annually might suffice to shoot all the able-bodied Paupers that had accumulated within the year. Let Governments think of this. The expense were trifling: nay the very carcasses would pay it. Have them salted and barrelled; could not you victual therewith, if not Army and Navy, yet richly such infirm Paupers, in workhouses and elsewhere, as enlightened Charity, dreading no evil of them, might see good to keep alive?'

'And yet,' writes he farther on, 'there must be something wrong. A full-formed Horse will, in any market, bring from twenty to as high as two-hundred Friedrichs d'or: such is his worth to the world. A full-formed Man is not only worth nothing to the world, but the world could afford him a round sum would he simply engage to go and hang himself. Nevertheless, which of the two was the more cunningly-devised article, even as an Engine? Good Heavens! A white European Man, standing on his two Legs, with his two five-fingered Hands at his shackle-bones, and miraculous Head on his shoulders, is worth, I should say, from fifty to a hundred Horses'!

'True, thou Gold-Hofrath,' cries the Professor elsewhere: 'too

---

[2] Helots were a people enslaved by the Spartans, who periodically murdered large numbers as a means of population control.

crowded indeed! Meanwhile, what portion of this inconsiderable terraqueous Globe have ye actually tilled and delved, till it will grow no more? How thick stands your Population in the Pampas and Savannas of America; round ancient Carthage, and in the interior of Africa; on both slopes of the Altaic chain, in the central Platform of Asia; in Spain, Greece, Turkey, Crim Tartary, the Curragh of Kildare? One man, in one year, as I have understood it, if you lend him Earth, will feed himself and nine others. Alas, where now are the Hengsts and Alarics[3] of our still-glowing, still-expanding Europe; who, when their home is grown too narrow, will enlist, and, like Fire-pillars, guide onwards those superfluous masses of indomitable living Valour; equipped, not now with the battle-axe and war-chariot, but with the steam-engine and ploughshare? Where are they?—Preserving their Game!'

Chapter V
The Phoenix[1]

Teufelsdröckh considers Society as *dead*; its soul (Religion) gone, its body (existing Institutions) going. Utilitarianism, needing little farther preaching, is now in full activity of destruction.—Teufelsdröckh would yield to the Inevitable, accounting that the best: Assurance of a fairer Living Society, arising, Phoenix-like, out of the ruins of the old dead one. Before that Phoenix death-birth is accomplished, long time, struggle, and suffering must intervene.

Putting which four singular Chapters together, and alongside of them numerous hints, and even direct utterances, scattered

---

[3] Hengst: See Book I, Chapter 3, n. 14. Alaric: King of the Visigoths who sacked Rome in 410.

[1] A legendary bird which is said to live for 500 years in the Arabian Desert and then consume itself by fire, rising from its ashes young again.

over these Writings of his, we come upon the startling yet not quite unlooked-for conclusion, that Teufelsdröckh is one of those who consider Society, properly so called, to be as good as extinct; and that only the gregarious feelings, and old inherited habitudes, at this juncture, hold us from Dispersion, and universal national, civil, domestic and personal war! He says expressly: 'For the last three centuries, above all for the last three quarters of a century, that same Pericardial Nervous Tissue (as we named it) of Religion, where lies the Life-essence of Society, has been smote-at and perforated, needfully and needlessly; till now it is quite rent into shreds; and Society, long pining, diabetic, consumptive, can be regarded as defunct; for those spasmodic, galvanic sprawlings are not life; neither indeed will they endure, galvanise as you may, beyond two days.'

'Call ye that a Society,' cries he again, 'where there is no longer any Social Idea extant; not so much as the Idea of a common Home, but only of a common over-crowded Lodging-house? Where each, isolated, regardless of his neighbour, turned against his neighbour, clutches what he can get, and cries "Mine!" and calls it Peace, because, in the cut-purse and cut-throat Scramble, no steel knives, but only a far cunninger sort, can be employed? Where Friendship, Communion, has become an incredible tradition; and your holiest Sacramental Supper is a smoking Tavern Dinner, with Cook for Evangelist? Where your Priest has no tongue but for platelicking: and your high Guides and Governors cannot guide; but on all hands hear it passionately proclaimed: *Laissez faire*; Leave us alone of *your* guidance, such light is darker than darkness; eat you your wages, and sleep!

'Thus, too,' continues he, 'does an observant eye discern everywhere that saddest spectacle: The Poor perishing, like neglected, foundered Draught-Cattle, of Hunger and Over-work; the Rich, still more wretchedly, of Idleness, Satiety, and Over-growth. The Highest in rank, at length, without honour from the Lowest; scarcely, with a little mouth-honour, as from tavern-waiters who expect to put it in the bill. Once-sacred Symbols fluttering as empty Pageants, whereof men grudge even the expense; a World becoming dismantled: in one word   the

CHURCH fallen speechless, from obesity and apoplexy; the
STATE shrunken into a Police-Office, straitened to get its pay!'

We might ask, are there many 'observant eyes,' belonging to
practical men in England or elsewhere, which have descried
these phenomena; or is it only from the mystic elevation of a
German *Wahngasse* that such wonders are visible? Teufelsdröckh contends that the aspect of a 'deceased or expiring Society' fronts us everywhere, so that whoso runs may read. 'What,
for example,' says he, 'is the universally-arrogated Virtue, almost
the sole remaining Catholic Virtue, of these days? For some
half century, it has been the thing you name "Independence."
Suspicion of "Servility," of reverence for Superiors, the very
dogleech is anxious to disavow. Fools! Were your Superiors
worthy to govern, and you worthy to obey, reverence for them
were even your only possible freedom. Independence, in all
kinds, is rebellion; if unjust rebellion, why parade it, and everywhere prescribe it?'

But what then? Are we returning, as Rousseau prayed, to the
state of Nature? 'The Soul Politic having departed,' says Teufelsdröckh, 'what can follow but that the Body Politic be decently
interred, to avoid putrescence? Liberals, Economists, Utilitarians enough I see marching with its bier, and chanting loud
pæans, towards the funeral-pile, where, amid wailings from
some, and saturnalian revelries from the most, the venerable
Corpse is to be burnt. Or, in plain words, that these men,
Liberals, Utilitarians, or whatsoever they are called, will ultimately carry their point, and dissever and destroy most existing
Institutions of Society, seems a thing which has some time ago
ceased to be doubtful.

'Do we not see a little subdivision of the grand Utilitarian
Armament come to light even in insulated England? A living
nucleus, that will attract and grow, does at length appear there
also; and under curious phasis; properly as the inconsiderable
fag-end, and so far in the rear of the others as to fancy itself
the van. Our European Mechanisers are a sect of boundless
diffusion, activity, and coöperative spirit: has not Utilitarianism
flourished in high places of Thought, here among ourselves, and
in every European country, at some time or other, within the

last fifty years? If now in all countries, except perhaps England, it has ceased to flourish, or indeed to exist, among Thinkers, and sunk to Journalists and the popular mass,—who sees not that, as hereby it no longer preaches, so the reason is, it now needs no Preaching, but is in full universal Action, the doctine everywhere known, and enthusiastically laid to heart? The fit pabulum, in these times, for a certain rugged workshop intellect and heart, nowise without their corresponding workshop strength and ferocity, it requires but to be stated in such scenes to make proselytes enough.—Admirably calculated for destroying, only not for rebuilding! It spreads like a sort of Dog-madness; till the whole World-kennel will be rabid: then woe to the Huntsmen, with or without their whips! They should have given the quadrupeds water,' adds he; 'the water, namely, of Knowledge and of Life, while it was yet time.'

Thus, if Professor Teufelsdröckh can be relied on, we are at this hour in a most critical condition; beleaguered by that boundless 'Armament of Mechanisers' and Unbelievers, threatening to strip us bare! 'The World,' says he, 'as it needs must, is under a process of devastation and waste, which, whether by silent assiduous corrosion, or open quicker combustion, as the case chances, will effectually enough annihilate the past Forms of Society; replace them with what it may. For the present, it is contemplated that when man's whole Spiritual Interests are once *divested*, these innumerable stript-off Garments shall mostly be burnt; but the sounder Rags among them be quilted together into one huge Irish watch-coat for the defence of the Body only!'—This, we think, is but Job's-news[2] to the humane reader.

'Nevertheless,' cries Teufelsdröckh, 'who can hinder it; who is there that can clutch into the wheelspokes of Destiny, and say to the Spirit of the Time: Turn back, I command thee?—Wiser were it that we yielded to the Inevitable and Inexorable, and accounted even this the best.'

Nay, might not an attentive Editor, drawing his own inferences from what stands written, conjecture that Teufelsdröckh individually had yielded to this same 'Inevitable and Inexorable'

---

[2] Bad news (Job, i, 13–19).

heartily enough; and now sat waiting the issue, with his natural diabolico-angelical Indifference, if not even Placidity? Did we not hear him complain that the World was a 'huge Ragfair,' and the 'rags and tatters of old Symbols' were raining-down everywhere, like to drift him in, and suffocate him? What with those 'unhunted Helots' of his; and the uneven *sic vos non vobis*[3] pressure and hard-crashing collision he is pleased to discern in existing things; what with the so hateful 'empty Masks,' full of beetles and spiders, yet glaring out on him, from their glass eyes, 'with a ghastly affectation of life,'—we feel entitled to conclude him even willing that much should be thrown to the Devil, so it were but done gently! Safe himself in that 'Pinnacle of Weissnichtwo,' he would consent, with a tragic solemnity, that the monster UTILITARIA, held back, indeed, and moderated by nose-rings, halters, foot-shackles, and every conceivable modification of rope, should go forth to do her work;—to tread down old ruinous Palaces and Temples with her broad hoof, till the whole were trodden down, that new and better might be built! Remarkable in this point of view are the following sentences.

'Society,' says he, 'is not dead: that Carcass, which you call dead Society, is but her mortal coil which she has shuffled-off, to assume a nobler; she herself, through perpetual metamorphoses, in fairer and fairer development, has to live till Time also merge in Eternity. Wheresoever two or three Living Men are gathered together, there is Society; or there it will be, with its cunning mechanisms and stupendous structures, overspreading this little Globe, and reaching upwards to Heaven and downwards to Gehenna: for always, under one of the other figure, it has two authentic Revelations, of a God and of a Devil; the Pulpit, namely, and the Gallows.'

Indeed, we already heard him speak of 'Religion, in unnoticed nooks, weaving for herself new Vestures';—Teufelsdröckh himself being one of the loom-treadles? Elsewhere he quotes without censure that strange aphorism of Saint-Simon's,[4]

---

[3] "Thus do ye, but not for yourselves."
[4] Comte Claude Henri de Saint-Simon (1760–1825): French rationalistic philosopher and socialist reformer. His work strongly influenced the young Carlyle.

concerning which and whom so much were to be said: '*L'âge d'or, qu'une aveugle tradition a placé jusqu'ici dans le passé, est devant nous*; The golden age, which a blind tradition has hitherto placed in the Past, is Before us.'—But listen again:

'When the Phœnix is fanning her funeral pyre, will there not be sparks flying! Alas, some millions of men, and among them such as a Napoleon, have already been licked into that high-eddying Flame, and like moths consumed there. Still also have we to fear that incautious beards will get singed.

'For the rest, in what year of grace such Phœnix-cremation will be completed, you need not ask. The law of Perseverance is among the deepest in man: by nature he hates change; seldom will he quit his old house till it has actually fallen about his ears. Thus have I seen Solemnities linger as Ceremonies, sacred Symbols as idle Pageants, to the extent of three-hundred years and more after all life and sacredness had evaporated out of them. And then, finally, what time the Phœnix Death-Birth itself will require, depends on unseen contingenices.—Meanwhile, would Destiny offer Mankind, that after, say two centuries of convulsion and conflagration, more or less vivid, the fire-creation should be accomplished, and we to find ourselves again in a Living Society, and no longer fighting but working,—were it not perhaps prudent in Mankind to strike the bargain?'

Thus is Teufelsdröckh content that old sick Society should be deliberately burnt (alas, with quite other fuel than spicewood); in the faith that she is a Phœnix; and that a new heavenborn young one will rise out of her ashes! We ourselves, restricted to the duty of Indicator, shall forbear commentary. Meanwhile, will not the judicious reader shake his head, and reproachfully, yet more in sorrow than in anger, say or think: From a *Doctor utriusque Juris*, titular Professor in a University, and man to whom hitherto, for his services, Society, bad as she is, has given not only food and raiment (of a kind), but books, tobacco and gukguk, we expected more gratitude to his benefactress; and less of a blind trust in the future, which resembles that rather of a philosophical Fatalist and Enthusiast, than of a solid house-holder paying scot-and-lot[5] in a Christian country.

[5] A British tax imposed on all inhabitants of a borough according to their ability to pay.

Chapter VI
Old Clothes

Courtesy due from all men to all men: The Body of Man a
Revelation in the Flesh. Teufelsdröckh's respect for Old
Clothes, as the 'Ghosts of life.' Walk in Monmouth Street,
and meditations there.

As mentioned above, Teufelsdröckh, though a sansculottist, is
in practice probably the politest man extant: his whole heart
and life are penetrated and informed with the spirit of politeness; a noble natural Courtesy shines through him, beautifying
his vagaries; like sun-light, making a rosy-fingered, rainbow-
dyed Aurora out of mere aqueous clouds; nay brightening
London-smoke itself into gold vapour, as from the crucible of
an alchemist. Hear in what earnest though fantastic wise he
expresses himself on this head:

'Shall Courtesy be done only to the rich, and only by the
rich? In Good-breeding, which differs, if at all, from High-
breeding, only as it gracefully remembers the rights of others,
rather than gracefully insists on its own rights, I discern no
special connexion with wealth or birth: but rather that it lies in
human nature itself, and is due from all men towards all men.
Of a truth, were your Schoolmaster at his post, and worth anything when there, this, with so much else, would be reformed.
Nay, each man were then also his neighbour's schoolmaster; till
at length a rude-visaged, unmannered Peasant could no more
be met with, than a Peasant unacquainted with botanical Physiology, or who felt not that the clod he broke was created in
Heaven.

'For whether thou bear a sceptre or a sledge-hammer, art not
thou ALIVE; is not this thy brother ALIVE? "There is but one
temple in the world," says Novalis, "and that temple is the

Body of Man. Nothing is holier than this high Form. Bending before men is a reverence done to this Revelation in the Flesh. We touch Heaven, when we lay our hands on a human Body."

'On which ground, I would fain carry it farther than most do; and whereas the English Johnson[1] only bowed to every Clergyman, or man with a shovel-hat, I would bow to every Man with any sort of hat, or with no hat whatever. Is not he a Temple, then; the visible Manifestation and Impersonation of the Divinity? And yet, alas, such indiscriminate bowing serves not. For there is a Devil dwells in man, as well as a Divinity; and too often the bow is but pocketed by the *former*. It would go to the pocket of Vanity (which is your clearest phasis of the Devil, in these times); therefore must we withhold it.

'The gladder am I, on the other hand, to do reverence to those Shells and outer Husks of the Body, wherein no devilish passion any longer lodges, but only the pure emblem and effigies of Man: I mean, to Empty, or even to Cast Clothes. Nay, is it not to Clothes that most men do reverence: to the fine frogged broadcloth, nowise to the "straddling animal with bandy legs" which it holds, and makes a Dignitary of? Who ever saw any Lord my-lorded in tattered blanket fastened with wooden skewer? Nevertheless, I say, there is in such worship a shade of hypocrisy, a practical deception: for how often does the Body appropriate what was meant for the Cloth only! Whoso would avoid falsehood, which is the essence of all Sin, will perhaps see good to take a different course. That reverence which cannot act without obstruction and perversion when the Clothes are full, may have free course when they are empty. Even as, for Hindoo Worshippers, the Pagoda is not less sacred than the God; so do I too worship the hollow cloth Garment with equal fervour, as when it contained the Man: nay, with more, for I now fear no deception, of myself or of others.

'Did not King *Toomtabard*, or, in other words, John Baliol,[2] reign long over Scotland; the man John Baliol being quite gone, and only the "Toom Tabard" (Empty Gown) remaining? What

---

[1] Boswell's *Life of Johnson* tells of Dr. Johnson's respect for the clergy, but not that he bowed to "every Clergyman."
[2] John Baliol reigned four years, 1292–1296.

still dignity dwells in a suit of Cast Clothes! How meekly it bears its honours! No haughty looks, no scornful gesture: silent and serene, it fronts the world; neither demanding worship, nor afraid to miss it. The Hat still carries the physiognomy of its Head: but the vanity and the stupidity, and goose-speech which was the sign of these two, are gone. The Coat-arm is stretched out, but not to strike; the Breeches, in modest simplicity, depend at ease, and now at last have a graceful flow; the Waistcoat hides no evil passion, no riotous desire; hunger or thirst now dwells not in it. Thus all is purged from the grossness of sense, from the carking cares and foul vices of the World; and rides there, on its Clothes-horse; as, on a Pegasus, might some skyey Messenger, or purified Apparition, visiting our low Earth.

'Often, while I sojourned in that monstrous tuberosity of Civilised Life, the Capital of England; and meditated, and questioned Destiny, under that ink-sea of vapour, black thick, and multifarious as Spartan broth; and was one lone soul amid those grinding millions;—often have I turned into their Old-Clothes Market to worship. With awe-struck heart I walk through that Monmouth Street,[3] with its empty Suits, as through a Sanhedrim of stainless Ghosts. Silent are they, but expressive in their silence: the past witnesses and instruments of Woe and Joy, of Passions, Virtues, Crimes, and all the fathomless tumult of Good and Evil in "the Prison men call Life." Friends! trust not the heart of that man for whom Old Clothes are not venerable. Watch, too, with reverence, that bearded Jewish Highpriest, who with hoarse voice, like some Angel of Doom, summons them from the four winds! On his head, like the Pope, he has three Hats,[4]—a real triple tiara; on either hand are the similitude of wings, whereon the summoned Garments come to alight; and ever, as he slowly cleaves the air, sounds forth his deep fateful note, as if through a trumpet he were proclaiming: "Ghosts of Life, come to Judgment!" Reck not, ye fluttering Ghosts: he will purify you in his Purgatory, with fire and with

---

[3] Street in London known for second-hand clothing stores.
[4] Carlyle is here humorously comparing a Jewish old-clothes seller of Monmouth Street to the Pope who traditionally wears a triple crown.

water; and, one day, new-created ye shall reappear. O, let him in whom the flame of Devotion is ready to go out, who has never worshipped, and knows not what to worship, pace and repace, with austerest thought, the pavement of Monmouth Street, and say whether his heart and his eyes still continue dry. If Field Lane,[5] with its long fluttering rows of yellow handkerchiefs, be a Dionysius' Ear,[6] where, in stifled jarring hubbub, we hear the Indictment which Poverty and Vice bring against lazy Wealth, that it has left them there cast-out and trodden under foot of Want, Darkness and the Devil,—then is Monmouth Street a Mirza's Hill, where, in motley vision, the whole Pageant of Existence passes awfully before us; with its wail and jubilee, mad loves and mad hatreds, church-bells and gallows-ropes, farce-tragedy, beast-godhood,—the Bedlam of Creation!'

To most men, as it does to ourselves, all this will seem over-charged. We too have walked through Monmouth Street; but with little feeling of 'Devotion': probably in part because the contemplative process is so fatally broken in upon by the brood of money-changers who nestle in that Church, and importune the worshipper with merely secular proposals. Whereas Teufels-dröckh might be in that happy middle state, which leaves to the Clothes-broker no hope either of sale or of purchase, and so be allowed to linger there without molestation.—Something we would have given to see the little philosophical figure, with its steeple-hat and loose flowing skirts, and eyes in a fine frenzy, 'pacing and repacing in austerest thought' that foolish Street; which to him was a true Delphic avenue, and supernatural Whispering-gallery, where the 'Ghosts of Life' rounded strange secrets in his ear. O thou philosophic Teufelsdröckh, that lis-tenest while others only gabble, and with thy quick tympanum hearest the grass grow!

At the same time, is it not strange that, in Paper-bag Docu-ments destined for an English work, there exists nothing like an

---

[5] A street in London known for its dealings in stolen goods, espe-cially handkerchiefs.
[6] Dionysius, Greek Tyrant of Syracuse (c. 430–367 B.C.) built a subterranean cave, called "Dionysius' Ear," where he could listen to the conversation of prisoners he had confined there.

authentic diary of this his sojourn in London; and of his Meditations among the Clothes-shops only the obscurest emblematic shadows? Neither, in conversation (for, indeed, he was not a man to pester you with his Travels), have we heard him more than allude to the subject.

For the rest, however, it cannot be uninteresting that we here find how early the significance of Clothes had dawned on the now so distinguished Clothes-Professor. Might we but fancy it to have been even in Monmouth Street, at the bottom of our own English 'ink-sea,' that this remarkable Volume first took being, and shot forth its salient point in his soul,—as in Chaos did the Egg of Eros,[7] one day to be hatched into a Universe!

Chapter VII
Organic Filaments

Destruction and Creation ever proceed together; and organic filaments of the Future are even now spinning. Wonderful connection of each man with all men; and of each generation with all generations, before and after: Mankind is One. Sequence and progress of all human work, whether of creation or destruction, from age to age.—Titles, hitherto derived from Fighting, must give way to others. Kings will remain and their title. Political Freedom, not to be attained by any mechanical contrivance. Hero-worship, perennial amongst men; the cornerstone of politics in the Future. Organic filaments of the New Religion: Newspapers and Literature. Let the faithful soul take courage!

For us, who happen to live while the World-Phœnix is burning herself, and burning so slowly that, as Teufelsdröckh calculates, it were a handsome bargain would she engage to have done

[7] In early Greek myths, Eros, the generative principle, was born from an egg laid in the unformed world of Chaos.

'within two centuries,' there seems to lie but an ashy prospect. Not altogether so, however, does the Professor figure it. 'In the living subject,' says he, 'change is wont to be gradual: thus, while the serpent sheds its old skin, the new is already formed beneath. Little knowest thou of the burning of a World-Phœnix, who fanciest that she must first burn-out, and lie as a dead cinereous heap; and therefrom the young one start-up by miracle, and fly heavenward. Far otherwise! In that Fire-whirlwind, Creation and Destruction proceed together; ever as the ashes of the Old are blown about, do organic filaments of the New mysteriously spin themselves: and amid the rushing and the waving of the Whirlwind-element come tones of a melodious Deathsong, which end not but in tones of a more melodious Birthsong. Nay, look into the Fire-whirlwind with thy own eyes, and thou wilt see.' Let us actually look, then: to poor individuals, who cannot expect to live two centuries, those same organic filaments, mysteriously spinning themselves, will be the best part of the spectacle. First, therefore, this of Mankind in general:

'In vain thou deniest it,' says the Professor; 'thou *art* my Brother. Thy very Hatred, thy very Envy, those foolish Lies thou tellest of me in thy splenetic humour: what is all this but an inverted Sympathy? Were I a Steam-engine, wouldst thou take the trouble to tell lies of me? Not thou! I should grind all unheeded, whether badly or well.

'Wondrous truly are the bonds that unite us one and all; whether by the soft binding of Love, or the iron chaining of Necessity, as we like to choose it. More than once have I said to myself, of some perhaps whimsically strutting Figure, such as provokes whimsical thoughts: "Wert thou, my little Brotherkin, suddenly covered-up within the largest imaginable Glass-bell,—what a thing it were, not for thyself only, but for the world! Post Letters, more or fewer, from all the four winds, impinge against thy Glass walls, but have to drop unread: neither from within comes there question or response into any Postbag; thy Thoughts fall into no friendly ear or heart, thy Manufacture into no purchasing hand: thou art no longer a circulating venous-arterial Heart, that, taking and giving, circulatest through all

Space and all Time: there has a Hole fallen-out in the immeasurable, universal World-tissue, which must be darned-up again!"

'Such venous-arterial circulation, of Letters, verbal Messages, paper and other Packages, going out from him and coming in, are a blood-circulation, visible to the eye: but the finer nervous circulation, by which all things the minutest that he does, minutely influence all men, and the very look of his face blesses or curses whomso it lights on, and so generates even new blessing or new cursing: all this you cannot see, but only imagine. I say, there is not a red Indian, hunting by Lake Winnipic, can quarrel with his squaw, but the whole world must smart for it: will not the price of beaver rise?[1] It is a mathematical fact that the casting of this pebble from my hand alters the centre of gravity of the Universe.

'If now an existing generation of men stand so woven together, not less indissolubly does generation with generation. Hast thou ever meditated on that word, Tradition: how we inherit not Life only, but all the garniture and form of Life; and work, and speak, and even think and feel, as our Fathers, and primeval grandfathers, from the beginning, have given it us?—Who printed thee, for example, this unpretending Volume on the Philosophy of Clothes? Not the Herren Stillschweigen and Company; but Cadmus of Thebes, Faust of Mentz,[2] and innumerable others whom thou knowest not. Had there been no Mœsogothic Ulfila,[3] there had been no English Shakespeare, or a different one. Simpleton! it was Tubalcain[4] that made thy very Tailor's needle, and sewed that court-suit of thine.

'Yes, truly, if Nature is one, and a living indivisible whole, much more is Mankind, the Image that reflects and creates Nature, without which Nature were not. As palpable life-

[1] Carlyle is here alluding to the extensive fur-trade with Canada (Lake Winnipeg).
[2] Cadmus: legendary founder of Thebes, said to have introduced the alphabet into Greece. Faust of Mentz (c. 1400–1466): partner of Johann Gutenberg and considered inventor of movable types.
[3] Ulfila or Wulfila (c. 311–383), a missionary to the Gothic tribes settled in Moesia on the Danube, translated the Bible into Gothic. Carlyle erroneously believed that Gothic was the language from which emerged all the Teutonic languages, including English.
[4] According to Old Testament, first worker in iron (Genesis, iv, 22).

streams in that wondrous Individual Mankind, among so many life-streams that are not palpable, flow on those main-currents of what we call Opinion; as preserved in Institutions, Polities, Churches, above all in Books. Beautiful it is to understand and know that a Thought did never yet die; that as thou, the originator thereof, hast gathered it and created it from the whole Past, so thou wilt transmit it to the whole Future. It is thus that the heroic heart, the seeing eye of the first times, still feels and sees in us of the latest; that the Wise Man stands ever encompassed, and spiritually embraced, by a cloud of witnesses and brothers; and there is a living, literal *Communion of Saints,* wide as the World itself, and as the History of the World.

'Noteworthy also, and serviceable for the progress of this same Individual, wilt thou find his subdivision into Generations. Generations are as the Days of toilsome Mankind: Death and Birth are the vesper and the matin bells, that summon Mankind to sleep, and to rise refreshed for new advancement. What the Father has made, the Son can make and enjoy; but has also work of his own appointed him. Thus all things wax, and roll onwards; Arts, Establishments, Opinions, nothing is completed, but ever completing. Newton has learned to see what Kepler[5] saw; but there is also a fresh heaven-derived force in Newton; he must mount to still higher points of vision. So too the Hebrew Lawgiver is, in due time, followed by an Apostle of the Gentiles. In the business of Destruction, as this also is from time to time a necessary work, thou findest a like sequence and perseverance: for Luther it was as yet hot enough to stand by that burning of the Pope's Bull; Voltaire could not warm himself at the glimmering ashes, but required quite other fuel. Thus likewise, I note, the English Whig has, in the second generation, become an English Radical; who, in the third again, it is to be hoped, will become an English Rebuilder. Find Mankind where thou wilt, thou findest it in living movement, in progress faster or slower: the Phœnix soars aloft, hovers with outstretched wings, filling Earth with her music; or, as now, she sinks, and with spheral swan-song immolates herself in flame, that she may soar the higher and sing the clearer.'

[5] See "Signs of the Times," n. 24.

Let the friends of social order, in such a disastrous period, lay this to heart, and derive from it any little comfort they can. We subjoin another passage, concerning Titles:

'Remark, not without surprise,' says Teufelsdröckh, 'how all high Titles of Honour come hitherto from Fighting. Your *Herzog* (Duke, *Dux*) is Leader of Armies; your Earl (*Jarl*) is Strong Man; your Marshal cavalry Horse-shoer. A Millennium, or reign of Peace and Wisdom, having from of old been prophesied, and becoming now daily more and more indubitable, may it not be apprehended that such Fighting-titles will cease to be palatable, and new and higher need to be devised?

'The only Title wherein I, with confidence, trace eternity, is that of King. *König* (King), anciently *Könning*, means Kenning (Cunning), or which is the same thing, Can-ning.[6] Ever must the Sovereign of Mankind be fitly entitled King.'

'Well, also,' says he elsewhere, 'was it written by Theologians: a King rules by divine right. He carries in him an authority from God, or man will never give it him. Can I choose my own King? I can choose my own King Popinjay, and play what farce or tragedy I may with him: but he who is to be my Ruler, whose will is to be higher than my will, was chosen for me in Heaven. Neither except in such Obedience to the Heaven-chosen is Freedom so much as conceivable.'

The Editor will here admit that, among all the wondrous provinces of Teufelsdröckh's spiritual world, there is none he walks in with such astonishment, hesitation, and even pain, as in the Political. How, with our English love of Ministry and Opposition, and that generous conflict of Parties, mind warming itself against mind in their mutual wrestle for the Public Good, by which wrestle, indeed, is our invaluable Consitution kept warm and alive; how shall we domesticate ourselves in this spectral Necropolis, or rather City both of the Dead and of the Unborn, where the Present seems little other than an inconsiderable Film dividing the Past and the Future? In those dim long-drawn expanses, all is so immeasurable; much so disastrous, ghastly; your very radiances and straggling light-beams have a supernatural character. And then with such an indifference,

[6] Carlyle's etymology is no longer accepted.

such a prophetic peacefulness (accounting the inevitably coming as already here, to him all one whether it be distant by centuries or only by days), does he sit;—and live, you would say, rather in any other age than in his own! It is our painful duty to announce, or repeat, that, looking into this man, we discern a deep, silent, slow-burning, inextinguishable Radicalism, such as fills us with shuddering admiration.

Thus, for example, he appears to make little even of the Elective Franchise;[7] at least so we interpret the following: 'Satisfy yourselves,' he says, 'by universal, indubitable experiment, even as ye are now doing or will do, whether FREEDOM, heavenborn and leading heavenward, and so vitally essential for us all, cannot peradventure be mechanically hatched and brought to light in that same Ballot-Box of yours; or at worst, in some other discoverable or devisable Box, Edifice, or Steam-mechanism. It were a mighty convenience; and beyond all feats of manufacture witnessed hitherto.' Is Teufelsdröckh acquainted with the British Constitution, even slightly?—He says under another figure: 'But after all, were the problem, as indeed it now everywhere is, To rebuild your old House from the top downwards (since you must live in it the while), what better, what other, than the Representative Machine will serve your turn? Meanwhile, however, mock me not with the name of Free, "when you have but knit-up my chains into ornamental festoons." '—Or what will any member of the Peace Society[8] make of such as assertion as this: 'The lower people everywhere desire War. Not so unwisely; there is then a demand for lower people—to be shot!'

Gladly, therefore, do we emerge from those soul-confusing labyrinths of speculative Radicalism, into somewhat clearer regions. Here, looking round, as was our hest, for 'organic filaments,' we ask, May not this, touching 'Hero-worship,' be of the number? It seems of a cheerful character; yet so quaint, so mystical, one knows not what or how little, may lie under it. Our readers shall look with their own eyes:

'True is it that, in these days, man can do almost all things,

[7] The Reform Bill of 1832 had recently extended the franchise.
[8] Organization established in London in 1816 by Society of Friends (Quakers) to promote peaceful settlement of international disputes.

only not obey. True likewise that whoso cannot obey cannot be free, still less bear rule; he that is the inferior of nothing, can be the superior of nothing, the equal of nothing. Nevertheless, believe not that man has lost his faculty of Reverence; that if it slumber in him, it has gone dead. Painful for man is that same rebellious Independence, when it has become inevitable; only in loving companionship with his fellows does he feel safe; only in reverently bowing down before the Higher does he feel himself exalted.

'Or what if the character of our so troublous Era lay even in this: that man had forever cast away Fear, which is the lower; but not yet risen into perennial Reverence, which is the higher and highest?

'Meanwhile, observe with joy, so cunningly has Nature ordered it, that whatsoever man ought to obey, he cannot but obey. Before no faintest revelation of the Godlike did he ever stand irreverent; least of all, when the Godlike showed itself revealed in his fellow-man. Thus is there a true religious Loyalty forever rooted in his heart; nay in all ages, even in ours, it manifests itself as a more or less orthodox *Hero-worship*. In which fact, that Hero-worship exists, has existed, and will forever exist, universally among Mankind, mayest thou discern the corner-stone of living-rock, whereon all Polities for the remotest time may stand secure.'

Do our readers discern any such corner-stone, or even so much as what Teufelsdröckh is looking at? He exclaims, 'Or hast thou forgotten Paris and Voltaire?[9] How the aged, withered man, though but a Sceptic, Mocker, and millinery Court-poet, yet because even he seemed the Wisest, Best, could drag mankind at his chariot-wheels, so that princes coveted a smile from him, and the loveliest of France would have laid their hair beneath his feet! All Paris was one vast Temple of Hero-worship; though their Divinity, moreover, was of feature too apish.

'But if such things,' continues he, 'were done in the dry tree, what will be done in the green? If, in the most parched season of Man's History, in the most parched spot of Europe, when

[9] When Voltaire returned to Paris in 1778 after an absence of thirty years, he was received in triumph.

Parisian life was at best but a scientific *Hortus Siccus*, bedizened with some Italian Gumflowers,[10] such virtue could come out of it; what is to be looked for when Life again waves leafy and bloomy, and your Hero-Divinity shall have nothing apelike, but be wholly human? Know that there is in man a quite indestructible Reverence for whatsoever holds of Heaven, or even plausibly counterfeits such holding. Show the dullest clodpole, show the haughtiest featherhead, that a soul higher than himself is actually here; were his knees stiffened into brass, he must down and worship.'

Organic filaments, of a more authentic sort, mysteriously spinning themselves, some will perhaps discover in the following passage:

'There is no Church, sayest thou? The voice of Prophecy has gone dumb? This is even what I dispute: but in any case, hast thou not still Preaching enough? A Preaching Friar settles himself in every village; and builds a pulpit, which he calls Newspaper. Therefrom he preaches what most momentous doctrine is in him, for man's salvation; and dost not thou listen, and believe? Look well, thou seest everywhere a new Clergy of the Mendicant Orders, some bare-footed, some almost bare-backed, fashion itself into shape, and teach and preach, zealously enough, for copper alms and the love of God. These break in pieces the ancient idols; and, though themselves too often reprobate, as idol-breakers are wont to be, mark out the sites of new Churches, where the true God-ordained, that are to follow, may find audience, and minister. Said I not, Before the old skin was shed, the new had formed itself beneath it?'

Perhaps also in the following; wherewith we now hasten to knit-up this ravelled sleeve:

'But there is no Religion?' reiterates the Professor. 'Fool! I tell thee, there is. Hast thou well considered all that lies in this immeasurable froth-ocean we name LITERATURE? Fragments of a genuine Church-*Homiletic* lie scattered there, which Time will assort: nay fractions even of a *Liturgy* could I point out. And knowest thou no Prophet, even in the vesture, environment, and dialect of this age? None to whom the Godlike had

[10] Hortus Siccus: collection of dried plants. Gumflowers: artificial flowers.

revealed itself, through all meanest and highest forms of the Common; and by him been again prophetically revealed: in whose inspired melody, even in these rag-gathering and rag-burning days. Man's Life again begins, were it but afar off, to be divine? Knowest thou none such? I know him, and name him—Goethe.

'But thou as yet standest in no Temple; joinest in no Psalm-worship; feelest well that, where there is no ministering Priest, the people perish? Be of comfort! Thou art not alone, if thou have Faith. Spake we not of a Communion of Saints, unseen, yet not unreal, accompanying and brotherlike embracing thee, so thou be worthy? Their heroic Sufferings rise up melodiously together to Heaven, out of all lands, and out of all times as a sacred *Miserere*; their heroic Actions also, as a boundless ever-lasting Psalm of Triumph. Neither say that thou hast now no Symbol of the Godlike. Is not God's Universe a Symbol of the Godlike; is not Immensity a Temple; is not Man's History, and Men's History, a perpetual Evangel? Listen, and for organ-music thou wilt ever, as of old, hear the Morning Stars sing together.'

Chapter VIII
Natural Supernaturalism

Deep significance of Miracles. Littleness of human Science: Divine incomprehensibility of Nature. Custom blinds us to the miraculousness of daily-recurring miracles; so do Names. Space and Time, appearances only; forms of human Thought: A glimpse of Immortality. How Space hides from us the won-drousness of our commonest powers; and Time, the divinely miraculous course of human history.

It is in his stupendous Section, headed *Natural Super-naturalism*, that the Professor first becomes a Seer; and, after long effort, such as we have witnessed, finally subdues under his feet this refractory Clothes-Philosophy, and takes victorious possession thereof. Phantasms enough he has had to struggle with; 'Cloth-webs and Cob-webs,' of Imperial Mantles, Superannuate Symbols, and what not: yet still did he courageously pierce through. Nay, worst of all, two quite mysterious, world-embracing Phantasms, TIME and SPACE, have ever hovered round him, perplexing and bewildering: but with these also he now resolutely grapples, these also he victoriously rends asunder. In a word, he has looked fixedly on Existence, till, one after the other, its earthly hulls and garnitures have all melted away; and now, to his rapt vision, the interior celestial Holy of Holies lies disclosed.

Here, therefore, properly it is that the Philosophy of Clothes attains to Transcendentalism; this last leap, can we but clear it, takes us safe into the promised land, where *Palingenesia*,[1] in all senses, may be considered as beginning. 'Courage, then!' may our Diogenes exclaim, with better right than Diogenes the First once did.[2] This stupendous Section we, after long painful meditation, have found not to be unintelligible; but, on the contrary, to grow clear, nay radiant, and all-illuminating. Let the reader, turning on it what utmost force of speculative intellect is in him, do his part; as we, by judicious selection and adjustment, shall study to do ours:

'Deep has been, and is, the significance of Miracles,' thus quietly begins the Professor; 'far deeper perhaps than we imagine. Meanwhile, the question of questions were: What specially is a Miracle? To that Dutch King of Siam, an icicle had been a miracle; whoso had carried with him an air-pump, and vial of vitriolic ether, might have worked a miracle. To my Horse, again, who unhappily is still more unscientific, do not I work a miracle, and magical *"Open sesame!"* every time I please to pay twopence, and open for him an impassable *Schlagbaum*, or shut Turnpike?

' "But is not a real Miracle simply a violation of the Laws

---

[1] "New birth or regeneration."
[2] Diogenes, the philosopher, is said to have exclaimed near the end of a tedious lecture, "Courage, friends! I see land."

of Nature?" ask several. Whom I answer by this new question: Where are the Laws of Nature? To me perhaps the rising of one from the dead were no violation of these Laws, but a confirmation; were some far deeper Law, now first penetrated into, and by Spiritual Force, even as the rest have all been, brought to bear on us with its Material Force.

'Here too may some inquire, not without astonishment: On what ground shall one, that can make Iron swim, come and declare that therefore he can teach Religion? To us, truly, of the Nineteenth Century, such declaration were inept enough; which nevertheless to our fathers, of the First Century, was full of meaning.

' "But is it not the deepest Law of Nature that she be constant?" cries an illuminated class: "Is not the Machine of the Universe fixed to move by unalterable rules?" Probable enough, good friends: nay I, too, must believe that the God, whom ancient inspired men assert to be "without variableness or shadow of turning," does indeed never change; that Nature, that the Universe, which no one whom it so pleases can be prevented from calling a Machine, does move by the most unalterable rules. And now of you, too, I make the old inquiry: What those same unalterable rules, forming the complete Statute-Book of Nature, may possibly be?

'They stand written in our Works of Science, say you; in the accumulated records of Man's Experience?—Was Man with his Experience present at the Creation, then, to see how it all went on? Have any deepest scientific individuals yet dived down to the foundations of the Universe, and gauged everything there? Did the Maker take them into His counsel; that they read His groundplan of the incomprehensible All; and can say, This stands marked therein, and no more than this? Alas, not in anywise! These scientific individuals have been nowhere but where we also are; have seen some handbreadths deeper than we see into the Deep that is infinite, without bottom as without shore.

'Laplace's Book on the Stars, wherein he exhibits that certain Planets, with their Satellites, gyrate round our worthy Sun, at a rate and in a course, which, by greatest good fortune, he and the like of him have succeeded in detecting,—is to me as precious as to another. But is this what thou namest "Mechanism of the Heavens," and "System of the World"; this, wherein Sirius and the Pleiades, and all Herschel's Fifteen-thousand Suns per minute,[3] being left out, some paltry handful of Moons, and inert Balls, had been—looked at, nicknamed, and marked in the Zodiacal Way-bill; so that we can now prate of their Whereabout; their How, their Why, their What, being hid from us, as in the signless Inane?

'System of Nature! To the wisest man, wide as is his vision, Nature remains of quite *infinite* depth, of quite infinite expansion; and all Experience thereof limits itself to some few computed centuries and measured square-miles. The course of Nature's phases, on this our little fraction of a Planet, is partially known to us: but who knows what deeper courses these depend on; what infinitely larger Cycle (of causes) our little Epicycles revolves on? To the Minnow every cranny and pebble, and quality and accident, of its little native Creek may have become familiar: but does the Minnow understand the Ocean Tides and periodic Currents, the Trade-winds, and Monsoons, and Moon's Eclipses; by all which the condition of its little Creek is regulated, and may, from time to time (*un*miraculously enough), be quite overset and reversed? Such a minnow is Man; his Creek this Planet Earth; his Ocean the immeasureable All; his Monsoons and periodic Currents the mysterious Course of Providence through Æons of Æons.

'We speak of the Volume of Nature: and truly a Volume it is,—whose Author and Writer is God. To read it! Dost thou, does man, so much as well know the Alphabet thereof? With its Words, Sentences, and grand descriptive Pages, poetical and philosophical, spread out through Solar Systems, and Thousands of Years, we shall not try thee. It is a Volume written in celestial hieroglyphs, in the true Sacred-writing; of which even Prophets

---

[3] A minute is an astronomical unit of measure, the sixtieth part of a degree. Sir William Herschel (1738–1822), English astronomer, discovered a great number of stars through the use of new telescopic equipment.

are happy that they can read here a line and there a line. As for your Institutes, and Academies of Science, they strive bravely; and, from amid the thick-crowded, inextricably intertwisted hieroglyphic writing, pick out, by dextrous combination, some Letters in the vulgar Character, and therefrom put together this and the other economic Recipe, of high avail in Practice. That Nature is more than some boundless Volume of such Recipes, or huge, well-nigh inexhaustible Domestic-Cookery Book, of which the whole secret will in this manner one day evolve itself, the fewest dream.

'Custom,' continues the Professor, 'doth make dotards of us all. Consider well, thou wilt find that Custom is the greatest of Weavers; and weaves air-raiment for all the Spirits of the Universe; whereby indeed these dwell with us visibly, as ministering servants, in our houses and workshops; but their spiritual nature becomes, to the most, forever hidden. Philosophy complains that Custom has hoodwinked us, from the first; that we do everything by Custom, even Believe by it; that our very Axioms, let us boast of Free-thinking as we may, are oftenest simply such Beliefs as we have never heard questioned. Nay, what is Philosophy throughout but a continual battle against Custom; an ever-renewed effort to *transcend* the sphere of blind Custom, and so become Transcendental?

'Innumerable are the illusions and legerdemain-tricks of Custom: but of all these, perhaps the cleverest is her knack of persuading us that the Miraculous, by simple repetition, ceases to be Miraculous. True, it is by this means we live; for man must work as well as wonder: and herein is Custom so far a kind nurse, guiding him to his true benefit. But she is a fond foolish nurse, or rather we are false foolish nurselings, when, in our resting and reflecting hours, we prolong the same deception. Am I to view the Stupendous with stupid indifference, because I have seen it twice, or two-hundred, or two-million times? There is no reason in Nature or in Art why I should: unless, indeed, I am a mere Work-Machine, for whom the divine gift of Thought were no other than the terrestrial gift of Steam is to the Steam-engine; a power whereby cotton might be spun, and money and money's worth realised.

'Notable enough too, here as elsewhere, wilt thou find the potency of Names; which indeed are but one kind of such custom-woven, wonder-hiding Garments. Witchcraft, and all manner of Spectre-work, and Demonology, we have now named Madness and Diseases of the Nerves. Seldom reflecting that still the new question comes upon us: What is Madness, what are Nerves? Ever, as before, does Madness remain a mysterious-terrific, altogether *infernal* boiling-up of the Nether Chaotic Deep, through this fair-painted Vision of Creation, which swims thereon, which we name the Real. Was Luther's Picture of the Devil[4] less a Reality, whether it were formed within the bodily eye, or without it? In every the wisest Soul lies a whole world of internal Madness, an authentic Demon-Empire; out of which, indeed, his world of Wisdom has been creatively built together, and now rests there, as on its dark foundations does a habitable flowery Earth-rind.

'But deepest of all illusory Appearances, for hiding Wonder, as for many other ends, are your two grand fundamental world-enveloping Appearances, SPACE and TIME. These, as spun and woven for us from before Birth itself, to clothe our celestial ME for dwelling here, and yet to blind it,—lie all-embracing, as the universal canvas, or warp and woof, whereby all minor Illusions, in this Phantasm Existence, weave and paint themselves. In vain, while here on Earth, shall you en-deavour to strip them off; you can, at best, but rend them asun-der for moments, and look through.

'Fortunatus had a wishing Hat, which when he put on, and wished himself Anywhere, behold he was There. By this means had Fortunatus triumphed over Space, he had annihilated Space; for him there was no Where, but all was Here. Were a Hatter to establish himself, in the Wahngasse of Weissnichtwo, and make felts of this sort for all mankind, what a world we should have of it! Still stranger, should, on the opposite side of

---

[4] Martin Luther is said to have thrown an inkstand at the Devil when he appeared while Luther was translating the Bible.

the street, another Hatter establish himself; and, as his fellow-craftsman made Space-annihilating Hats, make Time-annihilating! Of both would I purchase, were it with my last groschen; but chiefly of this latter. To clap-on your felt, and, simply by wishing that you were Any*where*, straightway to be *There*! Next to clap-on your other felt, and, simply by wishing that you were Any*when*, straightway to be *Then*! This were indeed the grander: shooting at will from the Fire-Creation of the World to its Fire-Consummation; here historically present in the First Century, conversing face to face with Paul and Seneca;[5] there prophetically in the Thirty-first, conversing also face to face with other Pauls and Senecas, who as yet stand hidden in the depth of that late Time!

'Or thinkest thou it were impossible, unimaginable? Is the Past annihilated, then, or only past; is the Future nonextant, or only future? Those mystic faculties of thine, Memory and Hope, already answer: already through those mystic avenues, thou the Earth-blinded summonest both Past and Future, and communest with them, though as yet darkly, and with mute beckonings. The curtains of Yesterday drop down, the curtains of Tomorrow roll up; but Yesterday and Tomorrow both *are*. Pierce through the Time-element, glance into the Eternal. Believe what thou findest written in the sanctuaries of Man's Soul, even as all thinkers, in all ages, have devoutly read it there: that Time and Space are not God, but creations of God; that with God as it is a universal HERE, so is it an everlasting Now.

'And seest thou therein any glimpse of IMMORTALITY?—O Heaven! Is the white Tomb of our Loved One, who died from our arms, and had to be left behind us there, which rises in the distance, like a pale, mournfully receding Milestone, to tell how many toilsome uncheered miles we have journeyed on alone,—but a pale spectral Illusion! Is the lost Friend still mysteriously Here, even as we are Here mysteriously, with God!—Know of a truth that only the Time-shadows have perished, or are perishable; that the real Being of whatever was, and whatever is, and

---

[5] Lucius Seneca (4 B.C.–65 A.D.) Roman Stoic philosopher. Carlyle is referring to Seneca's legendary meeting with his contemporary, St. Paul.

whatever will be, *is* even now and forever. This, should it unhappily seem new, thou mayest ponder at thy leisure; for the next twenty years, or the next twenty centuries: believe it thou must; understand it thou canst not.

'That the Thought-forms, Space and Time, wherein, once for all, we are sent into this Earth to live, should condition and determine our whole Practical reasonings, conceptions, and imagings or imaginings, seems altogether fit, just, and unavoidable. But that they should furthermore, usurp such sway over pure spiritual Meditation, and blind us to the wonder everywhere lying close on us, seems nowise so. Admit Space and Time to their due rank as Forms of Thought; nay even, if thou wilt, to their quite undue rank of Realities: and consider, then, with thyself how their thin disguises hide from us the brightest God-effulgences! Thus, were it not miraculous, could I stretch forth my hand and clutch the Sun? Yet thou seest me daily stretch forth my hand and therewith clutch many a thing, and swing it hither and thither. Art thou a grown baby, then, to fancy that the Miracle lies in miles of distance, or in pounds avoirdupois of weight; and not to see that the true inexplicable God-revealing Miracle lies in this, that I can stretch forth my hand at all; that I have free Force to clutch aught therewith? Innumerable other of this sort are the deceptions, and wonder-hiding stupefactions, which Space practises on us.

'Still worse is it with regard to Time. Your grand antimagician, and universal wonder-hider, is this same lying Time. Had we but the Time-annihilating Hat, to put on for once only, we should see ourselves in a World of Miracles, wherein all fabled or authentic Thaumaturgy, and feats of Magic, were outdone. But unhappily we have not such a Hat; and man, poor fool that he is, can seldom and scantily help himself without one.

'Were it not wonderful, for instance, had Orpheus, or Amphion,[6] built the walls of Thebes by the mere sound of his

---

[6] Orpheus: in Greek mythology, a legendary poet who could charm wild beasts with his singing to the music of the lyre. Amphion: Son of Zeus who caused the wall of Thebes to be built by the sound of a magic lyre.

Lyre? Yet tell me, Who built these walls of Weissnichtwo;
summoning out all the sandstone rocks, to dance along from
the *Steinbruch*[7] (now a huge Troglodyte Chasm, with frightful
green-mantled pools); and shape themselves into Doric and
Ionic pillars, squared ashlar houses and noble streets? Was it
not the still higher Orpheus, or Orpheuses, who, in past centuries, by the divine Music of Wisdom, succeeded in civilising
Man? Our highest Orpheus walked in Judea, eighteen-hundred
years ago: his sphere-melody, flowing in wild native tones, took
captive the ravished souls of men; and, being of a true sphere-
melody still flows and sounds, though now with thousandfold
accompaniments, and rich symphonies, through all our hearts;
and modulates, and divinely leads them. Is that a wonder,
which happens in two hours; and does it cease to be wonderful
if happening in two million? Not only was Thebes built by the
music of an Orpheus; but without the music of some inspired
Orpheus was no city ever built, no work that man glories in ever
done.

'Sweep away the Illusion of Time; glance, if thou have eyes,
from the near moving-cause to its far-distant Mover: The stroke
that came transmitted through a whole galaxy of elastic balls,
was it less a stroke than if the last ball only had been struck,
and sent flying? O, could I (with the Time-annihilating Hat)
transport thee direct from the Beginnings to the Endings, how
were thy eyesight unsealed, and thy heart set flaming in the
Light-sea of celestial wonder! Then sawest thou that this fair
Universe, were it in the meanest province thereof, is in very
deed the star-domed City of God; that through every star,
through every grass-blade, and most through every Living Soul,
the glory of a present God still beams. But Nature, which is the
Time-vesture of God, and reveals Him to the wise, hides Him
from the foolish.

'Again, could anything be more miraculous than an actual
authentic Ghost? The English Johnson[8] longed, all his life, to
see one; but could not, though he went to Cock Lane, and

[7] "Quarry."
[8] Allusion to incident in Boswell's *Life of Johnson*.

thence to the church-vaults, and tapped on coffins. Foolish Doctor! Did he never, with the mind's eye as well as with the body's, look round him into that full tide of human Life he so loved; did he never so much as look into Himself? The good Doctor was a Ghost, as actual and authentic as heart could wish; well-nigh a million of Ghosts were travelling the streets by his side. Once more I say, sweep away the illusion of Time; compress the threescore years into three minutes: what else was he, what else are we? Are we not Spirits, that are shaped into a body, into an Appearance; and that fade away again into air and Invisibility? This is no metaphor, it is a simple scientific *fact*; we start out of Nothingness, take figure, and are Apparitions; round us, as round the veriest spectre, is Eternity; and to Eternity minutes are as years and æons. Come there not tones of Love and Faith, as from celestial harp-strings, like the Song of beatified Souls? And again, do not we squeak and jibber (in our discordant, screech-owlish debatings and recriminatings); and glide bodeful, and feeble, and fearful; or uproar (*poltern*), and revel in our mad Dance of the Dead,—till the scent of the morning air summons us to our still Home; and dreamy Night becomes awake and Day? Where now is Alexander of Macedon: does the steel Host, that yelled in fierce battle-shouts at Issus and Arbela, remain behind him; or have they all vanished utterly, even as perturbed Goblins must? Napoleon too, and his Moscow Retreats and Austerlitz Campaigns! Was it all other than the veriest Spectrehunt; which has now, with its howling tumult that made Night hideous, flitted away?—Ghosts! There are nigh a thousand-million walking the Earth openly at noon-tide; some half-hundred have vanished from it, some half-hundred have arisen in it, ere thy watch ticks once.

'O Heaven, it is mysterious, it is awful to consider that we not only carry each a future Ghost within Him; but are, in very deed, Ghosts! These Limbs, whence had we them; this stormy Force; this life-blood with its burning Passion? They are dust and shadow; a Shadow-system gathered round our ME; wherein, through some moments or years, the Divine Essence is to be revealed in the Flesh. That warrior on his strong war-horse, fire flashes through his eyes; force dwells in his arm and heart: but warrior and war-horse are a vision; a revealed Force, nothing more. Stately they tread the Earth, as if it were a firm substance: fool! the Earth is but a film; it cracks in twain, and warrior and war-horse sink beyond plummet's sounding. Plummet's? Fantasy herself will not follow them: A little while ago, they were not; a little while, and they are not, their very ashes are not.

'So has it been from the beginning, so will it be to the end. Generation after generation takes to itself the Form of a Body; and forth-issuing from Cimmerian Night, on Heaven's mission APPEARS. What Force and Fire is in each he expends: one grinding in the mill of Industry; one hunter-like climbing the giddy Alpine heights of Science; one madly dashed in pieces on the rocks of Strife, in war with his fellow:—and then the Heaven-sent is recalled; his earthly Vesture falls away, and soon even to sense becomes a vanished Shadow. Thus, like some wild-flaming, wild-thundering train of Heaven's Artillery, does this mysterious MANKIND thunder and flame, in long-drawn, quick-succeeding grandeur, through the unknown Deep. Thus, like a God-created, fire-breathing Spirit-host, we emerge from the Inane; haste stormfully across the astonished Earth; then plunge again into the Inane. Earth's mountains are levelled, and her seas filled up, in our passage: can the Earth, which is but dead and a vision, resist Spirits which have reality and are alive? On the hardest adamant some footprint of us is stamped-in; the last Rear of the host will read traces of the earliest Van. But whence?—O Heaven, whither? Sense knows not; Faith knows not; only that it is through Mystery to Mystery, from God and to God.

> "We *are such stuff*
> As dreams are made of, and our little Life
> Is rounded with a sleep!"[9]

[9] *The Tempest*, V, i, 156–158.

Thomas Carlyle

Chapter IX
Circumspective

Recapitulation. Editor congratulates the few British readers
who have accompanied Teufelsdröckh through all his speculations. The true use of the *Sartor Resartus*, to exhibit the
Wonder of daily life and common things; and to show that
all Forms are but Clothes, and temporary. Practical inferences enough will follow.

Here, then, arises the so momentous question: Have many
British Readers actually arrived with us at the new promised
country; is the Philosophy of Clothes now at last opening around
them? Long and adventurous has the journey been: from those
outmost vulgar, palpable Woollen Hulls of Man; through his
wondrous Flesh-Garment, and his wondrous Social Garnitures;
inwards to the Garments of his very Soul's Soul, to Time and
Space themselves! And now does the spiritual, eternal Essence
of Man, and of Mankind, bared of such wrappages, begin in
any measure to reveal itself? Can many readers discern, as
through a glass darkly, in huge wavering outlines, some primeval rudiments of Man's Being, what is changeable divided
from what is unchangeable? Does that Earth-Spirit's speech in
Faust,—

> 'Tis thus at the roaring Loom of Time I ply,
> And weave for God the Garment thou see'st Him by';

or that other thousand-times repeated speech of the Magician,
Shakspeare,—

> 'And like the baseless fabric of this vision,
> The cloudcapt Towers, the gorgeous Palaces,

The solemn Temples, the great Globe itself,
And all which it inherit, shall dissolve;
And like this unsubstantial pageant faded,
Leave not a wrack behind';[1]

begin to have some meaning for us? In a word, do we at length
stand safe in the far region of Poetic Creation and Palingenesia,
where that Phœnix Death-Birth of Human Society, and of all
Human Things, appears possible, is seen to be inevitable?

Along this most insufficent, unheard-of Bridge, which the
Editor, by Heaven's blessing, has now seen himself enabled to
conclude if not complete, it cannot be his sober calculation, but
only his fond hope, that many have travelled without accident.
No firm arch, overspanning the Impassable with paved highway,
could the Editor construct; only, as was said, some zigzag
series of rafts floating tumultuously thereon. Alas, and the leaps
from raft to raft, were too often of a breakneck character; the
darkness, the nature of the element, all was against us!

Nevertheless, may not here and there one of a thousand,
provided with a discursiveness of intellect rare in our day, have
cleared the passage, in spite of all? Happy few! little band of
Friends! be welcome, be of courage. By degrees, the eye grows
accustomed to its new Whereabout; the hand can stretch itself
forth to work there: it is in this grand and indeed highest work
of Palingenesia that ye shall labour, each according to ability.
New labourers will arrive; new Bridges will be built; nay, may
not our own poor rope-and-raft Bridge, in your passings and
repassings, be mended in many a point, till it grows quite firm,
passable even for the halt?

Meanwhile, of the innumerable multitude that started with
us, joyous and full of hope, where now is the innumerable
remainder, whom we see no longer by our side? The most have
recoiled, and stand gazing afar off, in unsympathetic astonishment, at our career: not a few, pressing forward with more
courage, have missed footing, or leaped short; and now swim
weltering in the Chaos-flood, some towards this shore, some to-

[1] *The Tempest*, IV, i, 151–156.

245

wards that. To these also a helping hand should be held out; at least some word of encouragement be said.

Or, to speak without metaphor, with which mode of utterance Teufelsdröckh unhappily has somewhat infected us,—can it be hidden from the Editor that many a British reader sits reading quite bewildered in head, and afflicted rather than instructed by the present Work? Yes, long ago has many a British Reader been, as now, demanding with something like a snarl: Whereto does all this lead; or what use is in it?

In the way of replenishing thy purse, or otherwise aiding thy digestive faculty, O British Reader, it leads to nothing, and there is no use in it; but rather the reverse, for it costs thee somewhat. Nevertheless, if through this unpromising Horn-gate,[2] Teufelsdröckh, and we by means of him, have led thee into the true Land of Dreams; and through the Clothes-Screen, as through a magical *Pierre-Pertuis*,[3] thou lookest, even for moments, into the region of the Wonderful, and seest and feelest that thy daily life is girt with Wonder, and based on Wonder, and thy very blankets and breeches are Miracles,—then art thou profited beyond money's worth; and hast a thankfulness towards our Professor; nay, perhaps in many a literary Tea-circle wilt open thy kind lips, and audibly express that same.

Nay further, art not thou too perhaps by this time made aware that all Symbols are properly Clothes; that all Forms whereby Spirit manifests itself to sense, whether outwardly or in the imagination, are Clothes; and thus not only the parchment Magna Charta, which a Tailor was nigh cutting into measures, but the Pomp and Authority of Law, the sacredness of Majesty, and all inferior Worships (Worthships) are properly a Vesture and Raiment; and the Thirty-nine Articles[4] themselves are articles of wearing-apparel (for the Religious Idea)? In which case, must it not also be admitted that this Science of Clothes is a high one, and may with infinitely deeper study on thy part

---

[2] The gate of sleep from which true dreams issue.
[3] A large natural opening in a rock in the Alps.
[4] Statement of doctrine subscribed to by members of the Church of England.

yield richer fruit: that it takes scientific rank beside Codification,[5] and Political Economy, and the Theory of the British Constitution; nay rather, from its prophetic height looks down on all these, as on so many weaving-shops and spinning-mills, where the Vestures which *it* has to fashion, and consecrate and distribute, are, too often by haggard hungry operatives who see no farther than their nose, mechanically woven and spun?

But omitting all this, much more all that concerns Natural Supernaturalism, and indeed whatever has reference to the Ulterior or Transcendental portion of the Science, or bears never so remotely on that promised Volume of the *Palingenesie der menschlichen Gesellschaft* (Newbirth of Society),—we humbly suggest that no province of Clothes-Philosophy, even the lowest, is without its direct value, but that innumerable inferences of a practical nature may be drawn therefrom. To say nothing of those pregnant considerations, ethical, political, symbolical, which crowd on the Clothes-Philosopher from the very threshold of his Science; nothing even of those 'architectural ideas,' which, as we have seen, lurk at the bottom of all Modes, and will one day, better unfolding themselves, lead to important revolutions,—let us glance for a moment, and with the faintest light of Clothes-Philosophy, on what may be called the Habilatory Class of our fellow-men. Here too overlooking, where so much were to be looked on, the million spinners, weavers, fullers, dyers, washers, and wringers, that puddle and muddle in their dark recesses, to make us Clothes, and die that we may live,—let us but turn the reader's attention upon two small divisions of mankind, who, like moths, may be regarded as Cloth-animals, creatures that live, move, and have their being in Cloth: we mean, Dandies and Tailors.

In regard to both which small divisions it may be asserted without scruple, that the public feeling, unenlightened by Philosophy, is at fault; and even that the dictates of humanity are violated. As will perhaps abundantly appear to readers of the two following Chapters.

[5] One of the Benthamites' main endeavors was codification, or the establishing of codes of laws.

Thomas Carlyle

Chapter X
The Dandiacal Body

The Dandy defined. The Dandiacal Sect a new modification of the primeval superstition Self-worship: How to be distinguished. Their Sacred Books (Fashionable Novels) unreadable. Dandyism's Articles of Faith.—Brotherhood of Poor-Slaves; vowed to perpetual Poverty; worshippers of Earth; distinguished by peculiar costume and diet. Picture of a Poor-Slave Household; and of a Dandiacal. Teufelsdröckh fears these two Sects may spread, till they part all England between them, and then frightfully collide.

First, touching Dandies, let us consider, with some scientific strictness, what a Dandy specially is. A Dandy is a Clothes-wearing Man, a Man whose trade, office, and existence consists in the wearing of Clothes. Every faculty of his soul, spirit, purse, and person is heroically consecrated to this one object, the wearing of Clothes wisely and well: so that as others dress to live, he lives to dress. The all-importance of Clothes, which a German Professor, of unequalled learning and acumen, writes his enormous Volume to demonstrate, has sprung up in the intellect of the Dandy without effort, like an instinct of genius; he is inspired with Cloth, a Poet of Cloth. What Teufelsdröckh would call a 'Divine Idea of Cloth' is born with him; and this, like other such Ideas, will express itself outwardly, or wring his heart asunder with unutterable throes.

But, like a generous, creative enthusiast, he fearlessly makes his Idea an Action; shows himself in peculiar guise to mankind; walks forth, a witness and living Martyr to the eternal world of Clothes. We called him a Poet: is not his body the (stuffed) parchment-skin whereon he writes, with cunning Huddersfield

248

dyes, a Sonnet to his mistress' eyebrow? Say, rather, an Epos, and *Clotha Virumque cano*,[1] to the whole world, in Macaronic[2] verses, which he that runs may read. Nay, if you grant, what seems to be admissible, that the Dandy has a Thinking-principle in him, and some notions of Time and Space, is there not in this Life-devotedness to Cloth, in this so willing sacrifice of the Immortal to the Perishable, something (though in reverse order) of that blending and identification of Eternity with Time, which, as we have seen, constitutes the Prophetic character?

And now, for all this perennial Martyrdom, and Poesy, and even Prophecy, what is it that the Dandy asks in return? Solely, we may say, that you would recognise his existence; would admit him to be a living object; or even failing this, a visual object, or thing that will reflect rays of light. Your silver or your gold (beyond what the niggardly Law has already secured him) he solicits not; simply the glance of your eyes. Understand his mystic significance, or altogether miss and misinterpret it; do but look at him, and he is contented. May we not well cry shame on an ungrateful world, which refuses even this poor boon; which will waste its optic faculty on dried Crocodiles, and Siamese Twins; and over the domestic wonderful wonder of wonders, a live Dandy, glance with hasty indifference, and a scarcely concealed contempt! Him no Zoologist classes among the Mammalia, no Anatomist dissects with care: when did we see any injected Preparation of the Dandy in our Museums; any specimen of him preserved in spirits? Lord Herringbone may dress himself in a snuff-brown suit, with snuff-brown shirt and shoes: it skills not; the undiscerning public, occupied with grosser wants, passes by regardless on the other side.

The age of Curiosity, like that of Chivalry, is indeed, properly speaking, gone. Yet perhaps only gone to sleep: for here arises the Clothes-Philosophy to resuscitate, strangely enough, both the one and the other! Should sound views of this Science come to prevail, the essential nature of the British Dandy, and the

[1] "Of clothes and the man I sing," parody of opening lines of *The Aeneid*, "Of arms and the man I sing."

[2] Poetry composed in a medley of languages. Also pun on macaroni, a term for dandy.

mystic significance that lies in him, cannot always remain hidden under laughable and lamentable hallucination. The following long Extract from Professor Teufelsdröckh may set the matter, if not in its true light, yet in the way towards such. It is to be regretted, however, that here, as so often elsewhere, the Professor's keen philosophic perspicacity is somewhat marred by a certain mixture of almost owlish purblindness, or else of some perverse, ineffectual, ironic tendency; our readers shall judge which:

'In these distracted times,' writes he, 'when the Religious Principle, driven out of most Churches, either lies unseen in the hearts of good men, looking and longing and silently working there towards some new Revelation; or else wanders homeless over the world, like a disembodied soul seeking its terrestrial organisation,—into how many strange shapes, of Superstition and Fanaticism, does it not tentatively and errantly cast itself! The higher Enthusiasm of man's nature is for the while without Exponent; yet does it continue indestructible, unweariedly active, and work blindly in the great chaotic deep: thus Sect after Sect, and Church after Church, bodies itself forth, and melts again into new metamorphosis.

'Chiefly is this observable in England, which, as the wealthiest and worst-instructed of European nations, offers precisely the elements (of Heat, namely, and of Darkness), in which such moon-calves and monstrosities are best generated. Among the newer Sects of that country, one of the most notable, and closely connected with our present subject, is that of the *Dandies*; concerning which, what little information I have been able to procure may fitly stand here.

'It is true, certain of the English Journalists, men generally without sense for the Religious Principle, or judgment for its manifestations, speak, in their brief enigmatic notices, as if this were perhaps rather a Secular Sect, and not a Religious one; nevertheless, to the psychologic eye its devotional and even sacrificial character plainly enough reveals itself. Whether it belongs to the class of Fetich-worships, or of Hero-worships or Polytheisms, or to what other class, may in the present state of our intelligence remain undecided (*schweben*). A certain

touch of Manicheism, not indeed in the Gnostic shape, is discernible enough: also (for human Error walks in a cycle, and
reappears at intervals) a not-inconsiderable resemblance to that
Superstition of the Athos Monks, who by fasting from all
nourishment, and looking intensely for a length of time into
their own navels, came to discern therein the true Apocalypse
of Nature, and Heaven Unveiled. To my own surmise, it appears
as if this Dandiacal Sect were but a new modification, adapted to
the new time, of that primeval Supersision, *Self-worship*; which
Zerdusht, Quangfoutchee,³ Mohamed, and others, strove rather
to subordinate and restrain than to eradicate, and which only in
the purer forms of Religion has been altogether rejected. Wherefore, if any one chooses to name it revived Ahrimanism,⁴ or a
new figure of Demon-worship, I have, so far as is yet visible, no
objection.

'For the rest, these people, animated with the zeal of a new
Sect, display courage and perseverance, and what force there is
in man's nature, though never so enslaved. They affect great
purity and separatism; distinguish themselves by a particular
costume (whereof some notices were given in the earlier part
of this Volume); likewise, so far as possible, by a particular
speech (apparently some broken *Lingua-franca*,⁵ or English-
French); and, on the whole, strive to maintain a true Nazarene
deportment, and keep themselves unspotted from the world.

'They have their Temples, whereof the chief, as the Jewish
Temple did, stands in their metropolis; and is named *Almack's*,⁶
a word of uncertain etymology. They worship principally by
night; and have their Highpriests and Highpriestesses, who,
however, do not continue for life. The rites, by some supposed
to be of the Menadic⁷ sort, or perhaps with an Eleusinian or
Cabiric character,⁸ are held strictly secret. Nor are Sacred Books
wanting to the Sect; these they call *Fashionable Novels*: how-

³ Zerdusht: Zoroaster. Quangfoutchee: Confucius.
⁴ Ahriman is the principle of evil in the ancient Persian religion.
⁵ Any mixed language used in commercial transactions among people
of different languages within an area. Also refers to the use of French
words by English dandies.
⁶ A fashionable assembly room in the nineteenth century.
⁷ Maenads were female priests of Bacchus, god of wine.
⁸ Referring to secret rites in the classical world.

ever, the Canon is not completed, and some are canonical and others not.

'Of such Sacred Books I, not without expense, procured myself some samples; and in hope of true insight, and with the zeal which beseems an Inquirer into Clothes, set to interpret and study them. But wholly to no purpose: that tough faculty of reading, for which the world will not refuse me credit, was here for the first time foiled and set at naught. In vain that I summoned my whole energies (*mich weidlich anstrengte*), and did my very utmost; at the end of some short space, I was uniformly seized with not so much what I can call a drumming in my ears, as a kind of infinite, unsufferable, Jew's harping and scrannel-piping there; to which the frightfullest species of Magnetic Sleep soon supervened. And if I strove to shake this away, and absolutely would not yield, there came a hitherto unfelt sensation, as of *Delirium Tremens*, and a melting into total deliquium: till at last, by order of the Doctor, dreading ruin to my whole intellectual and bodily faculties, and a general breaking-up of the constitution, I reluctantly but determinedly forbore. Was there some miracle at work here; like those Fireballs, and supernal and infernal prodigies, which, in the case of the Jewish Mysteries, have also more than once scared-back the Alien? Be this as it may, such failure on my part, after best efforts, must excuse the imperfection of this sketch; altogether incomplete, yet the completest I could give of a Sect too singular to be omitted.

'Loving my own life and senses as I do, no power shall induce me, as a private individual, to open another *Fashionable Novel*. But luckily, in this dilemma, comes a hand from the clouds; whereby if not victory, deliverance is held out to me. Round one of those Book-packages, which the *Stillschweigen'sche Buchhandlung* is in the habit of importing from England, come, as is usual, various waste printed-sheets (*Maculaturblätter*), by way of interior wrappage: into these the Clothes-Philosopher, with a certain Mohamedan reverence even for waste-paper, which curious knowledge will sometimes hover, disdains not to cast his eye. Readers may judge of his astonishment when on such a defaced stray-sheet, probably the outcast fraction of some English Periodical, such as they name *Maga-*

zine, appears something like a Dissertation on this very subject of *Fashionable Novels*! It sets out, indeed, chiefly from a Secular point of view; directing itself, not without asperity, against some to me unknown individual named *Pelham*,[9] who seems to be a Mystagogue, and leading Teacher and Preacher of the Sect; so that, what indeed otherwise was not to be expected in such a fugitive fragmentary sheet, the true secret, the Religious physiognomy and physiology of the Dandiacal Body, is nowise laid fully open there. Nevertheless, scattered lights do from time to time sparkle out, whereby I have endeavoured to profit. Nay, in one passage selected from the Prophecies, or Mythic Theogonies, or whatever they are (for the style seems very mixed) of this Mystagogue, I find what appears to be a Confession of Faith, or Whole Duty of Man, according to the tenets of that Sect. Which Confession or Whole Duty, therefore, as proceeding from a source so authentic, I shall here arrange under Seven distinct Articles, and in very abridged shape lay before the German world; therewith taking leave of this matter. Observe also, that to avoid possibility of error, I, as far as may be, quote literally from the Original:[10]

Articles of Faith

"1. Coats should have nothing of the triangle about them; at the same time, wrinkles behind should be carefully avoided.

"2. The collar is a very important point: it should be low behind, and slightly rolled.

"3. No licence of fashion can allow a man of delicate taste to adopt the posterial luxuriance of a Hottentot.

"4. There is safety in a swallow-tail.

"5. The good sense of a gentleman is nowhere more finely developed than in his rings.

"6. It is permitted to mankind, under certain restrictions, to wear white waistcoats.

"7. The trousers must be exceedingly tight across the hips."

---

[9] *Pelham, or The Adventures of a Gentleman*, a novel by Bulwer Lytton published in 1828.
[10] The following consists of direct quotation from *Pelham*.

'All which Propositions I, for the present, content myself with modestly but peremptorily and irrevocably denying.

'In strange contrast with this Dandiacal Body stands another British Sect, originally, as I understand, of Ireland, where its chief seat still is; but known also in the main Island, and indeed everywhere rapidly spreading. As this Sect has hitherto emitted no Canonical Books, it remains to me in the same state of obscurity as the Dandiacal, which has published Books that the unassisted human faculties are inadequate to read. The members appear to be designated by a considerable diversity of names, according to their various places of establishment: in England they are generally called the *Drudge* Sect; also, unphilosophically enough, the *White Negroes*; and, chiefly in scorn by those of other communions, the *Ragged-Beggar* Sect. In Scotland, again, I find them entitled *Hallanshakers*,[11] or the *Stook of Duds* Sect; any individual communicant is named *Stook of Duds* (that is, Shock of Rags), in allusion, doubtless, to their professional Costume. While in Ireland, which, as mentioned, is their grand parent hive, they go by a perplexing multiplicity of designations, such as *Bogtrotters, Redshanks, Ribbonmen, Cottiers, Peep-of-Day Boys, Babes of the Wood, Rockites, Poor-Slaves*:[12] which last, however, seems to be the primary and generic name; whereto, probably enough, the others are only subsidiary species, or slight varieties; or, at most, propagated offsets from the parent stem, whose minute subdivisions, and shades of difference, it were here loss of time to dwell on. Enough for us to understand, what seems indubitable, that the original Sect is that of the *Poor-Slaves*; whose doctrines, practices, and fundamental characteristics pervade and animate the whole Body, howsoever denominated our outwardly diversified.

'The precise speculative tenets of this Brotherhood: how the Universe, and Man, and Man's Life, picture themselves to the mind of an Irish Poor-Slave; with what feelings and opinions he looks forward on the Future, round on the Present, back on

[11] Scottish for sturdy beggars.
[12] Names applied to different groups of oppressed and insurgent Irishmen.

the Past, it were extremely difficult to specify. Something Monastic there appears to be in their Constitution: we find them bound by the two Monastic Vows, of Poverty and Obedience; which Vows, especially the former, it is said, they observe with great strictness; nay, as I have understood it, they are pledged, and be it by any solemn Nazarene ordination or not, irrevocably consecrated thereto, even *before* birth. That the third Monastic Vow, of Chastity, is rigidly enforced among them, I find no ground to conjecture.

'Furthermore, they appear to imitate the Dandiacal Sect in their grand principle of wearing a peculiar Costume. Of which Irish Poor-Slave Costume no description will indeed be found in the present Volume; for this reason, that by the imperfect organ of Language it did not seem describable. Their raiment consists of innumerable skirts, lappets and irregular wings, of all cloths and of all colours; through the labyrinthic intricacies of which their bodies are introduced by some unknown process. It is fastened together by a multiplex combination of buttons, thrums, and skewers; to which frequently is added a girdle of leather, of hempen or even of straw rope, round the loins. To straw rope, indeed, they seem partial, and often wear it by way of sandals. In headdress they affect a certain freedom: hats with partial brim, without crown, or with only a loose, hinged, or valved crown; in the former case, they sometimes invert the hat, and wear it brim uppermost, like a University-cap, with what view is unknown.

'The name Poor-Slaves seems to indicate a Slavonic, Polish, or Russian origin: not so, however, the interior essence and spirit of their Superstition, which rather displays a Teutonic or Druidical character. One might fancy them worshippers of Hertha, or the Earth: for they dig and affectionately work continually in her bosom; or else, shut-up in private Oratories,[13] meditate and manipulate the substances derived from her; seldom looking-up towards the Heavenly Luminaries, and then with comparative indifference. Like the Druids, on the other hand, they live in dark dwellings; often even breaking their

---

[13] A chapel, here used as ironic term for factories.

glass-windows, where they find such, and stuffing them up with pieces of raiment or other opaque substances, till the fit obscurity is restored. Again, like all followers of Nature-Worship, they are liable to outbreakings of an enthusiasm rising to ferocity; and burn men, if not in wicker idols, yet in sod cottages.

'In respect of diet, they have also their observances. All Poor-Slaves are Rhizophagous (or Root-eaters); a few are Ichthyophagous, and use Salted Herrings: other animal food they abstain from; except indeed, with perhaps some strange inverted fragment of a Brahminical feeling, such animals as die a natural death. Their universal sustenance is the root named Potato, cooked by fire alone; and generally without condiment or relish of any kind, save an unknown condiment named *Point*, into the meaning of which I have vainly inquired; the victual *Potatoes-and-Point*[14] not appearing, at least not with specific accuracy of description, in any European Cookery-Book whatever. For drink, they use, with an almost epigrammatic counterpoise of taste, Milk, which is the mildest of liquors, and *Potheen*,[15] which is the fiercest. This latter I have tasted, as well as the English *Blue-Ruin*, and the Scotch *Whisky*, analogous fluid used by the Sect in those countries: it evidently contains some form of alcohol, in the highest state of concentration, though disguised with acrid oils; and is, on the whole, the most pungent substance known to me,—indeed, a perfect liquid fire. In all their Religious Solemnities, Potheen is said to be an indispensable requisite, and largely consumed.

'An Irish Traveller, of perhaps common veracity, who presents himself under the to me unmeaning title of *The late John Bernard*, offers the following sketch of a domestic establishment, the inmates whereof, though such is not stated expressly, appear to have been of that Faith. Thereby shall my German readers now behold an Irish Poor-Slave, as it were with their own eyes; and even see him at meat. Moreover, in the so precious waste-paper sheet above mentioned, I have found some

---

[14] It was an Irish joke to point to a piece of bacon saved for a future meal, before eating a meal composed solely of potatoes.
[15] Whiskey distilled from potatoes.

corresponding picture of a Dandiacal Household, painted by that same Dandiacal Mystagogue, or Theogonist: this also, by way of counterpart and contrast, the world shall look into.

'First, therefore, of the Poor-Slave, who appears likewise to have been a species of Innkeeper. I quote from the original:[16]

Poor-Slave Household

' "The furniture of this Caravansera consisted of a large iron Pot, two oaken Tables, two Benches, two Chairs, and a Potheen Noggin. There was a Loft above (attainable by a ladder), upon which the inmates slept; and the space below was divided by a hurdle into two Apartments; the one for their cow and pig, the other for themselves and guests. On entering the house we discovered the family, eleven in number, at dinner: the father sitting at the top, the mother at the bottom, the children on each side of a large oaken Board, which was scooped-out in the middle, like a trough, to receive the contents of their Pot of Potatoes. Little holes were cut at equal distances to contain Salt; and a bowl of Milk stood on the table: all the luxuries of meat and beer, bread, knives and dishes were dispensed with." The Poor-Slave himself our Traveller found, as he says, broad-backed, black-browed, of great personal strength, and mouth from ear to ear. His Wife was a sun-browned but well-featured woman; and his young ones, bare and chubby, had the appetite of ravens. Of their Philosophical or Religious tenets or observances, no notice or hint.

'But now, secondly, of the Dandiacal Household; in which, truly, that often-mentioned Mystagogue and inspired Penman himself has his abode:[17]

Dandiacal Household

' "A Dressing-room splendidly furnished; violet-coloured curtains, chairs and ottomans of the same hue. Two full-length Mirrors are placed, one on each side of a table, which supports

---

[16] The quotation is taken from the accounts of travel in Ireland in John Bernard, *Retrospections of the Stage* (1830).
[17] The quotation is taken from the introduction to Bulwer Lytton's novel, *The Disowned* (1828).

the luxuries of the Toilet. Several Bottles of Perfumes, arranged in a peculiar fashion, stand upon a smaller table of mother-of-pearl: opposite to these are placed the appurtenances of Lavation richly wrought in frosted silver. A Wardrobe of Buhl is on the left; the doors of which, being partly open, discover a profusion of Clothes; Shoes of a singularly small size monopolise the lower shelves. Fronting the wardrobe a door ajar gives some slight glimpse of a Bathroom. Folding-doors in the background.—Enter the Author," our Theogonist in person, "obsequiously preceded by a French Valet, in white silk Jacket and cambric Apron."

'Such are the two Sects which, at this moment, divide the more unsettled portion of the British People; and agitate that ever-vexed country. To the eye of the political Seer, their mutual relation, pregnant with the elements of discord and hostility, is far from consoling. These two principles of Dandiacal Self-worship or Demon-worship, and Poor-Slavish or Drudgical Earth-worship, or whatever that same Drudgism may be, do as yet indeed manifest themselves under distant and nowise considerable shapes: nevertheless, in their roots and subterranean ramifications, they extend through the entire structure of Society, and work unweariedly in the secret depths of English national Existence; striving to separate and isolate it into two contradictory, uncommunicating masses.

'In numbers, and even individual strength, the Poor-Slaves or Drudges, it would seem, are hourly increasing. The Dandiacal, again, is by nature no proselytising Sect; but it boasts of great hereditary resources, and is strong by union; whereas the Drudges, split into parties, have as yet no rallying-point; or at best only coöperate by means of partial secret affiliations. If, indeed, there were to arise a *Communion of Drudges*, as there is already a Communion of Saints, what strangest effects would follow therefrom! Dandyism as yet affects to look-down on Drudgism: but perhaps the hour of trial, when it will be practically seen which ought to look down, and which up, is not so distant.

'To me it seems probable that the two Sects will one day part England between them; each recruiting itself from the intermediate ranks, till there be none left to enlist on either side. Those Dandiacal Manicheans, with the host of Dandyising Christians, will form one body: the Drudges, gathering round them whosoever is Drudgical, be he Christian or Infidel Pagan: sweeping-up likewise all manner of Utilitarians, Radicals, refractory Potwallopers, and so forth, into their general mass, will form another. I could liken Dandyism and Drudgism to two bottomless boiling Whirlpools that had broken-out on opposite quarters of the firm land: as yet they appear only disquieted, foolishly bubbling wells, which man's art might cover-in; yet mark them, their diameter is daily widening: they are hollow Cones that boil-up from the infinite Deep, over which your firm land is but a thin crust or rind! Thus daily is the intermediate land crumbling-in, daily the empire of the two Buchan-Bullers[18] extending; till now there is but a foot-plank, a mere film of Land between them; this too is washed away: and then —we have the true Hell of Waters, and Noah's Deluge is outdeluged!

'Or better, I might call them two boundless, and indeed unexampled Electric Machines (turned by the "Machinery of Society"), with batteries of opposite quality; Drudgism the Negative, Dandyism the Positive: one attracts hourly towards it and appropriates all the Positive Electricity of the nation (namely, the Money thereof); the other is equally busy with the Negative (that is to say the Hunger), which is equally potent. Hitherto you see only partial transient sparkles and sputters: but wait a little, till the entire nation is in an electric state; till your whole vital Electricity, no longer healthfully Neutral, is cut into two isolated portions of Positive and Negative (of Money and of Hunger); and stands there bottled-up in two World-Batteries! The stirring of a child's finger brings the two together; and then—What then? The Earth is but shivered into impalpable smoke by that Doom's-thunderpeal;

---

[18] Bullers of Buchan is a whirlpool on the coast of Scotland.

the Sun misses one of his Planets in Space, and thenceforth
there are no eclipses of the Moon.—Or better still, I might
liken——'

O, enough, enough of likenings and similitudes; in excess of
which, truly, it is hard to say whether Teufelsdröckh or ourselves sin the more.

We have often blamed him for a habit of wire-drawing and
over-refining; from of old we have been familiar with his tendency to Mysticism and Religiosity, whereby in everything he
was still scenting-out Religion: but never perhaps did these
amaurosis-suffusions so cloud and distort his otherwise most
piercing vision, as in this of the *Dandiacal Body*! Or was there
something of intended satire; is the Professor and Seer not quite
the blinkard he affects to be? Of an ordinary mortal we should
have decisively answered in the affirmative; but with a Teufelsdröckh there ever hovers some shade of doubt. In the meanwhile, if satire were actually intended, the case is little better.
There are not wanting men who will answer: Does your Professor take us for simpletons? His irony has overshot itself; we
see through it, and perhaps through him.

Chapter XI
Tailors

Injustice done to Tailors, actual and metaphorical. Their
rights and great services will one day be duly recognized.

Thus, however, has our first Practical Inference from the
Clothes-Philosophy, that which respects Dandies, been suffi-
ciently drawn; and we come now to the second concerning
Tailors. On this latter our opinion happily quite coincides with

that of Teufelsdröckh himself, as expressed in the concluding page of his Volume, to whom, therefore, we willingly give place. Let him speak his own last words, in his own way:

'Upwards of a century,' says he, 'must elapse, and still the bleeding fight of Freedom be fought, whoso is noblest perishing in the van, and thrones be hurled on altars like Pelion on Ossa, and the Moloch of Iniquity have his victims, and the Michael of Justice his martyrs, before Tailors can be admitted to their true prerogatives of manhood, and this last wound of suffering Humanity be closed.

'If aught in the history of the world's blindness could surprise us, here might we indeed pause and wonder. An idea has gone abroad, and fixed itself down into a wide-spreading rooted error, that Tailors are a distinct species in Physiology, not Men, but fractional Parts of a Man. Call any one a *Schneider* (Cutter, Tailor), is it not, in our dislocated, hoodwinked, and indeed delirious condition of Society, equivalent to defying his perpetual fellest enmity? The epithet *schneidermässig* (tailor-like) betokens an otherwise unapproachable degree of pusillanimity: we introduce a *Tailor's-Melancholy*, more opprobrious than any Leprosy, into our Books of Medicine; and fable I know not what of his generating it by living on Cabbage. Why should I speak of Hans Sachs (himself a Shoemaker, or kind of Leather-Tailor), with his *Schneider mit dem Panier*?[1] Why of Shakespeare, in his *Taming of the Shrew*, and elsewhere? Does it not stand on record that the English Queen Elizabeth, receiving a deputation of Eighteen Tailors, addressed them with a "Good-morning, gentlemen both!" Did not the same virago boast that she had a Cavalry Regiment, whereof neither horse nor man could be injured; her Regiment, namely, of Tailors on Mares? Thus everywhere is the falsehood taken for granted, and acted on as an indisputable fact.

'Nevertheless, need I put the question to any Physiologist, whether it is disputable or not? Seems it not at least presum-

---

[1] Hans Sachs: sixteenth century German poet who wrote "Tailor with a Banner."

able, that, under his Clothes, the Tailor has bones and viscera, and other muscles than the sartorious?[2] Which function of manhood is the Tailor not conjectured to perform? Can he not arrest for debt? Is he not in most countries a tax-paying animal?

'To no reader of this Volume can it be doubtful which conviction is mine. Nay if the fruit of these long vigils, and almost preternatural Inquiries, is not to perish utterly, the world will have approximated towards a higher Truth; and the doctrine, which Swift,[3] with the keen forecast of genius, dimly anticipated, will stand revealed in clear light: that the Tailor is not only a Man, but something of a Creator or Divinity. Of Franklin it was said, that "he snatched the Thunder from Heaven and the Sceptre from Kings": but which is greater, I would ask, he that lends, or he that snatches? For, looking away from individual cases, and how a Man is by the Tailor new-created into a Nobleman, and clothed not only with Wool but with Dignity and a Mystic Dominion,—is not the fair fabric of Society itself, with all its royal mantles and pontifical stoles, whereby, from nakedness and dismemberment, we are organised into Polities, into nations, and a whole coöperating Mankind, the creation, as has here been often irrefragably evinced, of the Tailor alone?— What too are all Poets and moral Teachers, but a species of Metaphorical Tailors? Touching which high Guild the greatest living Guild-brother has triumphantly asked us: "Nay if thou wilt have it, who but the Poet first made Gods for men; brought them down to us; and raised us up to them?"

'And this is he, whom sitting downcast, on the hard basis of his Shopboard, the world treats with contumely, as the ninth part of a man! Look up, thou much-injured one, look up with the kindling eye of hope, and prophetic bodings of a noble better time. Too long hast thou sat there, on crossed legs, wearing thy ankle-joints to horn; like some sacred Anchorite, or Catholic Fakir, doing penance, drawing down Heaven's richest blessings, for a world that scoffed at thee. Be of hope! Already

---

[2] Longest muscle in the body, crossing the front of the thigh.
[3] *Tale of a Tub*, Section ii. This section in Swift is one of the chief sources of *Sartor*.

streaks of blue peer through our clouds; the thick gloom of Ignorance is rolling asunder, and it will be Day. Mankind will repay with interest their long-accumulated debt: the Anchorite that was scoffed at will be worshipped; the Fraction will become not an Integer only, but a Square and Cube. With astonishment the world will recognise that the Tailor is its Hierophant and Hierarch, or even its God.

'As I stood in the Mosque of St. Sophia,[4] and looked upon these Four-and-Twenty Tailors, sewing and embroidering that rich Cloth, which the Sultan sends yearly for the Caaba[5] of Mecca, I thought within myself: How many other Unholies has your covering Art made holy, besides this Arabian Whinstone!

'Still more touching was it when, turning the corner of a lane, in the Scottish Town of Edinburgh, I came upon a Sign-post, whereon stood written that such and such a one was "Breeches-Maker to his Majesty"; and stood painted the Effigies of a Pair of Leather Breeches, and between the knees these memorable words, SIC ITUR AD ASTRA.[6] Was not this the martyr prison-speech of a Tailor signing indeed in bonds, yet sighing towards deliverance, and prophetically appealing to a better day? A day of justice, when the worth of Breeches would be revealed to man, and the Scissors become forever venerable.

'Neither, perhaps, may I now say, has his appeal been alto-gether in vain. It was in this high moment, when the soul, rent, as it were, and shed asunder, is open to inspiring influence, that I first conceived this Work on Clothes: the greatest I can ever hope to do; which has already, after long retardations, occupied, and will yet occupy, so large a section of my Life; and of which the Primary and simpler Portion may here find its conclusion.'

[4] Located in Istanbul.
[5] Shrine at Mecca.
[6] "Thus one goes to the stars."

Thomas Carlyle

Chapter XII
Farewell

Teufelsdröckh's strange manner of speech, but resolute, truthful character: His purpose seemingly to proselytise, to unite the wakeful earnest in these dark times. Letter from Hofrath Heuschrecke announcing that Teufelsdröckh has disappeared from Weissnichtwo. Editor guesses he will appear again. Friendly Farewell.

So have we endeavoured, from the enormous, amorphous Plum-pudding, more like a Scottish Haggis,[1] which Herr Teufelsdröckh had kneaded for his fellow-mortals, to pick out the choicest Plums, and present them separately on a cover of our own. A laborious, perhaps a thankless enterprise; in which, however, something of hope has occasionally cheered us, and of which we can now wash our hands not altogether without satisfaction. If hereby, though in barbaric wise, some morsel of spiritual nourishment have been added to the scanty ration of our beloved British world, what nobler recompense could the Editor desire? If it prove otherwise, why should he murmur? Was not this a Task which Destiny, in any case, had appointed him; which having now done with, he sees his general Day's work so much the lighter, so much the shorter?

Of Professor Teufelsdröckh it seems impossible to take leave without a mingled feeling of astonishment, gratitude, and disapproval. Who will not regret that talents, which might have profited in the higher walks of Philosophy, or in Art itself, have been so much devoted to a rummaging among lumber-rooms;

[1] A Scottish pudding made of sheep's vitals mixed with suet, oatmeal and onions and boiled in a sheep's stomach.

nay too often to a scraping in kennels, where lost rings and diamond-necklaces are nowise the sole conquests? Regret is unavoidable; yet censure were loss of time. To cure him of his mad humours British Criticism would essay in vain: enough for her if she can, by vigilance, prevent the spreading of such among ourselves. What a result, should this piebald, entangled, hypermetaphorical style of writing, not to say of thinking, become general among our Literary men! As it might so easily do. Thus has not the Editor himself, working over Teufelsdröckh's German, lost much of his own English purity? Even as the smaller whirlpool is sucked into the larger, and made to whirl along with it, so has the lesser mind, in this instance, been forced to become portion of the greater, and, like it, see all things figuratively: which habit time and assiduous effort will be needed to eradicate.

Nevertheless, wayward as our Professor shows himself, is there any reader that can part with him in declared enmity? Let us confess, there is that in the wild, much-suffering, much-inflicting man, which almost attaches us. His attitude, we will hope and believe, is that of a man who had said to Cant, Begone; and to Dilettantism, Here thou canst not be; and to Truth, Be thou in place of all to me: a man who had manfully defied the 'Time-prince,' or Devil, to his face; nay perhaps, Hannibal-like, was mysteriously consecrated from birth to that warfare, and now stood minded to wage the same, by all weapons, in all places, at all times. In such a cause, any soldier, were he but a Polack Scythe-man, shall be welcome.

Still the question returns on us: How could a man occasionally of keen insight, not without keen sense of propriety, who had real Thoughts to communicate, resolve to emit them in a shape bordering so closely on the absurd? Which question he were wiser than the present Editor who should satisfactorily answer. Our conjecture has sometimes been, that perhaps Necessity as well as Choice was concerned in it. Seems it not conceivable that, in a Life like our Professor's, where so much bountifully given by Nature had in Practice failed and misgone, Literature also would never rightly prosper: that striving with his characteristic vehemence to paint this and the other Picture, and ever without success, he at last desperately dashes his sponge, full of all colours, against the canvas, to try whether it will paint Foam?[2] With all his stillness, there were perhaps in Teufelsdröckh desperation enough for this.

A second conjecture we hazard with even less warranty. It is, that Teufelsdröckh is not without some touch of the universal feeling, a wish to proselytise. How often already have we paused, uncertain whether the basis of this so enigmatic nature were really Stoicism and Despair, or Love and Hope only seared into the figure of these! Remarkable, moreover, is this saying of his: 'How were Friendship possible? In mutual devotedness to the Good and True: otherwise impossible; except as Armed Neutrality, or hollow Commercial League. A man, be the Heavens ever praised, is sufficient for himself; yet were ten men, united in Love, capable of being and of doing what ten thousand singly would fail in. Infinite is the help man can yield to man.' And now in conjunction therewith consider this other: 'It is the Night of the World, and still long till it be Day: we wander amid the glimmer of smoking ruins, and the Sun and the Stars of Heaven are as if blotted out for a season; and two immeasurable Phantoms, HYPOCRISY and ATHEISM, with the Gowl,[3] SENSUALITY, stalk abroad over the Earth, and call it theirs: well at ease are the Sleepers for whom Existence is a shallow Dream.'

But what of the awestruck Wakeful who find it a Reality? Should not these unite; since even an authentic Spectre is not visible to Two?—In which case were this enormous Clothes-Volume properly an enormous Pitchpan, which our Teufelsdröckh in his lone watchtower had kindled, that it might flame far and wide through the Night, and many a disconsolately wandering spirit be guided thither to a Brother's bosom!—We say as before, with all his malign Indifference, who knows what mad Hopes this man may harbour?

Meanwhile there is one fact to be stated here, which harmonises ill with such conjecture; and, indeed, were Teufelsdröckh made like other men, might as good as altogether sub-

---

[2] Apelles, a Greek painter, is said to have finally been able to paint foam in this manner.

[3] Ghoul.

vert it. Namely, that while the Beacon-fire blazed its brightest, the Watchman had quitted it; that no pilgrim could now ask him: Watchman, what of the Night? Professor Teufelsdröckh, be it known, is no longer visibly present at Weissnichtwo, but again to all appearance lost in space! Some time ago, the Hofrath Heuschrecke was pleased to favour us with another copious Epistle; wherein much is said about the 'Population-Institute'; much repeated in praise of the Paper-bag Documents, the hieroglyphic nature of which our Hofrath still seems not to have surmised; and, lastly, the strangest occurrence communicated, to us for the first time, in the following paragraph:

'*Ew. Wohlgeboren*[4] will have seen from the public Prints, with what affectionate and hitherto fruitless solicitude Weissnichtwo regards the disappearance of her Sage. Might but the united voice of Germany prevail on him to return; nay could we but so much as elucidate for ourselves by what mystery he went away! But, alas, old Lieschen experiences or affects the profoundest deafness, the profoundest ignorance: in the Wahngasse all lies swept, silent, sealed up; the Privy Council itself can hitherto elicit no answer.

'It had been remarked that while the agitating news of those Parisian Three Days[5] flew from mouth to mouth, and dinned every ear in Weissnichtwo, Herr Teufelsdröckh was not known, at the *Gans* or elsewhere, to have spoken, for a whole week, any syllable except once these three: *Es geht an* (It is beginning). Shortly after, as *Ew. Wohlgeboren* knows, was the public tranquillity here, as in Berlin, threatened by a Sedition of the Tailors. Nor did there want Evil-wishers, or perhaps mere desperate Alarmists, who asserted that the closing Chapter of the Clothes-Volume was to blame. In this appalling crisis, the serenity of our Philosopher was indescribable: nay, perhaps through one humble individual, something thereof might pass into the *Rath* (Council) itself, and so contribute to the country's deliverance. The Tailors are now entirely pacificated.—

'To neither of these two incidents can I attribute our loss; yet still comes there the shadow of a suspicion out of Paris and its

---

[4] "Your honor."
[5] French Revolution of 1830.

Politics. For example, when the *Saint-Simonian Society* transmitted its Propositions hither, and the whole *Gans* was one vast cackle of laughter, lamentation, and astonishment, our Sage sat mute; and at the end of the third evening said merely: "Here also are men who have discovered, not without amazement, that Man is still Man; of which high, long-forgotten Truth you already see them make a false application." Since then, as has been ascertained by examination of the Post-Director, there passed at least one Letter with its Answer between the Messieurs Bazard-Enfantin[6] and our Professor himself; of what tenor can now only be conjectured. On the fifth night following, he was seen for the last time!

'Has this invaluable man, so obnoxious to most of the hostile Sects that convulse our Era, been spirited away by certain of their emissaries; or did he go forth voluntarily to their headquarters to confer with them and confront them? Reason we have, at least of a negative sort, to believe the Lost still living; our widowed heart also whispers that ere long he will himself give a sign. Otherwise, indeed, his archives must, one day, be opened by Authority; where much, perhaps the *Palingenesie* itself, is thought to be reposited.'

Thus far the Hofrath; who vanishes, as is his wont, too like an Ignis Fatuus, leaving the dark still darker.

So that Teufelsdröckh's public History were not done, then, or reduced to an even, unromantic tenor: nay, perhaps the better part thereof were only beginning? We stand in a region of conjectures, where substance has melted into shadow, and one cannot be distinguished from the other. May Time, which solves or suppresses all problems, throw glad light on this also! Our own private conjecture, now amounting almost to certainty, is that, safe-moored in some stillest obscurity, not to lie always still, Teufelsdröckh is actually in London!

Here, however, can the present Editor, with an ambroisial joy as of over-weariness falling into sleep, lay down his pen. Well does he know, if human testimony be worth aught, that to

[6] Amand Bazard (1791–1832) and Barthélemy Prosper Enfantin (1796–1864): followers of Saint-Simon.

innumerable British readers likewise, this is a satisfying con-summation; that innumerable British readers consider him, during these current months, but as an uneasy interruption to their ways of thought and digestion; and indicate so much, not without a certain irritancy and even spoken invective. For which, as for other mercies, ought not he to thank the Upper Powers? To one and all of you, O irritated readers, he, with outstretched arms and open heart, will wave a kind farewell. Thou too, miraculous Entity, who namest thyself YORKE and OLIVER,[7] and with thy vivacities and genialities, with thy all-too Irish mirth and madness, and odour of palled punch, mak-est such strange work, farewell; long as thou canst, fare-*well*! Have we not, in the course of Eternity, travelled some months of our Life-journey in partial sight of one another; have we not existed together, though in a state of quarrel?

[7] See Book I, Chapter 2, n. 6.

Past and Present

Past and Present was written and published in 1843.
The work is divided into four parts: "Proem,"
"The Ancient Monk," "The Modern Worker," "Horoscope."
The last three parts illustrate Carlyle's vision of the past,
the present and the future, and this anthology includes
selections from each of these parts.

Book Second

※

The Ancient Monk

Chapter X
Government

How Abbot Samson, giving his new subjects seriatim the kiss of fatherhood in the St. Edmundsbury chapterhouse, proceeded with cautious energy to set about reforming their disjointed distracted way· of life; how he managed with his Fifty rough *Milites* (Feudal Knights), with his lazy Farmers, remiss refractory Monks, with Pope's Legates, Viscounts, Bishops, Kings; how on all sides he laid about him like a man, and putting consequence on premiss, and everywhere the saddle on the right horse, struggled incessantly to educe organic method out of lazily fermenting wreck,—the careful reader will discern, not without true interest, in these pages of Jocelin Boswell.[1] In most antiquarian quaint costume, not of garments alone, but of thought, word, action, outlook and position, the substantial figure of a man with eminent nose, bushy brows and clear-

[1] Carlyle often compares Jocelin, the author of the medieval chronicle, to James Boswell, author of *The Life of Samuel Johnson*.

flashing eyes, his russet beard growing daily grayer, is visible, engaged in true governing of men. It is beautiful how the chrysalis governing-soul, shaking off its dusty slough and prison, starts forth winged, a true royal soul! Our new Abbot has a right honest unconscious feeling, without insolence as without fear or flutter, of what he is and what others are. A courage to quell the proudest, an honest pity to encourage the humblest. Withal there is a noble reticence in this Lord Abbot: much vain unreason he hears; lays up without response. He is not there to expect reason and nobleness of others; he is there to give them of his own reason and nobleness. Is he not their servant, as we said, who can suffer them, and for them; bear the burden their poor spindle-limbs totter and stagger under; and, in virtue of *being* their servant, govern them, lead them out of weakness into strength, out of defeat into victory!

One of the first Herculean Labours Abbot Samson undertook, or the very first, was to institute a strenuous review and radical reform of his economics. It is the first labour of every governing man, from *Paterfamilias* to *Dominus Rex*.[2] To get the rain thatched out from you is the preliminary of whatever farther, in the way of speculation or of action, you may mean to do. Old Abbot Hugo's budget, as we saw, had become empty, filled with deficit and wind. To see his account-books clear, be delivered from those ravening flights of Jew and Christian creditors, pouncing on him like obscene harpies wherever he showed face, was a necessity for Abbot Samson.

On the morrow after his instalment he brings in a load of money-bonds, all duly stamped, sealed with this or the other Convent Seal: frightful, unmanageable, a bottomless confusion of Convent finance. There they are;—but there at least they all are; all that shall be of them. Our Lord Abbot demands that all the official seals in use among us be now produced and delivered to him. Three-and-thirty seals turn up; are straightway broken, and shall seal no more: the Abbot only, and those duly authorized by him shall seal any bond. There are but two ways of

[2] "Head of a family to King."

paying debt: increase of industry in raising income, increase of thrift in laying it out. With iron energy, in slow but steady undeviating perseverance, Abbot Samson sets to work in both directions. His troubles are manifold: cunning *milites*, unjust bailiffs, lazy sockmen, he an inexperienced Abbot; relaxed lazy monks, not disinclined to mutiny in mass: but continued vigilance, rigorous method, what we call 'the eye of the master,' work wonders. The clear-beaming eyesight of Abbot Samson, steadfast, severe, all-penetrating,—it is like *Fiat lux*[3] in that inorganic waste whirlpool; penetrates gradually to all nooks, and of the chaos makes a *kosmos* or ordered world!

He arranges everywhere, struggles unweariedly to arrange, and place on some intelligible footing, the 'affairs and dues, *res ac redditus*,' of his dominion. The Lakenheath eels cease to breed squabbles between human beings; the penny of *reap-silver* to explode into the streets the Female Chartism of St. Edmundsbury.[4] These and innumerable greater things. Wheresoever Disorder may stand or lie, let it have a care; here is the man that has declared war with it, that never will make peace with it. Man is the Missionary of Order; he is the servant not of the Devil and Chaos, but of God and the Universe! Let all sluggards, and cowards, remiss, false-spoken, unjust, and otherwise diabolic persons have a care: this is a dangerous man for them. He has a mild grave face; a thoughtful sternness, a sorrowful pity: but there is a terrible flash of anger in him too; lazy monks often have to murmur, '*Sævit ut lupus*, He rages like a wolf; was not our Dream true!' 'To repress and hold-in such sudden anger he was continually careful,' and succeeded well: —right, Samson; that it may become in thee as noble central heat, fruitful, strong, beneficent; not blaze out, or the seldomest possible blaze out, as wasteful volcanoism to scorch and consume!

[3] "Let there be light" (Genesis, i, 3).
[4] A tax demanded for the reaping of the convent grain. Carlyle earlier describes the violent attack by the women of the town on the collector of this tax, and here compares this direct action to contemporary Chartism.

'We must first creep, and gradually learn to walk,' had Abbot Samson said of himself, at starting. In four years he has become a great walker; striding prosperously along; driving much before him. In less than four years, says Jocelin, the' Convent Debts were all liquidated: the harpy Jews not only settled with, but banished, bag and baggage, out of the *Bannaleuca* (Liberties, *Banlieue*) of St. Edmundsbury,—so has the King's Majesty been persuaded to permit. Farewell to *you*, at any rate; let us, in no extremity, apply again to you! Armed men march them over the borders, dismiss them under stern penalties,—sentence of excommunication on all that shall again harbour them here: there were many dry eyes at their departure.

New life enters everywhere, springs up beneficent, the Incubus of Debt once rolled away. Samson hastes not; but neither does he pause to rest. This of the Finance is a lifelong business with him;—Jocelin's anecdotes are filled to weariness with it. As indeed to Jocelin it was of very primary interest.

But we have to record also, with a lively satisfaction, that spiritual rubbish is as little tolerated in Samson's Monastery as material. With due rigour, Willelmus Sacrista, and his bibations and *tacenda* are, at the earliest opportunity, softly yet irrevocably put an end to.[5] The bibations, namely, had to end; even the building where they used to be carried on was razed from the soil of St. Edmundsbury, and 'on its place grow rows of beans': Willelmus himself, deposed from the Sacristy and all offices, retires into obscurity, into absolute taciturnity unbroken thenceforth to this hour. Whether the poor Willelmus did not still, by secret channels, occasionally get some slight wetting of vinous or alcoholic liquor,—now grown, in a manner, indispensable to the poor man? Jocelin hints not; one knows not how to hope, what to hope! But if he did, it was in silence and darkness; with an ever-present feeling that teetotalism was his only true course. Drunken dissolute Monks are a class of persons who had better keep out of Abbot Samson's way. *Sævit ut lupus*; was not the Dream true! murmured many a Monk. Nay

[5] An earlier chapter describes William the Sacristan, the monk in charge of the maintenance of the Abbey, as drinking (bibations) and doing "Things not to be spoken" (tacenda).

Ranulf de Glanvill, Justiciary in Chief, took umbrage at him, seeing these strict ways; and watched farther with suspicion: but discerned gradually that there was nothing wrong, that there was much the opposite of wrong.

Book Third

The Modern Worker

Chapter XI
Labour

For there is a perennial nobleness, and even sacredness, in Work. Were he never so benighted, forgetful of his high calling, there is always hope in a man that actually and earnestly works: in Idleness alone is there perpetual despair. Work, never so Mammonish, mean, *is* in communication with Nature; the real desire to get Work done will itself lead one more and more to truth, to Nature's appointments and regulations, which are truth.

The latest Gospel in this world is, Know thy work and do it. 'Know thyself': long enough has that poor 'self' of thine tormented thee; thou wilt never get to 'know' it, I believe! Think it not thy business, this of knowing thyself; thou art an unknowable individual: know what thou canst work at; and work at it, like a Hercules! That will be thy better plan.

It has been written, 'an endless significance lies in Work'; a man perfects himself by working. Foul jungles are cleared away, fair seedfields rise instead, and stately cities; and withal the man himself first ceases to be a jungle and foul unwholesome desert thereby. Consider how, even in the meanest sorts of Labour, the whole soul of a man is composed into a kind of real harmony, the instant he sets himself to work! Doubt, Desire, Sorrow, Remorse, Indignation, Despair itself, all these like helldogs lie beleaguering the soul of the poor dayworker, as of every man: but he bends himself with free valour against his task, and all these are stilled, all these shrink murmuring far off into their caves. The man is now a man. The blessed glow of Labour in him, is it not as purifying fire, wherein all poison is burnt up, and of sour smoke itself there is made bright blessed flame!

Destiny, on the whole, has no other way of cultivating us. A formless Chaos, once set it *revolving*, grows round and ever rounder; ranges itself, by mere force of gravity, into strata, spherical courses; is no longer a Chaos, but a round compacted World. What would become of the Earth, did she cease to revolve? In the poor old Earth, so long as she revolves, all inequalities, irregularities disperse themselves; all irregularities are incessantly becoming regular. Hast thou looked on the Potter's wheel,—one of the venerablest objects; old as the Prophet Ezechiel and far older? Rude lumps of clay, how they spin themselves up, by mere quick whirling, into beautiful circular dishes. And fancy the most assiduous Potter, but without his wheel; reduced to make dishes, or rather amorphous botches, by mere kneading and baking! Even such a Potter were Destiny, with a human soul that would rest and lie at ease, that would not work and spin! Of an idle unrevolving man the kindest Destiny, like the most assiduous Potter without wheel, can bake and knead nothing other than a botch; let her spend on him what expensive colouring, what gilding and enamelling she will, he is but a botch. Not a dish; no, a bulging, kneaded, crooked, shambling, squint-cornered, amorphous botch,—a mere enamelled vessel of dishonour! Let the idle think of this.

Blessed is he who has found his work; let him ask no other blessedness. He has a work, a life-purpose; he has found it, and will follow it! How, as a free-flowing channel, dug and torn by noble force through the sour mud-swamp of one's existence, like an ever-deepening river there, it runs and flows;—draining-off the sour festering water, gradually from the root of the remotest grass-blade; making, instead of pestilential swamp, a green fruitful meadow with its clear-flowing stream. How blessed for the meadow itself, let the stream and *its* value be great or small! Labour is Life: from the inmost heart of the Worker rises his god-given Force, the sacred celestial Life-essence breathed into him by Almighty God; from his inmost heart awakens him to all nobleness,—to all knowledge, 'self-knowledge' and much else, so soon as Work fitly begins. Knowledge? The knowledge that will hold good in working, cleave thou to that; for Nature herself accredits that, says Yea to that. Properly thou hast no other knowledge but what thou hast got by working: the rest is yet all a hypothesis of knowledge; a thing to be argued of in schools, a thing floating in the clouds, in endless logic-vortices, till we try it and fix it. 'Doubt, of whatever kind, can be ended by Action alone.'[1]

And again, hast thou valued Patience, Courage, Persever-ance, Openness to light; readiness to own thyself mistaken, to do better next time? All these, all virtues, in wrestling with the dim brute Powers of Fact, in ordering of thy fellows in such wrestle, there and elsewhere not at all, thou wilt continually learn. Set down a brave Sir Christopher in the middle of black ruined Stone-heaps, of foolish unarchitectural Bishops, redtape Officials, idle Nell-Gwyn Defenders of the Faith; and see whether he will ever raise a Paul's Cathedral out of all that, yea or no![2] Rough, rude, contradictory are all things and persons, from the mutinous masons and Irish hodmen, up to the idle Nell-Gwyn Defenders, to blustering redtape Officials, foolish unarchitectural Bishops. All these things and persons are there not for Christopher's sake and his Cathedral's; they are there for their own sake mainly! Christopher will have to conquer and constrain all these,—if he be able. All these are against him. Equitable Nature herself, who carries her mathematics and

---

[1] Goethe, *Wilhelm Meister's Apprenticeship.*
[2] Sir Christopher Wren rebuilt St. Paul's Cathedral after the London fire of 1666.

architectonics not on the face of her, but deep in the hidden heart of her,—Nature herself is but partially for him; will be wholly against him, if he constrain her not! His very money, where is it to come from? The pious munificence of England lies far-scattered, distant, unable to speak, and say, 'I am here'; —must be spoken to before it can speak. Pious munificence, and all help, is so silent, invisible like the gods; impediment, contradictions manifold are so loud and near! O brave Sir Christopher, trust thou in those notwithstanding, and front all these; understand all these; by valiant patience, noble effort, insight, by man's-strength, vanquish and compel all these,—and, on the whole, strike down victoriously the last topstone of that Paul's Edifice; thy monument for certain centuries, the stamp 'Great Man' impressed very legibly on Portland-stone there!—

Yes, all manner of help, and pious response from Men or Nature, is always what we call silent; cannot speak or come to light, till it be seen, till it be spoken to. Every noble work is at first 'impossible.' In very truth, for every noble work the possibilities will lie diffused through Immensity; inarticulate, undiscoverable except to faith. Like Gideon thou shalt spread out thy fleece at the door of thy tent; see whether under the wide arch of Heaven there be any bounteous moisture, or none. Thy heart and life-purpose shall be as a miraculous Gideon's fleece, spread out in silent appeal to Heaven: and from the kind Immensities, what from the poor unkind Localities and town and country Parishes there never could, blessed dew-moisture to suffice thee shall have fallen!

Work is of a religious nature:—work is of a *brave* nature; which it is the aim of all religion to be. All work of man is as the swimmer's: a waste ocean threatens to devour him; if he front it not bravely, it will keep its word. By incessant wise defiance of it, lusty rebuke and buffet of it, behold how it loyally supports him, bears him as its conqueror along. 'It is so,' says Goethe, 'with all things that man undertakes in this world.'

Brave Sea-captain, Norse Sea-King,—Columbus, my hero, royalest Sea-king of all! it is no friendly environment this of thine, in the waste deep waters; around thee mutinous discouraged souls, behind thee disgrace and ruin, before thee the unpenetrated veil of Night. Brother, these wild water-mountains,

bounding from their deep bases (ten miles deep, I am told),
are not entirely there on thy behalf! Meseems *they* have other
work than floating thee forward:—and the huge Winds, that
sweep from Ursa Major to the Tropics and Equators, dancing
their giant-waltz through the kingdoms of Chaos and Immensity, they care little about filling rightly or filling wrongly the
small shoulder-of-mutton sails in this cockle-skiff of thine! Thou
art not among articulate-speaking friends, my brother; thou art
wide as the world here. Secret, far off, invisible to all hearts but
thine, there lies a help in them: see how thou wilt get at that.
Patiently thou wilt wait till the mad Southwester spend itself,
saving thyself by dextrous science of defence, the while: valiantly, with swift decision, wilt thou strike in, when the favour-
ing East, the Possible, springs up. Mutiny of men thou wilt
sternly repress; weakness, despondency, thou wilt cheerily encourage: thou wilt swallow down complaint, unreason, weariness, weakness of others and thyself;—how much wilt thou
swallow down! There shall be a depth of Silence in thee, deeper
than this Sea, which is but ten miles deep: a Silence unsound-
able; known to God only. Thou shall be a Great man. Yes, my
World-Soldier, thou of the World Marine-service,—thou wilt
have to be *greater* than this tumultuous unmeasured World
here round thee is: thou, in thy strong soul, as with wrestler's
arms, shalt embrace it, harness it down; and make it bear thee
on,—to new Americas, or whither God wills!

Chapter XIII
Democracy

If the Serene Highnesses and Majesties do not take note of
that, then, as I perceive, *that* will take note of itself! The time
for levity, insincerity, and idle babble and play-acting, in all

kinds, is gone by; it is a serious, grave time. Old long-vexed questions, not yet solved in logical words or parliamentary laws, are fast solving themselves in facts, somewhat unblessed to behold! This largest of questions, this question of Work and Wages, which ought, had we heeded Heaven's voice, to have begun two generations ago or more, cannot be delayed longer without hearing Earth's voice. 'Labour' will verily need to be somewhat 'organised,' as they say,—God knows with what difficulty. Man will actually need to have his debts and earnings a little better paid by man; which, let Parliaments speak of them or be silent of them, are eternally his due from man, and cannot, without penalty and at length not without death-penalty, be withheld. How much ought to cease among us straightway; how much ought to begin straightway, while the hours yet are!

Truly they are strange results to which this of leaving all to 'Cash'; of quietly shutting-up the God's Temple, and gradually opening wide-open the Mammon's Temple, with 'Laissez-faire, and Every man for himself,'—have led us in these days! We have Upper, speaking Classes, who indeed do 'speak' as never man spake before; the withered flimsiness, the godless baseness and barrenness of whose Speech might of itself indicate what kind of Doing and practical Governing went on under it! For speech is the gaseous element out of which most kinds of Practice and Performance, especially all kinds of moral Performance, condense themselves, and take shape; as the one is, so will the other be. Descending, accordingly, into the Dumb Class in its Stockport Cellars[1] and Poor-Law Bastilles,[2] have we not to announce that they also are hitherto unexampled in the History of Adam's Posterity?

Life was never a May-game for men: in all times the lot of the dumb millions born to toil was defaced with manifold sufferings, injustices, heavy burdens, avoidable and unavoidable; not play at all, but hard work that made the sinews sore

---

[1] Earlier in the book, Carlyle tells of an actual case in which a mother and father in Stockport, a small manufacturing city, murdered their children in order to receive funds from the Burial society.

[2] Carlyle compares to the famous French prison the workhouses, established under the Poor Laws, in which the poor had to live in order to receive government support.

and the heart sore. As bond-slaves, *villani, bordarii, soche-manni*, nay indeed as dukes, earls and kings, men were often-times made weary of their life; and had to say, in the sweat of their brow and of their soul, Behold, it is not sport, it is grim earnest, and our back can bear no more! Who knows not what massacrings and harryings there have been; grinding, long-continuing, unbearable injustices,—till the heart had to rise in madness, and some *'Eu Sachsen, nimith euer sachses*, You Saxons, out with your gully-knives, then!' You Saxons, some 'arrestment,' partial 'arrestment of the Knaves and Dastards' has become indispensable!—The page of Dryasdust[3] is heavy with such details.

And yet I will venture to believe that in no time, since the beginnings of Society, was the lot of those same dumb millions of toilers so entirely unbearable as it is even in the days now passing over us. It is not to die, or even to die of hunger, that makes a man wretched; many men have died; all men must die,—the last exit of us all is in a Fire-Chariot of Pain. But it is to live miserable we know not why; to work sore and yet gain nothing; to be heart-worn, weary, yet isolated, unrelated, girt-in with a cold universal Laissez-faire: it is to die slowly all our life long, imprisoned in a deaf, dead, Infinite Injustice, as in the accursed iron belly of a Phalaris' Bull![4] This is and re-mains forever intolerable to all men whom God has made. Do we wonder at French Revolutions, Chartisms, Revolts of Three Days?[5] The times, if we will consider them, are really unexampled.

Never before did I hear of an Irish Widow reduced to 'prove her sisterhood by dying of typhus-fever and infecting seventeen persons,'—saying in such undeniable way, 'You *see* I was your sister!' Sisterhood, brotherhood, was often forgotten; but not till the rise of these ultimate Mammon and Shotbelt Gospels did I ever see it so expressly denied. If no pious Lord or *Law-ward* would remember it, always some pious Lady ('*Hlaf-dig*,' Bene-

[3] Carlyle's term for the pedantic historian.
[4] Legendary hollow metal bull in which Phalaris, a Sicilian king, burned malefactors.
[5] The revolution of 1830 in France.

factress, '*Loaf-giveress*,' they say she is,—blessings on her beautiful heart!) was there, with mild mother-voice and hand, to remember it; some pious thoughtful *Elder*, what we now call 'Prester,' *Presbyter* or 'Priest,' was there to put all men in mind of it, in the name of the God who had made all.

Not even in Black Dahomey was it ever, I think, forgotten to the typhus-fever length. Mungo Park,[6] resourceless, had sunk down to die under the Negro Village-Tree, a horrible White object in the eyes of all. But in the poor Black Woman, and her daughter who stood aghast at him, whose earthly wealth and funded capital consisted of one small calabash of rice, there lived a heart richer than *Laissez-faire*: they, with a royal munificence, boiled their rice for him; they sang all night to him, spinning assiduous on their cotton distaffs, as he lay to sleep: 'Let us pity the poor white man; no mother has he to fetch him milk, no sister to grind him corn!' Thou poor black Noble One, —thou *Lady* too: did not a God make thee too; was there not in thee too something of a God!—

Gurth, born thrall of Cedric the Saxon,[7] has been greatly pitied by Dryasdust and others. Gurth, with the brass collar round his neck, tending Cedric's pigs in the glades of the wood, is not what I call an exemplar of human felicity: but Gurth, with the sky above him, with the free air and tinted boscage and umbrage round him, and in him at least the certainty of supper and social lodging when he came home; Gurth to me seems happy, in comparison with many a Lancashire and Buckinghamshire man of these days, not born thrall of anybody! Gurth's brass collar did not gall him: Cedric *deserved* to be his master. The pigs were Cedric's, but Gurth too would get his parings of them. Gurth had the inexpressible satisfaction of feeling himself related indissolubly, though in a rude brass-collar way, to his fellow-mortals in this Earth. He had superiors, inferiors, equals. —Gurth is now 'emancipated' long since; has what we call 'Liberty.' Liberty, I am told, is a divine thing. Liberty when it becomes the 'Liberty to die by starvation' is not so divine!

[6] Mungo Park (1771–1806): Scottish explorer of Africa.
[7] Characters in Sir Walter Scott's *Ivanhoe*.

Liberty? The true liberty of a man, you would say, consisted in his finding out, or being forced to find out the right path, and to walk thereon. To learn, or to be taught, what work he actually was able for; and then by permission, persuasion, and even compulsion, to set about doing of the same! That is his true blessedness, honour, 'liberty' and maximum of wellbeing: if liberty be not that, I for one have small care about liberty. You do not allow a palpable madman to leap over precipices; you violate his liberty, you that are wise; and keep him, were it in strait-waistoats, away from the precipices! Every stupid, every cowardly and foolish man is but a less palpable madman: his true liberty were that a wiser man, that any and every wiser man, could, by brass collars, or in whatever milder or sharper way, lay hold of him when he was going wrong, and order and compel him to go a little righter. O, if thou really art my *Senior*, Seigneur, my *Elder*, Presbyter or Priest,—if thou art in very deed my *Wiser*, may a beneficent instinct lead and impel thee to 'conquer' me, to command me! If thou do know better than I what is good and right, I conjure thee in the name of God, force me to do it; were it by never such brass collars, whips and handcuffs, leave me not to walk over precipices! That I have been called, by all the Newspapers, a 'free man' will avail me little, if my pilgrimage had ended in death and wreck. O that the Newspapers had called me slave, coward, fool, or what it pleased their sweet voices to name me, and I had attained not death, but life!—Liberty requies new definitions.

A conscious abhorrence and intolerance of Folly, of Baseness, Stupidity, Poltroonery and all that brood of things, dwells deep in some men: still deeper in others an *un*conscious abhorrence and intolerance, clothed moreover by the beneficent Supreme Powers in what stout appetites, energies, egoisms so-called, are suitable to it;—these latter are your Conquerors, Romans, Normans, Russians, Indo-English; Founders of what we call Aristocracies. Which indeed have they not the most 'divine right' to found;—being themselves very truly Ἄριστοι, BRAVEST, BEST; and conquering generally a confused rabble of WORST, or at lowest, clearly enough, of WORSE? I think their divine right, tried, with affirmatory verdict, in the greatest Law-Court known to me, was good! A class of men who are dreadfully exclaimed against by Dryasdust; of whom nevertheless beneficent Nature has oftentimes had need; and may, alas, again have need.

When, across the hundredfold poor scepticisms, trivialisms and constitutional cobwebberies of Dryasdust, you catch any glimpse of a William the Conqueror, a Tancred of Hauteville[8] or suchlike,—do you not discern veritably some rude outline of a true God-made King; whom not the Champion of England cased in tin, but all Nature and the Universe were calling to the throne?[9] It is absolutely necessary that he get thither. Nature does not mean her poor Saxon children to perish, of obesity, stupor or other malady, as yet: a stern Ruler and Line of Rulers therefore is called in,—a stern but most beneficent *perpetual House-Surgeon* is by Nature herself called in, and even the appropriate *fees* are provided for him! Dryasdust talks lamentably about Hereward and the Fen Counties; fate of Earl Waltheof;[10] Yorkshire and the North reduced to ashes: all which is undoubtedly lamentable. But even Dryasdust apprises me of one fact: 'A child, in this William's reign, might have carried a purse of gold from end to end of England.' My erudite friend, it is a fact which outweighs a thousand! Sweep away thy constitutional, sentimental and other cobwebberies; look eye to eye, if thou still have any eye, in the face of this big burly William Bastard: thou wilt see a fellow of most flashing discernment, of most strong lionheart;—in whom, as it were, within a frame of oak and iron, the gods have planted the soul of 'a man of genius'! Dost thou call that nothing? I call it an immense thing!—Rage enough was in this Willelmus Conquæstor, rage enough for his occasions;—and yet the essential element of him, as of all such men, is not scorching *fire*, but shining illuminative *light*. Fire and light are strangely interchangeable; nay, at bottom, I have found them different forms of the same most god-

---

[8] A leader of the first Crusade.
[9] See *Sartor*, Book III, Chapter 3, n. 11.
[10] Hereward the Wake and Waltheof both led rebellions against William the Conqueror in 1069–1070. After putting down the rebellions, William plundered the northern part of England.

like 'elementary substance' in our world: a thing worth stating in these days. The essential element of this Conquæstor is, first of all, the most sun-eyed perception of what *is* really what on this God's-Earth;—which, thou wilt find, does mean at bottom 'Justice,' and 'Virtues' not a few: *Conformity* to what the Maker has seen good to make; that, I suppose, will mean Justice and a Virtue or two?—

Dost thou think Willelmus Conquæstor would have tolerated ten years' jargon, one hour's jargon, on the propriety of killing Cotton-manufacturers by partridge Corn-Laws?[11] I fancy, this was not the man to knock out of his night's-rest with nothing but a noisy bedlamism in your mouth! 'Assist us still better to hush the partridges; strangle Plugson who spins the shirts?'— '*Par la Splendeur de Dieu!*'[12]—Dost thou think Willelmus Conquæstor, in this new time, with Steamengine Captains of Industry on one hand of him, and Joe-Manton Captains of Idleness on the other, would have doubted which *was* really the BEST; which did deserve strangling, and which not?

I have a certain indestructible regard for Willelmus Conquæstor. A resident House-Surgeon, provided by Nature for her beloved English People, and even furnished with the requisite fees, as I said; for he by no means felt himself doing Nature's work, this Willelmus, but his own work exclusively! And his own work withal it was; informed '*par la Splendeur de Dieu.*'—I say, it is necessary to get the work out of such a man, however harsh that be! When a world, not yet doomed for death, is rushing down to ever-deeper Baseness and Confusion, it is a dire necessity of Nature's to bring in her ARISTOCRACIES, her BEST, even by forcible methods. When their descendants or representatives cease entirely to *be* the Best, Nature's poor world will very soon rush down again to Baseness; and it becomes a

[11] Allusion to the extended Parliamentary debates over the Corn Laws in which the agricultural interests of the aristocracy, whom Carlyle sees as interested only in hunting partridges, wanted to maintain high grain prices. The manufacturers, represented in *Past and Present* by the name Plugson of Undershot, wanted to reduce the price of grain in order to be able to pay lower wages and thus compete in foreign markets.

[12] "By the Glory of God."

dire necessity of Nature's to cast them out. Hence French Revolutions, Five-point Charters,[13] Democracies, and a mournful list of *Etceteras*, in these our afflicted times.

To what extent Democracy has now reached, how it advances irresistible with ominous, ever-increasing speed, he that will open his eyes on any province of human affairs may discern. Democracy is everywhere the inexorable demand of these ages, swiftly fulfilling itself. From the thunder of Napoleon battles, to the jabbering of Open-vestry in St. Mary Axe,[14] all things announce Democracy. A distinguished man, whom some of my readers will hear again with pleasure, thus writes to me what in these days he notes from the Wahngasse of Weissnichtwo, where our London fashions seem to be in full vogue. Let us hear the Herr Teufelsdröckh again, were it but the smallest word!

'Democracy, which means despair of finding any Heroes to govern you, and contented putting-up with the want of them, —alas, thou too, *mein Lieber*, seest well how close it is of kin to *Atheism*, and other sad *Isms*: he who discovers no God whatever, how shall he discover Heroes, the visible Temples of God? —Strange enough meanwhile it is, to observe with what thoughtlessness, here in our rigidly Conservative Country, men rush into Democracy with full cry. Beyond doubt, his Excellenz the Titular-Herr Ritter Kauderwälsch von Pferdefuss-Quacksalber,[15] he our distinguished Conservative Premier himself, and all but the thicker-headed of his Party, discern Democracy to be inevitable as death, and are even desperate of delaying it much!

'You cannot walk the streets without beholding Democracy announce itself: the very Tailor has become, if not properly Sansculottic,[16] which to him would be ruinous, yet a Tailor unconsciously symbolising, and prophesying with his scissors, the reign of Equality. What now is our fashionable coat? A thing of superfinest texture, of deeply meditated cut; with

[13] The five Chartist demands for social reform.
[14] A London parish.
[15] "Sir Gibberish of Horsefoot-Quack Doctor."
[16] See *Sartor*, Book I, Chapter 3, n. 8.

Malines-lace cuffs; quilted with gold; so that a man can carry, without difficulty, an estate of land on his back? *Keineswegs*, By no manner of means! The Sumptuary Laws have fallen into such a state of desuetude as was never before seen. Our fashionable coat is an amphibium between barnsack and drayman's doublet. The cloth of it is studiously coarse; the colour a speckled soot-black or rust-brown gray; the nearest approach to a Peasant's. And for shape,—thou shouldst see it! The last consummation of the year now passing over us is definable as Three Bags; a big bag for the body, two small bags for the arms, and by way of collar a hem! The first Antique Cheruscan who, of felt-cloth or bear's-hide, with bone or metal needle, set about making himself a coat, before Tailors had yet awakened out of Nothing,—did not he make it even so? A loose wide poke for body, with two holes to let out the arms; this was his original coat: to which holes it was soon visible that two small loose pokes, or sleeves, easily appended, would be an improvement.

'Thus has the Tailor-art, so to speak, overset itself, like most other things; changed its centre-of-gravity; whirled suddenly over from zenith to nadir. Your Stulz,[17] with huge somerset, vaults from his high shopboard down to the depths of primal savagery,—carrying much along with him! For I will invite thee to reflect that the Tailor, as topmost ultimate froth of Human Society, is indeed swift-passing, evanescent, slippery to decipher; yet significant of much, nay of all. Topmost evanescent froth, he is churned-up from the very lees, and from all intermediate regions of the liquor. The general outcome he, visible to the eye, of what men aimed to do, and were obliged and enabled to do, in this one public department of symbolising themselves to each other by covering of their skins. A smack of all Human Life lies in the Tailor: its wild struggles towards beauty, dignity, freedom, victory; and how, hemmed-in by Sedan and Huddersfield[18] by Nescience, Dulness, Prurience, and other sad necessities and laws of Nature, it has attained just to this: Gray savagery of Three Sacks with a hem!

'When the very Tailor verges towards Sansculottism, is it not

---

[17] Fashionable Tailor.
[18] Textile-manufacturing towns.

ominous? The last Divinity of poor mankind dethroning himself; sinking *his* taper too, flame downmost, like the Genius of Sleep or of Death; admonitory that Tailor time shall be no more! —For, little as one could advise Sumptuary Laws at the present epoch, yet nothing is clearer than that where ranks do actually exist, strict division of costumes will also be enforced; that if we ever have a new Hierarchy and Aristocracy, acknowledged veritably as such, for which I daily pray Heaven, the Tailor will reawaken; and be, by volunteering and appointment, consciously and unconsciously, a safeguard of that same.'—Certain farther observations, from the same invaluable pen, on our never-ending changes of mode, our 'perpetual nomadic and even ape-like appetite for change and mere change' in all the equipments of our existence, and the 'fatal revolutionary character' thereby manifested, we suppress for the present. It may be admitted that Democracy, in all meanings of the word, is in full career; irresistible by any Ritter Kauderwälsch or other Son of Adam, as times go. 'Liberty' is a thing men are determined to have.

But truly, as I had to remark in the mean while, 'the liberty of not being oppressed by your fellow man' is an indispensable, yet one of the most insignificant fractional parts of Human Liberty. No man oppresses thee, can bid thee fetch or carry, come or go, without reason shown. True; from all men thou art emancipated: but from Thyself and from the Devil—? No man, wiser, unwiser, can make thee come or go: but thy own futilities, bewilderments, thy false appetites for Money, Windsor Georges[19] and suchlike? No man oppresses thee, O free and independent Franchiser: but does not this stupid Porter-pot oppress thee? No Son of Adam can bid thee come or go; but this absurd Pot of Heavy-wet, this can and does! Thou art the thrall not of Cedric the Saxon, but of thy own brutal appetites and this scoured dish of liquor. And thou pratest of thy 'liberty'? Thou entire blockhead!

Heavy-wet and gin: alas, these are not the only kinds of

---

[19] The medal of the Order of the Garter.

thraldom. Thou who walkest in a vain show, looking out with ornamental dilettante sniff and serene supremacy at all Life and all Death; and amblest jauntily; perking up thy poor talk into crotchets, thy poor conduct into fatuous somnambulisms;—and *art* as an 'enchanted Ape' under God's sky, where thou mightest have been a man, had proper Schoolmasters and Conquerors, and Constables with cat-o'-nine tails, been vouchsafed thee; dost thou call that 'liberty'? Or your unreposing Mammon-worshipper again, driven, as if by Galvanisms, by Devils and Fixed-Ideas, who rises early and sits late, chasing the impossible; straining every faculty to 'fill himself with the east wind,'—how merciful were it, could you, by mild persuasion, or by the severest tyranny so-called, check him in his mad path, and turn him into a wiser one! All painful tyranny, in that case again, were but mild 'surgery'; the pain of it cheap, as health and life, instead of galvanism and fixed-idea, are cheap at any price.

Sure enough, of all paths a man could strike into, there *is*, at any given moment, a *best path* for every man; a thing which, here and now, it were of all things *wisest* for him to do;—which could he be but led or driven to do, he were then doing 'like a man,' as we phrase it; all men and gods agreeing with him, the whole Universe virtually exclaiming Well-done to him! His success, in such case, were complete; his felicity a maximum. This path, to find this path and walk in it, is the one thing needful for him. Whatsoever forwards him in that, let it come to him even in the shape of blows and spurnings, is liberty: whatsoever hinders him, were it wardmotes,[20] open-vestries, poll-booths, tremendous cheers, rivers of heavy-wet, is slavery.

The notion that a man's liberty consists in giving his vote at election-hustings, and saying, 'Behold, now I too have my twenty-thousandth part of a Talker in our National Palaver;[21] will not all the gods be good to me?'—is one of the pleasantest! Nature nevertheless is kind at present; and puts it into the heads of many, almost of all. The liberty especially which has to purchase itself by social isolation, and each man standing separate from the other, having 'no business with him' but a

[20] Meetings of wards, political divisions of a city.
[21] Carlylean term for Parliament.

cash-account: this is such a liberty as the Earth seldom saw;—as the Earth will not long put up with, recommend it how you may. This liberty turns out, before it have long continued in action, with all men flinging up their caps round it, to be, for the Working Millions a liberty to die by want of food; for the Idle Thousands and Units, alas, a still more fatal liberty to live in want of work; to have no earnest duty to do in this God's-World any more. What becomes of a man in such predicament? Earth's Laws are silent; and Heaven's speak in a voice which is not heard. No work, and the ineradicable need of work, give rise to new very wondrous life-philosophies, new very wondrous life-practices! Dilettantism, Pococurantism, Beau-Brummelism,[22] with perhaps an occasional, half-mad, protesting burst of Byronism, establish themselves: at the end of a certain period,—if you go back to 'the Dead Sea,' there is, say our Moslem friends, a very strange 'Sabbath-day' transacting itself there!—Brethren, we know but imperfectly yet, after ages of Constitutional Government, what Liberty and Slavery are.

Democracy, the chase of Liberty in that direction, shall go its full course; unrestrainable by him of Pferdefuss-Quacksalber, or any of *his* household. The Toiling Millions of Mankind, in most vital need and passionate instinctive desire of Guidance, shall cast away False-Guidance; and hope, for an hour, that No-Guidance will suffice them: but it can be for an hour only. The smallest item of human Slavery is the oppression of man by his Mock-Superiors; the palpablest, but I say at bottom the smallest. Let him shake-off such oppression, trample it indignantly under his feet; I blame him not, I pity and commend him. But oppression by your Mock-Superiors well shaken off, the grand problem yet remains to solve: That of finding government by your Real-Superiors! Alas, how shall we ever learn the solution of that, benighted, bewildered, sniffing, sneering, godforgetting unfortunates as we are? It is a work for centuries; to be taught us by tribulations, confusions, insurrections, obstructions; who knows if not by conflagration and despair! It is a lesson inclusive of all other lessons; the hardest of all lessons to learn.

[22] See "Signs of the Times," n. 30.

One thing I do know: Those Apes, chattering on the branches by the Dead Sea, never got it learned; but chatter there to this day. To them no Moses need come a second time; a thousand Moseses would be but so many painted Phantasms, interesting Fellow-Apes of new strange aspect,—whom they would 'invite to dinner,' be glad to meet with in lion-soirées.[23] To them the voice of Prophecy, of heavenly monition, is quite ended. They chatter there, all Heaven shut to them, to the end of the world. The unfortunates! Oh, what is dying of hunger, with honest tools in your hand, with a manful purpose in your heart, and much real labour lying round you done, in comparison? You honestly quit your tools; quit a most muddy confused coil of sore work, short rations, of sorrows, dispiritments and contradictions, having now honestly done with it all;—and await, not entirely in a distracted manner, what the Supreme Powers, and the Silences and the Eternities may have to say to you.

A second thing I know: This lesson will have to be learned, —under penalties! England will either learn it, or England also will cease to exist among Nations. England will either learn to reverence its Heroes, and discriminate them from its Sham-Heroes and Valets and gaslighted Histrios; and to prize them as the audible God's-voice, amid all inane jargons and temporary market-cries, and say to them with heart-loyalty, 'Be ye King and Priest, and Gospel and Guidance for us': or else England will continue to worship new and ever-new forms of Quackhood,—and so, with what resiliences and reboundings matters little, go down to the Father of Quacks! Can I dread such things of England? Wretched, thick-eyed, gross-hearted mortals, why will ye worship lies, and 'Stuffed Clothes-suits created by the ninth-parts of men'! It is not your purses that suffer; your farm-rents, your commerces, your mill-revenues, loud as ye lament over these; no, it is not these alone, but a far deeper than these: it is your souls that lie dead, crushed down under despicable Nightmares, Atheisms, Brain-fumes; and are not souls at all, but mere succedanea for *salt* to keep your bodies and their appetites from putrefying! Your cotton-spinning and thrice-

---

[23] An evening party to meet a famous person (a "lion").

miraculous mechanism, what is this too, by itself, but a larger kind of Animalism? Spiders can spin, Beavers can build and show contrivance; the Ant lays-up accumulation of capital, and has, for aught I know, a Bank of Antland. If there is no soul in man higher than all that, did it reach to sailing on the cloud-rack, and spinning sea-sand; then I say, man is but an animal, a more cunning kind of brute: he has no soul, but only a succe-daneum for salt. Whereupon, seeing himself to be truly of the beasts that perish, he ought to admit it, I think;—and also straightway universally to kill himself; and so, in a manlike manner at least *end*, and wave these brute-worlds *his* dignified farewell!—

Book Fourth

Horoscope

Chapter IV
Captains of Industry

If I believed that Mammonism with its adjuncts was to continue henceforth the one serious principle of our existence, I should reckon it idle to solicit remedial measures from any Government, the disease being insusceptible of remedy. Government can do much, but it can in nowise do all. Government, as the most conspicuous object in Society, is called upon to give signal of what shall be done; and, in many ways, to preside over, further, and command the doing of it. But the Government cannot do, by all its signaling and commanding, what the Society is radically indisposed to do. In the long-run every Government is the exact symbol of its People, with their wisdom and unwisdom; we have to say, Like People Like Government.— The main substance of this immense Problem of Organising Labour, and first of all of Managing the Working Classes, will, it is very clear, have to be solved by those who stand practically in the middle of it; by those who themselves work and preside

over work. Of all that can be enacted by any Parliament in regard to it, the germs must already lie potentially extant in those
two Classes, who are to obey such enactment. A Human Chaos
in which there is no light, you vainly attempt to irradiate by
light shed *on* it: order never can arise there.

But it is my firm conviction that the 'Hell of England' will
cease to be that of 'not making money'; that we shall get a
nobler Hell and a nobler Heaven! I anticipate light *in* the Human
Chaos, glimmering, shining more and more; under manifold
true signals from without That light shall shine. Our deity no
longer being Mammon,—O Heavens, each man will then say to
himself: 'Why such deadly haste to make money? I shall not go
to Hell, even if I do not make money! There is another Hell, I
am told!' Competition, at railway-speed, in all branches of commerce and work will then abate:—good felt-hats for the head,
in every sense, instead of seven-feet lath-and-plaster hats on
wheels,[1] will then be discoverable! Bubble-periods,[2] with their
panics and commercial crises, will again become infrequent;
steady modest industry will take the place of gambling speculation. To be a noble Master, among noble Workers, will again be
the first ambition with some few; to be a rich Master only the
second. How the Inventive Genius of England, with the whirr of
its bobbins and billy-rollers[3] shoved somewhat into the back-
grounds of the brain, will contrive and devise, not cheaper
produce exclusively, but fairer distribution of the produce at its
present cheapness! By degrees, we shall again have a Society
with something of Heroism in it, something of Heaven's Blessing on it; we shall again have, as my German friend asserts,
'instead of Mammon-Feudalism with unsold cotton-shirts and
Preservation of the Game, noble just Industrialism and Government by the Wisest!'

It is with the hope of awakening here and there a British
man to know himself for a man and divine soul, that a few
words of parting admonition, to all persons to whom the
Heavenly Powers have lent power of any kind in this land, may

[1] This mobile hat served as an advertisement for a London hatter.
[2] Period of financial speculation in worthless schemes.
[3] Parts of textile machinery.

now be addressed. And first to those same Master-Workers, Leaders of Industry; who stand nearest and in fact powerfulest, though not most prominent, being as yet in too many senses a Virtuality rather than an Actuality.

The Leaders of Industry, if Industry is ever to be led, are virtually the Captains of the World! if there be no nobleness in them, there will never be an Aristocracy more. But let the Captains of Industry consider: once again, are they born of other clay than the old Captains of Slaughter; doomed forever to be no Chivalry, but a mere gold-plated *Doggery*,—what the French well name *Canaille*, 'Doggery' with more or less gold carrion at its disposal! Captains of Industry are the true Fighters, henceforth recognisable as the only true ones: Fighters against Chaos, Necessity and the Devils and Jötuns,[4] and lead on Mankind in that great, and alone true, and universal warfare; the stars in their courses fighting for them, and all Heaven and all Earth saying audibly, Well done! Let the Captains of Industry retire into their own hearts, and ask solemnly, If there is nothing but vulturous hunger, for fine wines, valet reputation and gilt carriages, discoverable there? Of hearts made by the Almighty God I will not believe such a thing. Deep-hidden under wretchedest god-forgetting Cants, Epicurisms, Dead-Sea Apisms; forgotten as under foulest fat Lethe mud and weeds, there is yet, in all hearts born into this God's-World, a spark of the Godlike slumbering. Awake, O nightmare sleepers; awake, arise, or be forever fallen! This is not playhouse poetry; it is sober fact. Our England, our world cannot live as it is. It will connect itself with a God again, or go down with nameless throes and fire-consummation to the Devils. Thou who feelest aught of such a Godlike stirring in thee, any faintest intimation of it as through heavy-laden dreams, follow *it*, I conjure thee. Arise, save thyself, be one of those that save thy country.

Bucaniers, Chactaw Indians, whose supreme aim in fighting is that they may get the scalps, the money, that they may amass scalps and money: out of such came no Chivalry, and never

---

[4] Giants in Norse mythology.

will! Out of such came only gore and wreck, infernal rage and misery; desperation quenched in annihilation. Behold it, I bid thee, behold there, and consider! What is it that thou have a hundred thousand-pound bills laid-up in thy strong-room, a hundred scalps hung-up in thy wigwam? I value not them or thee. Thy scalps and thy thousand-pound bills are as yet nothing, if no nobleness from within irradiate them; if no Chivalry, in action, or in embryo ever struggling towards birth and action, be there.

Love of men cannot be bought by cash-payment; and without Love men cannot endure to be together. You cannot lead a Fighting World without having it regimented, chivalried: the thing, in a day, becomes impossible; all men in it, the highest at first, the very lowest at last, discern consciously, or by a noble instinct, this necessity. And can you any more continue to lead a Working World unregimented, anarchic? I answer, and the Heavens and Earth are now answering, No! The thing becomes not 'in a day' impossible; but in some two generations it does. Yes, when fathers and mothers, in Stockport hunger-cellars, begin to eat their children, and Irish widows have to prove their relationship by dying of typhus-fever; and amid Governing 'Corporations of the Best and Bravest,' busy to preserve their game by 'bushing,' dark millions of God's human creatures start up in mad Chartisms, impracticable Sacred-Months,[5] and Manchester Insurrections;—and there is a virtual Industrial Aristocracy as yet only half-alive, spell-bound amid money-bags and ledgers; and an actual Idle Aristocracy seemingly near dead in somnolent delusions, in trespasses and double-barrels; 'sliding,' as on inclined-planes, which every new year they *soap* with new Hansard's-jargon[6] under God's sky, and so are 'sliding,' ever faster, towards a 'scale' and balance-scale whereon is written *Thou art found Wanting*:—in such days, after a generation or two, I say, it does become, even to the low and simple, very palpably impossible! No Working World, any more than a Fighting World, can be led on without a noble Chivalry of

[5] Name used by Chartists in asking for a month-long strike.
[6] Carlyle's terms for Parliamentary debate. Hansard was the name given to the record of Parliamentary debate.

Work, and laws and fixed rules which follow out of that,—far nobler than any Chivalry of Fighting was. As an anarchic multitude on mere Supply-and-demand, it is becoming inevitable that we dwindle in horrid suicidal convulsion and self-abrasion, frightful to the imagination, into *Chactaw* Workers. With wigwams and scalps,—with palaces and thousand-pound bills; with savagery, depopulation, chaotic desolation! Good Heavens, will not one French Revolution and Reign of Terror suffice us, but must there be two? There will be two if needed; there will be twenty if needed; there will be precisely as many as are needed. The Laws of Nature will have themselves fulfilled. That is a thing certain to me.

Your gallant battle-hosts and work-hosts, as the others did, will need to be made loyally yours; they must and will be regulated, methodically secured in their just share of conquest under you;—joined with you in veritable brotherhood, sonhood, by quite other and deeper ties than those of temporary day's wages! How would mere red-coated regiments, to say nothing of chivalries, fight for you, if you could discharge them on the evening of the battle, on payment of the stipulated shillings,—and they discharge you on the morning of it! Chelsea Hospitals,[7] pensions, promotions, rigorous lasting covenant on the one side and on the other, are indispensable even for a hired fighter. The Feudal Baron, much more,—how could he subsist with mere temporary mercenaries round him, at sixpence a day; ready to go over to the other side, if sevenpence were offered? He could not have subsisted;—and his noble instinct saved him from the necessity of even trying! The Feudal Baron had a Man's Soul in him; to which anarchy, mutiny, and the other fruits of temporary mercenaries, were intolerable: he had never been a Baron otherwise, but had continued a Chactaw and Bucanier. He felt it precious, and at last it became habitual, and his fruitful enlarged existence included it as a necessity, to have men round him who in heart loved him; whose life he watched over with rigour yet with love; who were prepared to give their life for him, if need came. It was beautiful; it was human! Man lives not

---

[7] A Government-supported home in London for retired or disabled soldiers.

otherwise, nor can live contented, anywhere or anywhen. Isolation is the sum-total of wretchedness to man. To be cut off, to be left solitary: to have a world alien, not your world; all a hostile camp for you; not a home at all, of hearts and faces who are yours, whose you are! It is the frightfulest enchantment; too truly a work of the Evil One. To have neither superior, nor inferior, nor equal, united manlike to you. Without father, without child, without brother. Man knows no sadder destiny. 'How is each of us,' exclaims Jean Paul,[8] 'so lonely in the wide bosom of the all!' Encased each as in his transparent 'ice-palace'; our brother visible in his, making signals and gesticulations to us;—visible, but forever unattainable: on his bosom we shall never rest, nor he on ours. It was not a God that did this; no!

Awake, ye noble Workers, warriors in the one true war: all this must be remedied. It is you who are already half-alive, whom I will welcome into life; whom I will conjure, in God's name, to shake off your enchanted sleep, and live wholly! Cease to count scalps, gold-purses; not in these lies your or our salvation. Even these, if you count only these will not long be left. Let bucaniering be put far from you; alter, speedily abrogate all laws of the bucaniers, if you would gain any victory that shall endure. Let God's justice, let pity, nobleness and manly valour, with more gold-purses or with fewer, testify themselves in this your brief Life-transit to all the Eternities, the Gods and Silences. It is to you I call; for ye are not dead, ye are already half-alive: there is in you a sleepless dauntless energy, the prime-matter of all nobleness in man. Honour to you in your kind. It is to you I call: yet know at least this, That the mandate of God to His creature man is: Work! The future Epic of the World rests not with those that are near dead, but with those that are alive, and those that are coming into life.

Look around you. Your world-hosts are all in mutiny, in confusion, destitution; on the eve of fiery wreck and madness! They will not march farther for you, on the sixpence a day and supply-and-demand principle: they will not; nor ought they,

---

[8] Jean Paul Richter. See *Sartor*, Book I, Chapter 4, n. 6.

nor can they. Ye shall reduce them to order, begin reducing them. To order, to just subordination; noble loyalty in return for noble guidance. Their souls are driven nigh mad; let yours be sane and ever saner. Not as a bewildered bewildering mob; but as a firm regimented mass, with real captains over them, will these men march any more. All human interests, combined human endeavours, and social growths in this world, have, at a certain stage of their development, required organising; and Work, the grandest of human interests, does now require it.

God knows, the task will be hard: but no noble task was ever easy. This task will wear away your lives, and the lives of your sons and grandsons: but for what purpose, if not for tasks like this, were lives given to men? Ye shall cease to count your thousand-pound scalps, the noble of you shall cease! Nay the very scalps, as I say, will not long be left if you count only these. Ye shall cease wholly to be barbarous vulturous Chactaws, and become noble European Nineteenth-Century Men. Ye shall know that Mammon, in never such gigs[9] and flunky 'respectabilities,' is not the alone God; that of himself he is but a Devil, and even a Brute-god.

Difficult? Yes, it will be difficult. The short-fibre cotton; that too was difficult. The waste cotton-shrub, long useless, disobedient, as the thistle by the wayside,—have ye not conquered it: made it into beautiful bandana webs; white woven shirts for men; bright-tinted air-garments wherein flit goddesses? Ye have shivered mountains asunder, made the hard iron pliant to you as soft putty: the Forest-giants, Marsh-jötuns bear sheaves of golden-grain; Ægir the Sea-demon[10] himself stretches his back for a sleek highway to you, and on Firehorses and Windhorses ye career. Ye are most strong. Thor red-bearded, with his blue sun-eyes, with his cheery heart and strong thunderhammer, he and you have prevailed. Ye are most strong, ye Sons of the icy North, of the far East,—far marching from your rugged Eastern Wildernesses, hitherward from the gray Dawn of Time! Ye are Sons of the *Jötun*-land; the land of

---

[9] Light, two-wheeled carriage which Carlyle uses as the symbol of middle-class respectability.

[10] Giant in Norse mythology.

Difficulties Conquered. Difficult? You must try this thing. Once try it with the understanding that it will and shall have to be done. Try it as ye try the paltrier thing, making of money! I will bet on you once more, against all Jötuns, Tailor-gods, Double-barrelled Law-wards, and Denizens of Chaos whatsoever!

Rinehart Editions